At the thought she felt pain in the pit of her stomach.

And then she heard it.

"Hello, Mother."

Out of the shadows from the far end of the room walked a large man dressed in black. His head was shaved and he was deeply tanned.

For several seconds she did not recognize him. The light from the one table lamp was dim and the figure remained at the end of the room. As she became adjusted to the light and the object of her gaze, she realized why the man appeared to be a stranger. The face had changed. The shining black hair was shaved off; the nose was altered, smaller and the nostrils wider; even the eyes—where before there had been a Neapolitan droop to the lids—these eyes were wide, as if no lids existed. There were reddish splotches around the mouth and forehead. It was not a face. It was the mask of a face. It was striking. It was monstrous. And it was her son.

"Ulster! My God!"

"Mother, if you die right now from heart failure, you'll make fools out of several highly paid assassins."

THE SCARLATTI INHERITANCE

"What makes this book fascinating is the rapidity of its narration and the scope of the story . . . A gripping tale."
                                                    —*Best Sellers*

Bantam Books by Robert Ludlum
Ask your bookseller for the books you have missed.

THE AQUITAINE PROGRESSION
THE BOURNE IDENTITY
THE BOURNE SUPREMACY
THE CHANCELLOR MANUSCRIPT
THE GEMINI CONTENDERS
THE HOLCROFT COVENANT
THE ICARUS AGENDA
THE MATARESE CIRCLE
THE MATLOCK PAPER
THE OSTERMAN WEEKEND
THE PARSIFAL MOSAIC
THE RHINEMANN EXCHANGE
THE ROAD TO GANDOLFO
THE SCARLATTI INHERITANCE
TREVAYNE
THE BOURNE ULTIMATUM

THE
SCARLATTI
INHERITANCE

ROBERT LUDLUM

BANTAM BOOKS

NEW YORK · TORONTO · LONDON · SYDNEY · AUCKLAND

THE SCARLATTI INHERITANCE

A Bantam Book / published by arrangement with the author

Bantam edition / March 1982

ISBN 0-553-27146-6

Published simultaneously in the United States and Canada

Bantam Books are published by Bantam Books, a division of Bantam Doubleday Dell Publishing Group, Inc. Its trademark, consisting of the words ''Bantam Books'' and the portrayal of a rooster, is Registered in U.S. Patent and Trademark Office and in other countries. Marca Registrada. Bantam Books, 666 Fifth Avenue, New York, New York 10103.

PRINTED IN THE UNITED STATES OF AMERICA

KR   23   22   21   20   19   18   17

For Mary:

For all those reasons she must know so well—
"Above all, there was Mary."

NEW YORKER MISSING

New York, May 21—The scion of one of America's wealthiest industrial families, who was decorated for bravery at the Meuse-Argonne, disappeared from his Manhattan brownstone over five weeks ago, it was learned today. Mr. . . .

HITLER AIDE DISRUPTS I. G. FARBEN CONFERENCE

Berlin, July 10—An unidentified member of Reichschancellor Hitler's Ministry of War today startled negotiators of I. G. Farben and U.S. firms during their reciprocal trade agreements conference. In a surprising display of invective, spoken clearly in the English language, he branded the progress as unacceptable. The unknown observer then departed with his staff. . . .

THE NEW YORK TIMES, February 18, 1948   (Page 6)

NAZI OFFICIAL DEFECTED IN 1944

Washington, D.C., February 18— A little-known story from World War II was partially revealed to-day when it was learned that a high-ranking Nazi figure, using the code name "Saxon," defected to the Allies in October, 1944. A Senate subcommittee . . .

THE NEW YORK TIMES, May 26, 1951   (Page 58)

WAR DOCUMENT FOUND

*Kreuzlingen, Switz., May 26—*An oilcloth packet containing maps of armament installations in and around wartime Berlin was found buried in the ground near a small inn in this Swiss village on the Rhine. The inn is being razed for a resort hotel. No iden-tification was found; just the word "Saxon" imprinted on a strip of the tape attached to the packet. . . .

THE
SCARLATTI
INHERITANCE

PART ONE

CHAPTER 1

The brigadier general sat stiffly on the deacon's bench, preferring the hard surface of the pine to the soft leather of the armchairs. It was nine twenty in the morning and he had not slept well, no more than an hour.

As each half hour had been marked by the single chime of the small mantel clock, he had found himself, to his surprise, wanting the time to pass more swiftly. Because nine thirty had to come, he wanted to reckon with it.

At nine thirty he was to appear before the secretary of state, Cordell S. Hull.

As he sat in the secretary's outer office, facing the large black door with its gleaming brass hardware, he fingered the white folder, which he had taken out of his attaché case. When the time came for him to produce it, he did not want an awkward moment of silence while he opened the case to extract the folder. He wanted to be able to thrust it, if necessary, into the hands of the secretary of state with assurance.

On the other hand, Hull might not ask for it. He might demand only a verbal explanation and then proceed to use the authority of his office to term the spoken words unacceptable. If such was the case the brigadier could do no more than protest. Mildly, to be sure. The information in the folder did not constitute proof, only data that could or could not bolster the conjectures he had made.

The brigadier general looked at his watch. It was nine twenty-four and he wondered if Hull's reputation for

3

punctuality would apply to his appointment. He had reached his own office at seven thirty, approximately half an hour before his normal arrival time. Normal, that was, except for periods of crisis when he often stayed through the night awaiting the latest development of critical information. These past three days were not unlike those periods of crisis. In a different way.

His memorandum to the secretary, the memorandum that had resulted in his appointment this morning, might put him to the test. Ways could be found to place him out of communication, far from any center of influence. He might well be made to appear a total incompetent. But he knew he was right.

He bent the top of the folder back, just enough to read the typed title page: "Canfield, Matthew. Major, United States Army Reserve. Department of Military Intelligence."

Canfield, Matthew. . . . Matthew Canfield. He was the proof.

A buzzer rang on the intercom on the desk of a middle-aged receptionist.

"Brigadier General Ellis?" She barely looked up from the paper.

"Right here."

"The secretary will see you now."

Ellis looked at his wristwatch. It was nine thirty-two.

He rose, walked toward the ominous black-enameled door, and opened it.

"You'll forgive me, General Ellis. I felt that the nature of your memorandum required the presence of a third party. May I introduce Undersecretary Brayduck?"

The brigadier was startled. He had not anticipated a third party; he had specifically requested that the audience be between the secretary and himself alone.

Undersecretary Brayduck stood about ten feet to the right of Hull's desk. He obviously was one of those White House–State Department university men so prevalent in the Roosevelt administration. Even his clothes—the light gray flannels and the wide herringbone jacket—were casually emphasized in the silent counterpoint to the creased uniform of the brigadier.

"Certainly, Mr. Secretary. . . . Mr. Brayduck." The brigadier nodded.

Cordell S. Hull sat behind the wide desk. His familiar

features—the very light skin, almost white, the thinning white hair, the steel-rimmed pince-nez in front of his blue-green eyes—all seemed larger than life because they were an everyday image. The newspapers and the motion picture newsreels were rarely without photographs of him. Even the more inclusive election posters—ponderously asking, Do you want to change horses in the middle of the stream?—had his reassuring, intelligent face prominently displayed beneath Roosevelt's; sometimes more prominently than the unknown Harry Truman's.

Brayduck took a tobacco pouch out of his pocket and began stuffing his pipe. Hull arranged several papers on his desk and slowly opened a folder, identical to the one in the brigadier's hand, and looked down at it. Ellis recognized it. It was the confidential memorandum he had had hand-delivered to the secretary of state.

Brayduck lit his pipe and the odor of the tobacco caused Ellis to look at the man once again. That smell belonged to one of those strange mixtures considered so original by the university people but generally offensive to anyone else in the room. Brigadier Ellis would be relieved when the war was over. Roosevelt would then be out and so would the so-called intellectuals and their bad-smelling tobaccos.

The Brain Trust. Pinks, every one of them.

But first the war.

Hull looked up at the brigadier. "Needless to say, General, your memorandum is very disturbing."

"The information was disturbing to me, Mr. Secretary."

"No doubt. No doubt. . . . The question would appear to be, Is there any foundation for your conclusions? I mean, anything concrete?"

"I believe so, sir."

"How many others in Intelligence know about this, Ellis?" Brayduck interrupted and the absence of the word "General" was not lost on the brigadier.

"I've spoken to no one. I didn't think I'd be speaking to anyone but the secretary this morning, to be perfectly frank with you."

"Mr. Brayduck has my confidence, General Ellis. He's here at my request. . . . My orders, if you like."

"I understand."

Cordell Hull leaned back in his chair. "Without offense, I wonder if you do. . . . You send a classified memorandum, delivered under the highest priority to this office—to my own person, to be exact—and the substance of what you say is nothing short of incredible."

"A preposterous charge you admit you can't prove," interjected Brayduck, sucking on his pipe as he approached the desk.

"That's precisely why we're here." Hull had requested Brayduck's presence but he was not going to suffer undue interference, much less insolence.

Brayduck, however, was not to be put off. "Mr. Secretary, Army Intelligence is hardly without its inaccuracies. We've learned that at great cost. My only concern is to prevent another inaccuracy, a misinformed speculation, from becoming ammunition for this administration's political opponents. There's an election less than four weeks away!"

Hull shifted his large head no more than several inches. He did not look at Brayduck as he spoke. "You don't have to remind me of such pragmatic considerations. . . . However, I may have to remind *you* that we have other responsibilities. . . . Other than those to practical politics. Do I make myself clear?"

"Of course." Brayduck stopped in his tracks.

Hull continued. "As I understand your memorandum, General Ellis, you submit that an influential member of the German High Command is an American citizen operating under the assumed name—and a name well-known to us—of Heinrich Kroeger."

"I do, sir. Except that I qualified my statement by saying he *might* be."

"You also imply that Heinrich Kroeger is associated with, or connected to, a number of large corporations in this country. Industries involved with government contracts, armaments appropriations."

"Yes, Mr. Secretary. Except, again, I stated that he *was*, not necessarily *is*."

"Tenses have ways of becoming blurred with such accusations." Cordell Hull took off his steel-rimmed spectacles and placed them beside the folder. "Especially in time of war."

Undersecretary Brayduck struck a match and spoke between puffs on his pipe. "You also state quite clearly that you have no specific proof."

"I have what I believe would be termed circumstantial evidence. Of such a nature I felt I'd be derelict in my duty if I didn't bring it to the secretary's attention." The brigadier took a deep breath before continuing. He knew that once he began he was committed.

"I'd like to point out a few salient facts about Heinrich Kroeger. . . . To begin with, the dossier on him is incomplete. He's received no party recognition as most of the others have. And yet when others have come and gone, he's remained at the center. Obviously he has a great deal of influence with Hitler."

"We know this." Hull did not like restatements of known information simply to bolster an argument.

"The name itself, Mr. Secretary. Heinrich is as common as William or John, and Kroeger no more unusual than Smith or Jones in our own country."

"Oh, come, General." Brayduck's pipe was curling smoke. "Such an inference would make half our field commanders suspect."

Ellis turned and gave Brayduck the full benefit of his military scorn. "I believe the fact is relevant, Mr. Undersecretary."

Hull began to wonder if it had been such a good idea to have Brayduck present. "There's no point in being hostile, gentlemen."

"I'm sorry you feel that way, Mr. Secretary." Brayduck again would not accept a rebuke. "I believe my function here this morning is that of the devil's advocate. None of us, least of all you, Mr. Secretary, have the time to waste . . ."

Hull looked over at the undersecretary, moving his swivel chair as he did so. "Let's make the time. Please continue, General."

"Thank you, Mr. Secretary. A month ago word was relayed through Lisbon that Kroeger wanted to make contact with us. Channels were arranged and we expected the normal procedures to be followed. . . . Instead Kroeger rejected these procedures—refused any contact with British or French units—insisted on direct communication with Washington."

"If I may?" Brayduck's tone was courteous. "I don't think that's an abnormal decision. We're the predominant factor, after all."

"It was abnormal, Mr. Brayduck, insofar as Kroeger

7

would communicate with no one other than a Major Canfield. . . . Major Matthew Canfield who is, or was, an efficient minor officer in Army Intelligence stationed in Washington."

Brayduck held his pipe motionless and looked at the brigadier general. Cordell Hull leaned forward in his chair, his elbows resting on the desk.

"There's no mention of this in your memorandum."

"I realize that, sir. I omitted it in the conceivable event that the memorandum might be read by someone other than yourself."

"You have my apologies, General." Brayduck was sincere.

Ellis smiled at the victory.

Hull leaned back in his chair. "A ranking member of the Nazi High Command insists upon communicating only with an obscure major in Army Intelligence. Most unusual!"

"Unusual, but not unheard of. . . . We've all known German nationals; we merely assumed that Major Canfield had met Kroeger before the war. In Germany."

Brayduck stepped forward toward the brigadier. "Yet you tell us that Kroeger may not be a German. Therefore between Kroeger's request from Lisbon and your memorandum to the secretary something changed your mind. What was it? Canfield?"

"Major Canfield is a competent, at times excellent Intelligence officer. An experienced man. However, since the channel between him and Kroeger was opened, he's displayed marked tendencies of being under emotional strain. He's become extremely nervous and hasn't functioned in the manner of an officer with his background and experience. . . . He has also, Mr. Secretary, instructed me to make a most unusual request of the president of the United States."

"Which is?"

"That a classified file from the archives of the State Department be delivered to him with the seals unbroken, before he makes contact with Heinrich Kroeger."

Brayduck took his pipe from his mouth, about to object.

"Just one minute, Mr. Brayduck." Brayduck may be brilliant, thought Hull, but did he have any idea of what it meant to a career officer such as Ellis to face the two

8

of them and make a statement? For his statement was an undisguised petition for the White House and the State Department to seriously consider granting Canfield's request. Many officers would have rejected the illegal proposition rather than allow themselves to be placed in such a position. That was the army way. "Am I correct in assuming that you recommended the release of this file to Major Canfield?"

"That judgment would have to be yours. I only point out that Heinrich Kroeger has been instrumental in every important decision made by the Nazi hierarchy since its inception."

"Could the defection of Heinrich Kroeger shorten the war?"

"I don't know. The possibility brought me to your office."

"What is the file this Major Canfield demands?" Brayduck was annoyed.

"I know only the number and the classification stated by the archives section of the State Department."

"What are they?" Cordell Hull again leaned forward on his desk.

Ellis hesitated. It would be inviting personal as well as professional embarrassment to state the terms of the file without giving Hull the data on Canfield. He would have been able to do that had Brayduck not been there. Goddamn college boys. Ellis was always uncomfortable with the fast talkers. Damn! he thought. He'd be direct with Hull.

"Before I answer you, may I take the opportunity to fill in some background material I believe is most relevant. . . . Not only relevant, sir, but intrinsic to the file itself."

"By all means." Hull wasn't sure whether he was irritated or fascinated.

"The final communication from Heinrich Kroeger to Major Canfield demands a preliminary meeting with someone identified only as . . . April Red. This meeting is to take place in Bern, Switzerland, prior to any negotiations between Kroeger and Canfield."

"Who is April Red, General? I gather from the tone of your voice that you have an idea who he may be." Very little was lost on Undersecretary Brayduck, and Brigadier Ellis was painfully aware of the fact.

9

"We . . . or more specifically . . . I think I do." Ellis opened the white folder in his hands and flipped the top page over the cardboard. "If I may have the secretary's permission, I have extracted the following from Major Canfield's security check."

"Of course, General."

"Matthew Canfield—entered government service, Department of the Interior, in March, nineteen seventeen. Education—one year University of Oklahoma, one and one-half years night school extension courses, Washington, D.C. Employed as a junior accountant government frauds section of Interior. Promoted to field accountant in nineteen eighteen. Attached to Group Twenty division, which, as you know . . ."

Cordell Hull interrupted quietly. "A small, highly trained unit assigned to conflicts of interests, misappropriations, et cetera, during the First World War. Very effective too. . . . Until, as most such units, it became overly impressed with itself. Disbanded in twenty-nine or thirty, I believe."

"In nineteen thirty-two, Mr. Secretary." General Ellis was pleased that he had the facts at his command. He flipped a second page over the top of the folder and continued to read.

"Canfield remained with Interior for a period of ten years, rising four pay grades. Superior performance. Excellent rating. In May of nineteen twenty-seven he resigned from government service to enter employment with the Scarlatti Industries."

At the mention of the name Scarlatti, both Hull and Brayduck reacted as if stung.

"Which of the Scarlatti companies?"

"Executive Offices, five twenty-five Fifth Avenue, New York."

Cordell Hull toyed with the thin black cord of his pince-nez. "Quite a jump for our Mr. Canfield. From night school in Washington to the executive offices of Scarlatti." He glanced downward, taking his eyes off the general.

"Is Scarlatti one of the corporations you referred to in your memorandum?" Brayduck was impatient.

Before the brigadier could answer, Cordell Hull rose from his chair. Hull was tall and imposing. Much larger

10

than the other two. "General Ellis, I instruct you not to answer any further questions!"

Brayduck looked as though he'd been slapped. He stared at Hull, confused and startled by the secretary's order to the brigadier. Hull returned his gaze and spoke softly.

"My apologies, Mr. Brayduck. I cannot guarantee it, but I hope to have an explanation for you later in the day. Until then, will you be so kind as to leave us alone?"

"Of course." Brayduck knew that this good and honest old man had his reasons. "No explanation is necessary, sir."

"However, one is deserved."

"Thank you, Mr. Secretary. You may be assured of my confidence regarding this meeting."

Hull's eyes followed Brayduck until the door was closed. He then returned to the brigadier general, who stood quietly, not comprehending. "Undersecretary Brayduck is an extraordinary public servant. My dismissing him is not to be construed as a reflection on either his character or his work."

"Yes, sir."

Hull slowly and in some pain sat down once more in his chair. "I asked Mr. Brayduck to leave because I believe I may know something of what you're about to discuss. If I'm right, it's best we be alone."

The brigadier general was unsettled. He did not think it possible for Hull to know.

"Don't be alarmed, General. I'm no mind reader. . . . I was in the House of Representatives during the period you speak of. Your words evoked a memory. An almost forgotten memory of a very warm afternoon in the House. . . . But perhaps I'm in error. Please continue where you left off. I believe our Major Canfield had entered employment with the Scarlatti Industries. . . . A most unusual step, I think you'll agree."

"There is a logical explanation. Canfield married the widow of Ulster Stewart Scarlett six months after Scarlett's death in Zurich, Switzerland, in nineteen twenty-six. Scarlett was the youngest of two surviving sons of Giovanni and Elizabeth Scarlatti, founders of the Scarlatti Industries."

Cordell Hull briefly closed his eyes. "Go on."

11

"Ulster Scarlett and his wife Janet Saxon Scarlett had a son, Andrew Roland, subsequently adopted by Matthew Canfield after his marriage to Scarlett's widow. Adopted but not separated from the Scarlatti estates. . . . Canfield continued in the employ of Scarlatti until August, nineteen forty, when he returned to government service and was commissioned in Army Intelligence."

General Ellis paused and looked over the folder at Cordell Hull. He wondered if Hull was beginning to understand, but the secretary's face betrayed no expression.

"You spoke of the file Canfield has requested from the archives. What is it?"

"That was my next consideration, Mr. Secretary." Ellis folded over another page. "The file is only a number to us, but the number gives us the year of its entry. . . . It's nineteen twenty-six, the fourth quarter of twenty-six to be exact."

"And what are the terms of classification?"

"Maximum. It can be released only by an executive order signed by the president for reasons of national security."

"I presume that one of the signators—witnesses to the file—was a man then employed by the Department of the Interior by the name of Matthew Canfield."

The brigadier was visibly upset but continued to hold the white folder firmly between his thumb and forefinger. "That is correct."

"And now he wants it back or he refuses to make contact with Kroeger."

"Yes, sir."

"I trust you have pointed out to him the illegality of his position?"

"I have personally threatened him with a court-martial. . . . His only reply was that it's our choice to refuse him."

"And then no contact is made with Kroeger?"

"Yes, sir. . . . It's my opinion that Major Canfield would rather face spending the rest of his life in a military prison than alter his position."

Cordell Hull rose from his chair and faced the general. "Would you care to summarize?"

"It is my belief that the April Red referred to by Heinrich Kroeger is the boy, Andrew Roland. I think he's Kroeger's son. The initials are the same. The boy was

12

born in April, nineteen twenty-six. I believe that Heinrich Kroeger is Ulster Scarlett."

"He died in Zurich." Hull watched the general closely.

"The circumstances are suspect. There is on record only a death certificate from an obscure court in a small village thirty miles outside of Zurich and untraceable affidavits of witnesses never heard of before or since."

Hull stared coolly into the general's eyes. "You realize what you're saying? Scarlatti is one of the corporate giants."

"I do, sir. I contend further that Major Canfield is aware of Kroeger's identity and intends to destroy the file."

"Do you believe that it's a conspiracy? A conspiracy to conceal the identity of Kroeger?"

"I don't know. . . . I'm not very good at putting into words another person's motives. But Major Canfield's reactions seem so intensely private that I'm inclined to believe that it's a highly personal matter."

Hull smiled. "I think you're very good with words. . . . However, you do believe that the truth is in the file? And if it is, why would Canfield bring it to our attention? Certainly he knows that if we can get it for him, we certainly can get it for ourselves. We might never have been aware of it, had he kept silent."

"As I said, Canfield's an experienced man. I'm sure he's acting on the premise that we soon will be aware of it."

"How?"

"Through Kroeger. . . . And Canfield has set the condition that the file's seals be intact. He's an expert, sir. He'd know if they were tampered with."

Cordell Hull walked around his desk past the brigadier with his hands clasped behind his back. His gait was stiff, his health obviously failing. Brayduck had been right, thought the secretary of state. If even the specter of a relationship between the powerful American industrialists and the German High Command became known, regardless of how remote or how long in the past, it could tear the country apart. Especially during a national election.

"In your judgment if we delivered the file to Major Canfield, would he produce . . . April Red . . . for this meeting with Kroeger?"

"I believe he would."

13

"Why? It's a cruel thing to do to an eighteen-year-old boy."

The general hesitated. "I'm not sure he has an alternative. There's nothing to prevent Kroeger from making other arrangements."

Hull stopped pacing and looked at the brigadier general. He had made up his mind. "I shall have the president sign an executive order for the file. However, and frankly I place this as a condition for his signature, your suppositions are to remain between the two of us."

"The two of us?"

"I shall brief President Roosevelt on the substance of our conversation, but I will not burden him with conjectures which may prove to be unfounded. Your theory may be nothing more than a series of recorded coincidences easily explained."

"I understand."

"But if you are correct, Heinrich Kroeger could trigger an internal collapse in Berlin. Germany's in a death struggle. . . . As you've pointed out, he's had extraordinary staying power. He's part of the elite corps surrounding Hitler. The Praetorian Guard revolts against Caesar. If you're wrong, however, then we must both think of two people who will soon be on their way to Bern. And may God have mercy on our souls."

Brigadier General Ellis replaced the pages in the white folder, picked up the attaché case at his feet, and walked to the large black door. As he closed it behind him, he saw that Hull was staring at him. He had an uncomfortable feeling in the pit of his stomach.

Hull was not thinking about the general, however. He was remembering that warm afternoon long ago in the House of Representatives. Member after member had gotten up and read glowing tributes into the *Congressional Record* eulogizing a brave young American who was presumed dead. Everyone from both parties had expected him, the honorable member from the great state of Tennessee, to add his comments. Heads kept turning toward his desk in anticipation.

Cordell Hull was the only member of the house who was on a first-name basis with the renowned Elizabeth Scarlatti, that legend in her own time. The mother of the brave young man being glorified for posterity in the Congress of the United States.

For in spite of their political differences, Hull and his wife had been friends with Elizabeth Scarlatti for years.

Yet he had remained silent that warm afternoon.

He had known Ulster Stewart Scarlett, and he had despised him.

CHAPTER 2

The brown sedan with the United States Army insignia on both doors turned right on Twenty-second Street and entered Gramercy Square.

In the back seat Matthew Canfield leaned forward, taking the briefcase off his lap and placing it at his feet. He pulled the right sleeve of his overcoat down to conceal the thick silver chain, which was tightly wound around his wrist and looped through the metal handle of the case.

He knew that the contents of the briefcase, or more specifically, his possession of its contents, signified the end for him. When it was all over, and if he were still alive, they would crucify him if a way could be found that would exonerate the military.

The army car made two left turns and stopped by the entrance of the Gramercy Arms Apartments. A uniformed doorman opened the rear door and Canfield stepped out.

"I want you back here in half an hour," he told his driver. "No later."

The pale sergeant, obviously conditioned by his superior's habits, replied, "I'll be back in twenty minutes, sir."

The major nodded appreciatively, turned, and went into the building. As he rode the elevator up, the major numbly realized how tired he was. Each number seemed to stay lighted far longer than it should have; the time lapse between the floors seemed interminable. And yet he was in no hurry. No hurry, whatsoever.

16

Eighteen years. The end of the lie but not the end of the fear. That would come only when Kroeger was dead. What would be left was guilt. He could live with the guilt, for it would be his alone and not the boy's or Janet's.

It would be his death, too. Not Janet's. Not Andrew's. If death was called for, it would be his. He'd make sure of that.

He would not leave Bern, Switzerland, until Kroeger was dead.

Kroeger or himself.

In all likelihood, both of them.

Out of the elevator he turned left and stepped down the short hallway to a door. He unlocked the door and stepped into a large, comfortable living room, furnished in Italian provincial style. Two huge bay windows overlooked the park, and various doors led to the bedrooms, dining room, the pantry, and the library. Canfield stood for a moment and thought unavoidably that all this, too, went back eighteen years.

The library door opened and a young man walked out. He nodded to Canfield without enthusiasm. "Hello, Dad."

Canfield stared at the boy. It took a great deal of strength not to rush to his son and hold him.

His son.

And not his son.

He knew if he attempted such a gesture it would be rejected. The boy was wary now and, although he tried not to show it, afraid.

"Hello," said the major. "Give me a hand with all this, will you?"

The young man crossed to the older one and mumbled, "Sure thing."

Between them they unfastened the primary lock on the chain, and the younger man held the briefcase out straight so Canfield could manipulate the secondary combination lock, which was secured on the flat of his wrist. The briefcase came loose, and Canfield removed his hat, overcoat, and uniform jacket, throwing them on an easy chair.

The boy held the briefcase, standing motionless before the major. He was extraordinarily good looking. He had bright blue eyes below very dark eyebrows, a straight but slightly upturned nose, and black hair combed neatly

17

back. His complexion was swarthy as though he had a perpetual tan. He stood just over six feet and was dressed in gray flannels, a blue shirt, and a tweed jacket.

"How do you feel?" asked Canfield.

The young man paused and replied softly. "Well, on my twelfth birthday you and Mother got me a new sailboat. I liked that better."

The older man returned the younger's smile. "I guess you did."

"Is this it?" The boy placed the briefcase on the table and fingered it.

"Everything."

"I suppose I should feel privileged."

"It took an executive order from the president to get it out of State."

"Really?" The boy looked up.

"Don't be alarmed. I doubt he knows what's in it."

"How come?"

"A deal was made. There was an understanding."

"I don't believe that."

"I think you will after you read it. No more than ten people have ever seen it in full, and most of them are dead. When we compiled the last quarter of the file, we did it in segments . . . in nineteen thirty-eight. It's in the separate folder with the lead seals. The pages are out of sequence and have to be collated. The key's on the first page." The major quickly loosened his tie and started unbuttoning his shirt.

"Was all that necessary?"

"We thought it was. As I recall, we used rotating pools of typists." The major started toward a bedroom door. "I suggest you arrange the pages before starting the last folder." He entered the bedroom, hastily took off his shirt, and unlaced his shoes. The young man followed and stood in the doorframe.

"When are we going?" asked the boy.

"Thursday."

"How?"

"Bomber Ferry Command. Matthews Air Force Base to Newfoundland, Iceland, Greenland, to Ireland. From Ireland, on a neutral, straight through to Lisbon."

"Lisbon?"

"The Swiss embassy takes over from there. They'll take us to Bern. . . . We're fully protected."

18

Canfield, having removed his trousers, selected a pair of light gray flannels from the closet and put them on.

"What's Mother going to be told?" asked the young man.

Canfield crossed into the bathroom without replying. He filled the washbowl with hot water and began lathering his face.

The boy's eyes followed him, but he did not move or break the silence. He sensed that the older man was far more upset than he wished to show.

"Get me a clean shirt from the second drawer over there, will you, please. Just put it on the bed."

"Sure." He selected a wide-collar broadcloth from the stack of shirts in the dresser drawer.

Canfield spoke while he shaved. "Today's Monday, so we'll have three days. I'll be making the final arrangements, and it'll give you time to digest the file. You'll have questions, and I don't have to tell you that you'll have to ask me. Not that you'll be speaking to anyone else who could answer you, anyway, but in case you get hot and want to pick up a phone, don't."

"Understood."

"Incidentally, don't feel you have to commit anything to memory. That's not important. I simply know that you have to understand."

Was he being honest with the boy? Was it really necessary to make him feel the weight of official truth? Canfield had convinced himself that it was, for no matter the years, no matter the affection between them, Andrew was a Scarlett. In a few years he would inherit one of the largest fortunes on earth. Such persons had to have responsibility thrust upon them when it was necessary, not when it was convenient.

Or did they?

Or was Canfield simply taking the easiest way for himself? Let the words come from someone else. Oh, God! Make somebody else speak!

Drying his face with a towel, the major splashed some Pinaud on his face and started putting on his shirt.

"If you're interested, you missed most of your beard."

"Not interested." He selected a tie from a rack on the closet door and pulled a dark blue blazer from a hanger. "When I leave, you can start reading. If you go out for dinner, put the briefcase in the cabinet to the right of the library door. Lock it. Here's the key." He unclipped a small key from his key ring.

The two men walked out of the bedroom, and Canfield started toward the front hall.

"You either didn't hear me or you don't want to answer, but what about Mother?"

"I heard you." Canfield turned toward the young man. "Janet isn't supposed to know anything."

"Why not? Supposing something happens?"

Canfield was visibly upset. "It's my judgment that she be told nothing."

"I don't agree with you." The young man remained subdued.

"That doesn't concern me!"

"Maybe it should. I'm pretty important to you now. . . . I didn't choose to be, Dad."

"And you think that gives you the right to issue orders?"

"I think I have a right to be heard. . . . Look, I know you're upset, but she's my mother."

"And my wife. Don't forget that part, will you, Andy?" The major took several steps toward the young man, but Andrew Scarlett turned away and walked to the table where the black leather case lay beside the lamp.

"You never showed me how to open your briefcase."

"It's unlocked. I unlocked it in the car. It opens like any other briefcase."

Young Scarlett fingered the clasps and they shot up. "I didn't believe you last night, you know," he said quietly while he opened the lid of the briefcase.

"That's not surprising."

"No. Not about him. I believe that part because it answered a lot of questions about you." He turned and looked at the older man. "Well, not questions really, because I always thought I knew why you acted the way you did. I figured you just resented the Scarletts. . . . Not me. The Scarletts. Uncle Chancellor, Aunt Allison, all the kids. You and Mom always laughed at all of them. So did I. . . . I remember how painful it was for you to tell me why my last name couldn't be the same as yours. Remember that?"

"Painfully." Canfield smiled gently.

"But the last couple of years . . . you changed. You got pretty vicious about the Scarletts. You hated it every time anyone mentioned the Scarlatti companies. You'd fly off the handle whenever the Scarlatti lawyers made appointments to discuss me with you and Mom. She got angry with you and said you were unreasonable. . . . Only she was wrong. I understand now. . . . So you see, I'm prepared to believe whatever's in here." He closed the lid on the briefcase.

"It won't be easy for you."

"It isn't easy now, and I'm just getting over the first shock." He tried lamely to smile. "Anyway, I'll learn to live with it, I guess. . . . I never knew him. He was never anything to me. I never paid much attention to Uncle Chancellor's stories. You see, I didn't want to know anything. Do you know why?"

The major watched the young man closely. "No, I don't," he replied.

"Because I never wanted to belong to anyone but you . . . and Janet."

Oh, God in your protective heaven, thought Canfield. "I've got to go." He started once again for the door.

"Not yet. We haven't settled anything."

"There's nothing to settle."

"You haven't heard what it was I didn't believe last night."

Canfield stopped, his hand on the doorknob. "What?"

"That mother . . . doesn't know about him."

Canfield removed his hand from the knob and stood by the door. When he spoke his voice was low and controlled. "I was hoping to avoid this until later. Until you'd read the file."

"It's got to be now, or I don't want the file. If anything's going to be kept from her, I want to know why before I go any further."

The major came back into the center of the room. "What do you want me to tell you? That it would kill her to find out?"

"Would it?"

"Probably not. But I haven't the courage to test that."

"How long have you known?"

Canfield walked to the window. The children had left the park. The gate was closed.

"On June twelfth, nineteen thirty-six, I made positive identification. I amended the file a year and a half later on January second, nineteen thirty-eight."

"Jesus Christ."

"Yes. . . . Jesus Christ."

"And you never told her?"

"No."

"Dad, why not?"

"I could give you twenty or thirty impressive reasons," said Canfield as he continued looking down at Gramercy Park. "But three have always stuck out in my mind. First—he'd done enough to her; he was her own personal hell. Second—once your grandmother died, no one else alive could identify him. And the third reason—your mother took my word . . . that I'd killed him."

"You!"

The major turned from the window. "Yes. Me. . . . I believed I had. . . . Enough so that I forced twenty-two witnesses to sign affidavits that he was dead. I bought a corrupt court outside of Zurich to issue the certificate of death. All very legal. . . . That June morning in thirty-six when I found out the truth we were at the bay house and I was on the patio having coffee. You and your mother were hosing down a catboat and calling for me to put it in the water. You kept splashing her with the hose, and she laughed and shrieked and ran around the boat with you following her. She was so happy! . . . I didn't tell her. I'm not proud of myself, but there it is."

The young man sat down in the chair next to the table. He started to speak several times, but each time the words fell short of making sense.

Canfield spoke quietly. "Are you sure you want to belong to me?"

The boy looked up from the chair. "You must have loved her a lot."

"I still do."

"Then I . . . still want to belong to you."

The shaded understatement of the young man's voice nearly caused Canfield to break. But he had promised himself he would not do that no matter what happened. There was too much left to go through.

"I thank you for that." He turned back to the window. The street lights had been turned on—every other one as if to remind people that it could happen here, but probably wouldn't so they could relax.

"Dad?"

"Yes?"

"Why did you go back and change the file?"

There was a long silence before Canfield answered. "I had to. . . . That sounds funny now—'I had to.' It took me eighteen months to make that decision. When I finally did make it, it took less than five minutes to convince myself." He stopped for a moment wondering if it was necessary to tell the boy. There was no point in not telling him. "On New Year's Day in nineteen thirty-eight your mother bought me a new Packard Roadster. Twelve cylinders. A beautiful automobile. I took it for a spin on the Southampton road. . . . I'm not sure what happened —I think the steering wheel locked. I don't know, but there was an accident. The car rolled over twice before I was thrown clear. It was a wreck, but I was okay. Except for a little blood, I was fine. But it occurred to me that I might have been killed."

"I remember that. You phoned from somebody's house and Mom and I drove over and picked you up. You were a mess."

"That's right. That was when I made up my mind to go down to Washington and amend the file."

"I don't understand."

Canfield sat on the window seat. "If anything did happen to me, Scarlett . . . Kroeger could have played out a horror story and would have if it served him. Janet was vulnerable because she didn't know anything. So somewhere the truth had to be told. . . . But told in such a way that would leave neither government any alternative but to have Kroeger eliminated . . . immediately. Speaking for this country, Kroeger made fools out of a lot of prominent men. Some of those distinguished gentlemen are at the policy level today. Others are manufacturing planes and tanks and ships. By identifying Kroeger as Scarlett, we move into a whole new set of questions. Questions our government won't want asked now. Or perhaps ever."

He slowly unbuttoned his tweed overcoat but he did not want to take it off.

"The Scarlatti lawyers have a letter which is to be delivered upon my death or disappearance to the most influential cabinet member of whatever administration is in Washington at the time. Scarlatti lawyers are good at that sort of thing. . . . I knew the war was coming. Everyone did. Remember, it was nineteen thirty-eight. . . . The letter directs that person to the file and the truth."

Canfield took a deep breath and looked at the ceiling.

"As you'll see, I outlined a specific course of action if we were at war and a variation if we weren't. Only in the last extremity was your mother to be told."

"Why should anyone pay attention to you after what you did?"

Andrew Scarlett was quick. Canfield liked that.

"There are times when countries . . . even countries in a state of war have the same objectives. Lines of communication are always open for such purposes . . . Heinrich Kroeger is a case in point. He represents too great an embarrassment to either side. . . . The file makes that clear."

"That seems cynical."

"It is. . . . I directed that within forty-eight hours after my death, the Third Reich's High Command be reached and told that a few of our top personnel in Military Intelligence have long suspected Heinrich Kroeger to be an American citizen."

Andrew Scarlett leaned forward on the edge of the chair. Canfield went on without apparently noticing the boy's growing concern.

"Since Kroeger consistently makes underground contacts with a number of Americans, these suspicions are believed to be confirmed. However, as a result of . . .'" Canfield paused to recall the exact wording. "'. . . 'the death of one Matthew Canfield, a former associate of the man known now as Heinrich Kroeger . . .' our government has in its possession . . . documents which state unequivocally that Heinrich Kroeger is . . . criminally insane. We want no part of him. Either as a former citizen or as a defector."

The young man rose from the chair, staring at his stepfather. "Is this true?"

"It would have been sufficient, which is more to the point. The combination is enough to guarantee a swift execution. A traitor as well as an insane man." .

"That's not what I asked."

"All the information's in the file."

"I'd like to know now. Is it true? Is he . . . was he insane? Or is it a trick?"

Canfield got up from the window seat. His reply was

24

barely above a whisper. "This is why I wanted to wait. You want a simple answer, and there isn't any."

"I want to know if my . . . father was insane."

"If you mean do we really have documented proof from medical authorities that he was unbalanced? . . . No, we do not. On the other hand, there were ten men left in Zurich, powerful men—six are still living—who had every reason in the world to want Kroeger, as they knew him, considered a lunatic. . . . It was their only way out. And being who they were, they made sure that was the case. The Heinrich Kroeger referred to in the original file is verified by all ten to be a maniac. A schizophrenic madman. It was a collective effort that left no room for doubt. They had no choice. . . . But if you ask me . . . Kroeger was the sanest man imaginable. And the cruelest. You'll read that, too."

"Why don't you call him by his right name?"

Suddenly, as if the strain had become more than he could bear, Canfield swiftly turned.

Andrew watched the angered, flushed, middle-aged man across the room. He had always loved him for he was a man to be loved. Positive, sure, capable, fun and—what was the word his stepfather had used?—vulnerable.

"You weren't just protecting Mother, were you? You were protecting me. You did what you did to protect me, too. . . . If he ever came back, I'd be a freak for the rest of my life."

Canfield slowly turned and faced his stepson. "Not just you. There'd be a lot of freaks. I counted on that."

"But not the same for them." Young Scarlett walked back to the briefcase.

"I grant you. Not the same." He followed the boy and stood behind him. "I'd have given anything not to have told you, I think you know that. I had no choice. By making you part of the final conditions, Kroeger—left me no choice but to tell you the truth. I couldn't fake that. . . . He believes that once you know the truth you'll be terrified, and I'll do anything short of killing you—perhaps even that—to keep you from going into panic. There is information in this file which could destroy your mother. Send me to prison, probably for the rest of my life. Oh, Kroeger thought it all out. But he misjudged. He didn't know you."

"Do I really have to see him? Talk to him?"

"I'll be in the room with you. That's where the deal is made."

Andrew Scarlett looked startled. "Then you're going to make a deal with him." It was a distasteful statement of fact.

"We have to know what he can deliver. Once he's satisfied that I've carried out my end of the bargain, you, we'll know what it is he's offering. And for what."

"Then I don't have to read this, do I." It was not a question. "All I have to do is be there. . . . Okay, I'll be there!"

"You'll read it because I'm ordering you to!"

"All right. All right, Dad. I'll read it."

"Thank you. . . . I'm sorry I had to speak that way." He began to button his overcoat.

"Sure. . . . I deserved it. . . . By the way, suppose Mother decides to call me at school? She does, you know."

"There's a tap on your phone as of this morning. An intercept, to be exact. Works fine. You have a new friend named Tom Ahrens."

"Who's he?"

"A lieutenant in CIC. Stationed in Boston. He has your schedule and will cover the phone. He knows what to say. You went to Smith for a long weekend."

"Jesus, you think of everything."

"Most of the time." Canfield had reached the door. "I may not be back tonight."

"Where are you going?"

"I've got some work to do. I'd rather you didn't go out but if you do, remember the cabinet. Put everything away." He opened the door.

"I won't go anywhere."

"Good. And Andy . . . you've got one hell of a responsibility ahead of you. I hope we've brought you up so you can handle it. I think you can." Canfield walked out the door and closed it behind him.

The young man knew that his stepfather spoke the wrong words. He was trying to say something else. The boy stared at the door and suddenly he knew what that something else was.

Matthew Canfield wasn't coming back.

What had he said? In the last extremity, Janet had to be told. His mother had to be told the truth. And there

26

was no one else now who could tell her.

Andrew Scarlett looked at the briefcase on the table.

The son and the stepfather were going to Bern, but only the son would come back.

Matthew Canfield was going to his death.

Canfield closed the apartment door and leaned against the hallway wall. He was heavy with sweat, and the rhythmic pounding in his chest was so loud he thought it might be heard back in the apartment.

He looked at his watch. It had taken him less than an hour, and he had remained remarkably calm. Now he wished to get as far away as possible. He knew that by any of the standards of courage or morality or responsibility, he should stay with the boy. But such demands could not be made on him now. One thing at a time or he'd go out of his mind. One item crossed off and then on to the next.

What was the next?

Tomorrow.

The courier to Lisbon with the detailed precautions. One mistake and everything could explode. The courier wasn't leaving until seven o'clock in the evening.

He could spend the night and most of the day with Janet. He rationalized that he had to. If Andy cracked, the first thing he'd do was try to reach his mother. Because he couldn't face staying with him, he had to be with her.

To hell with his office! To hell with the army! To hell with the United States government!

In light of his impending departure he was under voluntary surveillance twenty-four hours a day. God damn them!

They expected him to be no farther than ten minutes from a Teletype.

Well, he wasn't going to be.

He would spend every minute he could with Janet. She was closing up the Oyster Bay home for the winter. They'd be alone, perhaps for the last time.

Eighteen years and the charade was coming to a finish.

Fortunately for the state of his anxiety, the elevator came quickly. Because now he was in a hurry. To Janet.

The sergeant held the car door open and saluted as smartly as he could. Under ordinary circumstances, the major would have chuckled and reminded the sergeant that he was in civilian clothes. Instead, he returned the salute informally and hopped into the car.

"To the office, Major Canfield?"

"No, Sergeant. Oyster Bay."

CHAPTER 3

An American Success Story

On August 24, 1892, the social world of Chicago and Evanston, Illinois, was shaken to its foundations, which were not inordinately firm to begin with. For on this day Elizabeth Royce Wyckham, the twenty-seven-year-old daughter of industrialist Albert O. Wyckham, married an impoverished Sicilian immigrant by the name of Giovanni Merighi Scarlatti.

Elizabeth Wyckham was a tall, aristocratic girl who had been an ever-present source of worry to her parents. According to Albert O. Wyckham and his wife, the aging Elizabeth had thrown over every golden matrimonial opportunity a girl could ask for in Chicago, Illinois. Her reply had been:

"Fool's gold, Papa!"

So they had taken her on a grand tour of the Continent, expending great sums in great expectations. After four months of surveying the best matrimonial prospects from England, France, and Germany, her reply had been:

"Idiot's gold, Papa. I'd prefer a string of lovers!"

Her father had slapped his daughter resoundingly.

She proceeded, in turn, to kick him in the ankle.

Elizabeth first saw her future husband at one of those picnic outings the officers of her father's firm in Chicago held annually for deserving clerks and their families. He had been introduced to her as a serf might have been to the daughter of a feudal baron.

He was a huge man with massive, yet somehow gentle hands and sharp Italian features. His English was almost unintelligible, but instead of accompanying his broken speech with awkward humility, he radiated confidence and made no apologies. Elizabeth liked him immediately. Although young Scarlatti was neither a clerk nor had he a family, he had impressed the Wyckham executives with his knowledge of machinery and had actually submitted a design for a machine that would cut the cost of producing paper rolls by possibly 16 percent. He had been invited to the picnic.

Elizabeth's curiosity had already been aroused by her father's stories about him. The greaser had a knack for tinkering—absolutely incredible. He had spotted two machines in as many weeks wherein the addition of single levers eliminated the necessity of second men on the jobs. As there were eight of each machine, the Wyckham Company was able to lay off sixteen men who obviously were no longer pulling their weight. Further, Wyckham had had the foresight to hire a second-generation Italian from Chicago's Little Italy to accompany Giovanni Scarlatti wherever he wandered in the plant and literally act as his interpreter. Old Wyckham objected to the eight dollars a week he paid the conversant Italian but justified the salary on the basis that Giovanni would make other improvements. He had better. Wyckham was paying him fourteen dollars a week.

The first true inkling Elizabeth had about her future husband came several weeks after the picnic. Her father gloatingly announced at the dinner table that his big Italian simpleton had requested permission to come in Sundays! No additional pay, mind you; just that he had nothing better to do. Naturally, Wyckham had arranged it with his watchman, for it was his Christian duty to keep such a fellow occupied and away from all the wine and beer to which Italians were addicted.

On the second Sunday Elizabeth found a pretext to go from her elegant home in suburban Evanston to Chicago and then to the plant. There she found Giovanni, not in the machine shop but in one of the billing offices. He was laboriously copying down figures from a file marked clearly—CONFIDENTIAL. The drawer of a steel file cabinet on the left wall of the office was open. A long string of thin wire was still hanging from the small lock. Obviously the lock had been expertly picked.

At that moment, as she stood in the doorway watching

him, Elizabeth smiled. This large, black-haired Italian simpleton was far more complicated than her father thought. And, not incidentally, he was most attractive.

Startled, Giovanni looked up. Within a split second his attitude changed to one of defiance.

"Okay, Miss 'Lisbet! You tell you papa! I don't want to work here no more!"

Elizabeth then spoke her first words of love to Giovanni.

"Get me a chair, Mr. Scarlatti. I'll help you. . . . It'll be quicker that way."

And, indeed, it was.

The next several weeks were spent educating Giovanni in the legal and corporate structure of the American industrial organization. Just the facts devoid of theory, for Giovanni supplied his own philosophy. This land of opportunity was for those just a little bit quicker than the other opportunists. The period was one of enormous economic growth, and Giovanni understood that unless his machines enabled him to own a part of that growth, his position would remain that of a servant to masters rather than a master of servants. And he was ambitious.

Giovanni set to work with Elizabeth's help. He designed what old Albert Wyckham and his executives thought was a revolutionary impact-extrusion press that could turn out corrugated carton sides at a phenomenal rate of speed and at a cost approximating a 30 percent saving over the old process. Wyckham was delighted and gave Giovanni a ten-dollar raise.

While waiting for the new machinery to be tooled and put into assembly, Elizabeth convinced her father to ask Giovanni to dinner. At first, Albert Wyckham thought his daughter was playing a joke. A joke in poor taste for all concerned. Wyckham may have made fun of the Italian but he respected him. He did not wish to see his clever wop embarrassed at a dinner party. However, when Elizabeth told her father that embarrassment was the last thing she had in mind, that she had met Giovanni on several occasions since the company picnic—finding him quite amusing—her father consented to a small family dinner with suddenly new misgivings.

Three days after the dinner Wyckham's new machinery for corrugated carton sides was in operation and on that morning Giovanni Scarlatti did not show up for work.

None of the executives understood. It should have been the most important morning of his life.

It was.

For instead of Giovanni, a letter arrived at Albert Wyckham's office, typed by his own daughter. The letter outlined a second machine for corrugated carton sides that made Wyckham's new assembly totally obsolete.

Giovanni's conditions were frankly put. Either Wyckham assigned him a large block of company stock plus options for purchase of additional shares based upon current values, or he would take his second design for corrugated carton sides to Wyckham's competitor. Whoever possessed the second design would bury the other. It didn't matter to Giovanni Scarlatti, but he did feel it would be better kept in the family as he was formally requesting Albert's daughter in marriage. Again, Wyckham's answer did not really concern him, because Elizabeth and he would be united as man and wife within the month regardless of his position.

From this juncture on, the rise of Scarlatti was as rapid as it was clouded. The public facts indicate that for several years he continued to design newer and better machinery for a number of paper-producing companies throughout the Midwest. He did so always with the same conditions—minor royalties and shares of stock, with options to buy additional shares at the prices of stock prior to the installation of his new designs. All designs were subject to renegotiation of royalties after five-year periods. A reasonable item to be dealt with in reasonable good faith. A very acceptable legal expression, especially in light of the low royalty rates.

By this time, Elizabeth's father, exhausted by the tensions of business events and his daughter's marriage "to that wop," was content to retire. Giovanni and his wife were awarded the old man's entire voting stock in the Wyckham Company.

This was all Giovanni Scarlatti needed. Mathematics is a pure science, and never was this more apparent. Already possessing representation in eleven paper firms in Illinois, Ohio, and western Pennsylvania, and owning patents on thirty-seven different operating assemblies, Giovanni Scarlatti called a conference of the firms accountable to him. In what amounted to a slaughter of the uninformed, Giovanni suggested that a desirable course of action was the formation of one parent organization with himself and his wife as the principal stockholders.

Everyone would, of course, be well taken care of, and the single company would expand beyond their wildest dreams under his inventive genius.

If they didn't agree, they could take his machines out of their factories. He was a poor immigrant who had been deviously misled in his initial negotiations. The royalties paid for his designs were ridiculous in light of the profits. Also in several cases individual stocks had risen astronomically and by the terms of his contracts those particular firms had to make his options available at the previous stock prices. When one came right down to it, Giovanni Scarlatti was a major stockholder in a number of established paper companies.

Howls were heard in boardrooms throughout the three states. Impetuous challenges were flung at the arrogant Italian only to be muted by wiser legal counsel. Better a merging survival than isolated destruction. Scarlatti might be defeated in the courts, but it was quite possible that he might not be. In that latter event his demands could be excessive, and if rejected, the cost of retooling and loss of supply would plunge many of the firms into disastrous financial territory. Besides Scarlatti was a genius, and they all might do rather well.

So the mammoth Scarlatti Industries was formed, and the empire of Giovanni Merighi Scarlatti was born.

It was as its master—sprawling, energetic, insatiable. As his curiosity diversified, so did his companies. From paper it was an easy leap into packaging; from packaging into hauling and freight; from transportation into produce. And always a better idea came along with the purchase.

By the year 1904, after twelve years of marriage, Elizabeth Wyckham Scarlatti decided that it was prudent for her and her husband to go east. Although her husband's fortunes were secure and growing daily, his popularity was scarcely enviable. Among the financial powers of Chicago, Giovanni was the living proof of the Monroe Doctrine. The Irish were disagreeable, but this was intolerable.

Elizabeth's father and mother died; what few social loyalties that remained for her went with them. The consensus of the households of her lifelong friends was

33

described by Franklyn Fowler, recently of Fowler Paper Products:

"That black wop may own the mortgage on the club's building, but we'll be damned if we'll let him become a member!"

This general attitude had no effect on Giovanni, for he had neither the time nor the inclination for such indulgences. Neither did Elizabeth, for she had become Giovanni's partner in far more than the marriage bed. She was his censor, his sounding board, his constant interpreter of shaded meanings. But she differed from her husband regarding their banishment from the more normal social pursuits. Not for herself, but for the children.

Elizabeth and Giovanni had been blessed with three sons. They were Roland Wyckham, age nine; Chancellor Drew, eight; and Ulster Stewart, seven. And although they were only boys, Elizabeth saw the effects the family's ostracism was having on them. They attended the exclusive Evanston School for Boys, but except for their daily school associations, they saw no boys but each other. They were never asked to birthday parties but always told about them on the following days; invitations proferred to their classmates were invariably coolly received by calls from governesses; and, perhaps most cutting of all, was the repetitive ditty that greeted the boys each morning as they arrived:

"Scarlatti, spaghetti! Scarlatti, spaghetti!"

Elizabeth made up her mind that they should all have a fresh start. Even Giovanni and herself. She knew they could afford it even if it meant going back to his native Italy and buying Rome.

Instead of Rome, however, Elizabeth took a trip to New York City and discovered something quite unexpected.

New York was a very provincial town. Its interests were insular, and among those in the business world the reputation of Giovanni Merighi Scarlatti had taken a rather unusual twist; they weren't sure who he was other than the fact that he was an Italian inventor who had purchased a number of American companies in the Midwest.

Italian inventor. *American* companies.

Elizabeth found also that some of the more astute men on Wall Street believed Scarlatti's money had come

34

from one of the Italian ship lines. After all, he'd married the daughter of one of Chicago's best families.

New York it would be.

Elizabeth arranged for a temporary family residence at the Delmonico, and once settled, Elizabeth knew she had made the right decision. The children were bursting with excitement, anticipating new schools and new friends; and within a month Giovanni had purchased controlling interest in two failing, antiquated paper mills on the Hudson and was eagerly planning their joint resurrection.

The Scarlattis stayed at Delmonico's for nearly two years. It wasn't really necessary, for the uptown house might have been completed much sooner had Giovanni been able to give it proper attention. However, as a result of his lengthy conferences with the architects and contractors, he discovered another interest—land.

One evening while Elizabeth and Giovanni were having a late supper in their suite, Giovanni suddenly said, "Write out a check for two hundred ten thousand dollars. Put in the name East Island Real Estaters."

"Realtors, you mean?"

"That's right. Let me have the crackers."

Elizabeth passed the croutons. "That's a lot of money."

"We got a lot of money?"

"Well, yes, we do, but two hundred and ten thousand dollars. . . . Is it a new plant?"

"Just give me the check, Elizabeth. I've got a good surprise for you."

She stared at him. "You know I don't question your judgment but I must insist. . . ."

"All right, all right." Giovanni smiled. "You don't get a surprise. I tell you. . . . I'm going to be like a *barone*."

"A what?"

"A *barone*. A *conte*. You can be a *contessa!*"

"I simply don't understand. . . ."

"In Italy, a man who has a couple of fields, maybe a few pigs, he's practically a *barone*. Lots of men want to be *baroni*. I was talking to the East Island people. They're gonna sell me some meadows out on Long Island."

"Giovanni, they're worthless! They're simply the end of nowhere!"

"Woman, use your head! Already there's no place for the horses to stand. Tomorrow you give me the check.

35

Don't argue, please. Just'a smile and be the wife of a *barone*."

Elizabeth Scarlatti smiled.

Don Giovanni Merighi and Elizabeth Wyckham

Scarlatti of Ferrara

House of Ferrara d'Italia - American Residence

Delmonico - New York

Although Elizabeth did not take the cards seriously—they became a private joke between her and Giovanni—they did serve a purpose when not elaborated upon. They gave an identification befitting the Scarlatti wealth. Although no one who knew them ever referred to either as *conte* or *contessa*, there were many who weren't sure.

It was just possible. . . .

And one specific result—although the title did not appear on the cards—was that for the remainder of her long life Elizabeth was called madame.

Madame Elizabeth Scarlatti.

And Giovanni could no longer reach across the table and take his wife's bowl of soup.

Two years after the purchase of the land, on July 14, 1908, Giovanni Merighi Scarlatti died. The man was burnt out. And for weeks Elizabeth numbly tried to understand. There was no one to whom she could turn. She and Giovanni had been lovers, friends, partners, and each other's conscience. The thought of living without one another had been the only real fear in their lives.

But he was gone, and Elizabeth knew that they had not

built an empire for one to see it collapse with the other's absence.

Her first order of business was to consolidate the management of the widespread Scarlatti Industries into a single command post.

Top executives and their families were uprooted throughout the Midwest and brought to New York. Charts were prepared for Elizabeth's approval clearly defining all levels of decisions and areas of specific responsibility. A private network of telegraphic communications was set up between the New York offices and each plant, factory, yard, and subdivision office. Elizabeth was a good general and her army was a well-trained, headstrong organization. The times were on her side, and her shrewd analysis of people took care of the rest.

A magnificent town house was built, a country estate purchased in Newport, another seaside retreat constructed in a development called Oyster Bay, and every week she held a series of exhausting meetings with the executives of her late husband's companies.

Among her most important actions was her decision to help her children become totally identified with Protestant democracy. Her reasoning was simple. The name Scarlatti was out of place, even crude, in the circles her sons had entered and in which they would continue to live for the rest of their lives. Their names were legally altered to Scarlett.

Of course, for herself, in deep respect for Don Giovanni and in the tradition of Ferrara, she remained:

Elizabeth

Scarlatti of Ferrara

No residence was listed for it was difficult to know at which home she would be at a given time.

Elizabeth recognized the unpleasant fact that her two older sons had neither Giovanni's gift of imagination nor her own perception of their fellow man. It was difficult to know with the youngest, Ulster Stewart, for Ulster Stewart Scarlett was emerging as a problem.

In his early years it was merely the fact that he was a bully—a trait Elizabeth ascribed to his being the youngest, the most spoiled. But as he grew into his teens, Ulster's outlook changed subtly. He not only had to have his own way, he now demanded it. He was the only one of the brothers who used his wealth with cruelty. With brutality, perhaps, and that concerned Elizabeth. She first encountered this attitude on his thirteenth birthday. A few days before the event his teacher sent her a note.

Dear Madame Scarlatti:
Ulster's birthday invitations seem to have become a minor problem. The dear boy can't make up his mind who are his best friends—he has so many—and as a result he has given out a number of invitations and taken them back in favor of other boys. I'm sure the Parkleigh School would waive the twenty-five limit in Ulster Stewart's case.

That night Elizabeth asked Ulster about it.

"Yes. I took some of the invitations back. I changed my mind."

"Why? That's very discourteous."

"Why not? I didn't want them to come."

"Then why did you give them the invitations in the first place?"

"So they could all run home and tell their fathers and mothers they were coming over." The boy laughed. "Then they had to go back and say they weren't."

"That's terrible!"

"I don't think so. They don't want to come to my birthday party, they want to come to your house!"

38

While a freshman at Princeton, Ulster Stewart Scarlett displayed marked tendencies of hostility toward his brothers, his classmates, his teachers, and for Elizabeth the most unattractive, her servants. He was tolerated because he was the son of Elizabeth Scarlatti and for no other reason. Ulster was a monstrously spoiled young man, and Elizabeth knew she had to do something about it. In June of 1916 she ordered him to come home for a weekend, and told her son he had to take a job.

"I will not!"

"You *will!* You will *not* disobey me!"

And he didn't. Ulster spent the summer at the Hudson mill while his two brothers in Oyster Bay enjoyed the pleasures of Long Island Sound.

At the end of the summer, Elizabeth asked how he had done.

"You want the truth, Madame Scarlatti?" asked the youngish plant manager in Elizabeth's study one Saturday morning.

"Of course I do."

"It'll probably cost me my job."

"I doubt that."

"Very well, ma'am. Your son started out in raw baling as you ordered. It's a tough job but he's strong. . . . I yanked him out of there after he beat up a couple of men."

"Good Lord! Why wasn't I told?"

"I didn't know the circumstances. I thought that maybe the men had pushed him around. I didn't know."

"What did you find out?"

"The pushing was at the other end. . . . I put him in the upstairs presses and that was worse. He threatened the others, said he'd get them fired, made them do his work. He never let anyone forget who he was."

"You should have told me."

"I didn't know myself until the other week. Three men quit. We had to pay a dentist bill for one of them. Your son hit him with a lead strip."

"These are terrible things to hear. . . . Would you care to offer an opinion? Please, be frank. It will be to your advantage."

39

"Your son is big. He's a tough young fella. . . . But I'm not sure what else he is. I just have an idea he wants to start at the top and maybe that's what he should do. He's your son. His father built the mill."

"That gives him no such right. His father didn't start at the top!"

"Then maybe you should explain that to him. He doesn't seem to have much use for any of us."

"What you're saying is that my son has a birthright, a temper, certain animal strength . . . and no apparent talents. Am I correct?"

"If that costs me my job, I'll find another. Yes. I don't like your son. I don't like him at all."

Elizabeth studied the man carefully. "I'm not sure I do, either. You'll receive a raise starting next week."

Elizabeth sent Ulster Stewart back to Princeton that fall, and the day of his departure she confronted him with the summer's report.

"That dirty little Irish son of a bitch was out to get me! I knew that!"

"That dirty little Irish son of a bitch is an excellent plant manager."

"He lied! It's all lies!"

"It's the truth! He kept a number of men from pressing charges against you. You should be grateful for that."

"To hell with them! Groveling little snot-noses!"

"Your language is abhorrent! Who are you to call names? What have you contributed?"

"I don't have to!"

"Why? Because you're what you are? What are you? What extraordinary capabilities do you possess? I'd like to know."

"That's what you're looking for, isn't it? Isn't it!? What can you do, little man? What can you do to make money?"

"It's one measure of success."

"It's your only measure!"

"And you reject it?"

"You're damned right!"

"Then become a missionary."

"No, thanks!"

"Then don't cast aspersions at the marketplace. It takes a certain capability to survive there. Your father knew that."

40

"He knew how to maneuver. You think I haven't heard? How to manipulate, just like you!"

"He was a genius! He trained himself! What have you done? What have you ever done but live on what he provided? And you can't even do that graciously!"

"Shit!"

Elizabeth suddenly stopped for a moment, watching her son. "That's it! My God, that's it, isn't it? . . . You're frightened to death. You possess a great deal of arrogance but you have nothing—absolutely nothing—to be arrogant about! It must be very painful."

Her son raced out of the room, and Elizabeth sat for a long time pondering the exchange that had just taken place. She was genuinely afraid. Ulster was dangerous. He saw all around him the fruits of accomplishment without the talent or the ability to make his own contribution. He'd bear watching. Then she thought of all three sons. Shy, malleable Roland Wyckham; studious, precise Chancellor Drew; and the arrogant Ulster Stewart.

On April 6, 1917, the immediate answer was provided: America entered the World War.

The first to go was Roland Wyckham. He left his senior year at Princeton and sailed for France as Lieutenant Scarlett, AEF, Artillery. He was killed on his first day at the front.

The two remaining boys immediately made plans to avenge their brother's death. For Chancellor Drew the revenge had meaning; for Ulster Stewart it was an escape. And Elizabeth reasoned that she and Giovanni had not created an empire to have it terminated by war. One child must stay behind.

With cold calculation she commanded Chancellor Drew to remain a civilian. Ulster Stewart could go to war.

Ulster Stewart Scarlett sailed for France, had no mishaps at Cherbourg, and gave a fair account of himself at the front, especially at Meuse-Argonne. In the last days of the war he was decorated for bravery in action against the enemy.

CHAPTER 4

November 2, 1918

The Meuse-Argonne offensive was in its third or pursuit stage in the successful battle to break the Hindenburg line between Sedan and Mézières. The American First Army was deployed from Regneville to La Harasée in the Argonne Forest, a distance of some twenty miles. If the chief German supply lines in this sector were broken, the Kaiser's General Ludendorff would have no alternative but to sue for an armistice.

On November 2, the Third Army Corps under the command of General Robert Lee Bullard crashed through the demoralized German ranks on the right flank and took not only the territory but also eight thousand prisoners. Although other division commanders lived to dispute the conclusion, this breakthrough by the Third Army Corps signaled the final arrangements for the armistice a week later.

And for many in B Company, Fourteenth Battalion, Twenty-seventh Division, Third Corps, the performance of Second Lieutenant Ulster Scarlett was a superb example of the heroics that prevailed during those days of horror.

It started early in the morning. Scarlett's company had reached a field in front of a small forest of pine. The miniature forest was filled with Germans trying desperately to regroup under cover in order to execute an orderly retreat farther back into their own lines. The Americans dug three rows of shallow trenches to minimize their exposure.

Second Lieutenant Scarlett had one dug for himself just a bit deeper.

The captain of Scarlett's company did not like his second lieutenant, for the lieutenant was very good at issuing orders but very poor at executing them himself. Further, the captain suspected him of being less than enthusiastic about being shifted from a reserve division to the combat area. He also held it against his second lieutenant that throughout their reserve assignment—the major portion of their stay in France—he had been sought out by any number of ranking officers, all only too happy to have their photographs taken with him. It seemed to the captain that his second lieutenant was having a hell of a good time.

On this particular November morning, he was delighted to send him out on patrol.

"Scarlett. Take four men and scout out their positions."

"You're insane," said Scarlett laconically. "What positions? They're hightailing it out of the whole area."

"Did you hear what I said?"

"I don't give a God damn what you said. There's no point in a patrol."

Several of the men were sitting in the trenches watching the two officers.

"What's the matter, Lieutenant? No photographers around? No country club colonels to pat you on the back? Get four men and get out there."

"Go shag, *Captain!*"

"Are you disobeying your superior officer in the face of the enemy?"

Ulster Stewart looked at the smaller man with contempt. "Not disobeying. Just being insubordinate. Insulting, if you understand the term better. . . . I'm insulting you because I think you're stupid."

The captain reached for his holster, but Scarlett swiftly clamped his large hand on his superior's wrist.

"You don't shoot people for insubordination, *Captain*. It's not in the regulations. . . . I've got a better idea. Why waste four other men. . . ." He turned and glanced at the soldiers watching. "Unless four of you want to be candidates for Schnauzer bullets, I'll go myself."

The captain was stunned. He had no reply.

The men were similarly and gratefully surprised. Scarlett removed his hand from the captain's arm.

"I'll be back in half an hour. If not, I suggest you wait for some rear support. We're quite a bit ahead of the others."

Scarlett checked the magazine of his revolver and quickly crawled around the captain to the west flank, disappearing into the overgrown field.

The men mumbled to each other. They had misjudged the snotty lieutenant with all the fancy friends. The captain swore to himself and frankly hoped his second lieutenant would not return.

Which was precisely what Ulster Scarlett had in mind.

His plan was simple. He saw that about two hundred yards to the right of the wooded area in front of Company B was a clump of large rocks surrounded by autumn-foliaged trees. It was one of those rough-hewn spots that farmers can not dig out, so the fields were planted around it. Too small an area for any group but ample space for one or two individuals to hide themselves. He would make his way there.

As he crawled through the field, he came upon a number of dead infantrymen. The corpses had a strange effect upon him. He found himself removing personal items—wristwatches, rings, tags. Ripping them off and dropping them seconds later. He wasn't sure why he did it. He felt like a ruler in some mythical kingdom, and these were his subjects.

After ten minutes he wasn't sure of the direction of his refuge. He raised his head just high enough to orient himself, saw the tips of some small trees, and knew he was headed toward his sanctuary. He hurried forward, elbows and knees pounding the soft earth.

Suddenly he came to the foot of several large pines. He was not in the rocky knoll but on the edge of the small forest his company planned to attack. His preoccupation with the dead enemy had caused him to see what he wanted to see. The small trees had actually been the tall pines above him.

He was about to crawl back into the field when he saw, about fifteen feet to his left, a machine gun with a German soldier propped up against the trunk of a tree. He drew his revolver and remained still. Either the German had not seen him or he was dead. The gun was pointed directly at him.

Then the German moved. Only slightly with his right arm. He was trying to reach his weapon but in too much pain to accomplish the task.

Scarlett rushed forward and fell upon the wounded soldier, trying to make as little noise as possible. He could not let the German fire or raise an alarm. Awkwardly he pulled the man away from the gun and pinned him on the ground. Not wanting to fire his revolver and draw attention to himself, he began to choke him. Fingers and thumbs on his throat, the German tried to speak.

"Amerikaner! Amerikaner! Ich ergebe mich!" He held his palms up in desperation and gestured behind him.

Scarlett partially released his grip. He whispered. "What? What do you want?" He let the German raise himself as much as he was able to. The man had been left to die with his weapon, holding off whatever assault came while the rest of his company retreated.

He pushed the German machine gun out of the wounded man's reach and, while alternately looking forward and backward, crawled several yards into the forest. All around were signs of evacuation. Gas masks, emptied knapsacks, even bandoliers of ammunition. Anything too heavy to carry easily.

They'd all gone.

He rose and walked back to the German soldier. Something was becoming very clear to Ulster Scarlett.

"Amerikaner! Der Scheint ist fast zu Ende zu sein! Erlaube mir nach Hause zu gehen!"

Lieutenant Scarlett had made up his mind. The situation was perfect! More than perfect—it was extraordinary!

It would take an hour, perhaps longer, for the rest of the Fourteeenth Battalion to reach the area. B Company's Captain Jenkins was so determined to be a hero he had run hell out of them. Advance! Advance! Advance!

But this was his—Scarlett's—way out! Maybe they'd jump a rank and make him a captain. Why not? He'd be a hero.

Only he wouldn't be there.

Scarlett withdrew his revolver and as the German screamed he shot him in the forehead. Then he leapt to the machine gun. He started firing.

First to the rear, then to the right, then to the left.

The crackling, shattering noise echoed throughout the forest. The bullets entering trees thumped with a terrible finality. The sound was overpowering.

And then Scarlett pointed the weapon in the direction of his own men. He pulled the trigger and held it steady, swinging the gun from one flank to the other. Scare the living Jesus out of them! Maybe kill a few!

Who cared?

He was a power of death.

He enjoyed it.

He was entitled to it.

He laughed.

He withdrew his pressed finger and stood up.

He could see the mounds of dirt several hundred yards to the west. Soon he would be miles away and out of it all!

Suddenly he had the feeling he was being watched! Someone was watching him! He withdrew his pistol once again and crouched to the earth.

Snap!

A twig, a branch, a crushed stone!

He crawled on his knees slowly, cautiously into the woods.

Nothing.

He allowed his imagination to take over his reason. The sound was the sound of a tree limb cracked by the machine-gun fire. The sound was the sound of that same limb falling to the ground.

Nothing.

Scarlett retreated, still unsure, to the edge of the woods. He quickly picked up the remains of the dead German's helmet and began to run back to Company B's position.

What Ulster Stewart did not know was that he *was* being watched. He was being watched intently. With incredulity.

A German officer, the blood on his forehead slowly congealing, stood upright hidden from the American by the trunk of a wide pine tree. He had been about to kill the Yank lieutenant—as soon as his enemy left the gun—when he saw the man suddenly turn his fire on his own men. His own troops.

His own troops!

He had the American in his Luger's sight but he did not wish to kill this man.

Not yet.

For the German officer, the last man of his company in that small forest—left for dead—knew precisely what the American was doing.

It was a classic example under maximum conditions.

An infantry point, a commissioned officer at that, turning his information to his own advantage against his own troops!

He could put himself out of range of combat and get a medal in the bargain!

The German officer would follow this American.

Lieutenant Scarlett was halfway back to Company B's position when he heard the noise behind him. He flung himself to the ground and slowly turned his body around. He tried to stare through the slightly weaving tall grass.

Nothing.

Or was there nothing?

There was a corpse not twenty feet away—face down. But there were corpses everywhere.

Scarlett didn't remember this one. He remembered only the faces. He saw only the faces. He didn't remember.

Why should he?

Corpses everywhere. How could he remember? A single body with its face down. There must be dozens like that. He just didn't notice them.

He was letting his imagination overwork again! It was dawn. . . . Animals would come out of the ground, out of the trees.

Maybe.

Nothing moved.

He got up and raced to the mounds of dirt to Company B.

"Scarlett! My God, it's you!" said the captain, who was crouched in front of the first trench. "You're lucky we didn't shoot. We lost Fernald and Otis in the last fire! We couldn't return it because you were out there!"

Ulster remembered Fernald and Otis.

No loss. Not in exchange for his own escape.

He threw the German helmet he had carried from the forest to the ground. "Now, listen to me. I've wiped out one nest, but there are two others. They're waiting for

47

us. I know where they are and I can get them. But you've got to stay put! Down! Fire off to the left in ten minutes after I leave!"

"Where are you going?" asked the captain in consternation.

"Back where I can do some good! Give me ten minutes and then start firing. Keep it up for at least three or four minutes, but for Christ's sake, shoot *left*. Don't kill me. I need the diversion." He abruptly stopped and before the captain could speak reentered the field.

Once in the tall grass, Scarlett sprung from one German corpse to another, grabbing the helmets off the lifeless heads. After he had five helmets, he lay on the ground and waited for the firing to commence.

The captain did his part. One would have thought they were back at Château-Thierry. In four minutes the firing stopped.

Scarlett rose and ran back to his company's lines. As he appeared with the helmets in his hand, the men broke into spontaneous cheers. Even the captain, whose resentment disappeared with his newfound admiration, joined his men.

"God damn it to hell, Scarlett! That was the bravest act I've seen in the war!"

"Not so fast," Scarlett demurred with a humility not in evidence before. "We're clear in front and on the left flank, but a couple of Krauts ran off to the right. I'm going after them."

"You don't have to. Let 'em go. You've done enough." Captain Jenkins revised his opinion of Ulster Scarlett. The young lieutenant had met his challenge.

"If you don't mind, sir, I don't think I have."

"What do you mean?"

"My brother. . . . Rolly was his name. The Krauts got him eight months ago. Let me go after them and you take the ground."

Ulster Scarlett disappeared back into the field.

He knew exactly where he was going.

A few minutes later the American Lieutenant crouched by a large rock in his tiny island of stone and weeds. He waited for B Company to start its assault on the forest of pines. He leaned against the hard surface and looked up at the sky.

Then it came.

The men shouted to give themselves a touch more courage in the conceivable event they met the retreating enemy. Sporadic shots rang out. Several fingers were nervous. As the company reached the forest, a shattering volley from a score of rifles could be heard.

They were firing at dead men, thought Ulster Scarlett.

He was safe now.

For him the war was over.

"Stay where you are, *Amerikaner!*" The voice was thickly Germanic. "Don't move!"

Scarlett had reached for his pistol but the voice above him was emphatic. To touch his revolver meant death.

"You speak English." It was all Lieutenant Scarlett could think of to say.

"Reasonably well. Don't move! My gun is aimed at your skull. . . . The same area of the skull where you put a bullet into Corporal Kroeger."

Ulster Scarlett froze.

There *had* been someone! He *had* heard something! . . . The corpse in the field!

But why hadn't the German killed him?

"I did what I had to do." Again it was the only thing Scarlett could think of to say.

"I'm sure of that. Just as I am sure you had no alternative but to fire on your own troops. . . . You have . . . very strange concepts of your calling in this war, do you not?"

Scarlett was beginning to understand.

"This war . . . is over."

"I have a degree in military strategy from the Imperial Staff school in Berlin. I'm aware of our impending defeat. . . . Ludendorff will have no choice once the Mézières line is broken."

"Then why kill me?"

The German officer came from behind the huge rock and faced Ulster Scarlett, his pistol pointed at the American's head. Scarlett saw that he was a man not much older than himself, a young man with broad shoulders—like himself. Tall—like himself, with a confident look in his eyes, which were bright blue—like his own.

"We can be out of it, for Christ's sake! We can be out of it! Why the hell should we sacrifice each other? Or even one of us. . . . I can help you, you know!"

"Can you really?"

Scarlett looked at his captor. He knew he could not plead, could not show weakness. He had to remain calm, logical. "Listen to me. . . . If you're picked up, you'll be put in a camp with thousands of others. That is, if you're not shot. I wouldn't count on any officers' privileges if I were you. It'll take weeks, months, maybe a year or longer before they get to you! Before they let you go!"

"And you can change all this?"

"You're damned right I can!"

"But why would you?"

"Because I want to be out of it! . . . And so do you! . . . If you didn't, you would have killed me by now. . . . We need each other."

"What do you propose?"

"You're my prisoner. . . ."

"You think me insane?"

"Keep your pistol! Take the bullets out of mine. . . . If anyone comes across us, I'm taking you back for interrogation . . . far back. Until we can get you some clothes. . . . If we can get to Paris, I'll get you money."

"How?"

Ulster Scarlett grinned a confident smile. The smile of wealth. "That's my business. . . . What choice have you got? . . . Kill me and you're a prisoner anyway. Maybe a dead man. And you haven't much time. . . ."

"Get up! Put your arms out against the rock!"

Scarlett complied as the German officer took Scarlett's revolver out of his holster and removed the cartridges.

"Turn around!"

"In less than an hour others'll be coming up. We were an advance company but not that far ahead."

The German waved his pistol at Scarlett. "There are several farmhouses about a kilometer and a half southwest. Move! *Mach schnell!*" With his left hand he thrust Scarlett's empty revolver at him.

The two men ran across the fields.

The artillery to the north began its early morning barrage. The sun had broken through the clouds and the mist and was now bright.

About a mile to the southwest was a cluster of buildings. A barn and two small stone houses. It was necessary to cross a wide dirt road to reach the overgrown pasture, fenced for livestock, which were not now in evidence.

Chimney smoke curled from the larger of the two houses.

Someone had a fire going and that meant someone had food, warmth. Someone had supplies.

"Let's get into that shack," said Ulster.

"*Neim!* Your troops will be coming through."

"For Christ's sake, we've got to get you some clothes. Can't you see that?"

The German clicked the hammer of his Luger into firing position. "You're inconsistent. I thought you proposed taking me back—far back—through your own lines for interrogation? . . . It might be simpler to kill you now."

"Only until we could get you clothes! If I've got a Kraut officer in tow, there's nothing to prevent some fatass captain figuring out the same thing I have! Or a major or a colonel who wants to get the hell out of the area. . . . It's been done before. All they have to do is order me to turn you over and that's it! . . . If you're in civilian clothes, I can get us through easier. There's so damned much confusion!"

The German slowly released the hammer of his revolver, still staring at the lieutenant. "You really do want this war to be over for you, don't you?"

Inside the stone house was an old man, hard of hearing, confused and frightened by the strange pair. With little pretense, holding the unloaded revolver, the American lieutenant ordered the man to pack a supply of food and find clothes—any clothes for his "prisoner."

As Scarlett's French was poor, he turned to his captor. "Why don't you tell him we're both German? . . . We're trapped. We're trying to escape through the lines. Every Frenchman knows we're breaking through everywhere."

The German officer smiled. "I've already done that. It will add to the confusion. . . . You will be amused to learn that he said he presumed as much. Do you know why he said that?"

"Why?"

"He said we both had the filthy smell of the Boche about us."

The old man, who had edged near the open door, suddenly dashed outside and began—feebly—running toward the field.

"Jesus Christ! Stop him! God damn it, stop him!" yelled Scarlett.

The German officer, however, already had his pistol raised. "Don't be alarmed. He saves us making an unpleasant decision."

Two shots were fired.

The old man fell, and the young enemies looked at each other.

"What should I call you?" asked Scarlett.

"My own name will do. Strasser. . . . Gregor Strasser."

It was not difficult for the two officers to make their way through the Allied lines. The American push out of Regneville was electrifyingly swift, a headlong rush. But totally disconnected in its chain of command. Or so it seemed to Ulster Scarlett and Gregor Strasser.

At Reims the two men came across the remnants of the French Seventeenth Corps, bedraggled, hungry, weary of it all.

They had no trouble at Reims. The French merely shrugged shoulders after uninterested questions.

They headed west to Villers-Cotterêts, the roads to Epernay and Meaux jammed with upcoming supplies and replacements.

Let the other poor bastards take your deathbed bullets, thought Scarlett.

The two men reached the outskirts of Villers-Cotterêts at night. They left the road and cut across a field to the shelter of a cluster of trees.

"We'll rest here for a few hours," Strasser said. "Make no attempt to escape. I shall not sleep."

"You're crazy, sport! I need you as much as you need me! . . . A lone American officer forty miles from his company, which just happens to be at the front! Use your head!"

"You are persuasive, but I am not like our enfeebled imperial generals. I do not listen to empty, convincing arguments. I watch my flanks."

"Suit yourself. It's a good sixty miles from Cotterêts to Paris and we don't know what we're going to run into. We're going to need sleep. . . . We'd be smarter to take turns."

"Jawohl!" said Strasser with a contemptuous laugh. "You talk like the Jew bankers in Berlin. 'You do *this*. We'll do *that!* Why *argue?'* Thank you, no, *Amerikaner*. I shall not sleep."

"Whatever you say." Scarlett shrugged. "I'm beginning to understand why you guys lost the war." Scarlett rolled over on his side. "You're stubborn about being stubborn."

For a few minutes neither man spoke. Finally Gregor Strasser answered the American in a quiet voice. "We did not lose the war. We were betrayed."

"Sure. The bullets were blanks and your artillery backfired. I'm going to sleep."

The German officer spoke softly, as if to himself. "Many bullets were in empty cartridges. Many weapons did malfunction. . . . Betrayal. . . ."

Along the road several trucks lumbered out of Villers-Cotterêts followed by horses pulling caissons. The lights of the trucks danced flickeringly up and down. The animals whinnied; a few soldiers shouted at their charges.

More poor, stupid bastards, thought Ulster Scarlett as he watched from his sanctuary. "Hey, Strasser, what happens now?" Scarlett turned to his fellow deserter.

"Was ist?" Strasser had catnapped. He was furious with himself. "You speak?"

"Just wanted you to know I could have jumped you. . . . I asked you what happens now? I mean to you? . . . I know what happens to us. Parades, I guess. What about you?"

"No parades. No celebrations. . . . Much weeping. Much recrimination. Much drunkenness. . . . Many will be desperate. . . . Many will be killed also. You may be assured of that."

"Who? Who's going to be killed?"

"The traitors among us. They will be searched out and destroyed without mercy."

"You're crazy! I said you were crazy before and now I know it!"

"What would you have us do? You haven't been infected yet. But you will be! . . . The Bolsheviks! They are at our borders and they infiltrate! They eat away at our core! They rot inside us! . . . And the Jews! The Jews in Berlin make fortunes out of this war! The filthy Jew profiteers! The conniving Semites sell us out today, you tomorrow! . . . The Jews, the Bolsheviks, the stinking little people! We are all their victims and we do not know it! We fight each other when we should be fighting them!"

Ulster Scarlett spat. The son of Scarlatti was not interested in the problems of ordinary men. Ordinary men did not concern him.

And yet he was troubled.

Strasser was not an ordinary man. The arrogant German officer hated the ordinary man as much as he did. "What are you going to do when you shovel these people under ground? Play king of the mountain?"

"Of many mountains. . . . Of many, many mountains."

Scarlett rolled over away from the German officer.

But he did not close his eyes.

Of many, many mountains.

Ulster Scarlett had never thought of such a domain. . . . Scarlatti made millions upon millions but Scarlatti did not rule. Especially the sons of Scarlatti. They would never rule. . . . Elizabeth had made that clear.

"Strasser?"

"Yah?"

"Who are these people? Your people?"

"Dedicated men. Powerful men. The names can not be spoken of. Committed to rise out of defeat and unite the elite of Europe."

Scarlett turned his face up to the sky. Stars flickered through the low-flying gray clouds. Gray, black, dots of shimmering white.

"Strasser?"

"Was ist?"

"Where will you go? After it's over, I mean."

"To Heidenheim. My family lives there."

"Where is it?"

"Halfway between Munich and Stuttgart." The German officer looked at the strange, huge American deserter. Deserter, murderer, aider and abettor of his enemy.

"We'll be in Paris tomorrow night. I'll get you your money. There's a man in Argenteuil who keeps money for me."

"Danke."

Ulster Scarlett shifted his body. The earth was next to his face, and the smell was clean.

"Just . . . Strasser, Heidenheim. That's all?"

"That's all."

"Give me a name, Strasser."

"What do you mean? Give you a name?"

"Just that. A name you'll know is me when I get in touch with you."

Strasser thought for a moment. "Very well, *Amerikaner*. Let's choose a name you should find hard to forget—Kroeger."

"Who?"

"Kroeger—Corporal Heinrich Kroeger, whose head you shot off in the Meuse-Argonne."

On November 10 at three o'clock in the afternoon the cease-fire order went out.

Ulster Stewart Scarlett bought a motorcycle and began his swift journey to La Harasée and beyond. To B Company, Fourteenth Battalion.

He arrived in the area where most of the battalion was bivouacked and started his search for the company. It was difficult. The camp was filled with drunken, glassy-eyed, foul-breathed soldiers of every description. The order-of-the-early-morning was mass alcoholic hysteria.

Except for Company B.

B Company was holding a religious service. A commemoration for a fallen comrade.

For Lieutenant Ulster Stewart Scarlett, AEF.

Scarlett watched.

Captain Jenkins finished reading the beautiful Psalm for the Dead in a choked voice and then led the men in the Lord's Prayer.

"Our Father Who art in heaven . . ." Some of the men were weeping unashamedly.

It was a pity to spoil it all, thought Scarlett.

His citation read in part:

> . . . after single-handedly destroying three enemy machine-gun nests, he took out in pursuit of a fourth dangerous emplacement, destroying that also and thereby saving many Allied lives. He did not re-

turn and was presumed dead. However, until the fighting ceased a week hence, Second Lieutenant Scarlett provided B Company with an inspiring cry of battle. "For Old Rolly!" struck terror in the hearts of many an enemy. Through God's infinite wisdom, Second Lieutenant Scarlett rejoined his platoon the day following the cessation of hostilities. Exhausted and weak, he returned to glory. Through presidential order we hereby bestow . . .

CHAPTER 5

Back in New York, Ulster Stewart Scarlett discovered that being a hero let him do precisely as he wished. Not that he had been confined, far from it, but now even the minor restrictions such as punctuality and the normal acceptance of routine social courtesies were no longer expected of him. He had faced the supreme test of man's existence—the encounter with death. True, there were thousands like him in these respects but few were officially designated heroes, and none was a Scarlett. Elizabeth, startled beyond words, lavished upon him everything that money and power could make available. Even Chancellor Drew deferred to his young brother as the male leader of the family.

And so into the twenties bounded Ulster Stewart Scarlett.

From the pinnacles of society to the owners of speakeasies, Ulster Stewart was a welcome friend. He contributed neither much wit nor a great deal of understanding and yet his contribution was something very special. He was a man in working sympathy with his environment. His demands from life were certainly unreasonable but these were unreasonable times. The seeking of pleasure, the avoidance of pain, the enjoyment of existing without ambition were all that he seemed to require.

Seemed to require.

But not what Heinrich Kroeger required at all.

They corresponded twice a year, Strasser's letters addressed to a general post office box in mid-Manhattan.

April, 1920

My dear Kroeger:
It is official. We have given a name and a new life to the defunct Workers party. We are the National Socialist German Workers party—and, please, my dear Kroeger, don't take the words too seriously. It is a magnificent beginning. We attract so many. The Versailles restrictions are devastating. They reduce Germany to rubble. And yet it is good. It is good for us. The people are angry, they lash out not only at the victors—but at those who betrayed us from within.

June, 1921

Dear Strasser:
You have Versailles, we have the Volstead! And it's good for us, too. . . . Everyone's getting a slice of the pie and I'm not missing my share—our share! Everybody wants a favor, a payoff—a shipment! You have to know the right people. In a short time I'll be the "right people." I'm not interested in the money—screw the money! Leave that for the kikes and the greasers! I'm getting something else! Something far more important. . . .

January, 1922

My dear Kroeger:
It is all so slow. So painfully slow when it could be different. The depression is unbelievable and getting worse. Trunkfuls of currency virtually worthless. Adolf Hitler has literally assumed the position of chairman of the party over Ludendorff. You recall I once said to you that there were names I could not speak of? Ludendorff was one. I do not trust Hitler. There is something cheap about him, something opportunistic.

Dear Strasser:

It was a good summer and it'll be a better fall and a great winter! This Prohibition was tailor-made! It's madness! Have a little money up front and you're in business! . . . And what business! My organization is growing. The machinery is just the way you'd like it—perfect.

My dear Kroeger:

I am concerned. I have moved north and you can reach me at the address below. Hitler is a fool. The Ruhr take-over by Poincaré was his chance to unite all of Bavaria—politically. The people are ready. But they want order, not chaos. Instead, Hitler rants and raves and uses the old fool Ludendorff to give him stature. He will do something insane, I feel it. I wonder if there's room in the party for both of us? There is great activity in the north. A Major Buchrucker has formed the Black Reichswehr, a large armed force that may find sympathy wtih our cause. I meet with Buchrucker shortly. We'll see.

Dear Strasser:

Since last October it's been a better year than I ever thought possible! It's funny—but a person can find something in his past, something he may hate—and realize it's the best weapon he's got. I have. I lead two lives and neither meets the other! It is a brilliant manipulation if I do say so myself! I think you would be pleased that you didn't kill your friend Kroeger in France.

My dear Kroeger:

I head south immediately! Munich was a disaster.

I warned them not to attempt a forcible putsch. It has to be political—but they would not listen. Hitler will draw a long jail sentence, in spite of our "friends." God knows what will happen to poor old Ludendorff. Buchrucker's Black Reichswehr has been destroyed by von Seeckt. Why? We all want the same thing. The depression is nothing short of catastrophic now. Always it is the wrong people who fight each other. The Jews and the Communists enjoy it all, no doubt. It is an insane country.

April, 1924

Dear Strasser:
I've had my first contact with any real difficulty—but it's under control now. Remember, Strasser? Control. . . . The problem is a simple one—too many people are after the same thing. Everyone wants to be the big cheese! There's plenty for everybody but no one believes that. It's very much as you describe—the people who shouldn't fight each other are doing just that. Nevertheless, I've nearly accomplished what I set out to do. Soon I'll have a list of thousands! Thousands! Who'll do as we want!

January, 1925

My dear Kroeger:
This is my last letter. I write from Zurich. Since Herr Hitler's release he has once again assumed leadership of the party and I confess there are deep divisions between us. Perhaps they will be resolved. I, too, have my followers. To the point. We are all of us under the strongest surveillance. The Weimar is frightened of us—as well it should be. I am convinced my mail, my telephone, my every action is scrutinized. No more chances. But the time approaches. A bold plan is being conceived and I have taken the liberty of suggesting Heinrich Kroeger's inclusion. It is a master plan, a fantastic plan. You are to contact the Marquis Jacques Louis Bertholde

of Bertholde et Fils, London. By mid-April. The only name he knows—as myself—is Heinrich Kroeger.

A gray-haired man of sixty-three sat at his desk looking out the window over K Street in Washington. His name was Benjamin Reynolds and in two years he would retire. Until that time, however, he was responsible for the functions of an innocuous-sounding agency attached to the Department of the Interior. The agency was titled Field Services and Accounting. To less than five hundred people, it was known simply as Group Twenty.

The agency got its shortened name from its origins: a group of twenty field accountants sent out by Interior to look into the growing conflicts of interest between those politicians allocating federal funds and those of the electorate receiving them.

With America's entry into the war and the overnight industrial expansion necessary to sustain the war effort, Group Twenty became an overworked unit. The awarding of munitions and armament contracts to businesses throughout the country demanded an around-the-clock scrutiny beyond the capabilities of the limited number of field accountants. However, rather than expand the silent agency, it was decided to use it only in the most sensitive—or embarrassing—areas. There were a sufficient number of these. And the field accountants were specialists.

After the war there was talk of disbanding Group Twenty, but each time such action was considered problems arose that required its talents. Generally they were problems involving highly placed public servants who dipped a bit too greedily into the public jewel box. But in isolated cases Group Twenty assumed duties shunned by other departments for any number of reasons.

Such as the Treasury Department's reluctance to pursue a vapor called Scarlatti.

"Why, Glover?" asked the gray-haired man. "The question is why? Assuming there's an ounce of prosecutable proof, why?"

"Why does anyone break a law?" A man roughly ten years younger than Reynolds answered him with another question. "For profit. And there's a lot of profit in Prohibition."

"No! God damn it to hell, no!" Reynolds spun around in his chair and slammed his pipe on the desk blotter. "You're wrong! This Scarlatti has more money than our combined imaginations can conceive of. It's like saying the Mellons are going to open a bookmaking parlor in Philadelphia. It doesn't make sense. . . . Join me in a drink?"

It was after five and Group Twenty's staff was gone for the day. Only the man named Glover and Ben Reynolds remained.

"You shock me, Ben," Glover said with a grin.

"Then to hell with you. I'll save it for myself."

"You do that and I'll turn you in. . . . Good stuff?"

"Right off the boat from old Blighty, they tell me." Reynolds took a leather-bound flask out of his top drawer and two water glasses from a desk tray and poured.

"If you rule out profits, what the devil have you got left, Ben?"

"Damned if I know," replied the older man, drinking.

"What are you going to do? I gather no one else wants to do anything."

"Yes, siree! That is no, siree! Nobody wants to touch this. . . . Oh, they'll go after Mr. Smith and Mr. Jones with a vengeance. They'll prosecute the hell out of some poor slob in East Orange, New Jersey, with a case in his basement. But not this one!"

"You lost me, Ben."

"This is the Scarlatti Industries! This is big, powerful friends on the Hill! Remember, Treasury needs money, too. It gets it up there."

"What do you want to do, Ben?"

"I want to find out why the mammoth's tusk is plunging into bird feed."

"How?"

"With Canfield. He's partial to bird feed himself, the poor son of a bitch."

"He's a good man, Ben." Glover did not like the sound of Reynold's invective. He liked Matthew Canfield. He thought he was talented, quick. There but for the money to complete an education was a young man with a future. Too good for government service. A lot better than either of them. . . . Well, better than himself, better than a man named Glover who didn't care anymore. There weren't many people better than Reynolds.

Benjamin Reynolds looked up at his subordinate. He seemed to be reading his thoughts. "Yes, he's a good man. . . . He's in Chicago. Go out and call him. His routing must be somewhere."

"I have it in my desk."

"Then get him in here by tomorrow night."

CHAPTER 6

Matthew Canfield, field accountant, lay in his Pullman berth, and smoked the next to last thin cigar in his pack. They had no thin cigars on the New York–Chicago Limited and he inhaled each breath of smoke with a degree of sacrifice.

In the early morning he would reach New York, transfer to the next train south, and be in Washington ahead of schedule. That would make a better impression on Reynolds than arriving in the evening. That would show that he, Canfield, could close a problem quickly, with no loose ends left dangling. Of course, with his current assignment it wasn't difficult. He had completed it several days ago but had remained in Chicago as the guest of the senator he had been sent to confront about payroll allocations to nonexistent employees.

He wondered why he had been called back to Washington. He always wondered why he was called back. Probably because he believed deeply that it was never just another job but, instead, that someday, somehow Washington would be on to him. Group Twenty would be on to him.

They would confront him.

With evidence.

But it was unlikely. It hadn't happened. Matthew Canfield was a professional—minor level, he granted to himself—but still a professional. And he had no regrets whatsoever. He was entitled to every wooden nickel he could dig up.

Why not? He never took much. He and his mother deserved *something*. It had been a federal court in Tulsa, Oklahoma, which had pasted the sheriff's notice on his father's store. A federal judge who had rendered the determination—Involuntary Bankruptcy. The federal government hadn't listened to any explanations other than the fact that his father no longer had the ability to pay his debts.

For a quarter of a century a man could work, raise a family, get a son off to the state university—so many dreams fulfilled, only to be destroyed with the single banging of a wooden gavel upon a small marble plate in a courtroom.

Canfield had no regrets.

"You have a new occupation to get under your belt, Canfield. Simple procedures. Not difficult."

"Fine, Mr. Reynolds. Always ready."

"Yes. I know you are. . . . You start in three days at pier thirty-seven in New York City. Customs. I'll fill you in as best I can."

But, of course, Benjamin Reynolds did not "fill in" Matthew Canfield as thoroughly as he might have. He wanted Canfield to "fill in" the spaces he, Reynolds, left blank. The Scarlatti *pádrone* was operating out of the West Side piers—middle numbers—that much they knew. But someone had to see him. Someone had to identify him. Without being told.

That was very important.

And if anyone could do that it would be someone like Matthew Canfield, who seemed to gravitate to the nether world of the payoff, the bribe, the corrupt.

He did.

On the night shift of January 3, 1925.

Matthew Canfield, customs inspector, checked the invoices of the steamer *Genoa-Stella* and waved to the shakeup foreman to start unloading hold one of its crates of Como wool.

And then it happened.

At first an argument. Then a hook fight.

The *Genoa-Stella* crew would not tolerate a breach of unloading procedures. Their orders came from some-

65

one else. Certainly not from the American customs officials.

Two crates plummeted down from the cranes, and underneath the straw packing the stench of uncut alcohol was unmistakable.

The entire pier force froze. Several men then raced to phone booths and a hundred apelike bodies swarmed around the crates ready to fend off intruders with their hooks.

The first argument was forgotten. The hook fight was forgotten.

The contraband was their livelihood and they would die defending it.

Canfield, who had raced up the stairs to the glass-enclosed booth high above the pier, watched the angry crowd. A shouting match began between the men on the loading dock and the sailors of the *Genoa-Stella*. For fifteen minutes the opponents yelled at each other, accompanying their shouts with obscene gestures. But no one drew a weapon. No one threw a hook or knife. They were waiting.

Canfield realized that no one in the customs office made any move to call the authorities. "For Christ's sake! Someone get the police down!"

There was silence from the four men in the room with Canfield.

"Did you hear me? Call the police!"

Still the silence of the frightened men wearing the uniforms of the Customs Service.

Finally one man spoke. He stood by Matthew Canfield, looking out the glass partition at the gangster army below. "No one calls the police, young fella. Not if you want to show up at the docks tomorrow."

"Show up anywhere tomorrow," added another man, who calmly sat down and picked up a newspaper from his tiny desk.

"Why not? Somebody down there could get killed!"

"They'll settle it themselves," said the older customs man.

"What port did you come from again? . . . Erie? . . . You must have had different rules. Lake shipping has different rules. . . ."

"That's a lot of crap!"

A third man wandered over to Canfield. "Look, hick, just mind your own business, all right?"

"What the hell kind of talk is that? I mean, just what the hell kind of talk is that?"

"C'mere, hick." The third man, whose thin body and narrow face seemed lost in his loose-fitting uniform, took Canfield by the elbow and walked him to a corner. The others pretended not to notice but their eyes kept darting over to the two men. They were concerned, even worried. "You got a wife and kids?" the thin man asked quietly.

"No. . . . So what?"

"We do. That's what." The thin man put his hand into his pocket and withdrew several bills. "Here. Here's sixty bucks. . . . Just don't rock the boat, huh? . . . Calling the cops wouldn't do no good, anyhow. . . . They'd rat on you."

"Jesus! Sixty dollars!"

"Two weeks' pay, kid. Have a party."

"Okay. . . . Okay, I will."

"Here they come, Jesse." The older guard by the window spoke softly to the man next to Canfield.

"C'mon, hick. Get an education," said the man with the money, leading Canfield to the window overlooking the interior of the pier.

Down at the street-loading entrance, Canfield saw that two large automobiles, one behind the other, had pulled up—the first car halfway into the building. Several men in dark overcoats had gotten out of the lead car and were walking toward the phalanx of dock workers surrounding the damaged crates.

"What are they doing?"

"They're the goons, kid," answered the guard named Jesse. "They muscle."

"Muscle what?"

"Hah!" came a guttural laugh from the man at the tiny desk with the newspaper.

"They muscle what has to be put in line. No what—who!"

The men in overcoats—five in all—began wandering up to the various stevedores and talking quietly. Cheek to cheek, thought Canfield. With a few, they shoved them humorously and patted their thick necks. They were like zoo keepers, pacifying their animals. Two of the men walked up the gangplank onto the ship. The head man, who wore a white felt fedora and was now the central figure of the remaining three on the pier, looked back toward the automobiles and then up at the glass-enclosed booth. He nodded his head and started toward the stairs. The guard, Jesse, spoke.

"I'll handle this. Everyone stay put."

He opened the door and waited on the steel platform for the man in the white fedora.

Canfield could see the two men talking through the glass. The white fedora was smiling, even obsequious. But there was a hard look in his eyes, a serious look in his eyes. And then he seemed concerned, angry, and the two men looked into the office.

They looked at Matthew Canfield.

The door was opened by Jesse. "You. Cannon. Mitch Cannon, c'mere."

It was always easier to use a cover having one's own initials. You never could tell who'd send you a Christmas gift.

Canfield walked out onto the steel platform as the man in the white fedora descended the stairs to the cement floor of the pier.

"You go down and sign the search papers."

"The hell you say, buddy!"

"I said go down and sign the papers! They want to know you're clean." And then Jesse smiled. "The big boys are here. . . . You'll get another little dividend. . . . But I get fifty percent, understand?"

"Yeah," Canfield said reluctantly. "I understand." He started down the steps looking at the man who waited for him.

"New here, huh?"

"Yeah."

"Where ya' from?"

"Lake Erie. Lot of action in Lake Erie."

"What d'ya work?"

"Canadian stuff. What else? . . . Good hooch that Canadian stuff."

"We import wool! Como wool!"

"Yeah, sure, friend. In Erie it's Canadian pelts, fabric. . . ." Canfield winked at the waterfront subaltern. "Good soft packing, huh?"

"Look, fella. Nobody needs a wise guy."

"Okay. . . . Like I said. Wool."

"Come over to the dispatchers. . . . You sign for the loads."

Canfield walked with the large man to the dispatcher's booth where a second man thrust a clipboard filled with papers at him.

"Write clear and mark the dates and times perfect!" ordered the man in the booth.

After Canfield had complied, the first man spoke. "Okay. . . . C'mon with me." He led Canfield over to the automobiles. The field accountant could see two men talking in the back seat of the second vehicle. No one but a driver remained in the first car. "Wait here."

Canfield wondered why he had been singled out. Had anything gone wrong in Washington? There hadn't been enough time for anything to go wrong.

There was a commotion from the pier. The two goons who had boarded the ship were escorting a man in uniform down the gangplank. Canfield saw that it was the captain of the *Genoa-Stella.*

The man in the white fedora was now leaning into the window talking with the two men in the second car. They hadn't noticed the noise from the pier. The large man opened the car door and a short, very dark Italian stepped out. He was no more than five feet three.

The short man beckoned the field accountant to come over. He reached into his coat pocket, took out a billfold, and withdrew several bills from it. His speech was heavily accented. "You a new man?"

"Yes, sir."

"Lake Erie? That's right?"

"Yes, sir."

"What's name?"

"Cannon."

The Italian looked at the man in the white fedora.

The man shrugged. "Non conosco. . . ."

"Here." He handed Canfield two fifty-dollar bills. "You be a good boy. . . . We take care of good boys, don't we, Maggiore? . . . We also take care of boys who ain't so good. . . . *Capisce?*"

"You bet! Thanks very . . ."

It was as far as the field accountant got. The two men escorting the *Genoa-Stella* captain had reached the first automobile. They were now forcibly holding him, propelling him against his will.

"Lascia mi! Lascia mi! Maiali!" The captain tried to break the grip of the two hoodlums. He swung his shoulders back and forth but to no avail.

The small Italian brushed Canfield aside as the goons brought the captain up to him. The ship's officer and his two captors started shouting at the same time. The Italian listened and stared at the captain.

And then the other man, the man who remained in the back seat of the second automobile, leaned forward toward the window, half hidden in the shadows.

"What's the matter? What are they yelling about, Vitone?"

"This *comandante* doesn't like the way we do business, *Padrone*. He says he won't let us unload no more."

"Why not?"

"Si rifiuti!" shouted the captain, sensing what was being said though not understanding the words.

"He says he don't see anyone he knows. He says we don't have no rights with his ship! He wants to make telephone calls."

"I'll bet he does," the man in shadow said quietly. "I know just who he wants to call."

"You gonna let him?" asked the short Italian.

"Don't be foolish, Vitone. . . . Talk nice. Smile. Wave back at the ship. All of you! . . . That's a powder keg back there, you imbeciles! . . . Let them think everything's fine."

"Sure. Sure, *Padrone*."

All of them laughed and waved except the captain, who furiously tried to release his arms. The effect was comic, and Canfield found himself nearly smiling except that the face in the automobile window was now in his direct line of sight. The field accountant saw that it was a good-looking face—striking would be the word. Although the face was somewhat obscured by the wide brim of a hat, Canfield noticed that the features were sharp, aquiline, clean-cut. What particularly struck the field accountant were the eyes.

They were very light blue eyes. Yet he was addressed by the Italian "*padrone.*" Canfield assumed there were Italians with blue eyes but he had never met any. It was unusual.

"What do we do, *Padrone?*" asked the short man who had given Canfield the hundred dollars.

"What else, sport? He's a visitor to our shores, isn't he? Be courteous, Vitone. . . . Take the captain outside and let him . . . make his phone calls." Then the man with the light blue eyes lowered his voice. "And kill him!"

The small Italian nodded his head slightly in the direction of the pier entrance. The two men on each side of the uniformed officer pushed him forward, out the large door into the darkness of the night.

"Chiama le nostri amici . . ." said the goon on the captain's right arm.

But the captain resisted. Once outside, in the dim spill of the door's light, Canfield could see that he began violently thrashing his body against both escorts until the one on the left lost his balance. The captain then swung into the other man with both fists, shouting at him in Italian.

The man who had been shoved away regained his balance, and took something out of his pocket. Canfield couldn't distinguish its shape.

Then Canfield saw what it was.

A knife.

The man behind the captain plunged it into the officer's unguarded back.

Matthew Canfield pulled the visor of his customs cap down and began walking away from the automobiles. He walked slowly, casually.

"Hey! You! You! Customs!" It was the blue-eyed man from the back seat.

"You! Lake Erie!" the short Italian yelled.

Canfield turned. "I didn't see anything. Not a thing. Nothin'!" He tried to smile but no smile would come.

The man with the light blue eyes stared at him as Canfield squinted and pinched his face below the visor of his cap. The short Italian nodded to the driver of the first car.

The driver got out and came behind the field accountant.

"Porta lui fuori vicin' a l'acqua! Sensa fuccide! Corteddo!" said the short man.

The driver pushed Canfield in the small of the back toward the pier entrance. "Hey, c'mon! I didn't see nothin'! What d'you want with me! . . . C'mon, for Christ's sake!"

Matthew Canfield didn't have to be given an answer. He knew exactly what they wanted from him. His insignificant life.

The man behind him kept pushing, nudging him onward. Around the building. Along the deserted side of the pier.

Two rats scampered several yards in front of Canfield and his executioner. The growing sounds of arguments could be heard behind the walls of the cargo area. The Hudson River slapped against the huge pylons of the dock.

Canfield stopped. He wasn't sure why but he couldn't simply keep walking. The pain in his stomach was the pain of fear.

"A lesta chi! . . . Keep movin'!" said the man, poking a revolver into Canfield's ribs.

"Listen to me." Gone was Canfield's attempt to roughen his voice. "I'm a government man! You do anything to me, they'll get you! You won't get any protection from your friends when they find out. . . ."

"Keep movin'!"

A ship's horn sounded from the middle of the river. Another responded.

Then came a long, screeching, piercing whistle. It came from the *Genoa-Stella*. It was a signal, a desperate signal, which did not let up. The pitch of its scream was ear shattering.

It distracted—as it had to—the man with the gun beside Canfield.

The field accountant lashed out at the man's wrist and held it, twisted it with all his strength. The man reached up to Canfield's face and clawed at the sockets of his eyes while pushing him toward the steel wall of the building. Canfield gripped the wrist harder, harder, and then with his other hand clutched at the man's overcoat and pulled him toward the wall—the same direction the man was pushing—turning at the last second so that his executioner slammed into the steel.

The gun flew out of the Sicilian's hand and Canfield brought his knee crashing up into the man's groin.

The Italian screamed a guttural cry of anguish. Canfield threw him downward and the man lunged, writhing,

72

across the deck to the edge of the pier, curled up in agony. The field accountant grabbed his head and slammed it repeatedly against the thick wood. The skin broke and blood came pouring out of the man's skull.

It was over in less than a minute.

Matthew Canfield's executioner was dead.

The shrieking whistle from the *Genoa-Stella* kept up its now terrifying blast. The shouting from within the pier's loading area had reached a crescendo.

Canfield thought that the ship's crew must have openly revolted, must have demanded orders from their captain, and when they did not come, assumed him murdered—or at least held captive.

Several gunshots followed one after the other. The staccato sound of a submachine gun—more screaming, more cries of terror.

The field accountant couldn't return to the front of the building, and undoubtedly someone would come out looking for his executioner.

He rolled the body of the dead Sicilian over the edge of the dock and heard the splash below.

The whistle from the *Genoa-Stella* stopped. The shouting began to die down. Someone had assumed control. And at the front end of the pier two men came in sight. They called out.

"La Tona! Hey, La Tona! La Tona. . . ."

Matthew Canfield jumped into the filthy waters of the Hudson and started swimming, as best he could in his heavy customs uniform, toward the middle of the river.

"You're a very lucky fellow!" said Benjamin Reynolds.

"I know that, sir. And grateful it's over."

"We're not called on for this sort of thing, I realize. You take a week off. Relax."

"Thank you, sir."

"Glover will be here in a few minutes. It's still a bit early."

It was. It was six fifteen in the morning. Canfield hadn't reached Washington until four and he was afraid to go to his apartment. He had phoned Benjamin Reynolds at home and Reynolds had instructed the field accountant to go to the Group Twenty offices and wait for him.

73

The outer door opened and Reynolds called. "Glover? That you?"

"Yes, Ben. Jesus! It's not six thirty yet. . . . A lousy night. My son's kids are with us." The voice was weary, and when Glover reached Reynolds's door, it was apparent that the man was wearier. . . . "Hello, Canfield. What the hell happened to you?"

Matthew Canfield, field accountant, told the entire story.

When he had finished, Reynolds spoke to Glover. "I've phoned Lake Erie Customs—his personnel file's been removed. The boys in New York cleared out his room there. It hadn't been touched. Is there any other backup we should worry about?"

Glover thought for a moment. "Yes. Probably. . . . In case the Lake Erie employment file's gone after—and it will be—put out a rumor on the docks that Canfield . . . Cannon . . . was a fake name for a hit man. . . . That he was caught up with in Los Angeles or San Diego or someplace, and was shot. I'll take care of it."

"Good. . . . Now, Canfield, I'm going to show you several photographs. Without any comments on my part . . . see if you can identify them." Benjamin Reynolds walked to a file cabinet and opened it. He took out a folder and returned to his desk. "Here." He withdrew five photographs—three blowups from newspapers and two prison shots.

It took Canfield less than a second once they were arranged. "That's him! That's the one the little wop called *padrone!*"

"Il Scarlatti padrone," Glover said quietly.

"The identification's absolutely positive?"

"Sure. . . . And if he's got blue eyes, it's Holy Writ."

"You could swear to it in court?"

"Of course."

"Hey, Ben, come on!" interrupted Glover, who knew that such an action on Matthew Canfield's part was a death warrant.

"I'm only asking."

"Who is he?" said Canfield.

"Yes. Who is he? . . . What is he? . . . I'm not sure I should even answer the first, but if you found out some other way—and you could, easily—it might be dangerous."

Reynolds turned the photographs over. A name was printed in heavy black crayon.

"Ulster Stewart Scarlett—né Scarlatti," the field accountant read out loud. "He won a medal in the war, didn't he? A millionaire."

"Yes, he did and he is," answered Reynolds. "This identification's got to remain secret. And I mean *totally* classified! Is that understood?"

"Of course."

"Do you think anyone could recognize you from last night?"

"I doubt it. The light was bad and I wore my cap half over my face and tried to talk like a goon. . . . No, I don't think so."

"Good. You did a fine job. Get some sleep."

"Thank you." The field accountant walked out the door, closing it behind him.

Benjamin Reynolds looked at the photographs on his desk. "The Scarlatti *padrone*, Glover."

"Turn it back to Treasury. You've got all you need."

"You're not thinking. . . . We don't have a damned thing unless you want to consign Canfield to his grave. . . . And even assuming that, what is there? Scarlett doesn't write out checks. . . . He 'was observed in the company of . . .' He 'was heard to give an order . . .' To whom? On whose testimony? A minor government employee against the word of the celebrated war hero? The son of Scarlatti? . . . No, all we've got is a threat. . . . And perhaps that's enough."

"Who's going to threaten?"

Benjamin Reynolds leaned back in his chair and pressed the tips of his fingers against one another. "I am. . . . I'm going to talk with Elizabeth Scarlatti. . . . I want to know *why*."

CHAPTER 7

Ulster Stewart Scarlett got out of the taxi at the corner of Fifth Avenue and Fifty-fourth Street and walked the short distance to his brownstone house. He ran up the steps to the heavy front door and let himself in. He slammed the door shut and stood for a moment in the huge foyer, stamping his feet against the February cold. He threw his coat into a hallway chair, then walked through a pair of French doors into a spacious living room and turned on a table lamp. . . . It was only four in the afternoon but already growing dark.

He crossed from the table to the fireplace and noted with satisfaction that the servants had piled the logs and the kindling properly. He lit the fire and watched the flames leap to all corners of the fireplace. He gripped the mantel and leaned toward the warmth of the blaze. His eyes were on the level of his Silver Star citation, framed in gold in the center of the wall. He made a mental note to complete the display above the fireplace. The time would soon be here when that display should be in evidence.

A reminder to everyone who entered this house.

It was a momentary diversion. His thoughts returned to the source of his anger. His fury.

Stupid, God damn thick-headed scum!

Bilge! Garbage!

Four crewmen from the *Genoa-Stella* killed. The captain's body found in an abandoned waterfront barge.

They could have lived with that. They could have lived with the crew's rebellion. The docks were violent.

76

But not with the corpse of La Tona hooked to a cross post on the surface of the water fifty yards from the ship. The freighter bringing in the contraband.

La Tona!

Who had killed him? Not the slow-speaking, cloddish customs guard. . . . Christ, no! . . . La Tona would have eaten his balls off and spat them out laughing! La Tona was a sneak killer. The worst kind of homicidal brute.

There'd be a smell. A bad smell. No graft could stop it. Five murders on pier thirty-seven during a single night shift.

And with La Tona it would be traced to Vitone. Little Don Vitone Genovese. Dirty little guinea bastard, thought Scarlett.

Well, it was time for him to get out.

He had what he wanted. More than he needed. Strasser would be amazed. They'd all be amazed.

Ulster Scarlett lit a cigarette and walked to a small, thin door to the left of the fireplace. He took out a key, unlocked the door, and walked in.

The room, like the door to it, was small. It had once been a walk-in wine pantry; now it was a miniature office with a desk, a chair, and two heavy steel file cabinets. On each file drawer was a wide circular combination lock.

Scarlett turned on the desk lamp and went to the first cabinet. He crouched down to the bottom file, manipulated the combination numbers, and pulled out the drawer. He reached in and withdrew an extremely thick leather-bound notebook and placed it on the desk. He sat down and opened it.

It was his master work, the product of five years of meticulous scholarship.

He scanned the pages—delicately, precisely inserted into the rings with cloth circlets around each hole. Each entry was lettered clearly. After every name was a brief description, where available, and a briefer biography— position, finances, family, future—when the candidate warranted it.

The pages were titled and separated by cities and states. Index tabs of different colors descended from the top of the notebook to the bottom.

A masterpiece!

The record of every individual—important and unimportant—who had benefited in any way from the operations of the Scarlatti organization. From congressmen taking outright bribes from his subordinates to corporation heads "investing" in wildcat, highly illegal speculations proffered—again never by Ulster Stewart Scarlett—through his hired hands. All he had supplied was the capital. The honey. And the bees had flocked to it!

Politicians, bankers, lawyers, doctors, architects, writers, gangsters, office clerks, police, customs inspectors, firemen, bookmakers . . . the list of professions and occupations was endless.

The Volstead Act was the spine of the corruption, but there were other enterprises—all profitable.

Prostitution, abortion, oil, gold, political campaigns and patronage, the stock market, speakeasies, loan-sharking . . . this list, too, was endless.

The money-hungry little people could never walk away from their greed. It was the ultimate proof of his theories!

The money-grasping scum!

Everything documented. Everyone identified.

Nothing left to speculation.

The leather-bound notebook contained 4,263 names. In eighty-one cities and twenty-four states. . . . Twelve senators, ninety-eight congressmen, and three men in Coolidge's cabinet.

A directory of malfeasance.

Ulster Stewart picked up the desk phone and dialed a number.

"Put Vitone on. . . . Never mind who's calling! I wouldn't have this number if he didn't want me to have it!"

Scarlett crushed out his cigarette. He drew unconnected lines on a scratch pad while waiting for Genovese. He smiled when he saw that the lines converged—like knives—into a center spot. . . . No, not like knives. Like bolts of lightning.

"Vitone? It's me. . . . I'm aware of that. . . . There's not very much we *can* do, is there? . . . If you're questioned, you've got a story. You were in Westchester. You don't know where the hell La Tona was. . . . Just keep me out! Understand? Don't be a smart-ass. . . . I've got a proposition for you. You're going to like it. It makes everything worth while for you. . . . It's all yours. Everything! Make whatever deals you like. I'm out."

There was silence from the other end of the line. Ulster Scarlett drew the figure of a Christmas tree on the scratch pad.

"No hitches, no catches. It's yours! I don't want a thing. The organization's all yours. . . . No, I don't know anything! I just want out. If you're not interested, I can go elsewhere—say the Bronx or even out to Detroit. I'm not asking for a nickel. . . . Only this. Only one thing. You never saw me. You never met me. You don't know I exist! That's the price."

Don Vitone Genovese began chattering in Italian while Scarlett held the receiver several inches from his ear. The only word Scarlett really understood was the repeated, "Grazie, grazie, grazie."

He hung up the receiver and closed the leather-bound notebook. He sat for a moment and then opened the top drawer in the center of the desk. He took out the last letter he had received from Gregor Strasser. He reread it for the twentieth time. Or was it the hundred and twentieth?

"A fantastic plan . . . a bold plan . . . the Marquis Jacques Louis Bertholde . . . London . . . by mid-April . . ."

Was the time really here? At last!

If it was, Heinrich Kroeger had to have his own plan for Ulster Scarlett.

It wasn't so much bold as it was respectable. Immensely, thoroughly respectable. So proper, in fact, that Ulster Stewart Scarlett burst out laughing.

The scion of Scarlatti—the charming, handsome graduate of the cotillions, the hero of the Meuse-Argonne, New York society's most eligible bachelor—was going to be married.

CHAPTER 8

"You presume, Mr. Reynolds!" Elizabeth Scarlatti was seething. Her vehemence was directed at the old man who stood calmly in front of her, peering over his glasses. "I do not countenance presumptuous people and I will not abide liars!"

"I'm sorry. I really am."

"You got this appointment under false pretenses. Senator Brownlee told me you represented the Land Acquisition Agency and your business concerned the transactions between Scarlatti and the Department of the Interior."

"That's exactly what he believes."

"Then he's a bigger fool than I think he is. And now you threaten me! Threaten me with secondhand inflammatory gossip about my son! I trust you're prepared to be cross-examined in court."

"Is that what you want?"

"You may force me to it! . . . I don't know your position, but I do know a great many people in Washington and I've never heard of you. I can only conclude that if someone like you can carry such tales, others must have heard them too. Yes, you may force me into court. I won't tolerate such abuse!"

"Suppose it's true?"

"It isn't true and you know it as well as I do! There's no reason on earth why my son would involve himself in . . . in such activities. He's wealthy in his own right! Both my sons have trust funds that return annual incomes of— let's be honest—preposterous sums."

"Then we have to eliminate profit as a motive, don't we?" Benjamin Reynolds wrinkled his brow.

"We eliminate nothing for there *is* nothing! If my son has caroused a bit, he's to be criticized—not branded a criminal! And if you're using the gutter tactic of maligning the name Scarlatti because of its origin, you're contemptible and I'll have you dismissed!"

Benjamin Reynolds, slow to anger, was reaching a dangerous level of irritation. He had to remind himself that this old woman was guarding her house and was more difficult than she would have been in other circumstances.

"I wish you wouldn't think of me as an enemy. I'm neither an enemy nor a bigot. Frankly, I resent the second implication more than I do the first."

"Again you presume," interrupted Elizabeth Scarlatti. "I don't grant you the stature of an enemy. I think you're a little man using malicious slander for your own ends."

"Ordering a man's murder is not malicious slander!"

"What did you say?"

"It's the most serious charge we have. . . . But there are mitigating circumstances if it's any comfort to you."

The old woman stared at Benjamin Reynolds in contempt. He ignored the look.

"The man who was murdered—the one whose death your son ordered—was a known killer himself. . . . A captain of a freighter who worked with the worst elements on the waterfront. He was responsible for a great deal of killing."

Elizabeth Scarlatti rose from her chair. "I won't tolerate this," she said quietly. "You make the most damaging accusation possible and then you retreat behind a wall of implied judgment."

"These are strange times, Madame Scarlatti. We can't be everywhere. We don't want to be, frankly. We don't lament the gangster wars. Let's face it. Often they accomplish more than we can."

"And you put my son in this . . . this category?"

"I didn't put him anywhere. He did it himself."

Elizabeth walked slowly from her desk to a front window overlooking the street. "How many other people in Washington know about this outrageous gossip?"

"Everything I've told you?"

"Anything."

"There were a few rumors at Treasury. Nothing anyone wanted to run down. About the rest, only my immediate subordinate and the man who was the witness."

"Their names?"

"Oh, no."

"I can easily find out."

"It wouldn't do you any good."

Elizabeth turned. "I see."

"I wonder if you do?"

"Whatever you think, I'm not an idiot. I don't believe a word of this. But I don't want the name of Scarlatti impugned. . . . How much, Mr. Reynolds?"

Group Twenty's director returned Elizabeth's stare without giving quarter. "Nothing. Not a penny, thank you. . . . I'll go further. You tempt me to bring charges against you."

"You stupid old man!"

"Damn it to hell, cut it out! . . . All I want is the truth! . . . No, that's not all I want. I want it stopped. Before anyone else gets hurt. That much is due a decorated hero. Especially in these crazy times. . . . And I want to know why!"

"To speculate would be to grant your premise. I refuse to do that!"

"By Jesus! You're a rough bird."

"More than you realize!"

"Can't you understand? . . . It's not going any further! It ends here! That is, it will if you can stop any future . . . activity, as you call it. We figure you can do that. . . . But I'd think *you'd* want to know why. Since we both know your son is rich—why?"

Elizabeth simply stared at him and Reynolds knew she wouldn't answer. He'd done what he could, said what he had to say. The rest was up to her.

"Good day, Madame Scarlatti. . . . I should tell you. I'll be watching the Scarlatti *padrone*."

"The who?"

"Ask your son."

Reynolds trudged out of the room. People like Elizabeth Scarlatti tired him out. Probably, he thought, because he didn't believe they were worth it all. The giants never were.

Elizabeth—still by the window—watched the old man close the door behind him. She waited until she saw him descend the front steps and walk west toward Fifth Avenue.

The old man looked up at the figure in the window and their eyes met.

Neither acknowledged.

CHAPTER 9

Chancellor Drew Scarlett paced the thick oriental rug of his office at 525 Fifth Avenue. He kept breathing deeply, pushing his stomach out as he inhaled—the proper way—because the masseur at his club told him it was one method of calming down under pressure.

It wasn't working.

He would change masseurs.

He stopped in front of the mahogany-paneled wall between the two large windows overlooking Fifth Avenue. On the wall were various framed newspaper articles, all of them about the Scarwyck Foundation. Each prominently mentioned him—some with his name in bold print above the stories.

Whenever he was upset, which was quite often, he looked at these framed records of achievement. It always had a calming effect.

Chancellor Scarlett had assumed the role of husband to a dull wife as a matter of course. The conjugal bed had produced five children. Surprisingly—especially to Elizabeth—he had also become interested in the family enterprises. As if in answer to his celebrated brother's behavior, Chancellor retreated into the secure world of the quasi-inspired businessman. And he did have ideas.

Because the annual income from the Scarlatti holdings far exceeded the needs of a small nation, Chancellor convinced Elizabeth that the intelligent tax course was to establish a philanthropic foundation. Impressing his mother with irrefutable data—including the potential for antitrust suits—Chancellor won Elizabeth's consent for the

Scarwyck Foundation. Chancellor was installed as president and his mother as chairman of the board. Chancellor might never be a war hero, but his children would recognize his economic and cultural contributions.

The Scarwyck Foundation poured money into war memorials; preservation of Indian reservations; a *Dictionary of Great Patriots* to be distributed throughout selected prep schools; the Roland Scarlett Field Clubs, a chain of Episcopal youth camps dedicated to the outdoor life and high Christian principles of their democratic—but Episcopalian—patron. And scores of similar endeavors. One couldn't pick up a newspaper without noticing some new project endowed by Scarwyck.

Looking at the articles shored up Chancellor's undermined confidence, but the effect was short-lived. He could hear faintly through the office door the ring of his secretary's telephone and it immediately brought back the memory of his mother's angry call to him. She'd been trying to find Ulster since yesterday morning.

Chancellor picked up the intercom.

"Try my brother's home again, Miss Nesbit."

"Yes, sir."

He had to find Ulster. His mother was adamant. She insisted on seeing him before the afternoon was over.

Chancellor sat down in his chair and tried to breathe properly again. The masseur had told him it was good exercise while sitting down.

He took a deep breath, pushing his stomach out as far as possible. The middle button of his suit coat broke from the thread and fell on the soft carpet, bouncing first on the chair between his legs.

Damn!

Miss Nesbit rang him on the intercom.

"Yes!"

"The maid at your brother's house said he was on his way over to see you, Mr. Scarlett." Miss Nesbit's voice conveyed her pride in accomplishment.

"You mean he was there all the time?"

"I don't know, sir." Miss Nesbit was hurt.

Twenty agonizing minutes later Ulster Stewart Scarlett arrived.

"Good God! Where have you been? Mother's been trying to reach you since yesterday morning! We've called everywhere!"

"I've been out at Oyster Bay. Did any of you think of calling there?"

"In February? Of course not! . . . Or maybe she did, I don't know."

"You couldn't have reached me anyway. I was in one of the cottages."

"What the hell were you doing there? I mean, in February!"

"Let's say taking stock, brother mine. . . . Nice office, Chance. I can't remember when I was here last."

"About three years ago."

"What are all those gadgets?" asked Ulster, pointing at the desk.

"Newest equipment. See. . . . Here's an electric calendar that lights up on specific days to remind me of meetings. This is an intercommunicator setup with eighteen offices in the building. Now, right here a private wire to . . ."

"Never mind. I'm impressed. I haven't much time. I thought you might like to know. . . . I may get married."

"What! . . . Ulster, my God in heaven! You! Married! You're going to get married?"

"Seems to be a general request."

"Who, for God's sake!"

"Oh, I've whittled the numbers down, sport. Don't fret. She'll be acceptable."

Chancellor eyed his brother coldly. He was prepared to be told that Ulster had chosen some Broadway trollop from a Ziegfeld show, or, perhaps, one of those weird female writers in black sweaters and men's haircuts who were always at Ulster's parties.

"Acceptable to whom?"

"Well, let's see, I've tried out most of them."

"I'm not interested in your sex life! Who?"

"Oh, but you should be. Most of your wife's friends—married and otherwise—are lousy lays."

"Just tell me who you intend honoring, if you don't mind?"

"What would you say to the Saxon girl?"

"Janet! . . . Janet Saxon!" Chancellor cried out with delight.

"I think she'd do," murmured Ulster.

"Do! Why, she's wonderful! Mother will be so pleased! She's just terrific!"

"She'll do." Ulster was strangely quiet.

"Ulster, I can't tell you how pleased I am. You've asked her, of course." It was a statement.

"Why, Chance, how can you think that? . . . I wasn't sure she'd pass inspection."

"I see what you mean. Of course. . . . But I'm sure she will. Have you told Mother? Is that why she's calling so hysterically?"

"I've never seen Mother hysterical. That should be quite a sight."

"Really, you should phone her right away."

"I will. Give me a minute. . . . I want to say something. It's quite personal." Ulster Scarlett sat carelessly down in a chair in front of his brother's desk.

Chancellor, knowing that his brother rarely wanted to be personal, took his seat apprehensively. "What is it?"

"I was pulling your leg a few minutes ago. I mean about the lays."

"I'm relieved to hear that!"

"Oh, don't mistake me—I'm not saying it isn't true—just tasteless of me to discuss it. . . . I wanted to see you get upset. Take it easy, I had a reason. . . . I think it makes my case stronger."

"What case?"

"It's why I went out to the island. . . . To do a lot of thinking. . . . The aimless, crazy days are coming to an end. Not overnight, but they're slowly fading out."

Chancellor looked intently at his brother. "I've never heard you talk like this before."

"You do a lot of thinking in a cottage by yourself. No telephones, no one barging in on you. . . . Oh, I'm not making any big promises I can't keep. I don't have to do that. But I want to try. . . . I guess you're the only person I can turn to."

Chancellor Scarlett was touched. "What can I do?"

"I'd like to get some kind of position. Informal, at first. Nothing regimented. See if I can't get interested in something."

"Of course! I'll get you a job here! It'll be simply great working together."

"No. Not here. That'd be just another gift. No. I want to do what I should have done a long time ago. Do what you did. Start right at home."

"At home. What kind of position is that?"

"Figuratively speaking, I want to learn everything I

can about us. The family. Scarlatti. Its interests, businesses, that sort of thing. . . . That's what you did and I've always admired you for it."

"Did you really?" Chancellor was very serious.

"Yes, I did. . . . I took a lot of papers out to the island with me. Reports and things I picked up at mother's office. We do a lot of work with that bank downtown, don't we? What in hell is the name?"

"Waterman Trust. They execute all Scarlatti commitments. Have for years."

"Maybe I could start there. . . . Informally. Couple of hours a day."

"No problem at all! I'll arrange it this afternoon."

"Another thing. Do you think you might phone Mother. . . . Just as a favor. Tell her I'm on my way over. I won't bother to call. You might mention our discussion. Tell her about Janet, if you like." Ulster Scarlett stood up in front of his brother. There was something modestly heroic about him, about this errant who was trying to find his roots.

The effect was not lost on Chancellor, who rose from his chair and extended his hand. "Welcome home, Ulster. It's the start of a new life for you. Mark my words."

"Yes. I think it is. Not overnight, but it's a beginning."

Elizabeth Scarlatti slammed the flat of her hand down on the desk as she rose from her chair.

"You're sorry? Sorry? You don't fool me for a minute! You're frightened out of your wits and well you should be! You damned fool! You ass! What did you think you were doing? Playing games! Little boy games!"

Ulster Scarlett gripped the arm of the sofa in which he sat and repeated to himself over and over again, *Heinrich Kroeger, Heinrich Kroeger.*

"I demand an explanation, Ulster!"

"I told you. I was bored. Just plain bored."

"How involved are you?"

"Oh, Christ! I'm not. All I did was give some money for a supply. A shipment. That's all."

"Who did you give the money to?"

"Just—guys. Fellows I met at clubs."

"Were they criminals?"

"I don't know. Who isn't these days? Yes, I guess they were. They are. That's why I'm out of it. Completely out of it!"

"Did you ever sign anything?"

"Jesus, no! You think I'm crazy?"

"No. I think you're stupid."

Heinrich Kroeger, Heinrich Kroeger. Ulster Scarlett rose from the sofa and lit a cigarette. He walked to the fireplace and threw the match on the crackling logs.

"I'm not stupid, Mother," replied Elizabeth's son.

Elizabeth dismissed his pouting objection. "You only supplied money? You were never involved in any violence?"

"No! Of course not!"

"Then who was the ship's captain? The man who was murdered?"

"I don't know! Look, I told you. I admit I was down there. Some guys said I'd get a kick out of seeing how the stuff came in. But that's all, I swear it. There was trouble. The crew started fighting and I left. I got out of there as fast as I could."

"There's nothing more? That's the extent of it?"

"Yes. What do you want me to do? Bleed from my hands and feet?"

"That's not very likely." Elizabeth walked around the desk and approached her son. "What about this marriage, Ulster? Is it, too, because you're bored?"

"I thought you'd approve."

"Approve? I wasn't aware that my approval or disapproval concerned you."

"It does."

"I approve of the Saxon girl, but I doubt for the reasons Chancellor thinks I should. She seems to be a lovely girl from what I've seen of her. . . . I'm not at all sure I approve of you. . . . Do you love her?"

Ulster Scarlett looked casually at his mother. "I think she'll make a good wife."

"Since you avoid my question, do you think you'll make a good husband?"

"Why, Mother. I read in *Vanity Fair* where I was New York's most eligible bachelor."

"Good husbands and eligible bachelors are often mutually exclusive. . . . Why do you want to be married?"

"It's time I should be."

"I'd accept that answer from your brother. Not from you."

Scarlett walked away from his mother to the windows. This was the moment. This was the moment he had planned, the moment he had rehearsed. He had to do it simply, say it simply. He'd pull it off and one day Elizabeth would recognize how wrong she was.

He wasn't stupid; he was brilliant.

"I tried to tell Chance. I'll try again with you. I do want to get married. I do want to get interested in something. . . . You asked me if I love the girl. I think I do. I think I will. What's important to me now is that I get straightened out." He turned from the window and faced his mother. "I'd like to learn what you built for us. I want to know what the Scarlatti family's all about. Everyone seems to know but me. It's a place to start, Mother."

"Yes, it's a place to start. But I should caution you. When you speak of Scarlatti, don't be under any illusions that your name guarantees you a voice in its management. You'll have to prove your value before you receive any responsibility—or authority. In that decision, I am Scarlatti."

"Yes. You've always made that very clear."

Elizabeth Scarlatti circled the desk and sat down in her chair. "I've never been wedded to the idea that nothing changes. Everything changes. And it's possible you have talent. You are the son of Giovanni Scarlatti and, perhaps, I was a damned fool to change the surname. It seemed right at the time. He was a genius. . . . Go to work, Ulster. We'll see what happens."

Ulster Stewart Scarlett walked down Fifth Avenue. The sun was out and he left his topcoat open. He smiled to himself. Several passersby noticed the large, striking-looking man with the open coat in the February cold. He was arrogantly handsome, obviously successful. Some men were born to it.

Ulster Scarlett, seeing the looks of envy from the little people, agreed with the unspoken thoughts.

Heinrich Kroeger was on schedule.

CHAPTER 10

When Horace Boutier, president of Waterman Trust Company, received Chancellor's request for an indoctrination program for his brother Ulster, Boutier knew immediately who to make responsible.

Third vice-president Jefferson Cartwright.

Cartwright had been called on previously for duty with Ulster Scarlett and with good reason. He was, perhaps, the only executive at Waterman Trust who did not instantly irritate Ulster Scarlett. In a large measure this was due to Cartwright's unorthodox approach to his work. Quite unbankerlike.

For Jefferson Cartwright, a blondish, large, aging man, was a product of the playing fields of the University of Virginia and learned early in his career that the qualities that made him famous on the gridiron—and on the campus—served him extremely well in his chosen profession.

Briefly these were to learn the formations so thoroughly that one was always in the right position at the right time when on the field and always to press an advantage with the sheer bulk of one's size.

Off the field was merely an extension of the playing principles. Learn the surface formulas, wasting as little time as possible on complexities beyond one's grasp, and, again, impress everyone with the size—and attractiveness—of one's physical being.

These principles—when combined with an easy, outgoing Southern charm—guaranteed Jefferson Cartwright's sinecure at Waterman Trust. They even put his name on department letterheads.

For although Jefferson Cartwright's knowledge of banking hardly approached an expert vocabulary, his ability to commit adultery with some of the wealthiest women in Manhattan, Long Island, and southern Connecticut brought many excellent accounts to Waterman. Yet the bank's directors knew that their prime social stud was rarely a threat to any relatively secure marriage. Rather, he was a temporary divertissement, a charming, quick, and complete roll in the hay for the bored.

Most banking institutions had at least one Jefferson Cartwright on the executive payroll. However, such men often were overlooked when it came to club memberships and dinner parties. . . . One could never be sure.

It was the vague sense of ostracism that made Cartwright acceptable to Ulster Scarlett. Partly because he knew why it existed and it amused him, and partly because Cartwright—outside of a few mild lectures about the state of his accounts—never tried to tell him what to do with his money.

The bank's directors knew this, too. It was right that someone should advise Ulster Scarlett—if only to impress Elizabeth—but as no one could change him, why waste a committed man?

At the first session, as Cartwright called it, the banker discovered that Ulster Stewart Scarlett didn't know the difference between a debit and an asset. So a glossary of terms was prepared to give him a basic language to work with. From there another lexicon of stock market phraseology was written for him and in time he began to master it.

"Then, as I understand it, Mr. Cartwright, I have two separate incomes. Is that correct?"

"Indeed it is, Mr. Scarlett. The first trust fund, which is comprised of stocks—industrial and utility—is for your annual livin' expenses. Houses, clothes, trips abroad, purchases of any sort. . . . Of course, you certainly could invest this money if you wished. You have durin' the past several years if I'm not mistaken." Jefferson Cartwright smiled indulgently remembering a few of Ulster's extravagant withdrawals. "However, the second fund—the open-faced bonds and debentures—is designed for expansion. For reinvestment. Even speculation. That was your father's wish. Of course there's a degree of flexibility."

"What do you mean flexibility?"

"It's hardly conceivable, Mr. Scarlett, but should your livin' expenses exceed the income from the first trust we could, with your power of attorney, transfer capital from the second fund to the first. Of course, this is hardly conceivable."

"Of course."

Jefferson Cartwright laughed and gave his innocent pupil an exaggerated wink. "I have you there, haven't I?"

"What?"

"It did occur once. Don't you remember? The dirigible? . . . The dirigible you purchased several years ago?"

"Oh, yes. You were upset about that."

"As a banker I'm responsible to the Scarlatti Industries. After all, I'm your financial adviser. I'm held accountable. . . . We covered the purchase from the second fund but it wasn't proper. Not proper at all. A dirigible could hardly be called an investment."

"I apologize again."

"Just remember, Mr. Scarlett. Your father's wish was that the monies due from the open-faced securities were to be reinvested."

"How could anyone tell?"

"Those are the releases you sign semiannually."

"The hundred-odd signatures I have to sit through?"

"Yes. We convert the notes and invest the capital."

"In what?"

"Those are the portfolio statements we send you. We catalog all investments. We make the selection ourselves as you have not—with your busy schedule—ever answered our letters with regard to your preferences."

"I never understood them."

"Well, now, that can be overcome, can't it?"

"Suppose I didn't sign the releases?"

"Well . . . in that unlikely event the securities would remain in the vaults until the end of the year."

"Where?"

"The vaults. The Scarlatti vaults."

"I see."

"The releases are attached to the securities when we remove them."

"But no releases, no securities. No capital, no money."

"Exactly. They can't be converted. The releases are just what the name implies. You release to us with your power of attorney the right to invest the capital."

"Suppose, for imagination's sake, you didn't exist. There was no Waterman Trust. No bank at all. How could those securities be turned into money?"

"By signature again. Made payable to whomever you designated. It's all clearly set forth on each document."

"I see."

"One day—when you're more advanced, of course—you should see the vaults. The Scarlatti family occupies the entire east wing. The two remaining sons, yourself and Chancellor, have cubicles adjacent to each other. It's really quite touching."

Ulster considered. "Yes, I'd like to see the vaults. . . . When I'm more advanced, of course."

"For God's sake, are the Saxons preparing a wedding or a ceremonial convocation for the Archbishop of Canterbury?" Elizabeth Scarlatti had brought her oldest son to her house to discuss the various newspaper articles and the stack of invitations on her desk.

"You can't blame them. Ulster is hardly an ordinary catch."

"I'm aware of that. On the other hand the rest of New York can't stop functioning." Elizabeth walked to the library door and closed it. She turned and looked at her older son. "Chancellor, I want to discuss something with you. Very briefly and if you've got a brain in your head you won't repeat a word of what I'm going to mention."

"Of course."

Elizabeth kept looking at her son. She thought to herself that Chancellor was really a better man than she ever gave him credit for. His problem was that his outlook was so terribly provincial and yet so totally dependent. And his perpetual vacuous look whenever they had a conference made him seem like an ass.

A conference. Perhaps there had been too many conferences. Too few conversations. Perhaps it was her fault.

"Chancellor, I don't pretend to be on intimate terms with young people these days. There's a permissiveness that was absent from my own youth and, God knows, that's a step in the right direction, but I think it may have gone too far."

"I agree completely!" interrupted Chancellor Drew

94

Scarlett with fervor. "Today it is self-indulgence and I'll not have my children infected, let me tell you!"

"Well, perhaps it goes deeper than righteous indignation. The young, as the times, are what we shape them to be—willingly or unknowingly. . . . However, this is only an introduction." Elizabeth crossed to her desk and sat down. "I've been watching Janet Saxon during the past few weeks. . . . Watching, perhaps, is unfair. I've only seen her on half a dozen occasions starting with that absurd engagement party. It strikes me that she drinks quite heavily. Quite unnecessarily heavily. Yet she's a lovely girl. An intelligent, alert girl. Am I wrong?"

Chancellor Drew Scarlett was startled. He had never thought such a thing about Janet Saxon. It never crossed his mind. Everyone drank too much. It was all part of the self-indulgence and although he disapproved he never took it very seriously.

"I hadn't realized it, Mother."

"Then, obviously, I'm wrong and we'll drop the subject. I really am far removed from the times."

Elizabeth smiled, and for the first time in a long time she gave her oldest son an affectionate kiss. Yet something was bothering Janet Saxon and Elizabeth Scarlatti knew it.

The wedding ceremony of Janet Saxon and Ulster Stewart Scarlett was a triumph. Chancellor Drew was, naturally, his brother's best man and following the bride's train were Chancellor's five children. Chancellor's wife, Allison Demerest Scarlett, was unable to attend the wedding as she was in labor at Presbyterian Hospital.

The fact that it was an April wedding was a source of contention between Janet Saxon and her parents. They would have preferred June or, at least May, but Janet was adamant. Her fiancé insisted that they be in Europe by the middle of April and that's how it would be.

Besides, she had her own very valid reason for a short engagement.

She was pregnant.

Janet knew her mother suspected. She also knew that her mother was delighted, even admired her for what she believed was the proper use of the ultimate feminine ploy.

The prospect of this particular bridegroom entrapped, caged, irrefutably cornered, was enough for Marian Saxon to give in quickly to the April ceremony. Marian Saxon would have let her daughter be married in a synagogue on Good Friday if that ensured the Scarlatti heir.

Ulster Scarlett took a leave of absence from his sessions at the Waterman Trust Company. It was understood that following an extended honeymoon on the Continent he would plunge back into the world of finance with increased vigor. It positively touched—and amazed—Jefferson Cartwright that Ulster took with him—"on his sacred journey of love," as the Virginia cavalier put it—a large number of papers to study. He had gathered together literally hundreds of reports concerning the myriad interests of the Scarlatti Industries and promised Cartwright that he would master the complexities of the inexhaustible diversification by the time he returned.

Jefferson Cartwright was so moved by Ulster's earnestness that he presented him with a hand-tooled leather briefcase.

The first leg of the newlyweds' trip was marred by what appeared to be a severe case of seasickness on Janet's part. By a mildly amused ship's doctor, however, it was ascertained to be a miscarriage and as a result the bride spent the entire voyage to Southampton confined to her cabin.

In England they discovered that the English aristocracy was becoming quite tolerant of their invading American counterparts. It was all a question of degree. The crude but rich colonists were ripe for the taking and taken they were. The more acceptable—and this category included Ulster Scarlett and his wife—were absorbed without question.

Even the owners of Blenheim had to be impressed with someone who could wager the price of their best hunter on the turn of a single card. Especially when this particular gambler could tell at a glance which was the best hunter.

At about this time—the second month of their trip—the rumors began filtering back to New York. Brought mainly by returning members in good standing of the Four Hundred. It seemed Ulster Stewart was behaving very badly. He had taken to disappearing for days at a time and on one occasion was known to have been gone for the better part of two weeks, leaving his bride in a state of embarrassed anger.

However, even these extremes of gossip were not dwelled upon, for Ulster Stewart had done the same thing while a single man, and Janet Saxon, after all, had hooked herself Manhattan's most eligible bachelor. She should complain! A thousand girls would have settled for the ring and the ceremony and let him do as he pleased. All those millions and some said a titled family thrown into the bargain! No one had much sympathy for Janet Saxon.

And then the rumors took another turn.

The Scarletts uprooted themselves from London society and began what could only be described as an insanely planned itinerary throughout the Continent. From the frozen lakes of Scandinavia to the warm shores of the Mediterranean. From the still-cold streets of Berlin to the hot pavements of Madrid. From the mountain ranges of Bavaria to the flat, dirty ghettos of Cairo. From Paris in summer to the Scottish islands in autumn. One never knew where Ulster Scarlett and his wife would be next. It didn't make sense. There was no logic in their destinations.

Jefferson Cartwright was more concerned than anyone else. Alarmed. He was unsure of what to do and so he decided to do nothing but send carefully worded memorandums to Chancellor Drew Scarlett.

For Waterman Trust was sending thousands upon thousands of dollars in bank drafts to every conceivable and some inconceivable exchanges in Europe. Each letter of request from Ulster Scarlett was precisely worded and the instructions absolute. The demand for confidence, for silence, in the transactions was emphatic. The breaking of this confidence to be penalized by the immediate withdrawal of his interests from Waterman. . . . One-third of the Scarlett trusts. One-half of the Scarlatti inheritance.

There was no question about it. Ulster Scarlett had benefited from his sessions at the bank. He knew exactly how to expedite his financial demands and did it in the language of the banking profession. Still, Jefferson Cartwright was uneasy. He could be subject to criticism at a later date. There still remained two-thirds of the trusts and the second half of the inheritance. He solved his insoluble dilemma by sending the following—then variations of it—to Ulster Scarlett's brother.

Dear Chancellor:
Just to keep you up-to-date—as we so successfully established during your brother's sessions here at Waterman—Ulster is transferring considerable sums to European banks to cover what must be the finest honeymoon in the history of marriage. Nothing is too good for his beautiful wife! You'll be happy to learn that his correspondence is most businesslike.

A number of such notes were received by Chancellor Drew, who smiled indulgently at his reformed younger brother's devotion to his wife. And to think he was corresponding like a businessman. Progress had been made.

What Jefferson Cartwright did not explain was that Waterman Trust also received endless bills and charges validated by Ulster's signatures from countless hotels, railroads, stores, and lending institutions throughout Europe. What disturbed Cartwright was that the flexibility he had authorized during the dirigible incident would have to be employed again.

It was inconceivable but there it was! Ulster Scarlett's expenses were going to exceed the income from the trust fund. In the space of several months—when one added the charges to the transferals—Ulster Stewart Scarlett was reaching the eight-hundred-thousand-dollar mark.

Inconceivable!

Yet there it was.

And Waterman was subject to losing one-third of the Scarlatti interest if he divulged the information.

In August Ulster Stewart Scarlett sent word back to his mother and brother that Janet was pregnant. They would remain in Europe for a minimum of three more months as the doctors deemed it best that she do as little traveling as possible until the baby was well along.

Janet would remain in London, while Ulster traveled with friends to do some hunting in southern Germany.

98

He'd be gone for a month. Possibly a month and a half.

He'd cable when they decided to come home.

In mid-December the cable arrived. Ulster and Janet would be home for the holidays. Janet was to remain fairly inactive as the pregnancy was a difficult one, but Ulster hoped Chancellor had checked on the decorators and that his brownstone on Fifty-fourth Street would be comfortable for her.

He instructed Chancellor Drew to have someone meet a prior ship to escort a new housekeeper Ulster had found on the Continent. She had been highly recommended and Ulster wanted her to feel at home. Her name was Hannah.

Language would be no problem.

She spoke both English and German.

During the remaining three months of Janet's pregnancy Ulster resumed his sessions at Waterman Trust and his mere presence had a calming effect on Jefferson Cartwright. Although he never spent more than two hours at the bank, he seemed somewhat more subdued, less given to fits of irritation than he had been before his honeymoon.

He even began taking work home in the hand-tooled leather briefcase.

In reply to Cartwright's confidential and offhand questions about the large sums of money forwarded by the bank to Ulster in Europe, the Scarlatti heir reminded Waterman's third vice-president that it was he who had made it clear that nothing prohibited him from using the income from his trust fund for investments. He reiterated his request that all his European transactions remain confidential between the two of them.

"Of course. I understand completely. But you must realize that in the event we transfer funds from the second trust to cover your expenses—as surely we'll have to this year—I must record it for the Scarlatti records. . . .

We've paid enormous sums all over Europe on your signature."

"But you won't have to do that for a long time, will you?"

"At the end of the fiscal year, which for the Scarlatti Industries is June thirtieth. The same as the government's."

"Well"—the handsome man sighed as he looked at the agitated Southerner—"on June thirtieth I'll just have to stand up and face the music. It won't be the first time my family's been upset. I hope it's the last."

As the time approached for Janet's delivery, a constant procession of merchants passed through the doors of the Ulster Scarlett brownstone. A team of three doctors gave Janet constant attention and her own family saw her twice a day. What mattered was that the activity kept her occupied. It kept her mind off a frightening fact. A fact so personal she didn't know how to discuss it; there was no one to whom she felt close enough.

Her husband no longer spoke to her.

He had left her bed in her third month of pregnancy. In the south of France, to be exact. He had refused to have intercourse on the assumption that her miscarriage had been brought on by sex. She had wanted sex. She had wanted it desperately. She had wanted his body on hers because it was the only time she felt close to him. The only time her husband appeared to her to be without guile, without deceit, without the cold manipulation in his eyes. But even this was denied her.

Then he left their communal room, insisting upon separate rooms wherever they went.

And now he neither answered her questions nor asked any of his own.

He ignored her.

He was silent.

He was, if she wanted to be honest with herself, contemptuous of her.

He hated her.

Janet Saxon Scarlett. A reasonably intelligent product of Vassar. A graduate of the Pierre cotillions and a sane habitué of the hunt clubs. And always, always wondering why it was she and not someone else who enjoyed the privileges she had.

Not that she ever disclaimed them. She didn't. And

perhaps she was entitled to them. God knew she was a "looker." Everyone had said it for as long as she could remember. But she was what her mother always complained about—an observer.

"You never really enter into things, Janet! You must try to get over that!"

But it was hard to "get over." She looked upon her life as two sides of a stereopticon—both different, yet merging into one focus. On one plate was the well-appointed young lady with impeccable credentials, enormous wealth, and an obviously assured future with some well-appointed, enormously wealthy, impeccably credentialed husband. On the other was a girl with a frown on her forehead and a questioning look in her eyes.

For this girl thought the world was larger than the confined world presented to her. Larger and far more compelling. But no one had allowed her to see that larger world.

Except her husband.

And the part of it he let her see—forced her to see—was terrifying.

Which is why she drank.

While preparations for the birth continued, aided by a steady stream of Janet's friends and family, a strange passivity came over Ulster Stewart Scarlett. It was discernible especially to those who observed him closely, but even to others it was apparent that he had slowed down his normally frantic pace. He was quieter, less volatile, sometimes reflective. And for a while his periods of going off by himself became more frequent. Never very long, just three or four days at a time. Many, like Chancellor Drew, attributed it to impending fatherhood.

"I tell you, Mother, it's simply wonderful. He's a new man! And you know, I told him having children was the answer. Gives a man a purpose. You watch, when it's all over he'll be ready for a real man's job!"

"You have an acute ability to grasp the obvious, Chancellor. Your brother is quite convinced that he has a purpose in avoiding what you call a real man's job. I suspect he's bored to death by his imminent role as father. Or he's drinking bad whiskey."

101

"You're too hard on him."

"Quite the contrary," interrupted Elizabeth Scarlatti. "I think he's become far too hard on us."

Chancellor Drew looked bewildered. He changed the subject and began to read aloud a report of Scarwyck's newest project.

A week later a male child was born to Janet Scarlett at the French Hospital. Ten days later at the Cathedral of Saint John the Divine he was christened Andrew Roland Scarlett.

And a day after the christening, Ulster Stewart Scarlett disappeared.

CHAPTER 11

At first no one took much notice. Ulster had stayed away from home before. Although it was not the conventional behavior of a new father, Ulster hardly fit into any conventional pattern. It was presumed that the tribal rites attending the birth of a male child proved just too much for him and that he had taken refuge in activities best left undescribed. When after three weeks no word had been heard from him and no satisfactory explanations furnished by a variety of people, the family became concerned. On the twenty-fifth day after his disappearance, Janet asked Chancellor to call the police. Instead, Chancellor called Elizabeth, which was a far more positive action.

Elizabeth carefully weighed the alternatives. Calling the police would necessitate an investigation and probably a great deal of publicity. In light of Ulster's activities a year ago, that was undesirable. If Ulster's absence was his own doing, such action would only serve to provoke him. Without provocation her son was unpredictable; with it he might well be impossible. She decided to hire a discreet firm of investigators, which often had been called on to examine insurance claims against the family businesses. The owners understood completely and put only their most efficient and trusted men on the job.

Elizabeth gave them two weeks to unearth Ulster Stewart. Actually, she expected he'd show up by then, but if he didn't, she would turn the matter over to the police.

At the end of the first week, the investigators had compiled a multi-page report about Ulster's habits. The places he most frequently visited; his friends (many); his enemies (few); and, in as much detail as possible, a reconstruction of his movements during the last few days before he vanished. They gave this information to Elizabeth.

Elizabeth and Chancellor Drew studied the reports closely. They revealed nothing.

The second week proved equally unenlightening except to fill in Ulster's activities more minutely by the days and hours. Since his return from Europe, his daily rounds had become ritualistic. The squash courts and the steam rooms of the athletic club; the bank on lower Broadway, Waterman Trust; his cocktails on Fifty-third Street between 4:30 and 6:00 P.M. with five speakeasies sharing the five weekdays of his attendance; the nightly sorties into the entertainment world where a handful of entrepreneurs commandeered his indulgence (and financing); the almost routine early morning windups at a supper club on Fiftieth Street prior to his arrival home, never later than 2:00 A.M.

One bit of data did catch Elizabeth's attention as, indeed, it had the one who had reported it. It was incongruous. It appeared on Wednesday's sheet.

Left house at approximately 10:30 and immediately hailed a taxi in front of residence. Maid was sweeping front steps and believed she heard Mr. Scarlett direct the driver to a subway.

Elizabeth had never thought of Ulster in a subway. And yet, two hours later, according to a "Mr. Mascolo, head waiter at the Venezia Restaurant," he was having an early lunch with a "Miss Dempsey (See Acquaintances: Theatrical artists)." The restaurant was two blocks from Ulster's house. Of course there could be a dozen explanations and certainly nothing in the report indicated anything strange other than Ulster's decision to go to a subway. For the time being, Elizabeth attributed it to Ulster's meeting someone, probably Miss Dempsey.

At the end of the week, Elizabeth capitulated and instructed Chancellor Drew to contact the police.

The newspapers had a red-letter day.

The Bureau of Investigation joined with the Manhattan police on the premise that possibly interstate laws had been violated. Dozens of publicity seekers as well as many sincere individuals volunteered that they had seen Ulster during that last week before his disappearance. Some macabre souls telephoned, claiming knowledge of his whereabouts, demanding money for the information. Five letters arrived asking ransom for his return. All leads were checked out. All proved worthless.

Benjamin Reynolds saw the story on page two of the *Washington Herald*. Other than the wedding, it was the first news he'd read about Ulster Scarlett since his meeting with Elizabeth Scarlatti over a year ago. However, in keeping with his word, he had made discreet inquiries about the celebrated war hero during the past months— only to learn that he had rejoined his proper world. Elizabeth Scarlatti had done her job well. Her son had dropped out of the importing business and the rumors of his involvement with criminal elements had died away. He had gone so far as to assume some minor position— with New York's Waterman Trust.

It had seemed the affair Scarlatti was over for Ben Reynolds.

And now this.

Would this mean it was no longer dormant, no longer a closed wound? Would it signify a reopening of the harsh speculation he, Ben Reynolds, had dwelled upon? Would Group Twenty be called in?

A Scarlatti son did not simply disappear without the government at least alerted. Too many congressmen were indebted to Scarlatti for one thing or another—a factory here, a newspaper there, a good-sized campaign check most of the time. Sooner or later someone would remember that Group Twenty had looked into the man's activities once before.

They'd be back. Discreetly.

If Elizabeth Scarlatti said it was all right.

Reynolds put the newspaper down, got out of his chair, and walked to his office door.

"Glover," he asked his subordinate, "could you come in my office a minute?"

The older man walked back to his chair and sat down. "Did you read the story about Scarlatti?"

"This morning on the way to work," answered Glover, coming through the door.

"What do you make of it?"

"I knew you'd ask me. I think some of his last year's friends caught up with him."

"Why?"

Glover sat down in the chair in front of Reynolds's desk. "Because I can't think of anything else and it's logical. . . . And don't ask me why again because you know as well as I do."

"I do? I'm not sure of that."

"Oh, come on, Ben. The moneyman isn't having any more. Someone's stuck for a shipment and goes to him. He refuses. Sicilian sparks fly and that's that. . . . It's either something like that or a blackmail job. He decided to fight—and lost."

"I can't buy violence."

"Tell that to the Chicago police."

"Scarlett didn't deal with the lower echelons. That's why I can't buy a violence theory. There was too much to lose. Scarlett was too powerful; he had too many friends. . . . He might be used, not killed."

"Then what do you think?"

"I don't know. That's why I asked you. You jammed up this afternoon?"

"God damn it, yes. Still the same two things. No breaks coming our way."

"Arizona dam?"

"That's one. That son-of-a-bitch congressman keeps pushing through the appropriations and we know damned well he's getting paid, but we can't prove it. Can't even get anyone to admit they know anybody. . . . Incidentally, speaking of the Scarlett business, Canfield's on this one."

"Yes, I know. How's he doing?"

"Oh, we can't blame him. He's doing the best he can."

"What's the other problem?"

"The Pond memorandum from Stockholm."

"He's got to come through with something more than rumors, Glover. He's wasting our time until he gives us something concrete. I've told you that."

"I know, I know. But Pond sent word by courier—it arrived from State this morning—the transaction's been made. That's the word."

"Can't Pond get any names? Thirty million dollars' worth of securities and he can't get a single name?"

"A very tight syndicate, obviously. He hasn't come up with any."

"One hell of an ambassador. Coolidge appoints lousy ambassadors."

"He does think the whole shebang was manipulated by Donnenfeld."

"Well, that's a name! Who in hell is Donnenfeld?"

"Not a person. A firm. About the largest on the Stockholm exchange."

"How did he come to that conclusion?"

"Two reasons. The first is that only a large firm could handle it. Two—the whole thing can be buried easier that way. And it will have to be buried. American securities sold on the Stockholm exchange is touchy business."

"Touchy, hell! It can't be done!"

"All right. Rallied in Stockholm. Same thing as far as the money's concerned."

"What are you going to do about it?"

"Drudgery. Keep checking all the corporations with extensive ties in Sweden. You want to know something? There're a couple of dozen in Milwaukee alone. How do you like that? Make a bundle over here and do business with your cousins back home."

"If you want my opinion, Walter Pond's stirring up a quiet fuss so he gets some attention. Cal Coolidge doesn't make a friend an ambassador to the land of the midnight sun—or whatever the hell it's called—unless the fellow's not so good a friend as he thinks he is."

CHAPTER 12

After two months, with nothing further to write about or to broadcast, the novelty of Ulster Scarlett's disappearance wore off. For in truth, the only additional information uncovered by the combined efforts of the police, the Bureau of Missing Persons, and the federal investigators was of a character nature and led nowhere. It was as if he had literally decomposed, became vapor. Existing one minute, a colorful memory the next.

Ulster's life, possessions, prejudices, and anxieties were placed under the scrutiny of professionals. And the result of these labors etched an extraordinary portrait of pointlessness. A man who had just about everything a human being could ask for on this earth had apparently lived in a vacuum. A purposeless, aimless vacuum.

Elizabeth Scarlatti puzzled over the voluminous reports supplied her by the authorities. It had become a habit for her, a ritual, a hope. If her son had been killed, it would, of course, be painful; but she could accept the loss of life. And there were a thousand ways . . . fire, water, earth . . . to rid the world of a body. But she could not accept this conclusion. It was possible, of course. He had known the underworld, but on such a peripheral basis.

One morning Elizabeth stood by her library window watching the outside world come to grips with another day. The pedestrians always walked so rapidly in the morning. The automobiles were subject to far more backfiring after a night of idleness. Then Elizabeth saw one of her maids out on the front steps. The maid was sweeping the front steps.

As she watched the woman swing the broom back and forth, Elizabeth was reminded of another maid. On another set of steps.

A maid at Ulster's house. A maid who swept Ulster's steps one morning and remembered her son giving instructions to a taxi driver.

What were those instructions?

A subway. Ulster had to get to a subway.

Her son had to take a subway one morning and Elizabeth hadn't understood.

It was only a dim, flickering candle in a very dark forest but it was a light. Elizabeth crossed rapidly to the telephone.

Thirty minutes later, Third Vice-President Jefferson Cartwright stood before Elizabeth Scarlatti. He was still partially out of breath from the nervous pressures of rearranging his schedule in order to attend this command performance.

"Yes, indeed," drawled the Virginian. "All the accounts were thoroughly examined the minute Mr. Scarlett's disappearance was known to us. Wonderful boy. We became very close durin' his sessions at the bank."

"What is the state of his accounts?"

"Perfectly normal."

"I'm afraid I don't know what that means."

Cartwright hesitated for a few seconds—the thoughtful banker. "Of course, the final figures aren't complete but we have no reason at this point to believe he exceeded the annual income of his trust."

"What is that income, Mr. Cartwright?"

"Well, of course, the market fluctuates—happily upward—so it'd be difficult to give you a precise figure."

"Just an approximate one."

"Let me see now . . ." Jefferson Cartwright did not like the direction the conversation was taking. He was suddenly very thankful that he had had the foresight to send those vague memorandums to Chancellor Drew about his brother's expenditures in Europe. His Southern drawl became thicker. "I could call several executives more familiar with Mr. Scarlett's portfolio—but it was considerable, Madame Scarlatti."

109

"Then I expect you to have at least a rough figure at your command." Elizabeth did not like Jefferson Cartwright and the tone of her voice was ominous.

"Mr. Scarlett's income from the trust fund designated for personal expenditures as differentiated from the second trust fund designated for investments was in excess of seven hundred and eighty-three thousand dollars." Cartwright spoke rapidly, quietly.

"I'm very pleased that his personal needs rarely exceeded that trifling amount." Elizabeth shifted her position in the straight-backed chair so she could give Mr. Cartwright the full benefit of her stare. Jefferson Cartwright rattled on at an accelerated tempo. Phrases spilled over into others, his accent more pronounced than ever.

"Well, surely, you were aware of Mr. Scarlett's extravagances. I believe the newspapers reported many. As I say, I personally did my best to caution him, but he was a very headstrong young man. If you recall, just three years ago, Mr. Scarlett purchased a dirigible for nearly a half million dollars. We did our best to dissuade him, of course, but it was simply impossible. He said he had to have a dirigible! If you'll study your son's accounts, madame, you'll find many such rash purchases." Cartwright was decidedly on the defensive although he knew perfectly well Elizabeth could hardly hold him responsible.

"Just how many such . . . puchases were there?"

At an even faster rate of speed the banker replied, "Well, certainly none as extravagant as the dirigible! We were able to prevent similar incidents by explaining to Mr. Scarlett that it was improper to transfer monies from his second trust for such purposes. That he had to . . . limit his expenses to the income produced by the first trust. In our sessions at the bank we emphasized this aspect time and again. However, last year alone, while he was in Europe with the beautiful Mrs. Scarlett, we were in constant touch with the Continental banks over his personal accounts. To put it mildly, your son was most helpful to the European economy. . . . It also was necessary to make . . . numerous direct payments on his signature. . . . Certainly Mr. Chancellor Scarlett spoke of the many, many notes I sent him regarding the large sums of money we forwarded your son in Europe."

Elizabeth's eyebrows rose. "No, he told me nothing."

"Well, Madame Scarlatti, it was your son's honeymoon. There was no reason . . ."

"Mr. Cartwright," the old woman interrupted sharply, "do you have an accurate accounting of my son's bank drafts, here and abroad, for the past year?"

"Why, of course, madame."

"And a listing of the payments made directly by you on his signature?"

"Certainly."

"I shall expect them in my hands no later than tomorrow morning."

"But it would take several accountants a full week to compile everything. Mr. Scarlett was hardly the most precise individual when it came to such matters. . . ."

"Mr. Cartwright! I've dealt with Waterman Trust for over a quarter of a century. The Scarlatti Industries deal through Waterman Trust exclusively, because I direct that they should. I believe in Waterman Trust because it's never given me a reason not to. Do I make myself clear?"

"You do, indeed. Tomorrow mornin'." Jefferson Cartwright bowed out of the room as a pardoned slave might take leave of an Arabian sheikh.

"Oh, Mr. Cartwright."

"Yes?"

"I don't think I really commended you for keeping my son's expenses within the boundaries of his income."

"I'm sorry. . . ." Beads of perspiration appeared on Cartwright's forehead. "There was little . . ."

"I don't think you understand me, Mr. Cartwright. I'm quite sincere. I commend you. Good morning."

"Good day, Madame Scarlatti."

Cartwright and three Waterman bookkeepers stayed throughout the night in an attempt to bring the accounts of Ulster Stewart Scarlett up-to-date. It was a difficult chore.

By two thirty in the morning Jefferson Cartwright had on his desk a list of banks and exchanges where the Scarlatti heir either had or once had accounts. Opposite each were detailed figures and times of transference. The list seemed endless. The specific deposits might well have averaged yearly incomes for the large majority of middle-class Americans but for Ulster Stewart they were no more than weekly allowances. It would take days to ascertain what was left. The list included:

THE CHEMICAL CORN EXCHANGE, *900 Madison Avenue, New York City.*
MAISON DE BANQUE, *22 rue Violette, Paris.*
LA BANQUE AMÉRICAINE, *rue Nouveau, Marseilles.*
DEUTSCHE-AMERICANISCHE BANK, *Kurfuerstendamm, Berlin.*
BANCO-TURISTA, *Calle de la Sueños, Madrid.*
MAISON DE MONTE CARLO, *rue du Feuillage, Monaco.*
WIENER STAEDTISCHE SPARKASSE, *Salzburgerstrasse, Vienna.*
BANQUE-FRANCAISE-ALGÉRIE, *Harbor of Moons, Cairo, Egypt.*

And so it went. Ulster and his bride had seen Europe.

Of course, balancing this list of supposed assets was a second list of deficits in the form of accounts due. These included monies owed by signature to scores of hotels, department stores, shops, restaurants, automobile agencies, steamship lines, railroads, stables, private clubs, gambling establishments. They all had been paid by Waterman.

Jefferson Cartwright perused the detailed reports.

By civilized standards they were a conglomeration of financial nonsense, but the history of Ulster Stewart Scarlett bore out that for him this was perfectly normal. Cartwright reached the same conclusion as had the government accountants when they checked for the Bureau of Investigation soon after Ulster's disappearance.

Nothing unusual considering Ulster Scarlett's past life. Naturally, Waterman Trust would send letters of inquiry to the banks here and abroad to ascertain the amount of remaining deposits. It would be a simple matter to have the monies transferred under power of attorney back to Waterman Trust.

"Yes, indeed," muttered the Southerner to himself. "Mighty complete job under the circumstances."

Jefferson Cartwright was convinced that old Scarlatti would have a very different attitude toward him this morning. He would sleep for a few hours, take a long cold shower, and bring the reports to her himself. Secretly, he hoped that he would look tired, terribly tired. She might be impressed.

"My dear Mr. Cartwright," spat out Elizabeth Scarlatti, "it never occurred to you that while you were transferring thousands upon thousands to banks all over Europe, you were simultaneously settling debts which totaled nearly a quarter of a million dollars? It never crossed your mind that by combining these two figures my son accomplished the seemingly impossible! He went through the entire annual income from his trust in less than nine months! Damned near to the penny!"

"Naturally, Madame Scarlatti, letters are being sent this mornin' to the banks requestin' full information. Under our power of attorney, of course. I'm sure sizable amounts will be returned."

"I'm not at all sure."

"If I may be frank, Madame Scarlatti, what you're leadin' up to completely eludes me. . . ."

Elizabeth's tone became momentarily gentle, reflective. "To tell the truth, it eludes me also. Only I'm not leading, I'm being led. . . ."

"I beg your pardon?"

"During my son's sessions at Waterman could he have . . . come upon something . . . which might cause him to transfer such sums to Europe?"

"I asked myself the same question. As his adviser I felt it my duty to inquire. . . . Apparently Mr. Scarlett made a number of investments on the Continent."

"Investments? In Europe? That seems most unlikely!"

"He had a wide circle of friends, Madame Scarlatti. Friends who, I'm sure, didn't lack for projects. . . . And I must say, your son was becomin' more and more proficient in investment analysis. . . ."

"He what?"

"I refer to his studies of the Scarlatti portfolios. Why, he put his shoulder to the wheel and was unrelentin' on himself. I took great pride in his accomplishment. He was really takin' our sessions seriously. Tryin' so hard to understand the factor of diversification. . . . Why, on his honeymoon he took along hundreds of the Scarlatti corporate reports."

Elizabeth rose from her chair and walked slowly, deliberately toward the window overlooking the street, but her concentration was on the Southerner's sudden, incredible revelation. As had happened so often in the past, she realized that her instincts—abstract, unclear—were leading her to the truth. It was there; she was near it. But it remained out of her grasp.

"I assume you mean the statements—the breakdowns —of the Scarlatti Industries' holdings?"

"That, too, of course. But much, much more. He analyzed the trusts, both his and Chancellor's—even your own, Madame Scarlatti. It was his hope to write a complete report with special emphasis on the growth factors. It was a mighty ambitious task and he never wavered. . . ."

"Far more than ambitious, Mr. Cartwright," interrupted Elizabeth. "Without training, I'd say impossible." She continued to look out on the street.

"Actually, dear madame, we at the bank understood this. So we convinced him to limit his research to his own holdings. I felt it would be easier to explain and I certainly didn't wish to dampen his enthusiasm, so I . . ."

Elizabeth turned from the window and stared at the banker. Her look caused him to stop speaking. She knew the truth was now within her grasp. "Please clarify. How did my son . . . research his holdings?"

"From the securities in his trust fund. Primarily the bonds in his second trust—the investment fund—they're far more stable commodities. He cataloged them and then matched them with alternate choices, which might have been made when they were originally purchased. If I may add, he was most impressed with the selections. He told me so."

"He . . . cataloged them? What precisely do you mean?"

"He listed the securities separately. The amounts each represented and the years and months they were due. From the dates and the amounts he was able to compare with numerous other issues on the board."

"How did he do this?"

"As I mentioned, from the bonds and debentures themselves. From the yearly portfolios."

"Where?"

"The vaults, madame. The Scarlatti vaults."

114

My God! thought Elizabeth.

The old woman put her hand—trembling—on the windowsill. She spoke calmly in spite of the fear enveloping her. "How long did my son . . . do this research?"

"Why, for several months. Since his return from Europe to be exact."

"I see. Did anyone assist him? He was so inexperienced, I mean."

Jefferson Cartwright returned Elizabeth's look. He was not an utter fool. "There was no necessity. Catalogin' premature securities isn't difficult. It's a simple process of listin' names, figures, and dates. . . . And your son is . . . was a Scarlatti."

"Yes. . . . He was." Elizabeth knew the banker was beginning to read her thoughts. It didn't matter. Nothing mattered now but the truth.

The vaults.

"Mr. Cartwright, I'll be ready in ten minutes. I'll call for my car and we'll both return to your office."

"As you wish."

The ride downtown was made in silence. The banker and the matriarch sat next to each other in the back seat, but neither spoke. Each was preoccupied with his own thoughts.

Elizabeth's—the truth.

Cartwright's—survival. For if what he had begun to suspect was correct, he'd be ruined. Waterman Trust might be ruined. And he was the appointed adviser to Ulster Stewart Scarlett.

The chauffeur opened the door as the Southerner stepped out onto the curb and held his hand for Elizabeth. He noted that she grasped his hand tightly, too tightly, as she climbed—with difficulty—out of the automobile. She stared down at nothing.

The banker led the old woman rapidly through the bank. Past the cages, past the tellers, past the office doors to the rear of the building. They took the elevator down to the huge Waterman cellars. Out of the elevator they turned to the left and approached the east wing.

The walls were gray, the surfaces smooth, and the thick cement encased both sides of the gleaming steel bars. Above the portal was a simple inscription.

115

Elizabeth thought—once again—that the effect was tomblike. Beyond the bars was a narrow hallway lit from the ceiling with bright bulbs encased in wire mesh. Except for the doorways, two on either side, the corridor looked like a passageway to some pharaoh's final resting place in the center of an awesome pyramid. The door at the end led to the vault of the Scarlatti Industries itself.

Everything.

Giovanni.

The two doors on either side led to cubicles for the wife and the three children. Chancellor's and Ulster's were on the left. Elizabeth's and Roland's on the right. Elizabeth was next to Giovanni.

Elizabeth had never had Roland's consolidated. She knew that ultimately the courts would take care of that. It was her one gesture of sentiment to her lost son. It was proper. Roland, too, was part of the empire.

The uniformed guard nodded—funereally—and opened the steel-barred door.

Elizabeth stood in front of the entrance to the first cubicle on the left. The nameplate on the center of the metal door read, Ulster Stewart Scarlatti.

The guard opened this door and Elizabeth entered the small room. "You will relock the door and wait outside."

"Naturally."

She was alone in the cell-like enclosure. She reflected that only once before had she been in Ulster's cubicle. It had been with Giovanni. Years, histories ago. . . . He had coaxed her downtown to the bank without telling her of his arrangements for the east wing vaults. He had been so proud. He had taken her through the five rooms as a guide might usher tourists through a museum. He had elaborated on the intricacies of the various trusts. She remembered how he slapped the cabinets as if they were prize-winning cattle that would someday provide enormous herds.

He had been right.

The room hadn't changed. It might have been yesterday.

On one side, built into the wall, were the deposit boxes

holding the industrials—the stocks, the certificates of ownership in hundreds of corporations. The wherewithal for day-to-day living. Ulster's first trust fund. On two other walls stood file cabinets, seven on each side. Each file drawer was marked with a year date—changed each year by the Waterman executors. Each drawer contained hundreds of open-faced securities and each cabinet had six drawers.

Securities to be drawn on for the next eighty-four years.

The second trust. Earmarked for Scarlatti expansion.

Elizabeth studied the cards on the cabinets.

1926. 1927. 1928. 1929. 1930. 1931.

These were listed on the first cabinet.

She saw that there was a monk's stool pushed several feet away from the cabinet to the right. Whoever had used it last had been seated between the first and second file. She looked at the index cards on the adjacent cabinet.

1932. 1933. 1934. 1935. 1936. 1937.

She rreached down and pulled the stool in front of the first cabinet and sat down. She looked at the bottom file drawer.

1926.

She opened it.

The year was divided by the twelve months, each month separated by a small index tab. Before each tab was a thin metal carton with two miniature cleats joined by a single wire submerged in wax. On the face of the wax—branded—were the initials *W.T.* in old English lettering.

The year 1926 was intact. None of the thin metal cartons had been opened. Which meant that Ulster had not complied with the bank's request for investment instructions. At the end of December the executors would take the responsibility themselves and, no doubt, consult Elizabeth as they had always done in the past with Ulster's fund.

She pulled out the year 1927.

This, too, was untouched. None of the wax crests had been broken.

Elizabeth was about to close the file on 1927 when she stopped. Her eyes caught sight of a blur in the wax. A tiny, slight blemish that would have gone unnoticed had not a person's attention been on the crests.

117

The *T.* of the *W.T.* was ragged and slanted downward on the month of August. The same was true for September, October, November, and December.

She pulled out the August carton and shook it. Then she ripped the wire apart and the wax crest cracked and fell away.

The carton was empty.

She replaced it and drew out the remaining months of 1927.

All empty.

She replaced the cartons and opened the file for 1928. Every thin carton had the *T.* of the wax crest ragged and slanting downward.

All empty.

For how many months had Ulster carried out his extraordinary charade? Going from one harried banker to the next and always, always—at the last—coming down to the vaults. Document by document. Security by security.

Three hours ago she wouldn't have believed it. It was only because a maid sweeping her front steps had triggered the memory of another maid sweeping steps. A maid who remembered a short command given by her son to a cabdriver.

Ulster Scarlett had taken a subway.

One midmorning he could not take the chance of a taxi ride in traffic. He had been late for his session at the bank.

What better time than midmorning? The initial placing of orders, the chaos of early trading in the market.

Even Ulster Scarlett would be overlooked at midmorning.

She hadn't understood the subway.

Now she did.

As if performing a painful ritual she checked the remaining months and years of the first cabinet. Through December, 1931.

Empty.

She closed the drawer on 1931 and began at the bottom of the second cabinet. 1932.

Empty.

She had reached the middle of the cabinet—1934—when she heard the sound of the metal door opening. She quickly closed the file and turned around in anger.

Jefferson Cartwright entered and shut the door.

'I thought I told you to remain outside!"

"My word, Madame Scarlatti, you look like you've seen a dozen ghosts."

"Get out!"

Cartwright walked rapidly to the first cabinet and arbitrarily pulled out one of the middle drawers. He saw the broken seals on the metal cartons, lifted one out, and opened it. "Seems as if somethin's missin'."

"I'll have you dismissed!"

"Maybe. . . . Maybe you will." The Southerner pulled out another drawer and satisfied himself that several other cartons whose seals had been broken were empty also.

Elizabeth stood silently, contemptuously, next to the banker. When she spoke, it was with the intensity born of disgust. "You have just terminated your employment at Waterman Trust!"

"Maybe I have. Excuse me, please." The Virginian gently moved Elizabeth away from the second cabinet and continued his search. He reached the year 1936 and turned to the old woman. "Not much left, is there? I wonder how far it goes, don't you? Of course, I'll make a complete breakdown for you as soon as possible. For you and my superiors." He closed the drawer on 1936 and smiled.

"This is confidential family business. You'll do nothing! You can do nothing!"

"Oh, come now! These cabinets contained open-faced securities. Bearer bonds negotiable subject to signature. . . . Possession is ownership. They're the same as money. . . . Your disappearin' son took a whale of a hunk of the New York Exchange! And we haven't even finished lookin' around. Shall we open a few more cabinets?"

"I will not tolerate this!"

"Then don't. You go on your way, and I'll simply report to my superiors that Waterman Trust is in one hell of a pile of manure. Forgettin' very sizable commissions due the bank and puttin' aside any thoughts of the companies involved gettin' nervous over who owns what—there might even be a run on some stocks—I possess knowledge which I should report immediately to the authorities!"

"You can not! You must not!"

"Why not?" Jefferson Cartwright held out the palms of both hands.

Elizabeth turned away from him and tried to marshal her thoughts. "Estimate what's gone, Mr. Cartwright. . . ."

"I can estimate as far as we've looked. Eleven years, approximately three and a half million a year comes to something like forty million. But we may have only just begun."

"I said . . . prepare an estimate. I trust that I don't have to tell you that if you say a word to anyone—I shall destroy you. We'll arrive at mutually agreeable terms." She slowly turned and looked at Jefferson Cartwright. "You should know, Mr. Cartwright, that through an accident you're privileged to information that lifts you far above your talents or abilities. When men are so fortunate, they must be cautious."

Elizabeth Scarlatti spent a sleepless night.

Jefferson Cartwright also spent a sleepless night. But it wasn't in bed. It was on a monk's stool with reams of papers at his feet.

The figures mounted as he cautiously checked the file cabinets against the Scarlatti trusts reports.

Jefferson Cartwright thought he'd go mad.

Ulster Stewart Scarlett had removed securities worth over $270 million.

He totaled and retotaled the figures.

An amount that would cause a crisis on the exchange.

An international scandal, which could—if known—cripple the Scarlatti Industries. . . . And it would be known when the time came to convert the first missing securities. At the outside, barely a year.

Jefferson Cartwright folded the last of the pages together and stuffed them into his inner jacket pocket. He clamped his arm against his chest, making sure that the pressure between his flesh was stopped by the paper, and left the vaults.

He signaled the front guard with a short whistle. The man had been dozing on a black leather chair near the door.

"Oh, m'God, Mr. Cartwright! Y'startled me!"

Cartwright walked out onto the street.

He looked at the grayish white light of the sky. It was going to be morning soon. And the light was his signal.

For he—Jefferson Cartwright, fifty-year-old ex-football player from the University of Virginia, who had married first money and then lost it—held in his pocket carte blanche to everything he had ever wanted.

He was back in the stadium and the crowds were roaring.

Touchdown!

Nothing could be denied him now.

CHAPTER 13

At twenty minutes after one in the morning, Benjamin Reynolds sat comfortably in an armchair in his Georgetown apartment. He held on his lap one of the file folders the attorney general's office had sent Group Twenty. There had been sixteen in all and he divided the stack equally between Glover and himself.

With congressional pressure, especially New York's Senator Brownlee, the attorney general's office wasn't going to leave a single stone unturned. If the Scarlatti son had disappeared into a void, at least the AG men could write volumes explaining the fact. Because Group Twenty had touched—briefly—on the life of Ulster Scarlett, Reynolds, too, would be expected to add something. Even if it was nothing.

Reynolds felt a trace of guilt when he thought of Glover wading through the same nonsense.

Like all reports of investigations of missing persons, it was filled with trivia. Dates, hours, minutes, streets, houses, names, names, names. A record of the inconsequential made to seem important. And perhaps to someone, somewhere, it might be. A part, a section, a paragraph, a sentence, even a word could open a door for someone.

But certainly not for anyone at Group Twenty.

He'd apologize to Glover later that morning.

Suddenly the phone rang. The sound in the stillness at such an unexpected hour startled Reynolds.

"Ben? It's Glover. . . ."

"Jesus! You scared the hell out of me! What's wrong? Someone call in?"

"No, Ben. I suppose this could wait until morning, but I thought I'd give you the pleasure of laughing yourself to sleep, you bastard."

"You've been drinking, Glover. Fight with your wife, not me. What the hell have I done?"

"Gave me these eight Bibles from the attorney general's office, that's what you did. . . . I found something!"

"Good Christ! About the New York thing! The docks?"

"No. Nothing we've ever connected with Scarlett. Maybe nothing but it could be . . ."

"What?"

"Sweden. Stockholm."

"Stockholm? What the hell are you talking about?"

"I know the Pond file by rote."

"Walter Pond? The securities?"

"That's right. His first memorandum arrived last May. The initial word about the securities. . . . Remember now?"

"Yes, yes, I do. So what?"

"According to a report in the sixth file, Ulster Scarlett was in Sweden last year. Would you like to guess when?"

Reynolds paused before answering. His attention was riveted on the almost unimaginable amount of thirty million dollars. "It wasn't Christmas, was it." It was a statement spoken softly.

"Now that you mention it, some people might have looked at it that way. Perhaps Christmas in Sweden comes in May."

"Let's talk in the morning." Reynolds hung up without waiting for his subordinate to reply or say goodnight. He walked slowly back to the soft armchair and sat down.

As always Benjamin Reynolds's thought processes raced ahead of the information presented. To the complications, the ramifications.

If Glover had made a valid assumption, that Ulster Scarlett was involved with the Stockholm manipulation, then it had to follow that Scarlett was still alive. If that were true, then thirty million dollars' worth of American securities had been illegally offered by him for sale on the Stockholm exchange.

123

No one individual, not even Ulster Stewart Scarlett, could get his hands on thirty million dollars' worth of securities.

Unless there was a conspiracy.

But of what kind? For what purpose?

If Elizabeth Scarlatti herself were a part of it—she had to be considered in light of the magnitude of the capital—why?

Had he misread her completely?

It was possible.

It was also possible that he had been right over a year ago. The Scarlatti son had not done what he had done for thrills or because he'd met unsavory friends. Not if Stockholm was pertinent.

Glover paced the floor in front of Reynolds's desk. "It's there. Scarlett's visa shows he entered Sweden on May tenth. The Pond memorandum is dated the fifteenth."

"I see. I can read."

"What are you going to do?"

"Do? I can't do a damn thing. There's really nothing here at all. Simply a statement calling our attention to some rumors and the date of an American citizen's entry into Sweden. What else do *you* see?"

"Assuming there's a basis for the rumors, the connection's obvious and you know it as well as I do! Five will get you ten that if Pond's last communication is right, Scarlett's in Stockholm now."

"Assuming he's got something to sell."

"That's what I said."

"If I remember, somebody's got to say something's stolen before somebody else can yell thief! If we make accusations, all the Scarlattis have to say is they don't know what we're talking about and we're strung up on a high legal tree. And they don't even have to do that. They can simply refuse to dignify us with an answer—that's the way the old lady would put it—and the boys on the Hill will take care of the rest. . . . This agency—for those who know about it—is an abomination. The purpose we serve is generally at odds with a few other purposes in this town. We're one of the checks and balances—take your choice. A lot of people in Washington would like to see us out."

"Then we'd better let the AG's office have the information and let them draw their own conclusions. I guess that's the only thing left."

Benjamin Reynolds pushed his foot against the floor and his chair swung gently around to face the window. "We should do that. We will if you insist on it."

"What does that mean?" asked Glover, addressing his words to the back of his superior's head.

Reynolds shoved his chair around again and looked at his subordinate. "I think we can do the job better ourselves. Justice, Treasury, even the Bureau. They're accountable to a dozen committees. We're not."

"We're extending the lines of our authority."

"I don't think so. And as long as I sit in this chair that's pretty much my decision, isn't it?"

"Yes, it is. Why do you want us to take it on?"

"Because there's something diseased in all this. I saw it in the old woman's eyes.

"That's hardly clear logic."

"It's enough. I saw it."

"Ben? If anything turns up we think is beyond us, you'll go to the attorney general?"

"My word."

"You're on. What do we do now?"

Benjamin Reynolds rose from his chair. "Is Canfield still in Arizona?"

"Phoenix."

"Get him here."

Canfield. A complicated man for a complicated assignment. Reynolds did not like him, did not completely trust him: But he would make progress faster than any of the others.

And in the event he decided to sell out, Ben Reynolds would know it. He would spot it somehow. Canfield wasn't that experienced.

If that happened Reynolds would bear down on the field accountant and get to the truth of the Scarlatti business. Canfield was expendable.

Yes, Matthew Canfield was a good choice. If he pursued the Scarlattis on Group Twenty's terms, they could ask no more. If, on the other hand, he found different terms—terms too lucrative to refuse—he would be called in and broken.

Destroyed. But they would know the truth.

Ben Reynolds sat down and wondered at his own cynicism.

There was no question about it. The fastest way to solve the mystery behind the Scarlattis was for Matthew Canfield to be a pawn.

A pawn who trapped himself.

CHAPTER 14

It was difficult for Elizabeth to sleep. She repeatedly sat up in bed to write down whatever came into her head. She wrote down facts, conjectures, remote possibilities, even impossibilities. She drew little squares, inserted names, places, dates, and tried to match them with connecting lines. At about three in the morning, she had reduced the series of events to the following:

April, 1925. Ulster and Janet married after only three-week engagement. Why? . . . Ulster and Janet sailed Cunard Line to Southampton. Reservations made by Ulster in February. How did he know?

May to December, 1925. Approximately eight hundred thousand sent by Waterman Trust to sixteen different banks in England, France, Germany, Austria, Holland, Italy, Spain, and Algeria.

January to March, 1926. Securities valued at approximately 270 million taken from Waterman. Forced sale equivalent between 150 and 200 million. All bills and charges in Ulster's and Janet's name from European accounts settled in full by February, 1926. Month of March, Ulster's behavior considerably altered, withdrawn.

April, 1926. Andrew born. Andrew christened. Ulster disappears.

July, 1926. Confirmation received from fourteen European banks that all monies withdrawn previously. Generally within four weeks of deposit. Two banks, London and The Hague, report sums of twenty-six thousand and nineteen thousand, respectively, remain on deposit.

This was the chronological order of events relative to

Ulster's disappearance. The design was there. Premeditation of the whole sequence was apparent: the reservations made in February; the short engagement; the honeymoon tour; the constant deposits and prompt withdrawals; the removal of the securities and the final act of Ulster's disappearance itself. From February, 1925, to April, 1926. A plan conceived for fourteen months and executed with enormous precision, even to the point of assuring pregnancy, if Janet was to be believed. Was Ulster capable of such ingenuity? Elizabeth did not know. She really knew very little about him and the endless reports served only to cloud his image. For the person this research analyzed was seemingly capable of nothing save self-indulgence.

She knew there was only one place to start the search. Europe. The banks. Not all, she rationalized, but several. For regardless of the complexities of growth and the excesses of diversification, the fundamental practice of banking had remained constant since the time of the pharaohs. You put money in and you took money out. And whether for necessity or for pleasure the money withdrawn went someplace else. It was that other place, or those other places, that Elizabeth wanted to find. For it was this money, the money that Waterman Trust sent to the sixteen European banks, which would be used until such time as the securities might be sold.

At ten minutes to nine the butler opened the front door for Waterman Trust Company's newest second vice-president, Jefferson Cartwright. He showed Cartwright into the library where Elizabeth sat behind the desk with the inevitable cup of coffee in her hand.

Jefferson Cartwright sat on the small chair in front of the desk aware that it flatteringly accentuated his size. He put his briefcase by his side.

"Did you bring the letters?"

"I have them right here, Madame Scarlatti," answered the banker, lifting the briefcase to his lap and opening it. "May I take this opportunity to thank you for your kind intercession on my behalf at the office. It certainly was most generous of you."

"Thank you. I understand you've been made second vice-president."

"That's correct, ma'am, and I do believe the good word from you made it possible. I thank you again." He handed Elizabeth the papers.

She took them and started scanning the top pages. They seemed to be in order. In fact, they were excellent.

Cartwright spoke quietly. "The letters authorize you to receive all information regardin' any transactions made by your son, Ulster Stewart Scarlett, at the various banks. Deposits, withdrawals, transferals. They request access to all safety deposit boxes where they may exist. A coverin' letter has been sent to each bank with a photostat of your signature. I've signed these in my capacity as representin' Waterman's collective power of attorney for Mr. Scarlett. By doin' it, of course, I've taken a considerable risk."

"I congratulate you."

"It's simply incredible," the banker said quietly. "Securities worth over two hundred and seventy million dollars. Missin', unaccounted for. Just floatin' around somewhere. Who knows where? Even the largest bankin' syndicates have trouble raisin' such capital. Oh, it's a crisis, ma'am! Especially in a highly speculative market. I honestly don't know what to do."

"It's possible that by keeping your own counsel you'll spend many years drawing a remarkable salary for very little effort. Conversely, it's also possible—"

"I think I know what the other possibility is," interrupted Jefferson Cartwright. "As I see it, you're lookin' for information connected with the disappearance of your child. You may find it, if it exists. You may not. In either case, there're twelve months remainin' before the first of the bonds will be missed. Twelve months. Some of us might not be on God's good earth then. Others of us could be facin' ruin."

"Are you forecasting my demise?"

"I certainly hope not. But my own position is most delicate. I've violated the policies of my firm and the basic ethics of the bankin' business. As your son's financial adviser, the aspect of collusion will be raised—"

"And you'd feel more comfortable with a settlement, is that it?" Elizabeth put down the letters, angry with this

129

ungrateful Southerner. "I bribe you and you proceed to blackmail me on the strength of my bribe. It's clever strategy. How much?"

"I'm sorry I make such a poor impression. I don't want a settlement. That'd be demeanin'."

"Then what do you want?" Elizabeth was becoming exasperated.

"I've prepared a statement. In triplicate. One copy for you, one for the Scarwyck Foundation, and one, of course, for my lawyer. I'd appreciate your perusin' it for your approval."

Cartwright withdrew the papers from his briefcase and placed them before Elizabeth. She picked up the top copy and saw that it was a letter of agreement, addressed to the Scarwyck Foundation.

> This is to confirm an agreement between Mr. Jefferson Cartwright and myself, Mrs. Elizabeth Wyckham Scarlatti, in my position as chairman of the board of the Scarwyck Foundation, 525 Fifth Avenue, New York, New York.
>
> Whereas, Mr. Cartwright has given generously of his time and professional services in my behalf and in behalf of the Scarwyck Foundation, it is agreed that he be made advisory consultant to the foundation with an annual salary of fifty thousand dollars ($50,000), said position to be held throughout his natural life. Said position to be made effective as of the above date.
>
> Whereas, Mr. Jefferson Cartwright often has acted in my behalf and in behalf of the Scarwyck Foundation against his better judgment and in opposition to his own wishes, and,
>
> Whereas, Mr. Cartwright performed all services in the manner his client, myself, firmly believed was for the betterment of the Scarwyck Foundation, he did so without anticipating said responsibility and often without full knowledge of the transactions.
>
> Therefore, it is agreed that should there be at any future dates any fines, penalties, or judgments against Mr. Cartwright evolving from such actions, they will be paid in full from my personal accounts.
>
> It should be added that no such actions are anticipated, but as the interests of the Scarwyck Founda-

tion are international in scope, the demands excessive, and decisions often subject to my own opinion, the inclusion of such a statement is deemed proper.

It should be noted that Mr. Cartwright's exceptional services in my behalf have been rendered in confidence during the past months, but that from this date I have no objection to his position with the Scarwyck Foundation being made public knowledge.

There were two lines on the right for the signatures and a third line on the left for the signature of a witness. Elizabeth realized it was a professional document. It said nothing, but covered everything.

"You don't seriously expect me to sign this?"

"I honestly do. You see, if you don't, my overbearin' sense of responsibility would make me go right to the authorities. No doubt direct to the office of the district attorney with information I believe relevant to Mr. Scarlett's disappearance. . . . Can you imagine the international stir that would cause? The mere fact that the celebrated Madame Scarlatti was goin' to question the banks where her son did business—"

"I'll deny everything."

"Unfortunately, you couldn't deny the missin' securities. They don't have to be redeemed for a year, but they *are* missin'."

Elizabeth stared at the Southerner, knowing she was beaten. She sat down and silently reached for a pen. She signed the papers as he in turn took each page and did the same.

CHAPTER 15

Elizabeth's trunks were placed aboard the British liner
Calpurnia. She had told her family that the events of the
past few months had taken their toll of her patience and
health and she planned an extended stay in Europe—by
herself. She was sailing the next morning. Chancellor
Drew agreed that a trip might be beneficial, but he strongly urged his mother to take along a companion. After all,
Elizabeth was no longer young, and in her advanced
years someone should accompany her. He suggested
Janet.

Elizabeth suggested that Chancellor Drew save his sug-
gestions for the Scarwyck Foundation, but the issue of
Janet had to be faced.

She asked the girl to come to her house late in the
afternoon two days before the *Calpurnia* sailed.

"The things you tell me are hard to believe, Janet. Not
so much about my son, but about you. Did you love
him?"

"Yes. I think so. Or perhaps I was overwhelmed by
him. In the beginning there were so many people, so
many places. Everything went so fast. And then I realized
—slowly—that he didn't like me. He couldn't stand being in the same room with me. I was an irritating necessity. God! Don't ask me why!"

Elizabeth remembered her son's words. "It's time I was
married. . . . She'll make me a good wife." Why had he
said those words? Why had it been so important to him?

"Was he faithful?"

The girl threw back her head and laughed. "Do you

know what it's like to share your husband with——well, you're never quite sure?"

"The new psychology tells us that men often behave this way to compensate, Janet. To convince themselves that they're—adequate."

"Wrong again, Madame Scarlatti!" Janet emphasized Elizabeth's name with slight contempt. "Your son was adequate. In the extreme. I suppose I shouldn't say this, but we made love a great deal. The time, the place, it never mattered to Ulster. Or whether I wanted to or not. That was the last consideration. I mean I was the last consideration."

"Why did you put up with him? That's what I find difficult to understand."

Janet Scarlett reached into her purse. She withdrew a pack of cigarettes and nervously lit one. "I've told you this much. Why not the rest. . . . I was afraid."

"Of what?"

"I don't know. I've never thought it out. Why don't we call it—appearances."

"If you don't mind my saying so, that strikes me as foolish."

"You forget, I was the wife of the Ulster Stewart Scarlett. I'd caught him. . . . It's not so easy to admit that I wasn't able to hold him any longer than a few months."

"I see your point. . . . We both know that a divorce on the grounds of assumed desertion would be best for you, but you'd be criticized unmercifully. It would appear to be in the poorest taste."

"I know that. I've decided to wait until a year is up before I get the divorce. A year is a reasonable time. It would be understandable."

"I'm not sure that would be in your interest."

"Why not?"

"You'd completely separate yourself and partially separate your child from the Scarlatti family. I'll be frank with you. I don't trust Chancellor under these circumstances."

"I don't understand."

"Once you made the first move, he'd use every legal weapon available to have you declared unfit."

"What!"

"He'd control both the child and the inheritance. Fortunately . . ."

133

"You're mad!"

Elizabeth continued as if Janet had not interrupted. "Fortunately, Chancellor's sense of propriety—which borders on the ridiculous—would prevent him from initiating action that might cause embarrassment. But if you provoked. . . . No, Janet, a divorce isn't the answer."

"Do you know what you're saying?"

"I assure you I do. . . . If I could guarantee that I'd be alive a year from now I'd give you my blessing! I can't do that. And without me to stop him, Chancellor would be a conniving wild animal!"

"There is nothing, nothing Chancellor can do to me! Or my child!"

"Please, my dear. I'm no moralist. But your behavior hasn't been above reproach."

"I don't have to listen to this!" Janet rose from the sofa and opened her pocketbook, replacing the pack of cigarettes and taking out her gloves.

"I'm not making judgments. You're an intelligent girl. Whatever you do, I'm sure there are reasons. . . . If it's any comfort, I think you've spent a year in hell."

"Yes. A year in hell." Janet Scarlett began putting on her gloves.

Elizabeth spoke rapidly as she crossed to her desk by the window. "But let's be candid. If Ulster were here, or in evidence anywhere, an uncontested divorce could be arranged quietly, without difficulty. After all, neither is without blemish. But, as the law says, one of the parties is removed, perhaps deceased, but not legally declared dead. And there's a child, an only child. That child is Ulster's heir. This, Janet, is the problem."

Elizabeth wondered if the girl was beginning to understand. The trouble with the young rich, she decided, wasn't that they took their money for granted, but that they couldn't comprehend that money, though a by-product, was a true catalyst to power and, because of this, a frightening thing.

"Once you made the first move, the birds of prey from both camps would descend. In the final analysis, the Scarlatti name would become a joke in the back rooms of athletic clubs. And that I will not have!"

Elizabeth took out several folders from the desk drawer, selected one, and replaced the others. She sat down behind the desk and looked over at the girl.

"Do you understand what I'm saying?"

"Yes, I think I do," the girl said slowly, looking down at her gloved hands. "You want to conveniently tuck me away out of sight so nothing can disturb your precious Scarletts." She hesitated, lifting her head to return her mother-in-law's gaze. "And I thought for a minute you were going to be kind."

"You can't very well qualify as a charity case," said Elizabeth.

"No, I suppose not. But since I'm not looking for charity, that doesn't matter, does it? I guess you're trying to be kind, in your own way."

"Then you'll do as I suggest?" Elizabeth moved the folder to put it back in the drawer.

"No," Janet Saxon Scarlett said firmly. "I'll do exactly as I please. And I don't think I'll be a joke in athletic clubs."

"Don't be too sure of that!" Elizabeth slammed the folder back on the top of the desk.

"I'll wait until a year is up," said Janet, "and then do whatever I have to. My father will know what to do. I'll do what he says."

"Your father may have certain misgivings. He's a businessman."

"He's also my father!"

"I can very well understand that, my dear. I understand it so well that I suggest you allow me to ask you several questions before you go."

Elizabeth stood up and crossed to the library door. Closing it, she turned the brass lock.

Janet watched the old woman's movement with as much curiosity as fear. It was not like her mother-in-law to be the least concerned about interruptions. Any unwanted intruder was promptly ordered out.

"There's nothing more to say. I want to leave."

"I agree. You have little to say," broke in Elizabeth, who had returned to the desk. "You enjoyed Europe, my dear? Paris, Marseilles, Rome? I must say, though, New York's apparently a dull place for you. I suppose under the circumstances there's far more to offer across the ocean."

"What do you mean?"

"Just that. You seem to have enjoyed yourself somewhat unreasonably. My son found himself quite a likely

135

playmate for his escapades. However, if I do say so, he was frequently less obvious than you."

"I don't know what you're talking about."

Elizabeth opened the folder and flipped over several pages. "Let's see, now. There was a colored trumpet player in Paris. . . ."

"A what! What are you talking about?"

"He brought you back to your hotel, excuse me, yours and Ulster's hotel, at eight o'clock in the morning. Obviously, you'd been with him all night."

Janet stared at her mother-in-law in disbelief. Although dazed, she answered her rapidly, quietly. "Yes. Paris, yes! And I was with him, but not like that. I was trying to keep up with Ulster. Half the night trying to find him."

"That fact doesn't appear here. You were seen coming into the hotel with a colored man supporting you."

"I was exhausted."

"Drunk is the word used here. . . ."

"Then it's a lie!"

The old woman turned the page. "And then one week in the south of France? Do you remember that weekend, Janet?"

"No," the girl answered hesitantly. "What are you doing? What have you got there?"

Elizabeth rose, holding the folder away from the girl's eyes. "Oh, come now. That weekend at Madame Auriole's. What do they call her chateau—the Silhouette? Quite a dramatic name."

"She was a friend of Ulster!"

"And, of course, you had no idea what Auriole's Silhouette meant, and still means, I believe, throughout the south of France."

"You're not suggesting that I had anything to do with any of that?"

"Just what did people mean when they said they went to Auriole's Silhouette?"

"You can't mean it."

"What happens at Auriole's Silhouette?" Elizabeth's voice rose viciously.

"I don't . . . don't know. I don't know!"

"What happens?"

"I won't answer you!"

"That's very prudent, but I'm afraid it won't do! It's

common knowledge that the outstanding items on Madame Auriole's menus are opium, hashish, marijuana, heroin . . . a haven for the users of every form of narcotics!"

"I did not know that!"

"You didn't know anything about it? For an entire weekend? For three days during the height of her season?"

"No! . . . Yes, I found out and I left. I left as soon as I realized what they were doing!"

"Orgies for narcotics addicts. Marvelous opportunities for the sophisticated voyeur. Day and night. And Mrs. Scarlett knew nothing about it at all!"

"I swear I didn't!"

Elizabeth's voice changed to one of gentle firmness. "I'm sure you didn't, my dear, but I don't know who would believe you." She paused briefly. "There's a great deal more here." She flipped the pages, sitting down once more behind the desk. "Berlin, Vienna, Rome. Particularly Cairo."

Janet ran toward Elizabeth Scarlatti and leaned across the desk, her eyes wide with fright. "Ulster left me for almost two weeks! I didn't know where he was. I was petrified!"

"You were seen going into the strangest places, my dear. You even committed one of the gravest international crimes. You bought another human being. You purchased a slave."

"No! No, I didn't! That's not true!"

"Oh, yes, it is. You bought a thirteen-year-old Arab girl who was being sold into prostitution. As an American citizen there are specific laws . . ."

"It's a lie!" broke in Janet. "They told me that if I paid the money, the Arab could tell me where Ulster was! That's all I did!"

"No, it wasn't. You gave him a present. A little thirteen-year-old girl was your present to him and you know it. I wonder if you've ever thought about her."

"I just wanted to find Ulster! I was sick when I found out. I didn't understand! I didn't even know what they were talking about! All I wanted to do was find Ulster and get out of that awful place!"

"I wouldn't pretend to dispute you. Nevertheless, others would."

137

"Who?" The girl was shaking.

"The courts, for one. Newspapers, for another." Elizabeth stared at the frightened girl. "My friends. . . . Even your own friends."

"And you would allow . . . someone to use those lies against me?"

Elizabeth shrugged.

"And against your own grandchild?"

"I doubt that he would be your child, legally, that is, for very long. I'm sure he'd be declared a ward of the court until it was determined that Chancellor was the proper guardian for him."

Janet slowly sat down on the edge of the chair. Lips parted, she began to cry.

"Please, Janet. I'm not asking you to enroll in a nunnery. I'm not even asking you to do without the normal satisfactions of a woman of your age and appetites. You've hardly restricted yourself during the past several months, and I don't expect you to now. I'm only asking a fair amount of discretion, perhaps a bit more than you've been exercising, and a healthy degree of physical caution. In the absence of the latter, immediate remedy."

Janet Saxon Scarlett turned her head away, her eyes tightly shut. "You're horrible;" she whispered.

"I imagine I appear that way to you now. Someday I hope you may reconsider."

Janet sprang from the chair.

"Let me out of this house!"

"For heaven's sake try to understand. Chancellor and Allison will be here soon. I need you, my dear."

The girl raced to the door, forgetting the lock. She could not open it. Her voice was low in her panic. "What more could you possibly want?"

And Elizabeth knew she had won.

CHAPTER 16

Matthew Canfield leaned against the building on the southeast corner of Fifth Avenue at Sixty-third Street, about forty yards from the imposing entrance to the Scarlatti residence. He pulled his raincoat tightly around him to ward off the chill brought by the autumn rain and glanced at his watch: ten minutes to six. He had been at his post for over an hour. The girl had gone in at a quarter to five; and for all he knew, she would be there until midnight or, God forbid, until morning. He had arranged for a relief at two o'clock if nothing had happened by then. There was no particular reason for him to feel that something would happen by then, but his instincts told him otherwise. After five weeks of familiarizing himself with his subjects, he let his imagination fill in what observation precluded. The old lady was boarding ship the day after tomorrow, and not taking anyone with her. Her lament for her missing or dead son was international knowledge. Her grief was the subject of countless newspaper stories. However, the old woman hid her grief well and went about her business.

Scarlett's wife was different. If she mourned her missing husband, it was not apparent. But what was obvious was her disbelief in Ulster Scarlett's death. What was it she had said in the bar at the Oyster Bay Country Club? Although her voice was thick from whiskey, her pronouncement was clear.

"My dear mother-in-law thinks she's so smart. I hope the boat sinks! She'll find him."

Tonight there was a confrontation between the two

139

women, and Matthew Canfield wished he could be a witness.

The drizzle was letting up. Canfield decided to walk across Fifth Avenue to the park side of the street. He took a newspaper out of his raincoat pocket, spread it on the slatted bench in front of the Central Park wall, and sat down. A man and a woman stopped before the old lady's steps. It was fairly dark now, and he couldn't see who they were. The woman was animatedly explaining something, while the man seemed not to listen, more intent on pulling out his pocket watch and checking the time. Canfield looked again at his own watch and noted that it was two minutes to six. He slowly got up and began to saunter back across the avenue. The man turned toward the curb to get the spill of the streetlight on his watch. The woman kept talking.

Canfield saw with no surprise that it was the older brother Chancellor Drew Scarlett and his wife Allison.

Canfield kept walking east on Sixty-third as Chancellor Scarlett took his wife's elbow and marched her up the steps to the Scarlatti door. As he reached Madison Avenue, Canfield heard a sharp crash. He turned and saw that the front door of Elizabeth Scarlatti's house had been pulled open with such force that the collision against an unseen wall echoed throughout the street.

Janet Scarlett came running down the brick stairs, tripped, got up, and hobbled toward Fifth Avenue. Canfield started back toward her. She was hurt and the timing might just be perfect.

The field accountant was within thirty yards of Ulster Scarlett's wife when a roadster, a shiny black Pierce-Arrow, came racing down the block. The car veered close to the curb near the girl.

Canfield slowed down and watched. He could see the man in the roadster leaning forward toward the far window. The light from the overhead streetlamp shone directly on his face. He was a handsome man in his early fifties perhaps, with a perfectly groomed matted moustache. He appeared to be the sort of man Janet Scarlett might know. It struck Canfield that the man had been waiting—as he had been waiting—for Janet Scarlett.

Suddenly the man stopped the car, threw his door open, and quickly got out onto the street. He rapidly walked around the car toward the girl.

140

"Here, Mrs. Scarlett. Get in."

Janet Scarlett bent down to hold her injured knee. She looked up, bewildered, at the approaching man with the matted moustache. Canfield stopped. He stood in the shadows by a doorway.

"What? You're not a taxi. . . . No. I don't know you. . : ."

"Get in! I'll drive you home. Quickly, now!" The man spoke peremptorily. A disturbed voice. He grabbed Janet Scarlett's arm.

"No! No, I won't!" She tried to pull her arm away.

Canfield came out of the shadows. "Hello, Mrs. Scarlett. I thought it was you. Can I be of help?"

The well-groomed man released the girl and stared at Canfield. He seemed confused as well as angry. Instead of speaking, however, he suddenly ran back into the street and climbed into the car.

"Hey, wait a minute, mister!" The field accountant rushed to the curb and put his hand on the door handle. "We'll take you up on the ride. . . ."

The engine accelerated and the roadster sped off down the street throwing Canfield to the ground, his hand lacerated by the door handle wrenched from his grip.

He got up painfully and spoke to Janet Scarlett.

"Your friend's pretty damned chintzy."

Janet Scarlett looked at the field accountant with gratitude.

"I never saw him before. . . . At least, I don't think so. . . . Maybe. . . . I'm sorry to say, I don't remember your name. I am sorry and I do thank you."

"No apologies necessary. We've only met once. Oyster Bay club a couple of weeks ago."

"Oh!" The girl seemed not to want to recall the evening.

"Chris Newland introduced us. The name's Canfield."

"Oh, yes."

"Matthew Canfield. I'm the one from Chicago."

"Yes, I remember now."

"Come on. I'll get us a taxi."

"Your hand is bleeding."

"So's your knee."

"Mine's only a scratch."

"So's mine. Just scraped. Looks worse than it is."

"Perhaps you should see a doctor."

"All I need is a handkerchief and some ice. Handkerchief for the hand, ice for a Scotch." They reached Fifth Avenue and Canfield hailed a taxi. "That's all the doctoring I need, Mrs. Scarlett."

Janet Scarlett smiled hesitantly as they got into the cab. "That doctoring I can provide."

The entrance hall of the Scarlett home on Fifty-fourth Street was about what Canfield had imagined it would be. The ceilings were high, the main doors thick, and the staircase facing the entrance rose an imposing two stories. There were antique mirrors on either side of the hallway, double french doors beside each mirror facing each other across the foyer. The doors on the right were open and Canfield could see the furniture of a formal dining room. The doors on the left were closed and he presumed they led into a living room. Expensive oriental throw rugs were placed on the parquet floors. . . . This was all as it should be. However, what shocked the field accountant was the color scheme of the hallway itself. The wallpaper was a rich—too rich—red damask, and the drapes covering the french doors were black—a heavy black velvet that was out of character with the ornate delicacy of the French furniture.

Janet Scarlett noticed his reaction to the colors and before Canfield could disguise it, said, "Rather hits you in the eye, doesn't it?"

"I hadn't noticed," he said politely.

"My husband insisted on that hideous red and then replaced all my pink silks with those awful black drapes. He made a terrible scene about it when I objected." She parted the double doors and moved into the darkness to turn on a table lamp.

Canfield followed her into the extraordinarily ornate living room. It was the size of five squash courts, and the number of settees, sofas, and armchairs was staggering. Fringed lamps were silhouetted atop numerous tables placed conveniently by the seating places. The arrangement of the furniture was unrelated except for a semicircle of divans facing an enormous fireplace. In the dim light of the single lamp, Canfield's eyes were immediately drawn to a panoply of dull reflections above the mantel. They were photographs. Dozens of photographs of varying sizes placed in thin black frames. They were arranged as a floral spray, the focal point being a scroll encased in gold borders at the center of the mantel.

The girl noticed Canfield's stare but did not acknowledge it.

"There're drinks and ice over there," she said, pointing to a dry bar. "Just help yourself. Will you pardon me for a minute? I'll change my stockings." She disappeared into the main hall."

Canfield crossed to the glass-topped wheel cart and poured two small tumblers of Scotch. He withdrew a clean handkerchief from his trousers, doused it in ice water, and wrapped it around his slightly bleeding hand. Then he turned on another lamp to illuminate the display above the mantel. For the briefest of moments, he was shocked.

It was incredible. Over the mantel was a photographic presentation of Ulster Stewart Scarlett's army career. From officer's candidate school to embarkation; from his arrival in France to his assignments to the trenches. In some frames there were maps with heavy red and blue lines indicating positions. In a score of pictures Ulster was the energetic center of attraction.

He had seen photographs of Scarlett before, but they were generally snapshots taken at society parties or single shots of the socialite in his various athletic endeavors —polo, tennis, sailing—and he had looked precisely the way Brooks Brothers expected their clients to look. However, here he was among soldiers, and it annoyed Canfield to see that he was nearly a half a head taller than the largest soldier near him. And there were soldiers everywhere, of every rank and every degree of military bearing. Awkward citizen corporals having their weapons inspected, weary sergeants lining up wearier men, experienced-looking field officers listening intently—all were doing what they were doing for the benefit of the vigorous, lean lieutenant who somehow commanded their attention. In many pictures the young officer had his arms slung around half-smiling companions as if assuring them that happy days would soon be here again.

Judging by the expressions of those around him, Scarlett was not notably successful. However, his own countenance radiated optimism itself. Cool, and intensely self-satisfied as well, thought Canfield. The centerpiece was, indeed, a scroll. It was the Silver Star citation for gallantry at the Meuse-Argonne. To judge from the exhibition, Ulster Scarlett was the best-adjusted hero ever to have the good fortune to go to war. The disturbing aspect was the spectacle itself. It was grotesquely out of place. It belonged in the study of some celebrated warrior whose campaigns spanned half a century, not here on Fifty-fourth Street in the ornate living room of a pleasure-seeker.

"Interesting, aren't they?" Janet had reentered the room.

"Impressive, to say the least. He's quite a guy."

"You have no argument there. If anyone forgot, he just had to walk into this room to be reminded."

"I gather that this . . . this pictorial history of how the war was won wasn't your idea." He handed Janet her drink, which, he noted, she firmly clasped and brought immediately to her lips.

"It most certainly was not." She nearly finished the short, straight Scotch. "Sit down, won't you?"

Canfield quickly downed most of his own drink. "First let me freshen these." He took her glass. She sat on the large sofa facing the mantel while he crossed to the bar.

"I never thought your husband was subject to this kind of"—he paused and nodded to the fireplace—"hangover."

"That's an accurate analogy. Aftermath of a big binge. You're a philosopher."

"Don't mean to be. Just never thought of him as the type." He brought over the two drinks, handed one to her, and remained standing.

"Didn't you read his accounts of what happened? I thought the newspapers did a splendid job of making it perfectly clear who was really responsible for the Kaiser's defeat." She drank again.

"Oh, hell, that's the publishing boys. They have to sell papers. I read them but I didn't take them seriously. Never thought he did either."

"You talk as if you knew my husband."

Canfield purposely looked startled and took his glass away from his lips. "Didn't you know?"

"What?"

"Well, of course, I knew him. I knew him quite well. I just took it for granted that you knew. I'm sorry."

144

Janet concealed her surprise. "There's nothing to be sorry about. Ulster had a large circle of friends. I couldn't possibly know them all. Were you a New York friend of Ulster's? I don't remember his mentioning you."

"No, not really. Oh, we met now and then when I came east."

"Oh, that's right, you're from Chicago. It is Chicago?"

"It is. But to be honest with you, my job takes me all over the place." And certainly, he was honest about that.

"What do you do?"

Canfield returned with the drinks and sat down.

"Stripped of its frills, I'm a salesman. But we never strip the frills that obviously."

"What do you sell? I know lots of people who sell things. They don't worry about frills."

"Well, I don't sell stocks or bonds or buildings or even bridges. I sell tennis courts."

Janet laughed. It was a nice laugh. "You're joking!"

"No, seriously, I sell tennis courts."

He put his drink down and pretended to look in his pockets. "Let's see if I've got one on me. They're really very nice. Perfect bounce. Wimbledon standards except for the grass. That's the name of our company. Wimbledon. For your information, they're excellent courts. You've probably played on dozens of them and never knew who to give the credit to."

"I think that's fascinating. Why do people buy your tennis courts? Can't they just build their own?"

"Sure. We encourage them to. We make more money when we rip one out and replace it with ours."

"You're teasing me. A tennis court's a tennis court."

"Only the grass ones, my dear. And they're never quite ready by spring and they're always brown in the fall. Ours are year-round."

She laughed again.

"It's really very simple. My company's developed an asphalt composition that duplicates the bounce of a grass court. Never melts in heat. Never expands when frozen. Would you like the full sales pitch? Our trucks will be here in three days and during that time we'll contract for the first layer of gravel. We'll do that locally. Before you know it, you'll have a beautiful court right out there on Fifty-fourth Street."

They both laughed.

145

"And I assume you're a champion tennis player."

"No. I play. Not well. I don't particularly like the game. Naturally we have several internationally known whizzes on the payroll to vouch for the courts. Incidentally, we guarantee an exhibition match on yours the day we complete the job. You can ask your friends over and have a party. Some magnificent parties have been held on our courts. Now, that's generally the close that sells the job!"

"Very impressive."

"From Atlanta to Bar Harbor. Best courts. best parties." He raised his glass.

"Oh, so you sold Ulster a tennis court?"

"Never tried. I imagine I could have. He bought a dirigible once, and after all, what's a tennis court compared to that?"

"It's flatter." She giggled and held her glass out to him. He rose and went to the bar, unwrapping the handkerchief from his hand and putting it in his pocket. She slowly extinguished her cigarette in the ashtray in front of her.

"If you're not in the New York crowd, where did you know my husband?"

"We first met in college. Briefly, very briefly. I left in the middle of my first year." Canfield wondered if Washington had placed the proper records of a long-forgotten freshman down at Princeton University.

"Aversion to books?"

"Aversion to money. The wrong branch of the family had it. Then we met later in the army, again briefly."

"The army?"

"Yes. But in no way like that, I repeat, no way like that!" He gestured toward the mantel and returned to the sofa.

"Oh?"

"We parted company after training in New Jersey. He to France and glory. Me to Washington and boredom. But we had a helluva time before that." Canfield leaned ever so slightly toward her, permitting his voice the minor intimacy usually accompanying the second effects of alcohol. "All prior to his nuptials, of course."

"Not so prior, Matthew Canfield."

He looked at her closely, noting that the anticipated

146

response was positive but not necessarily liking the fact. "If that's the case, he was a bigger fool than I thought he was."

She looked into his eyes as one scans a letter, trying to read, not between the lines, but instead, beyond the words.

"You're a very attractive man." And then she rose quickly, a bit unsteadily, and put her drink down on the small table in front of the settee. "I haven't had dinner and if I don't eat soon I'll be incoherent. I don't like being incoherent."

"Let me take you out."

"And have you bleed all over some poor unsuspecting waiter?"

"No more blood." Canfield held out his hand. "I would like to have dinner with you."

"Yes, I'm sure you would." She picked up her drink and walked with ever so slight a list to the left side of the fireplace. "Do you know what I was about to do?"

"No." He remained seated, slouched deeply into the sofa.

"I was about to ask you to leave."

Canfield began to protest.

"No, wait. I wanted to be all by myself and nibble something all by myself and perhaps that's not such a good idea."

"I think that's a terrible idea."

"So I won't."

"Good."

"But I don't want to go out. Will you have, as they say, potluck with me here?"

"Won't that be a lot of trouble?"

Janet Scarlett yanked at a pull cord, which hung on the wall at the side of the mantel. "Only for the housekeeper. And she hasn't been overworked in the least since my husband—left."

The housekeeper answered her summons with such speed that the field accountant wondered if she were listening at the door. She was about the homeliest woman Matthew Canfield had ever seen. Her hands were huge.

"Yes, madame? We did not expect you home this evening. You did tell us you were dining with Madame Scarlatti."

"It seems I've changed my mind, doesn't it, Hannah? Mr. Canfield and I will dine here. I've told him potluck, so serve us whatever luck the pot holds."

"Very well, madame."

Her accent had a trace of Middle Europe, perhaps Swiss or German, thought Canfield. Her jowled face framed by her pulled-back gray hair should have been friendly. But it wasn't. It was somehow hard, masculine.

Nevertheless, she made sure the cook prepared an excellent meal.

"When that old bitch wants something, she makes them all quiver and quake until she gets it," said Janet. They had gone back to the living room and sat sipping brandy on the pillow-fluffed sofa, their shoulders touching.

"That's natural. From everything I've heard, she runs the whole show. They've got to cater to her. I know I would."

"My husband never thought so," the girl said quietly. "She'd get furious with him."

Canfield pretended disinterest. "Really? I never knew there was any trouble between them."

"Oh, not trouble. Ulster never cared enough about anything or anybody to cause trouble. That's why she'd get so angry. He wouldn't fight. He'd just do what he wanted to. He was the only person she couldn't control and she hated that."

"She could stop the money, couldn't she?" Canfield asked naïvely.

"He had his own."

"God knows that's exasperating. He probably drove her crazy."

The young wife was looking at the mantel. "He drove me crazy, too. She's no different."

"Well, she's his mother. . . ."

"And I'm his wife." She was now drunk and she stared with hatred at the photographs. "She has no right caging me up like an animal! Threatening me with stupid gossip! Lies! Millions of lies! My husband's friends, not mine! Though they might as well be mine, they're no God damn better!"

148

"Ulster's pals were always a little weird, I agree with you there. If they're being louses to you, ignore them. You don't need them."

Janet laughed. "That's what I'll do! I'll travel to Paris, Cairo, and wherever the hell else, and take ads in the papers. All you friends of that bastard Ulster Scarlett, I ignore you! Signed, J. Saxon Scarlett, widow. I hope!"

The field accountant pressed his luck. "She's got information about you from . . . places like that?"

"Oh, she doesn't miss a trick. You're nobody if the illustrious Madame Scarlatti hasn't got a dossier on you. Didn't you know that?"

And then almost as rapidly as she had flown into rage, she receded into calm reflection. "But it's not important. Let her go to hell."

"Why is she going to Europe?"

"Why do you care?"

Canfield shrugged. "I don't. I just read it in the columns."

"I haven't the vaguest idea."

"Has it anything to do with all that gossip, those lies she collected from Paris . . . and those places?" He tried, and it wasn't difficult, to slur his words.

"Ask her. Do you know, this brandy's good." She finished the remainder in her glass and set it down. The field accountant had most of his left. He held his breath and drank it.

"You're right. She's a bitch."

"She's a bitch." The girl pressed into Canfield's shoulder and arm, turning her face to his. "You're not a bitch, are you?"

"No, and the gender is wrong, anyway. Why is she going to Europe?"

"I've asked myself that lots of times and I can't think of an answer. And I don't care. Are you really a nice person?"

"The nicest, I think."

"I'm going to kiss you and find out. I can always tell."

"You're not that practiced. . . ."

"Oh, but I am." The girl reached across Canfield's neck and pulled him to her. She trembled.

His response was mild astonishment. The girl was desperate and for some senseless reason, he had the feeling of wanting to protect her.

She pulled her hand down from his shoulder. "Let's go upstairs," she said.

And upstairs they kissed and Janet Scarlett put her hands on his face.

"She said . . . fun of being a Scarlett without a Scarlett around. . . . That's what she said."

"Who? Who said that?"

"Mother Bitch. That's who."

"His mother?"

"Unless she finds him. . . . I'm free. . . . Take me, Matthew. Take me, please, for God's sake!"

As he led her to bed, Canfield made up his mind that he'd somehow convince his superiors that he had to get aboard that ship.

CHAPTER 17

Jefferson Cartwright draped a towel over his body and walked out of the club's steam room. He went into the needle shower and let the harsh spray beat down on the top of his head, turning his face upward until the tiny blasts of water hurt his skin. He adjusted the faucets so that the water slowly became colder, finally icy.

He had gotten very drunk the night before. Actually he had started drinking early in the afternoon and by midnight was so far gone he decided to stay at his club rather than go home. He had every reason to celebrate. Since his triumphant meeting with Elizabeth Scarlatti he'd spent several days analyzing to the best of his ability the affairs of the Scarwyck Foundation. Now he was prepared to walk among his peers. Elizabeth's agreement never left his mind. He kept it in his briefcase until he knew enough about Scarwyck so that even his own attorneys would be impressed. He remembered as the water splashed down on his head that he had put the briefcase in a locker at Grand Central Station. Many of his colleagues swore that the Grand Central lockers were safer than vaults. Certainly they were safer than the Scarlatti vaults!

He'd pick up the briefcase after lunch and take the agreement to his lawyers. They'd be astonished and he hoped they'd ask him questions about Scarwyck. He'd rattle off facts and figures so rapidly they'd be in shock.

He could hear them now.

"My God, ole Jeff! We had no idea!"

Cartwright laughed out loud in the shower.

He, Jefferson Cartwright, was the most cavalier of Virginia Cavaliers! These Northern pricks with their high-fallutin condescending ways, who couldn't even satisfy their own wives, had ole Jeff to reckon with now. On their level!

My God, he thought, he could buy and sell half the members in the club! It was a lovely day!

After his shower, Jefferson dressed and, feeling the full measure of his power, jauntily entered the private bar. Most of the members were gathered for lunch and with false graciousness several accepted his offer of a drink. However, their reluctance turned into minor enthusiasm when Jefferson announced casually that he had "taken over Scarwyck's financial chores."

Two or three suddenly found that the boorish Jefferson Cartwright had qualities that they had not noticed before. Indeed, not a bad chap, if you came to think about it. . . . Certainly must have something! Soon the heavy leather chairs surrounding the circular oak table to which Jefferson had repaired were occupied.

As the clock neared two thirty, the members excused themselves and headed to their offices and their telephones. The communications network was activated and the startling news of Cartwright's coup with the Scarwyck Foundation was spread.

One particular gentleman did not leave, however. He stayed on with a few diehards and joined the court of Jefferson Cartwright. He was perhaps fifty years old and the essence of that image so sought by aging socialites. Even to the graying moustache so perfectly overgroomed.

The funny thing was that no one at the table was quite sure of his name, but no one wanted to admit it. This was, after all, a club.

The gentleman gracefully propped himself into the chair next to Jefferson the minute it became available. He bantered with the Southerner and insisted upon ordering another round of drinks.

When the drinks arrived, the well-tailored gentleman reached for the martinis and in the middle of an anecdote placed them in front of him for a moment. As he finished his story, he handed one to Jefferson.

Jefferson took the drink and drank fully.

The gentleman excused himself. Two minutes later Jefferson Cartwright fell over on the table. His eyes were not drowsy or even closed as might become a man who had reached the limit of alcoholic capacity. Instead, they were wide open, bulging out of his skull.

Jefferson Cartwright was dead.

And the gentleman never returned.

Downtown in the press room of a New York tabloid an old typesetter punched out the letters of the short news story. It was to appear on page 10.

Banker Succumbs in Fashionable Men's Club

The typesetter was disinterested.

Several machines away another employee pushed the keys for another story. This one was sandwiched between retail advertisements on page 48.

Grand Central Locker Robbed

The man wondered. Isn't anything safe anymore?

CHAPTER 18

At the captain's table in the first-class dining room of the
Calpurnia, Elizabeth was somewhat surprised to find
that her companion to the right was a man no more than
thirty years old. The normal practice when she traveled
alone was for the ship line to provide her with an aging
diplomat or a retired broker, a good card player, someone with whom she'd have something in common.

She had no one to blame, however, as she had checked
the captain's list—a procedure she insisted upon so that
there would be no embarrassing business conflicts—and
had merely noted that one Matthew Canfield was an
executive with a sporting goods firm that purchased heavily in England. Someone with social connections, she had
assumed.

At any rate he was likable. A polite young man, very
shallow, she thought, and probably a good salesman,
which he refreshingly admitted he was.

Toward the end of dinner a deck officer approached
her chair; there was a cable for her.

"You may bring it to the table." Elizabeth was annoyed.

The officer spoke softly to Elizabeth.

"Very well." She rose from her chair.

"May I be of assistance, Madame Scarlatti?" asked Matthew Canfield, salesman, as he rose with the rest of the
table.

"No, thank you."

"Are you quite sure?"

"Quite, thank you." She followed the deck officer out of the salon.

In the radio room, Elizabeth was shown to a table behind the counter and handed the message. She noted the instructions at the top: "Emergency—have addressee brought to office for immediate reply."

She looked over at the deck officer who waited on the other side of the counter to escort her back to the salon. "My apologies, you were following orders."

She read the rest of the wireless.

> MADAME ELIZABETH SCARLATTI: H.M.S. CALPURNIA, HIGH SEAS
> VICE-PRESIDENT JEFFERSON CARTWRIGHT DEAD STOP CAUSE OF DEATH UNCERTAIN STOP AUTHORITIES SUSPECT ABNORMAL CIRCUMSTANCES STOP PRIOR TO DEATH CARTWRIGHT MADE PUBLIC A POSITION OF SIGNIFICANT RANK WITH SCARWYCK FOUNDATION STOP WE HAVE NO RECORD OF SUCH POSITION YET INFORMATION RECEIVED FROM RELIABLE SOURCES STOP IN LIGHT OF ABOVE DO YOU WISH TO COMMENT OR INSTRUCT US IN ANY WAY STOP EPISODE MOST TRAGIC AND EMBARRASSING TO WATERMAN CLIENTS STOP WE HAD NO KNOWLEDGE OF VICE-PRESIDENT CARTWRIGHT'S QUESTIONABLE ACTIVITIES STOP AWAITING YOUR REPLY STOP
> HORACE BOUTIER PRESIDENT WATERMAN TRUST COMPANY

Elizabeth was stunned. She wired Mr. Boutier that all announcements from the Scarlatti Industries would be issued by Chancellor Drew Scarlett within a week. Until then there would be no comment.

She sent a second wire to Chancellor Drew.

> C.D. SCARLETT, 129 EAST SIXTY-SECOND STREET, NEW YORK
> REGARDING JEFFERSON CARTWRIGHT NO STATEMENTS REPEAT NO STATEMENTS WILL BE ISSUED PUBLICLY OR PRIVATELY REPEAT PUBLICLY OR PRIVATELY UNTIL

Elizabeth felt she should reappear at the table if for
no other reason than to avoid calling too much attention
to the incident. But as she walked slowly back through
the narrow corridors with the deck officer, it came upon
her with progressive apprehension that what had happened was a warning. She immediately dismissed the
theory that Cartwright's "questionable activities" caused
his murder. He was a joke.

What Elizabeth had to be prepared for was the discovery of her agreement with Cartwright. There could be
several explanations, which she would issue without elabo-
ration. Of course, regardless of what she said, the consensus
would be that age had finally caught up with her. Such
an agreement with such a man as Jefferson Cartwright
was proof of eccentricity to the degree that raised questions of competence.

This did not concern Elizabeth Scarlatti. She was not
subject to the opinion of others.

What concerned her, and concerned her deeply, was
the cause of her profound fear: the fact that the agreement might not be found.

Back at the captain's table she dismissed her absence
with a short, sincere statement that one of her trusted
executives, of whom she was quite fond, had died. As
she obviously did not wish to dwell on the subject, her
dinner companions uttered their sympathies, and after an
appropriate pause in their conversations, resumed their
small talk. The captain of the *Calpurnia*, an overstuffed
Englishman with thickly matted eyebrows and enormous
jowls, noted ponderously that the loss of a good executive
must be akin to the transfer of a well-trained mate.

The young man next to Elizabeth leaned toward her
and spoke softly. "Right out of Gilbert and Sullivan, isn't
he?"

The old woman smiled back in agreeable conspiracy.
Beneath the babble of voices she answered him quietly.
"A monarch of the sea. Can't you picture him ordering
up the cat-o'-nine-tails?"

156

"No," replied the young man. "But I can picture him climbing out of his bathtub. It's funnier."

"You're a wicked boy. If we hit an iceberg, I shall avoid you."

"You couldn't. I'd be in the first lifeboat and certainly someone around here would reserve a seat for you." He smiled disarmingly.

Elizabeth laughed. The young man amused her and it was refreshing to be treated with a degree of good-humored insolence. They chatted pleasantly about their forthcoming itineraries in Europe. It was fascinating, in an offhand way, because neither had any intention of telling the other anything of consequence.

With dinner over, the captain's troupe of very important passengers made their way to the game room and paired off for bridge.

"I assume you're a terrible card player," Canfield said, smiling at Elizabeth. "Since I'm rather good, I'll carry you."

"It's difficult to refuse such a flattering invitation."

And then he inquired: "Who died? Anyone I might know?"

"I doubt it, young man."

"You never can tell. Who was it?"

"Now why in the world would you know an obscure executive in my bank?"

"I gathered he was a pretty important fellow."

"I imagine some people thought he was."

"Well, if he was rich enough, I might have sold him a tennis court."

"Really, Mr. Canfield, you're the limit." Elizabeth laughed as they reached the lounge.

During the game Elizabeth noted that although young Canfield had the quiet flair of a first-rate player, he really wasn't very good. At one point he made himself dummy, quite unnecessarily thought Elizabeth, but she put it down to a form of courtesy. He inquired of the lounge steward if there was a particular brand of cigars on hand, and when offered substitutes, excused himself saying that he'd get some from his stateroom.

Elizabeth remembered that back in the dining room during their coffee the charming Mr. Canfield had opened a fresh pack of thin cigars.

He returned several minutes after the hand was finished and apologized by explaining that he had helped an elderly gentleman, somewhat overcome by the sea, back to his cabin.

The opponents muttered complimentary phrases, but Elizabeth said nothing. She simply stared at the young man and noted with a degree of satisfaction, as well as alarm, that he avoided her gaze.

The game ended early; the pitch of the *Calpurnia* was now quite unsettling. Canfield escorted Elizabeth Scarlatti to her suite.

"You've been charming," she said. "I now release you to pursue the younger generation."

Canfield smiled and handed her the keys. "If you insist. But you condemn me to boredom. You know that."

"Times *have* changed, or perhaps the young men."

"Perhaps." It seemed to Elizabeth that he was anxious to leave.

"Well, an old woman thanks you."

"A not so young man thanks you. Good night, Madame Scarlatti."

She turned to him. "Are you still interested in who the man was who died?"

"I gathered you didn't want to tell me. It's not important. Good night."

"His name was Cartwright. Jefferson Cartwright. Did you know him?" She watched his eyes closely.

"No, I'm sorry, I didn't." His look was steady and entirely innocent. "Good night."

"Good night, young man." She entered her suite and closed the door. She could hear his footsteps fading away down the outside corridor. He was a man in a hurry.

Elizabeth removed her mink and walked into the large comfortable bedroom with its heavy furniture secured to the floor. She turned on a lamp attached to the nightstand and sat on the edge of the bed. She tried to recall more specifically what the *Calpurnia*'s captain had said of the young man when he had presented his table for her approval.

"And then there's a chap, very well connected, I might add, named Canfield."

Elizabeth paid no more attention to his abbreviated biography than she had to the others.

"He's associated with a sporting goods concern and crosses rather regularly. Wimbledon, I believe."

And then, if Elizabeth's memory served her well, the captain had added. "Priority request from the ship line. Probably the son of an old boy. School tie and that sort of thing. Had to drop Dr. Barstow for him."

Elizabeth had given her approval without any questions.

So the young man had a priority request for the captain's table from the owners of an English steamship company. And a fatuous captain, accustomed to associating with the social and professional leaders of both continents, had felt obliged to drop a highly regarded surgeon in his favor.

If for no other reason than to quell an inexhaustible imagination, Elizabeth picked up the stateroom phone and asked for the wireless room.

"*Calpurnia* radio, good evening." The British accent trailed off the word *evening* to a hum.

"This is Elizabeth Scarlatti, suite double A, three. May I speak with the officer in charge, if you please."

"This is Deck Officer Peters. May I help you?"

"Were you the officer who was on duty earlier this evening?"

"Yes, madame. Your wires to New York went out immediately. They should be delivered within the hour."

"Thank you. However, that's not why I'm calling. . . . I'm afraid I've missed someone I was to meet in the radio room. Has anyone asked for me?" She listened carefully for even the slightest hesitation. There was none.

"No, madame, no one's asked for you."

"Well, he might have been somewhat embarrassed. I really feel quite guilty."

"I'm sorry, Madame Scarlatti. Outside of yourself there've been only three passengers here all evening. First night out, y'know."

"Since there were only three, would you mind terribly describing them to me?"

"Oh, not at all. . . . Well, there was an elderly couple from tourist and a gentleman, a bit squiffed, I'm afraid, who wanted the wireless tour."

"The what?"

"The tour, madame. We have three a day for the first

159

class. Ten, twelve, and two. Nice chap, really. Just a pint too many."

"Was he a young man? In his late twenties, perhaps? Dressed in a dinner jacket?"

"That description would apply, madame."

"Thank you, Officer Peters. It's an inconsequential matter, but I'd appreciate your confidence."

"Of course."

Elizabeth rose and walked to the sitting room. Her bridge partner might not be very skilled at cards, but he was a superb actor.

CHAPTER 19

Matthew Canfield hurried down the corridor for the simple reason that his stomach was upset. Maybe the bar—and the crowd—on B deck would make him feel better. He found his way and ordered a brandy.

"Hell of a party, isn't it?"

A huge, broad-shouldered fullback-type crowded Canfield against the adjacent stool.

"Certainly is," Canfield replied with a meaningless grin.

"I know you! You're at the captain's table. We saw you at dinner."

"Good food there."

"Y'know something? I could have been at the captain's table, but I said shit on it."

"Well, that would have made an interesting hors d'oeuvre."

"No, I mean it." The accent, Canfield determined, was Tiffany-edged Park Avenue. "Uncle of mine owns a lot of stock. But I said shit on it."

"You can take my place, if you want to."

The fullback reeled slightly backward and grasped the bar for support. "Much too dull for us. Hey, barkeep! Bourbon and ginger!"

The fullback steadied himself and swayed back toward Canfield. His eyes were glazed and almost without muscular control. His very blond hair was falling over his forehead.

"What's your line, chum? Or are you still in school?"

"Thanks for the compliment. No, I'm with Wimbledon Sporting Goods. How about you?" Canfield backed himself into the stool, turning his head to continue surveying the crowd.

"Godwin and Rawlins. Securities. Father-in-law owns it. Fifth largest house in town."

"Very impressive."

"What's your drag?"

"What?"

"Drag. Pull. How come you're at the big table?"

"Oh, friends of the company, I guess. We work with English firms."

"Wimbledon. That's in Detroit."

"Chicago."

"Oh, yeah. Abercrombie of the sticks. Get it? Abercrombie of the sticks."

"We're solvent."

Canfield addressed this last remark directly to the drunken blond Adonis. He did not say it kindly.

"Don't get touchy. What's your name?"

Canfield was about to answer when his eyes were attracted to the drunk's tie. He didn't know why. Then Canfield noticed the man's cuff links. They, too, were large and striped with colors as intense as those of the tie. The colors were deep red and black.

"Cat got you?"

"What?"

"What's your name? Mine's Boothroyd. Chuck Boothroyd." He grasped the mahogany molding once again to steady himself. "You hustle for Abercrombie and . . . Oops, pardon me, Wimbledon?" Boothroyd seemed to lapse into a semistupor.

The field accountant decided that the brandy wasn't doing a thing for him, either. He really felt quite ill.

"Yeah, I hustle. Look, friend, I don't feel so good. Don't take offense, but I think I'd better get going before I have an accident. Good night, Mr. . . . ."

"Boothroyd."

"Right. Good night."

Mr. Boothroyd half opened his eyes and made a gesture of salute while reaching for his bourbon. Canfield made a swift but unsteady exit.

"Chucksie, sweetie!" A dark-haired woman slammed herself against the inebriated Mr. Boothroyd. "You disappear every God damn time I try to find you!"

"Don't be a bitch, love."

162

"I will be every time you do this!"

The bartender found unfinished business and walked rapidly away.

Mr. Boothroyd looked at his wife and for a few brief moments his wavering stopped. He fixed his eyes on her and his gaze was no longer unsteady, but very much alert. To the observer the two appeared to be nothing more than a husband and wife arguing over the former's drinking but with that quiet violence that keeps intruders away. Although he still maintained his bent-over posture, Chuck Boothroyd spoke clearly under the noise of the party. He was sober.

"No worries, pet."

"You're sure?"

"Positive."

"Who is he?"

"Glorified salesman. Just sucking up for business is my guess."

"If he's a salesman, why was he put at a table next to her?"

"Oh, come on, stop it. You're jittery."

"Just careful."

"I'll spell it out for you. He's with that sports store in Chicago. Wimbledon. They import half their stuff from a bunch of English companies." Boothroyd stopped as if explaining a simple problem to a child. "This is a British ship. The old lady's a hell of a contact and somebody's in on the take. Besides, he's drunk as a hoot owl and sick as a dog."

"Let me have a sip." Mrs. Boothroyd reached for her husband's glass.

"Help yourself."

"When are you going to do it?"

"In about twenty minutes."

"Why does it have to be tonight?"

"The whole ship's ginned up and there's some nice, lovely rotten weather. Anybody who isn't drunk is throwing up. Maybe both."

"What do you want me to do?"

"Slap me in the face good and hard. Then go back to whomever you were with and laugh it off. Tell them when I've gone this far, the end's in sight, or something like that. In a few minutes I'll pass out on the floor. Make sure two guys carry me to the stateroom. Three maybe."

"I don't know if anyone's sober enough."

"Then get the steward. Or the bartender, that's even better. The bartender. I've been giving him a hard time."

"All right. You've got the key?"

"Your daddy gave it to me on the pier this morning."

CHAPTER 20

Canfield reached his stateroom thinking he was going to be sick. The interminable and now violent motion of the ship had its effect on him. He wondered why people made jokes about seasickness. It was never funny to him. He never laughed at the cartoons.

He fell into bed removing only his shoes. Gratefully he realized that sleep was coming on. It had been twenty-four hours of never-ending pressure.

And then the knocking began.

At first quietly. So quietly it simply made Canfield shift his position. Then louder and louder and more rapid. It was a sharp knock, as if caused by a single knuckle and because of its sharpness it echoed throughout the stateroom.

Canfield, still half asleep, called out. "What is it?"

"I think you'd better open the door, mate."

"Who is it?" Canfield tried to stop the room from turning around.

The intense knocking started all over again.

"For Christ's sake, all right! All right!"

The field accountant struggled to his feet and lurched toward the stateroom door. It was a further struggle to unlatch the lock. The uniformed figure of a ship's radio operator sprang into his cabin.

Canfield gathered his sense as best he could and looked at the man now leaning against the door.

"What the hell do you want?"

"You told me to come to your cabin if I had somethin' worthwhile. You know. About what you're so interested in?"

"So?"

"Well, now, you wouldn't expect a British seaman to break regs without some reason, would you?"

"How much?"

"Ten quid."

"What in heaven's name is ten quid?"

"Fifty dollars to you."

"Pretty God damn expensive."

"It's worth it."

"Twenty bucks."

"Come on!" The cockney sailor whined.

"Thirty and that's it." Canfield started toward his bed.

"Sold. Gimme the cash."

Canfield withdrew his wallet and handed the radioman three ten-dollar bills. "Now, what's worth thirty dollars?"

"You were caught. By Madame Scarlatti." And he was gone.

Canfield washed in cold water to wake himself up and pondered the various alternatives.

He had been caught without an alibi that made sense. By all logic his usefulness was finished. He'd have to be replaced and that would take time. The least he could do was throw the old woman off the scent of where he came from.

He wished to God that Benjamin Reynolds was available for some good old sage advice. Then he remembered something Reynolds had once said to another field accountant who'd been exposed unmercifully. "Use part of the truth. See if it helps. Find some reason for what you're doing."

He left the stateroom and climbed the steps to A deck. He found her suite and knocked on the door.

Charles Conaway Boothroyd, executive vice-president of Godwin and Rawlins Securities, passed out cold on the deck of the lounge.

Three stewards, two inebriated male partygoers, his

wife, and a passing navigation officer managed to haul his immense body out of the lounge to his cabin. Laughing they removed the blond giant's shoes and trousers and covered him over with a blanket.

Mrs. Boothroyd brought out two bottles of champagne and poured for the rescuers. She filled a water glass for herself.

The stewards and the *Calpurnia* officer drank only at Mrs. Boothroyd's absolute insistence, and left as soon as they could. Not, however, before Mrs. Boothroyd had impressed upon them how totally unconscious her husband was.

Alone with the two volunteers, Mrs. Boothroyd made sure the last of the champagne was finished. "Who's got a cabin?" she asked.

It turned out that only one was a bachelor; the other had his wife at the party.

"Get 'er plastered and let's go on by ourselves!" She flung the challenge at both of them. "Think you boys can handle me?" asked Mrs. Boothroyd.

The boys responded as one, nodding like hamsters smelling cedar shavings.

"I warn you. I'll keep my skirts up for both of you, and you still won't be enough!" Mrs. Boothroyd swayed slightly as she opened the door. "God! I hope you all don't mind watching each other. I love it, myself!"

The two men nearly crushed each other following the lady out the stateroom door.

"Bitch!" Charles Conaway Boothroyd muttered.

He removed the blanket and got into his trousers. He then reached into a drawer and took out one of his wife's stockings.

As if for a practice run, he pulled the thigh end over his head, rose from the bed, and looked at himself in the mirror. He was pleased with what he saw. He removed the stocking and opened the suitcase.

Underneath several shirts were a pair of sneakers and a thin elasticized rope about four feet long.

Charles Conaway Boothroyd laced up the sneakers while the rope lay at his feet. He pulled a black knit sweater over his large frame. He was smiling. He was a happy man.

Elizabeth Scarlatti was already in bed when she heard the knocking. She reached into the bedside table drawer and withdrew a small revolver.

Elizabeth arose and walked to the door to the outer room. "Who is it?" she asked loudly.

"Matthew Canfield. I'd like very much to speak with you."

Elizabeth was confused. She had not expected him and she reached for words. "I'm sure you've had a touch too much to drink, Mr. Canfield. Can't it wait until morning?" She wasn't even convincing to herself.

"You know perfectly well I haven't and it can't. I think we should talk now." Canfield was counting on the wind and the sea to muffle his voice. He was also counting on the fact that he had business at hand to keep him from becoming very, very sick.

Elizabeth approached the door. "I can't think of a single reason why we should talk now. I hope it won't be necessary to call the ship's police."

"For God's sake, lady, will you open this door! Or shall *I* call the ship's police and say we're both interested in someone running around Europe with securities worth millions, none of which, incidentally, will I get."

"What did you say?" Elizabeth was now next to the stateroom door.

"Look, Madame Scarlatti"—Matthew cupped his hands against the wood of the door—"if my information is anywhere near correct, you have a revolver. All right. Open the door, and if I haven't got my hands over my head, and if there's anyone behind me, fire away! Can I be fairer than that?"

She opened the door and Canfield stood there with only the thought of the impending conversation keeping him from being sick. He closed the door and Elizabeth Scarlatti saw the state of his discomfort. As always, she knew the sequence of priorities under pressure.

"Use my bathroom, Mr. Canfield. It's in here. Straighten yourself up and then we'll talk."

Charles Conaway Boothroyd stuffed two pillows under the blanket of his bed. He picked up the rope and snapped the lines in a lasso loop. The crackle of the fibers

168

was sweet music to him. He placed his wife's silk stocking in his pocket and silently left his cabin. Because he was on A deck, starboard side, he had only to walk around the bow promenade to reach his destination. He ascertained the pitch and the roll of the ship in the rough seas and quickly determined the precise moment of side roll for a human body to reach the water below with the minimum of structural interference. Boothroyd was nothing if not a thorough professional. They would all soon learn his worth.

Canfield came out of Elizabeth Scarlatti's toilet feeling very much relieved. She stared at him from an easy chair several feet on the far side of the bed, pointing the revolver directly at him.

"If I sit down, will you put that damn thing away?"

"Probably not. But sit down and we'll talk about it."

Canfield sat on the bed and swung his legs over so that he faced her. The old woman cocked the hammer of her pistol.

"You spoke of something at the door, Mr. Canfield, which is the only reason this pistol hasn't been fired. Would you care to carry on?"

"Yes. The first thing I can think of saying is that I'm not . . ."

Canfield froze.

The lock in the outer room was being opened. The field accountant held up his hand to the old woman and she immediately, instinctively, handed him the pistol.

Swiftly Canfield took her hand and gently but firmly placed her on the bed. The look in his eyes instructed her and she obeyed.

She stretched out on the bed with only the table lamp illuminating her while Canfield backed into the shadows behind the open bedroom door. He signaled her to close her eyes, a command he did not really expect her to carry out, but she did. Elizabeth let her head fall to the left while the newspaper lay several inches from her right hand. She looked as though she had fallen asleep while reading.

The stateroom door was rapidly opened and closed.

Canfield pressed his back against the wall and gripped

the small pistol tightly in his hand. Through the overlapping steel lip of the door's inside border was a two-inch space that let Canfield look out. It struck him that the open space gave the intruder the same advantage, only Canfield was in shadow and, he hoped, unexpected.

And then the visitor was revealed and Canfield found himself involuntarily swallowing, partially from amazement, partially from fear.

The man was huge, several inches taller than Canfield, with immense chest and shoulders. He wore a black sweater, black gloves, and over his entire head was a translucent filmy cloth, silk, perhaps, which gave the giant an eerie, inhuman appearance and completely blurred his face.

The intruder passed through the bedroom door and stood at the foot of the bed barely three feet in front of Canfield. He seemed to be appraising the old woman while removing a thin rope from his trousers pocket.

He started toward the left side of the bed, hunching his body forward.

Canfield sprang forward, bringing his pistol down on the man's head as hard as he could. The downward impact of the blow caused an immediate break in the skin and a spurt of blood spread through the silk head covering. The intruder fell forward, breaking his fall with his hands, and whirled around to face Canfield. The man was stunned but only for seconds.

"You!" It was not an exclamation, but a damning recognition. "You son of a bitch!"

Canfield's memory mistly raced back, abstracting times and events, and yet he hadn't the remotest idea who this massive creature was. That he should know him was obvious; that he didn't possibly dangerous.

Madame Scarlatti crouched against the headboard of her bed observing the scene in fear but without panic. Instead she was angry because it was a situation she could not possibly control. "I'll phone for the ship's police," she said quietly.

"No!" Canfield's command was harsh. "Don't touch that phone! Please!"

"You must be insane, young man!"

"You want to make a deal, buddy?"

The voice, too, was vaguely familiar. The field accountant trained his pistol on the man's head.

"No deal. Just take off your Halloween mask."

The man slowly raised both arms.

"No, buddy! One hand. Sit on the other. With the palm up!"

"Smart guy." The intruder lowered one arm.

"Mr. Canfield, I really must insist! This man broke into my cabin. God knows he was probably going to rob or kill me. Not you. I must phone for the proper authorities!"

Canfield didn't quite know how to make the old woman understand. He was not the heroic type, and the thought of formal protection was inviting. But would it be protection? And even if it were, this hulk at his feet was the only connection, or possible connection, he or anyone in Group Twenty had with the missing Ulster Scarlett. Canfield realized that if the ship's authorities were called in, the intruder would simply be sacrificed as a thief. It was possible that the man was a thief, but Canfield doubted that strongly.

Sitting at the accountant's feet, the masked Charles Boothroyd came to the identical conclusion regarding his future. The prospect of failure coupled with jail began to trigger an uncontrollable desperation.

Canfield spoke quietly to the old woman. "I'd like to point out that this man did not break in. He unlocked the door, which presumes he was given a key."

"That's right! I was! You don't want to do anything stupid, do you, buddy? Let's make a deal. I'll pay you fifty times what you make selling baseball mitts! How about it?"

Canfield looked sharply down at the man. This was a new and disturbing note. Was his cover known? The sudden ache in Canfield's stomach came with the realization that there might well be two sacrificial goats in the stateroom.

"Take that God damn cloth off your head!"

"Mr. Canfield, thousands of passengers have traveled this ship. A key wouldn't be that difficult. I must insist . . ."

The giant intruder's right hand lashed out at Canfield's foot. Canfield fired into the man's shoulder as he was pulled forward. It was a small-caliber revolver and the shot was not loud.

The masked stranger's hand spastically released Canfield's ankle as he clutched his shoulder where the bullet was lodged. Canfield rose quickly and kicked the man with all his strength in the general area of the head. The toe of his patent-leather shoe caught the man on the side of the neck and ripped the skin beneath the stocking mask. Still the man lunged toward Canfield, hurling himself in a football cross-block at Canfield's midsection. Canfield fired again; this time the bullet entered the man's huge flank. Canfield pressed himself against the stateroom wall as the man fell against his shins, writhing in agony. The bone and muscle tissue in the path of the bullet had been shattered.

Canfield reached down to pull off the silk face covering, now drenched with blood, when the giant, on his knees, suddenly lashed out with his left arm pinning the field accountant back against the wall. Canfield pistol-whipped the man about the head, simultaneously trying to remove the steellike forearm. As he pulled upward on the man's wrist, the black sweater ripped revealing the sleeve of a white shirt. On the cuff was a large cuff link diagonally striped in red and black.

Briefly, Canfield stopped his assault, trying to assimilate his new knowledge. The creature, bloodied, wounded, was grunting in pain and desperation. But Canfield knew him and he was extraordinarily confused. While trying to steady his right hand, he aimed his revolver carefully at the man's kneecap. It was not easy; the strong arm was pressing into his upper groin with the power of a large piston. As he was about to fire, the intruder lurched upward, arching his back and heaving his frame against the smaller man. Canfield pulled the trigger, more as a reaction than intent. The bullet pierced the upper area of the stomach.

Charles Boothroyd fell again.

Matthew Canfield looked over at the old woman who was reaching for the bedside phone. He jumped over the man and forcibly took the instrument from her. He replaced the ear cup in its cradle. "Please! I know what I'm doing!"

"Are you sure?"

"Yes. Please! Believe me!"

"Good God! Look out!"

Canfield whirled, narrowly missing having his spine

172

crushed by the lurching, wounded Boothroyd, who had entwined his fingers into a single hammerlike weapon.

The man toppled on the end of the bed and rolled off. Canfield pulled the old woman away and leveled his pistol at the assailant.

"I don't know how you do it, but if you don't stop, the next shot goes right into your forehead. That's a marksman's promise, buddy!"

Canfield reflected that he was the only member of the training group to fail the small-arms target course twice in succession.

Lying on the floor, his vision impaired by the pain as well as the bloody silk covering his face, Charles Boothroyd knew there was next to nothing left. His breathing was erratic; blood was spilling into his windpipe. There was only one hope—to get to his cabin and reach his wife. She'd know what to do. She'd pay the ship's doctor a fortune to make him well. And somehow *they* would understand. No man could take this kind of punishment and be questioned.

With enormous effort he began to rise. He muttered incoherently as he steadied himself on the mattress.

"Don't try to stand, friend. Just answer a question," said Canfield.

"What . . . What? Quit. . . ."

"Where's Scarlett?" Canfield felt he was working against time. The man would collapse any second.

"Don't know . . ."

"Is he alive?"

"Who . . ."

"You know damn well who! Scarlett! Her son!"

With his last resource of strength, Boothroyd accomplished the seemingly impossible. Clutching the mattress, he staggered backward as if about to collapse. His movements pulled the heavy pad partially off the bed, loosening the hold of the blankets, and as Canfield stepped forward, Boothroyd suddenly lifted the mattress free of the bed and flung it at the field accountant. As the mattress rose in the air, Boothroyd rushed against it with his full weight. Canfield fired wildly into the ceiling as he and the old woman went down under the impact. Boothroyd gave a last push, crushing the two against the wall and the floor, letting his push spring him back onto his feet.

He turned, hardly able to see, and weaved out of the room. Once he reached the other stateroom he pulled off the stocking, opened the door, and rushed out.

Elizabeth Scarlatti moaned in pain, groping for her ankle. Canfield pushed against the mattress, and as it fell off, he tried to help the old woman to her feet.

"I think my ankle or some part of my foot is broken."

Canfield wanted only to go after Boothroyd but he couldn't leave the old woman like this. Too, if he did leave her, she'd be right back on the phone and at this juncture, that would never do. "I'll carry you to the bed."

"For God's sake put the mattress back first. I'm brittle!"

Canfield was torn between taking off his belt, binding the old woman's hands and running after Boothroyd, and carrying out her instructions. The former would be foolish—she'd scream bloody murder; he replaced the mattress and gently lifted her onto the bed.

"How does it feel?"

"Ghastly." She winced as he placed the pillows behind her.

"I guess I'd better call the ship's doctor." However, Canfield made no motion toward the phone. He tried to find the words to convince her to let him have his way.

"There's plenty of time for that. You want to go after that man, don't you?"

Canfield looked at her harshly. "Yes."

"Why? Do you think he has something to do with my son?"

"Every second I spend explaining lessens the possibility of our ever finding out."

"How do I know you'll be dealing in my interest? You didn't want me to phone for help when we certainly needed it. You nearly got us both killed, as a matter of fact. I think I deserve some explanation."

"There isn't time now. Please, trust me."

"Why should I?"

Canfield's eye caught sight of the rope dropped by Boothroyd. "Among other reasons too lengthy to go into, if I hadn't been here, you would have been killed." He pointed at the thin cord on the floor. "If you think that rope was meant to tie your hands with, remind me to explain the advantages of garroting with an elasticized cord as opposed to a piece of clothesline. Your wrists could wriggle out of this." He picked the cord up and thrust it in front of her. "Not your throat!"

She looked at him closely. "Who are you? Whom do you work for?"

Canfield remembered the purpose of his visit—to tell part of the truth. He had decided to say he was employed by a private firm interested in Ulster Scarlett—a magazine or some sort of publication. Under the present circumstances, that was obviously foolish. Boothroyd was no thief; he was a killer on assignment. Elizabeth Scarlatti was marked for assassination. She was no part of a conspiracy. Canfield needed all the resources available to him. "I'm a representative of the United States government."

"Oh, my God! That ass, Senator Brownlee! I had no idea!"

"Neither does he, I assure you. Without knowing it, he got us started, but that's as far as he goes."

"And now I presume all Washington is playing detective and not informing me!"

"If ten people in all Washington know about it, I'd be surprised. How's your ankle?"

"It will survive, as I shall under the circumstances."

"If I call the doctor, will you make up some story about falling? Just to give me time. That's all I ask."

"I'll do you one better, Mr. Canfield. I'll let you go now. We can call a doctor later if it's necessary." She opened the drawer in the bedside table and handed him the stateroom key.

Canfield started toward the door.

"Under one condition." The old woman raised her voice sufficiently to stop him.

"What's that?"

"That you give due consideration to a proposition I have to make to you."

Canfield turned and faced her quizzically. "What kind of proposition?"

"That you go to work for me."

"I'll be back soon," said the field accountant as he ran through the door.

CHAPTER 21

Three-quarters of an hour later Canfield let himself quietly back into Elizabeth Scarlatti's stateroom. The moment the old woman heard the key in the latch she cried out apprehensively.

"Who is it?"

"Canfield." He walked in.

"Did you find him?"

"I did. May I sit down?"

"Please."

"What happened? For heaven's sake, Mr. Canfield! What happened? Who is he?"

"His name was Boothroyd. He worked for a New York brokerage house. He obviously was hired, or assigned to kill you. He's dead and his earthly remains are behind us—I judge about three miles."

"Good God!" The old woman sat down.

"Shall we start at the beginning?"

"Young man, do you know what you've done? There'll be searches, inquiries! The ship will be in an uproar!"

"Oh, someone will be in an uproar, I grant you. But I doubt that there will be more than a routine, and I suspect, subdued inquiry. With a grieving, confused widow confined to her quarters."

"What do you mean?"

Canfield told her how he had located the body near Boothroyd's own stateroom. He then touched briefly on the grimmer aspects of searching the body and dispatching it overboard, but he described in fuller detail how he

176

had returned to the lounge and learned that Boothroyd supposedly passed out several hours earlier. The bartender, in what was probably exaggeration, said that it had taken half a dozen men to haul him away and put him to bed.

"You see, his highly noticeable alibi is the most logical explanation for his . . . disappearance."

"They'll search the ship until we reach port!"

"No, they won't."

"Why not?"

"I tore off part of his sweater and wedged it into a corner of the post railing outside his stateroom. It'll be apparent that the drunken Mr. Boothroyd tried to rejoin the party and that he had a tragic accident. A drunk plus rotten weather aboard ship is a bad combination." Canfield stopped and reflected. "If he was operating alone, we're all right. If he wasn't . . ." Canfield decided to be quiet.

"Was it necessary to throw the man overboard?"

"Would it have been better to have him found with four bullets in him?"

"Three. There's one lodged in the bedroom ceiling."

"That's even worse. He'd be traced to you. If he has a colleague aboard this ship, you'd be dead before morning!"

"I suppose you're right. What do we do now?"

"We wait. We talk and we wait."

"For what?"

"For someone to try to find out what happened. Perhaps his wife. Perhaps the one who gave him the key. Someone."

"You think they will?"

"I think they have to if there's anyone on board who was working with him. For the simple reason that everything went—poof."

"Perhaps he was just a burglar."

"He wasn't. He was a killer. I don't mean to alarm you."

The old woman looked carefully into Canfield's eyes. "Who is 'they,' Mr. Canfield?"

"I don't know. That's where the talking comes in."

"You believe they're connected with my son's disappearance, don't you?"

"Yes, I do. . . . Don't you?"

She did not answer directly. "You said we should start at the beginning. Where is that for you?"

"When we found out that millions of dollars' worth of American securities were being sold secretly on a foreign exchange."

"What has that to do with my son?"

"He was there. He was in the specific area when the rumors started. A year later, after his disappearance, we received reliable intelligence that the sale had been made. He was there again. Obvious, isn't it?"

"Or highly coincidental."

"That theory was knocked out of the box when you opened the door for me an hour ago."

The old woman stared at the field accountant as he slouched in the chair. He, in turn, watched her through half-closed eyes. He saw that she was furious but controlled.

"You presume, Mr. Canfield."

"I don't think so. And since we know who your would-be assassin was and who he worked for—Godwin-somebody-or-other, Wall Street—I think the picture's pretty clear. Someone, someone in the fifth largest brokerage house in New York, is angry enough with you or frightened enough of you to want you killed."

"That's speculation."

"Speculation, hell! I've got the bruises to prove it!"

"How did Washington make this . . . questionable connection?"

" 'Washington' takes in too many people. We're a very small department. Our normal concerns are quietly dealing with larcenous but highly placed government officials."

"You sound ominous, Mr. Canfield."

"Not at all. If an uncle of the Swedish ambassador makes a killing in Swedish imports, we'd rather straighten it out quietly." He watched her closely.

"Now you sound harmless."

"Neither I assure you."

"About the securities?"

"The Swedish ambassador, as a matter of fact." Canfield smiled. "Who, to the best of my knowledge, hasn't any uncle in the import business."

"The Swedish ambassador? I thought you said Senator Brownlee was the one."

"I didn't. You did. Brownlee caused enough of a fuss to make the Justice Department call in everyone who ever had anything to do with Ulster Scarlett. At one point, we did."

"You're with Reynolds!"

"Again, that's your statement. Not mine."

"Stop playing games. You work for that man, Reynolds, don't you?"

"One thing I'm not is your prisoner. I'm not going to be cross-examined."

"Very well. What about this Swedish ambassador?"

"You don't know him? You don't know anything about Stockholm?"

"Oh, for God's sake, of course I don't!"

The field accountant believed her. "Fourteen months ago Ambassador Walter Pond sent word to Washington that a Stockholm syndicate had pledged thirty million dollars for large blocks of American securities if they could be smuggled across. His report was dated May fifteenth. Your son's visa shows he entered Sweden on May tenth."

"Flimsy! My son was on his honeymoon. A trip to Sweden was not out of the ordinary."

"He was alone. His wife remained in London. That's out of the ordinary."

Elizabeth rose from the chaise longue. "It was over a year ago. The money was only pledged. . . ."

"Ambassador Pond has confirmed that the transaction was concluded."

"When?"

"Two months ago. Just after your son disappeared."

Elizabeth stopped pacing and looked at Canfield. "I asked you a question before you went after that man."

"I remember. You offered me a job."

"Could I receive cooperation from your agency on your approval alone? We have the same objective. There's no conflict."

"What does that mean?"

"Is it possible for you to report that I voluntarily offered to cooperate with you? The truth, Mr. Canfield, merely the truth. An attempt was made on my life. If it weren't for you, I'd be dead. I'm a frightened old woman."

"It'll be assumed that you know your son's alive."

179

"Not know. Suspect."

"Because of the securities?"

"I refuse to admit that."

"Then why?"

"First answer me. Could I use the influence of your agency without being questioned further? . . . Responsible only to you."

"Which means I'm responsible to you."

"Exactly."

"It's possible."

"In Europe as well?"

"We have reciprocal agreements with most—"

"Then here's my offer," interrupted Elizabeth. "I add that it's nonnegotiable. . . . One hundred thousand dollars. Paid in installments mutually agreeable."

Matthew Canfield stared at the confident old woman and suddenly found himself frightened. There was something terrifying about the sum Elizabeth Scarlatti had just mentioned. He repeated her words almost inaudibly. "One hundred thousand—"

" 'Dust thou wert,' Mr. Canfield. Take my offer and enjoy your life."

The field accountant was perspiring and it was neither warm nor humid in the suite. "You know my answer."

"Yes, I thought so. . . . Don't be overwhelmed. The transition to money takes but minor adjustments. You'll have enough to be comfortable, but not so much for responsibility. That would be uncomfortable. . . . Now, where were we?"

"What?"

"Oh, yes. Why do I suspect my son may be alive? Separate and apart from the securities you speak of."

"Why do you?"

"From April to December of the past year, my son had hundreds of thousands of dollars transferred to banks throughout Europe. I believe he intends to live on that money. I'm tracing those deposits. I'm following the trail of that money." Elizabeth saw that the field accountant did not believe her. "It happens to be the truth."

"But so are the securities, aren't they?"

"Speaking to someone on my payroll and knowing that I'll deny any knowledge of them outside of this stateroom . . . yes."

"Why deny it?"

"A fair question. I don't think you'll understand but I'll try. The missing securities won't be discovered for nearly a year. I have no legal right to question my son's trust—no one has—until the bonds mature. To do so would be to publicly accuse the Scarlatti family. It would tear the Scarlatti Industries apart. Make suspect all Scarlatti transactions in every banking institution in the civilized world. It's a heavy responsibility. Considering the amount of money involved, it could create panics in a hundred corporations."

Canfield reached the limits of his concentration. "Who was Jefferson Cartwright?"

"The only other person who knew about the securities."

"Oh, my God!" Canfield sat up in the chair.

"Do you really think he was killed for the reasons given?"

"I didn't know there were any."

"They were indirect. He was a notorious philanderer."

The field accountant looked into the old woman's eyes. "And you say he was the only other one who knew about the securities?"

"Yes."

"Then I think that was why he was killed. In your section of town, you don't kill a man for sleeping with your wife. You simply use it as an excuse to sleep with his."

"Then I do need you, don't I, Mr. Canfield?"

"What had you planned to do when we reach England?"

"Prescisely what I said I was going to do. Start with the banks."

"What would that tell you?"

"I'm not sure. But there were considerable sums of money by ordinary standards. This money had to go somewhere. It certainly wasn't going to be carried around in paper bags. Perhaps other accounts under false names; perhaps small businesses quickly established—I don't know. But I do know this is the money that will be used until the payments for the securities are liquid."

"Christ, he's got thirty million dollars in Stockholm!"

"Not necessarily. Accounts could be opened in Switzerland totaling thirty million—probably paid in bullion—but not released for a considerable length of time."

"How long?"

"As long as it takes to certify the authenticity of every

document. Since they were sold on a foreign exchange that could take months."

"So you're going to trace the accounts in the banks."

"That would appear to be the only starting point." Elizabeth Scarlatti opened the drawer of a writing desk and took out a vanity case. Unlocking it she took out a single sheet of paper.

"I assume you have a copy of this. I'd like you to read it over and refresh your memory." She handed him the paper. It was the list of foreign banks where monies had been deposited by Waterman Trust for Ulster Stewart Scarlett. Canfield remembered it from the material sent from the Justice Department.

"Yes, I've seen it, but I haven't got a copy. . . . Something less than a million dollars."

"Have you noticed the dates of the withdrawals?"

"I remember the last one was about two weeks before your son and his wife returned to New York. A couple of accounts are still open, aren't they? Yes, here . . ."

"London and The Hague." The old woman interrupted and continued without stopping. "That's not what I mean, but it could be valuable. What I'm referring to is the geographic pattern."

"What geographic pattern?"

"Starting with London, then north to Norway; then south again to England—Manchester; then east to Paris; north again to Denmark; south to Marseilles; west into Spain, Portugal; northeast to Berlin; south again into North Africa—Cairo; northwest through Italy—Rome; then the Balkans; reversing west back to Switzerland—it goes on. A patchwork." The old lady had recited by rote as Canfield tried to follow the list of dates.

"What's your point, Madame Scarlatti?"

"Nothing strikes you as unusual?"

"Your son was on his honeymoon. I don't know how you people go on honeymoons. All I know about is Niagara Falls."

"This is not a normal itinerary."

"I wouldn't know about that."

"Let me put it this way. . . . You wouldn't take a pleasure trip from Washington, D.C., to New York City, then return to Baltimore with your next stop Boston."

"I suppose not."

"My son crisscrossed within a semicircle. The final destination, the last and largest withdrawal was made at a point more logically reached months earlier."

Canfield was lost trying to follow the banks and dates.

"Don't bother, Mr. Canfield. It was Germany. An obscure town in southern Germany. It's called Tassing. . . . Why?"

PART TWO

CHAPTER 22

The second and third days of the *Calpurnia* voyage were calm, both the weather and the first-class section of the ship. The news of the death of a passenger cast a pall over the voyagers. Mrs. Charles Boothroyd was confined to quarters under the constant supervision of the ship's doctor and attending nurses. She had gone into hysterics upon hearing the news of her husband and it had been necessary to administer large doses of sedatives.

By the third day, with revived health, the optimism of most passengers revived.

Elizabeth Wyckham Scarlatti and her young table escort made it a point to part company after each meal. By ten thirty every night, however, Matthew Canfield let himself into her quarters to take up his post lest there be a recurrence of the Boothroyd attempt. It was an unsatisfactory arrangement.

"If I were a hundred years younger, you might pass yourself off as one of those distasteful men who perform services for middle-aged adventuresses."

"If you used some of your well-advertised money to buy your own ocean liner, I might get some sleep at night."

These late-hour conversations served one good purpose, however. Their plans began to take shape. Also Canfield's responsibilities as an employee of Elizabeth Scarlatti were diplomatically discussed.

"You understand," said Elizabeth, "I wouldn't expect you to do anything detrimental to the government. Or against your own conscience. I do believe in a man's conscience."

"But I gather you'd like to make the decision about what's detrimental and what isn't?"

"To a degree, yes. I believe I'm qualified."

"What happens if I don't agree with you?"

"We'll cross that bridge when we come to it."

"Oh, that's great!"

In essence, Matthew Canfield would continue submitting his reports to Washington's Group Twenty with one alteration—they first would be approved by Elizabeth Scarlatti. Together they would, through the field accountant, make certain requests of his office they both felt necessary. In all matters of physical well-being, the old woman would follow the instructions of the young man without argument.

Matthew Canfield would receive ten payments of ten thousand dollars each commencing with the first day in London. In small American bills.

"You realize, Mr. Canfield, that there's another way to look at this arrangement."

"What's that?"

"Your office is getting the benefit of my not inconsiderable talents for absolutely nothing. Extremely beneficial to the taxpayers."

"I'll put that in my next report."

The basic problem of the arrangement had not been resolved, however. For the field accountant to fulfill his obligations to both employers, a reason had to be found explaining his association with the old woman. It would become obvious as the weeks went by and it would be foolish to try to pass it off as either companionship or business. Both explanations would be suspect.

With a degree of self-interest, Matthew Canfield asked, "Can you get along with your daughter-in-law?"

"I assume you mean Ulster's wife. No one could stand Chancellor's."

"Yes."

"I like her. However, if you're thinking about her as a third party, I must tell you that she despises me. There are many reasons, most of them quite valid. In order to get what I want I've had to treat her quite badly. My only defense, if I felt I needed one—which I don't—is that what I wanted was for her benefit."

188

"I'm deeply moved, but do you think we could get her coopperation? I've met her on several occasions."

"She's not very responsible. But I suppose you know that."

"Yes. I also know that she suspects you of going to Europe on your son's account."

"I realize that. It would help to enlist her, I imagine. But I don't think I could manage it by cable, and I certainly wouldn't want to spell it out in a letter."

"I've a better way. I'll go back for her and I'll take a written . . . explanation from you. Not too involved, not too specific. I'll handle the rest."

"You must know her very well."

"Not so. I just think that if I can convince her that you—and I—are on her side . . . if someone's on her side, she'll help."

"She might be able to. She could show us places. . . ."

"She might recognize people. . . ."

"But what will I do while you're in America? I'll no doubt be dead when you come back."

Canfield had thought of that. "When we reach England, you should go into retreat."

"I beg your pardon?"

"For your immortal soul. And your son's as well, of course."

"I don't understand you."

"A convent. The whole world knows of your bereavement. It's a logical thing to do. We'll issue a statement to the press to the effect that you've gone to an undisclosed retreat in the north of England. Then send you somewhere down south. My office will help."

"It sounds positively ridiculous!"

"You'll be fetching in your black robes!"

The veiled, grieving Mrs. Boothroyd was led off with the first contingent of passengers. She was met by a man at customs who hurried her through the procedures and took her to a Rolls-Royce waiting on the street. Canfield followed the couple to the car.

Forty-five minutes later Canfield checked into the hotel. He had called his London contact from a public phone and they had agreed to meet as soon as the Londoner could drive down. The field accountant then spent a half hour enjoying the stability of a dry-land bed. He was depressed at the thought of going right back on board ship but he knew there was no other solution. Janet would supply the most reasonable explanation for his accompanying the old lady and it was logical that the wife and mother of the missing Ulster Scarlett should travel together. And certainly Canfield was not unhappy at the prospect of a continued association with Janet Scarlett. She was a tramp, no question; but he had begun to doubt his opinion that she was a bitch.

He was about to doze off when he looked at his watch and realized that he was late for his meeting. He picked up the phone and was delighted by the crisp British accent answering him.

"Madame Scarlatti is in suite five. Our instructions are to ring through prior to callers, sir."

"If you'll do that, please, I'll just go right up. Thank you."

Canfield said his name quite loudly before Elizabeth Scarlatti would open the door. The old woman motioned the young man inside to a chair while she sat on a huge Victorian sofa by the window.

"Well, what do we do now?"

"I phoned our London man nearly an hour ago. He should be here shortly."

"Who is he?"

"He said his name is James Derek."

"Don't you know him?"

"No. We're given an exchange to call and a man is assigned to us. It's a reciprocal arrangement."

"Isn't that convenient." A statement.

"We're billed for it."

"What will he want to know?"

"Only what we want to tell him. He won't ask any questions unless we request something either inimical to the· British government or so expensive he'd have to justify it; that's the point he'll be most concerned with."

"That strikes me as very amusing."

"Taxpayers' money." Canfield looked at his watch. "I asked him to bring along a list of religious retreats."

"You're really serious about that, aren't you?"

"Yes. Unless he has a better idea. I'll be gone for about

two and half weeks. Did you write the letter for your daughter-in-law?"

"Yes." She handed him an envelope.

Across the room on a table near the door, the telephone rang. Elizabeth walked rapidly to the table and answered it.

"Is that Derek?" asked Canfield, when she had hung up.

"Yes."

"Good. Now, please, Madame Scarlatti, let me do most of the talking. But if I ask you a question, you'll know I want an honest answer."

"Oh? We don't have signals?"

"No. He doesn't want to know anything. Believe that. Actually, we're a source of embarrassment to each other."

"Should I offer him a drink, or tea, or isn't that allowed?"

"I think a drink would be very much appreciated."

"I'll call room service and have a bar sent up."

"That's fine."

Elizabeth Scarlatti picked up the phone and ordered a complete selection of wines and liquors. Canfield smiled at the ways of the rich and lit one of his thin cigars.

James Derek was a pleasant-looking man in his early fifties, somewhat rotund, with the air of a prosperous merchant. He was terribly polite but essentially cool. His perpetual smile had a tendency to curve slowly into a strained straight line as he spoke.

"We traced the license of the Rolls at the pier. It belongs to a Marquis Jacques Louis Bertholde. French resident alien. We'll get information on him."

"Good. What about the retreats?"

The Britisher took out a paper from his inside coat pocket. "There're several we might suggest depending upon Madame Scarlatti's wishes to be in touch with the outside."

"Do you have any where contact is completely impossible? On both sides?" asked the field accountant.

"That would be Catholic, of course. There're two or three."

"Now, see here!" interrupted the imposing old lady.

"What are they?" asked Canfield.

"There's a Benedictine order and a Carmelite. They're

in the southwest, incidentally. One, the Carmelite, is near Cardiff."

"There are limits, Mr. Canfield, and I propose to establish them. I will not associate with such people!"

"What is the most fashionable, most sought after retreat in England, Mr. Derek?" asked the field accountant.

"Well, the duchess of Gloucester makes a yearly trek to the Abbey of York. Church of England, of course."

"Fine. We'll send out a story to all the wire services that Madame Scarlatti has entered for a month."

"That's far more acceptable," said the old woman.

"I haven't finished." He turned to the amused Londoner. "Then book us into the Carmelites. You'll escort Madame Scarlatti there tomorrow."

"As you say."

"Just one minute, gentlemen. I do not consent! I'm sure Mr. Derek will adhere to my wishes."

"Terribly sorry, madame. My instructions are to take orders from Mr. Canfield."

"And we have an agreement, Madame Scarlatti, or do you want to tear it up?"

"What can I possibly say to such people? I simply can not stand that voodoo mumbo jumbo coming from Rome!"

"You'll be spared that discomfort, madame," said Mr. Derek. "There's a vow of silence. You'll not hear from anyone."

"Contemplate," added the field accountant. "Good for the immortal soul."

CHAPTER 23

YORK, ENGLAND, *August 12, 1926—* The famed Abbey of York sustained a damaging explosion and fire at dawn this morning in its west wing, the residential quarters of the religious order. An undisclosed number of sisters and novices were killed in the tragic occurrence. It was believed that the explosion was due to a malfunction in the heating system recently installed by the order.

Canfield read the story in the ship's newspaper one day before arriving in New York.

They do their homework well, he thought. And although the price was painfully high, it proved two points conclusively: the press releases were read and Madame Scarlatti was marked.

The field accountant reached into his pocket and took out the old woman's letter to Janet Scarlett. He'd read it many times and thought it effective. He read it once more.

My dear Child:

I am aware that you are not particularly fond of me and I accept the fact as my loss. You have every right to feel as you do—the Scarlattis have not been pleasant people with whom to be associated. However, for whatever reasons and regardless of the pain you have been caused, you are now a Scarlatti and you have borne a Scarlatti into this world. Perhaps you will be the one who will make us better than we are.

I do not make this statement lightly or out of sentiment. History has shown that the least expected among us often emerge splendidly because of the grave responsibilities placed upon them. I ask you to consider this possibility.

I further ask you to give deep consideration to what Mr. Matthew Canfield will tell you. I trust him. I do so because he has saved my life and nearly lost his own in so doing. His interests and ours are inextricably bound together. He will tell you what he can and he will ask of you a great deal.

I am a very, very old woman, my dear, and do not have much time. What months or years I do have (precious perhaps only to me) may well be cut short in a fashion I'd like to believe is not the will of God. Naturally, I accept this risk gladly as the head of the house of Scarlatti, and if I can spend what time I have left preventing a great dishonor upon our family, I will join my husband with a grateful heart.

Through Mr. Canfield, I await your answer. If it is as I suspect, we will be together shortly and you will have gladdened me far beyond that which I deserve. If it is not, you still have my affection and, believe me when I say, my understanding.

Elizabeth Wyckham Scarlatti

Canfield replaced the letter in the envelope. It was quite good, he thought again. It explained nothing and asked for implicit trust that the unsaid explanation was vitally urgent. If he did his job, the girl would be coming back to England with him. If he failed to persuade her, an alternative would have to be found.

The Ulster Scarlett brownstone on Fifty-fourth Street was being repainted and sandblasted. There were several scaffolds lowered from the roof and a number of workmen diligently at their crafts. The heavy Checker cab pulled up in front of the entrance and Matthew Canfield walked up the steps. He rang the bell; the door was opened by the obese housekeeper.

"Good afternoon, Hannah. I don't know if you remember, but my name's Canfield. Matthew Canfield to see Mrs. Scarlett."

Hannah did not budge or offer entrance. "Does Mrs. Scarlett expect you?"

"Not formally, but I'm sure she'll see me." He had had no intention of phoning. It would have been too easy for her to refuse.

"I don't know if madame is in, sir."

"Then I'll just have to wait. Shall it be here on the stairs?"

Hannah reluctantly made way for the field accountant to step into the hideously colored hallway. Canfield was struck again by the intensity of the red wallpaper and the black drapes.

"I'll inquire, sir," said the housekeeper as she started toward the stairs.

In a few minutes Janet came down the long staircase, followed by a waddling Hannah. She was very much composed. Her eyes were clear, aware, and devoid of the panic he had remembered. She was in command and without question a beautiful woman.

Canfield felt a sudden sting of inferiority. He was outclassed.

"Why, Mr. Canfield, this is a surprise."

He could not determine whether her greeting was meant to be pleasant or not. It was friendly, but cool and reserved. This girl had learned the lessons of the old money well.

"I hope not an unwelcome one, Mrs. Scarlett."

"Not at all."

Hannah had reached the bottom step and walked toward the dining room doors. Canfield quickly spoke again. "During my trip I ran across a fellow whose company makes dirigibles. I knew you'd be interested." Canfield watched Hannah out of the corner of his eye without moving his head. Hannah had turned abruptly and looked at the field accountant.

"Really, Mr. Canfield? Why would that concern me?" The girl was mystified.

"I understood your friends on Oyster Bay were determined to buy one for their club. Here, I've brought all the information. Purchase price, rentals, specifications, the works. . . . Let me show you."

The field accountant took Janet Scarlett's elbow and led her swiftly toward the living room doors. Hannah hesitated ever so slightly but, with a glance from Canfield, retreated into the dining room. Canfield then closed the living room doors.

"What are you doing? I don't want to buy a dirigible."

The field accountant stood by the doors, motioning the girl to stop talking.

"What?"

"Be quiet for a minute. Please." He spoke softly.

Canfield waited about ten seconds and then opened the doors in one swinging motion.

Directly across the hallway, standing by the dining room table, was Hannah and a man in white overalls, obviously one of the painters. They were talking while looking over toward the living room doors. They were now in full view of Canfield's stare. Embarrassed, they moved away.

Canfield shut the door and turned to Janet Scarlett. "Interesting, isn't it?"

"What are you doing?"

"Just interesting that your help should be so curious."

"Oh, that." Janet turned and picked up a cigarette from a case on the coffee table. "Servants will talk and I think you've given them cause."

Canfield lit her cigarette. "Including the painters?"

"Hannah's friends are her own business. They're no concern of mine. Hannah's barely a concern of mine. . . ."

"You don't find it curious that Hannah nearly tripped when I mentioned a dirigible?"

"I simply don't understand you."

"I admit I'm getting ahead of myself."

"Why didn't you telephone?"

"If I had, would you have seen me?"

Janet thought for a minute. "Probably. . . . Whatever recriminations I had over your last visit wouldn't be any reason to insult you."

"I didn't want to take that gamble."

"That's sweet of you and I'm touched. But why this very odd behavior?"

There was no point in delaying any longer. He took the envelope out of his pocket. "I've been asked to give you this. May I sit down while you read it?"

Janet, startled, took the envelope and immediately rec-

196

ognized her mother-in-law's handwriting. She opened the envelope and read the letter.

If she was astonished or shocked, she hid her emotions well.

Slowly she sat down on the sofa and put out her cigarette. She looked down at the letter and up at Canfield, and then back to the letter. Without looking up, she asked quietly, "Who are you?"

"I work for the government. I'm an official . . . a minor official in the Department of the Interior."

"The government? You're not a salesman, then?"

"No, I'm not."

"You wanted to meet me and talk with me for the government?"

"Yes."

"Why did you tell me you sold tennis courts?"

"We sometimes find it necessary to conceal our employment. It's as simple as that."

"I see."

"I assume you want to know what your mother-in-law means in the letter?"

"Don't assume anything." She was cold as she continued. "It was your job to meet me and ask me all those amusing questions?"

"Frankly, yes."

The girl rose, took the necessary two steps toward the field accountant, and slapped him across the face with all her strength. It was a sharp and painful blow. "You son of a bitch! Get out of this house!" She still did not raise her voice. "Get out before I call the police!"

"Oh, my God, Janet, will you stop it!" He grabbed her shoulders as she tried to wriggle away. "Listen to me! I said listen or I'll slap you right back!"

Her eyes shone with hatred and, Canfield thought, a touch of melancholy. He held her firmly as he spoke. "Yes, I was assigned to meet you. Meet you and get whatever information I could."

She spat in his face. He did not bother to brush it away.

"I got the information I needed and I used that information because that's what I'm paid for! As far as my department is concerned, I left this house by nine o'clock after you served me two drinks. If they want to pick you up for illegal possession of alcohol, that's what they can get you for!"

"I don't believe you!"

"I don't give a good God damn whether you do or not! And for your further information I've had you under surveillance for weeks! You and the rest of your playmates. . . . It may interest you to know that I've omitted detailing the more . . . ludicrous aspects of your day-to-day activities!"

The girl's eyes began to fill with tears.

"I'm doing my job as best I can, and I'm not so sure you're the one who should scream 'violated virgin'! You may not realize it, but your husband, or former husband, or whatever the hell he is, could be very much alive. A lot of nice people who never heard of him—women like you and young girls—were burned to death because of him! Others were killed, too, but maybe they should have been."

"What are you saying?" He relaxed his grip on her but still held her firmly.

"I just know that I left your mother-in-law a week ago in England. It was a hell of a trip over! Someone tried to kill her the first night out on the ship. Oh, you can bet your life it would have been suicide! They would have said she had tearfully thrown herself overboard. No trace at all. . . . A week ago we let out a story to the newspapers saying she'd gone to a retreat in a place called York, in England, Two days ago the heating system blew up and killed Christ knows how many people! An accident, of course!"

"I don't know what to say."

"Do you want me to finish, or do you still want me to go?"

There was a sadness about Ulster Scarlett's wife as she tried to smile. "I guess you'd better stay and . . . finish."

They sat on the sofa and Canfield talked.

He talked as he had never talked before.

CHAPTER 24

Benjamin Reynolds sat forward in his chair, clipping a week-old article from the Sunday supplement of the *New York Herald*. It was a photograph of Janet Saxon Scarlett being escorted by "sportinggoods executive, M. Canfield" to a dog show at Madison Square Garden. Reynolds smiled as he recalled Canfield's remark on the telephone.

"I can stand everything but the God damn dog shows. Dogs are for the very rich or the very poor. Not for anyone in between!"

No matter, thought Group Twenty's head. The newspapers were doing an excellent job. Washington had ordered Canfield to spend an additional ten days in Manhattan thoroughly establishing his relationship with Ulster Scarlett's wife before returning to England.

The relationship was unmistakable and Benjamin Reynolds wondered if it was really a public facade. Or was it something else? Was Canfield in the process of trapping himself? The ease with which he had engineered a collaboration with Elizabeth Scarlatti bore watching.

"Ben"—Glover walked briskly into the office—"I think we've found what we've been looking for!" He closed the door firmly and approached Reynolds's desk.

"What have you got? About what?"

"A link with the Scarlatti business. I'm sure of it."

"Let me see."

Glover placed several pages on top of the spread-out newspaper. "Nice coverage, wasn't it?" he said, indicating the photograph of Canfield and the girl.

"Just what us dirty old men ordered. He's going to be the toast of society if he doesn't spit on the floor."

"He's doing a good job, Ben. They're back on board ship now, aren't they?"

"Sailed yesterday. . . . What is this?"

"Statistics found it. From Switzerland. Zurich area. Fourteen estates all purchased within the year. Look at these latitude and longitude marks. Every one of the properties is adjacent to another one. A borders on B, B on C, C on D, right down the line. Hundreds of thousands of acres forming an enormous compound."

"One of the buyers Scarlatti?"

"No. . . . But one of the estates was bought in the name of Boothroyd. Charles Boothroyd."

"You're sure? What do you mean 'bought in the name of'?"

"Father-in-law bought it for his daughter and her husband. Named Rawlins. Thomas Rawlins. Partner in the brokerage house of Godwin and Rawlins. His daughter's name is Cecily. Married to Boothroyd."

Reynolds picked up the page with the list of names. "Who are these people? How does it break down?"

Glover reached for the other two pages. "It's all here. Four Americans, two Swedes, three English, two French, and three German. Fourteen in all."

"Do you have any rundowns?"

"Only on the Americans. We've sent for information on the rest."

"Who are they? Besides Rawlins."

"A Howard Thornton, San Francisco. He's in construction. And two Texas oilmen. A Louis Gibson and Avery Landor. Between them they own more wells than fifty of their competitors combined."

"Any connections between them?"

"Nothing so far. We're checking that out now."

"What about the others? The Swedes, the French? . . . The English and the Germans?"

"Only the names."

"Anyone familiar?"

"Several. There's an Innes-Bowen, he's English, in textiles, I think. And I recognize the name of Daudet, French. Owns steamship lines. And two of the Germans. Kindorf—he's in the Ruhr Valley. Coal. And von Schritzler, speaks for I. G. Farben. Don't know the rest, never heard of the Swedes, either."

"In one respect they're all alike—"

"You bet your life they are. They're all as rich as a roomful of Astors. You don't buy places like these with mortgages. Shall I contact Canfield?"

"We'll have to. Send the list by courier. We'll cable him to stay in London until it arrives."

"Madame Scarlatti may know some of them."

"I'm counting on it. . . . But I see a problem."

"What's that?"

"It's going to be a temptation for the old girl to head right into Zurich. . . . If she does, she's dead. So's Canfield and Scarlett's wife."

"That's a pretty drastic assumption."

"Not really. We're presuming that a group of wealthy men have bought fourteen estates all adjoining one another because of a common interest. And Boothroyd— courtesy of a generous father-in-law—is one of them."

"Which ties Zurich to Scarlatti. . . ."

"We think so. We believe it because Boothroyd tried to kill her, right?"

"Of course."

"But the Scarlatti woman is alive. Boothroyd failed."

"Obviously."

"And the property was purchased before that fact."

"It must have been—"

"Then if Zurich is tied to Boothroyd, Zurich wants Scarlatti dead. They want to stop her. Also . . . Zurich presumed success. They expected Boothroyd to succeed."

"And now that he's gone," interrupted Glover, "Zurich will figure the old woman found out who he was. Maybe more. . . . Ben, perhaps we've gone too far. It might be better to call it off. Make a report to Justice and get Canfield back."

"Not yet. We're getting close to something. Elizabeth Scarlatti's the key right now. We'll get them plenty of protection."

"I don't want to make an alibi in advance, but this is your responsibility."

"I understand that. In our instructions to Canfield make one thing absolutely clear. He's to stay out of Zurich. Under no condition is he to go to Switzerland."

"I'll do that."

Reynolds turned from his desk and stared out the window. He spoke to his subordinate without looking at him. "And . . . keep a line open on this Rawlins. Boothroyd's father-in-law. He's the one who may have made the mistake."

CHAPTER 25

Twenty-five miles from the ancient limits of Cardiff, set in a remote glen in a Welsh forest, stands the Convent of the Virgin, the home of the Carmelite sisters. The walls rise in alabaster purity, like a new bride standing in holy expectation in a lush but serpentless Eden.

The field accountant and the young wife drove up to the entrance. Canfield got out of the car and walked to a small arched doorway set in the wall in which was centered a viewer. There was a black iron knocker on the side of the door that he used, then waited for several minutes until a nun answered.

"May I help you?"

The field accountant drew out his indentification card and held it up for the nun to see. "My name is Canfield, sister. I'm here for Madame Elizabeth Scarlatti. Her daughter-in-law is with me."

"If you'll wait, please. May I?" She indicated that she wished to take his identification card with her. He handed it to her through the small opening.

"If course."

The viewer was closed and bolted. Canfield wandered back to the car and spoke to Janet. "They're very cautious."

"What's happening?"

"She's taking my card in to make sure the photograph's me and not someone else."

"Lovely here, isn't it? So quiet."

"It is now. I make no promises when we finally see the old girl."

"Your callous, unfeeling disregard for my well-being, to say nothing of my comforts, is beyond anything I can describe! Do you have any idea what these idiots sleep on? I'll tell you! Army cots!"

"I'm sorry—" Canfield tried not to laugh.

"And do you know the slops they eat? I'll tell you! Food I'd prohibit in my stables!"

"I'm told they grow their own vegetables," the field accountant countered gently.

"They pluck up the fertilizer and leave the plants!"

At that moment the bells of the Angelus pealed out.

"That goes on night and day! I asked that damned fool, Mother MacCree, or whoever she is, why so early in the morning—and do you what know what she said?"

"What, Mother?" asked Janet.

"'That is the way of Christ,' that's what she said. 'Not a good Episcopal Christ!' I told her. . . . It's been intolerable! Why were you so late? Mr. Derek said you'd be here four days ago."

"I had to wait for a courier from Washington. Let's go. I'll tell you about it."

Elizabeth sat in the back seat of the Bentley reading the Zurich list.

"Know any of those people?" asked Canfield.

"Not personally. Most all of them by reputation, however."

"For instance?"

"The Americans, Louis Gibson and Avery Landor are two self-styled Texas Bunyans. They think they built the oil territories. Landor's a-pig, I'm told. Harold Leacock, one of the Englishmen, is a power on the British Stock Exchange. Very bright. Myrdal from Sweden is also in the European market. Stockholm. . . ." Elizabeth looked up and acknowledged Canfield's glance in the rearview mirror.

"Anybody else?"

"Yes. Thyssen in Germany. Fritz Thyssen. Steel companies. Everyone knows Kindorf—Ruhr Valley coal, and von Schnitzler. He's I. G. Farben now. . . . One of the Frenchmen, D'Almeida, has control of railroads, I think. I don't know Daudet but I recognize the name."

"He owns tankers. Steamships."

"Oh, yes. And Masterson. Sydney Masterson. English. Far East imports, I think. I don't know Innes-Bowen, but again I've heard the name."

"You didn't mention Rawlins. Thomas Rawlins."

"I didn't think I had to. Godwin and Rawlins. Booth-royd's father-in-law."

"You don't know the fourth American, Howard Thornton? He's from San Francisco."

"Never heard of him."

"Janet says your son knew a Thornton from San Francisco."

"I'm not at all surprised."

On the road from Pontypridd, on the outskirts of the Rhondda Valley, Canfield became aware of an automobile, which regularly appeared in his side mirror. It was far behind them, hardly more than a speck in the glass, but it was never out of sight except around curves. And whenever Canfield rounded one of the many turns, the automobile appeared subsequently much sooner than its previous distance would indicate. On long stretches it stayed far in the distance and whenever possible allowed other cars to come between them.

"What is it, Mr. Canfield?" Elizabeth was watching the field accountant, who kept shifting his eyes to the mirror outside his window.

"Nothing."

"Is someone following us?"

"Probably not. There aren't that many good roads leading to the English border."

Twenty minutes later Canfield saw that the automobile was drawing nearer. Five minutes after that he began to understand. There were no cars between the two vehicles now. Only a stretch of road—a very long curve—bordered on one side by the rocky slope of a small incline and on the other by a sheer drop of fifty feet into the waters of a Welsh lake.

Beyond the end of the curve, Canfield saw that the ground leveled off into a pasture or overgrown field. He accelerated the Bentley. He wanted to reach that level area.

The car behind shot forward closing the gap between them. It swung to the right on the side of the road by the rocky slope. Canfield knew that once the car came parallel it could easily force him off the road, over the edge, plunging the Bentley down the steep incline into the water. The field accountant held the pedal down and veered the car toward the center trying to cut off the pursuer.

"What is it? What are you doing?" Janet held on to the top of the dashboard.

"Brace yourselves! Both of you!"

Canfield held the Bentley in the center, crossing to the right each time the car behind him tried to squeeze between him and the solid ground. The level field was nearer now. Only another hundred yards.

There were two sharp, heavy crunches as the Bentley lurched spastically under the second car's impact. Janet Scarlett screamed. Her mother-in-law kept silent, clutching the girl's shoulders from behind, helping to brace her.

The level pasture was now on the left and Canfield suddenly swerved the car toward it, going off the road, holding to the dirt border beyond the pavement.

The pursuing car plunged forward at tremendous speed. Canfield riveted his eyes on the rapidly receding black-and-white license plate. He shouted, *"E, B . . . I* or *LI* Seven! Seven or nine! One, one, three!" He repeated the numbers again softly, quickly. He slowed the Bentley down and came to a stop.

Janet's back was arched against the seat. She held Elizabeth's arms with both her hands. The old woman sat forward, her cheek pressed against her daughter-in-law's head.

Elizabeth spoke.

"The letters you called out were *E, B, I* or *L,* the numbers, seven or nine, one, one, three."

"I couldn't tell the make of the car."

Elizabeth spoke again as she took her arms from Janet's shoulders.

"It was a Mercedes-Benz."

CHAPTER 26

"The automobile in question is a Mercedes-Benz coupé.
Nineteen twenty-five model. The license is EBI nine, one,
one, three. The vehicle is registered in the name of Jacques
Louis Bertholde. Once again, the Marquis de Bertholde."
James Derek stood by Canfield in front of Elizabeth and
Janet who sat on the sofa. He read from his notebook
and wondered if these curious Americans realized who
the marquis was. Bertholde, too, often stayed at the
Savoy and was probably as rich as Elizabeth Scarlatti.

"The same man who met Boothroyd's wife at the
pier?" asked Canfield.

"Yes. Or I should say, no. We assume it was Bertholde
at the pier from your description. It couldn't have been
yesterday. We've established that he was in London. However, the automobile is registered to him."

"What do you think, Mr. Derek?" Elizabeth smoothed
her dress and avoided looking at the Englishman. There
was something about the man that disturbed her.

"I don't know what to think. . . . However, I feel I
should tell you that the Marquis de Bertholde is a resident alien of considerable influence and position. . . ."

"He is the owner of Bertholde et Fils, as I recall."
Elizabeth rose from the sofa and gave her empty sherry
glass to Canfield. It was not that she wished more wine.
She was just too wrought up to sit still. "Bertholde et
Fils is an old established firm."

The field accountant went to the drinks table and
poured Elizabeth's sherry.

"Then you've met the marquis, Madame Scarlatti? Perhaps you know him?"

Elizabeth didn't like Derek's insinuation. "No, I do not know the marquis. I may have met his father. I'm not sure. The Bertholdes go back many years."

Canfield handed Elizabeth her glass aware that the old woman and the British operative were playing a mental tennis game. He broke in. "What's his business?"

"Plural. Businesses. Near East oil, mining and drilling in Africa, imports—Australia and South America. . . ."

"Why is he a resident alien?"

"I can answer that," said Elizabeth, returning to the couch. "The physical plants—his offices—are, no doubt, within Empire territories or protectorates."

"Quite correct, madame," said Derek. "Since the majority of his interests lie within the borders of British possessions, he deals continuously with Whitehall. He does so, most favorably."

"Is there a government dossier on Bertholde?"

"As a resident alien, of course there is."

"Can you get it for me?"

"I'd have to have a very sound reason. You know that."

"Mr. Derek!" interrupted Elizabeth. "An attempt was made on my life aboard the *Calpurnia!* Yesterday in Wales an automobile tried to run us off the road! In both instances the Marquis de Bertholde can be implicated. I would call these sound reasons!"

"I'm afraid I must disagree. What you describe are police matters. Anything I know to the contrary is privileged information and I respect it as such. Certainly no charges are being made in either case. It's a gray area, I grant you, but Canfield knows what I'm talking about."

The field accountant looked at Elizabeth and she knew the time had come to use his ploy. He had explained that eventually they would have to. He had called it—"part of the truth." The reason was simple. British Intelligence was not going to be used as someone's personal police force. There had to be other justifications. Justifications that Washington would confirm. Canfield looked at the Englishman and spoke softly.

"The United States government wouldn't involve any agency unless there were reasons beyond police matters. When Madame Scarlatti's son—Mrs. Scarlett's husband—

was in Europe last year, large sums of money, in the form of negotiable securities on a number of American corporations, were forwarded to him. We think they were sold undercover on the European markets. The British exchange included."

"Are you telling me that someone is forming an American monopoly over here?"

"The State Department thinks that the manipulation was handled by our own embassy personnel. They're right here in London now."

"Your own embassy personnel! And you think Scarlett was a party to it?"

"We think he was used." Elizabeth's voice pierced the air. "Used and then eliminated."

"He traveled in that crowd, Derek. So does the Marquis de Bertholde."

James Derek replaced his small notebook in his breast pocket. The explanation obviously was sufficient. The British operative was also very curious. "I'll have a copy of the dossier for you tomorrow, Canfield. . . . Good evening, ladies." He went out.

"I congratulate you, young man. Embassy personnel. Really very intelligent of you."

"I think he was remarkable!" said Janet Scarlett, smiling at him.

"It'll work," mumbled the field accountant, swallowing the major portion of a Scotch. "Now, may I suggest we all need some relief. Speaking for myself, I'm tired of thinking—and I wouldn't appreciate a comment on that, Madame Scarlatti. How about dinner at one of those places you upper class always go? I hate dancing but I swear I'll dance with you both until you drop."

Elizabeth and Janet laughed.

"No, but I thank you," said Elizabeth. "You two go and romp." She looked at the field accountant fondly. "An old woman thanks you again, Mr. Canfield."

"You'll lock the doors and windows?"

"Seven stories off the ground? Of course, if you like."

"I do," said Canfield.

CHAPTER 27

"It's heaven!" shrieked Janet over the din of voices at Claridge's. "Come on, Matthew, don't look so sour!"

"I'm not sour. I just can't hear you."

"Yes, you are. You didn't like it. Let me enjoy it."

"I will. I will! Do you want to dance?"

"No. You hate dancing. I just want to watch."

"No charge. Watch. It's good whiskey."

"Good what?"

"I said whiskey."

"No, thanks. See? I can be good. You're two up on me, you know."

"I may be sixty up on you if this keeps going."

"What, darling?"

"I said I may be sixty when we get out of here."

"Oh, stop it. Have fun!"

Canfield looked at the girl opposite him and felt once again a surge of joy. There was no other word but joy. She was a delight that filled him with pleasure, with warmth. Her eyes held the immediacy of commitment that only a lover can know. Yet Canfield tried so hard to disassociate, to isolate, to objectify, and found that he could not do it.

"I love you very much," he said.

She heard him through the music, the laughter, the undercurrent hum of movement.

"I know." She looked at him and her eyes had the hint of tears. "We love each other. Isn't that remarkable?"

"Do you want to dance, now?"

The girl threw back her head ever so slightly. "Oh,

Matthew! My dear, sweet Matthew. No, darling. You don't have to dance."

"Now, look, I will."

She clasped his hand. "We'll dance by ourselves, all by ourselves later."

Matthew Canfield made up his mind that he would have this woman for the rest of his life.

But he was a professional and his thoughts turned for a moment to the old woman at the Savoy.

Elizabeth Wyckham Scarlatti at that moment got out of her bed and into a dressing gown. She had been reading the *Manchester Guardian*. Turning its thin pages, she heard two sharp metallic clicks accompanied by a muffled sound of movement from the living room. She was not at first startled by the noise; she had bolted the hallway door and presumed that her daughter-in-law was fumbling with a key unable to enter because of the latch. After all, it was two o'clock in the morning and the girl should have returned by now. She called out.

"Just one minute, my dear. I'm up."

She had left a table lamp on and the fringe of the shade rippled as she passed it causing a flickering of minute shadows on the wall.

She reached the door and began to unbolt the latch. Remembering the field accountant, she halted momentarily.

"That is you, isn't it, my dear?"

There was no reply.

She automatically snapped back the bolt.

"Janet? Mr. Canfield? Is that you?"

Silence.

Fear gripped Elizabeth. She had heard the sound; age had not impaired her hearing.

Perhaps she had confused the clicking with the unfamiliar rustling of the thin English newspaper. That was not unreasonable and although she tried to believe it, she could not.

Was there someone else in the room?

At the thought she felt pain in the pit of her stomach.

As she turned to go back into the bedroom, she saw that one of the large french windows was partially

211

opened, no more than one or two inches but enough to cause the silk draperies to sway slightly from the incoming breeze.

In her confusion she tried to recall whether she had closed it before. She thought she had, but it had been an uninterested motion because she hadn't taken Canfield seriously. Why should she? They were seven stories high.

Of course, she hadn't closed it. Or, if she had, she hadn't secured the catch and it had slipped off. Nothing at all unusual. She crossed to the window and pushed it closed.

And then she heard it.

"Hello, Mother."

Out of the shadows from the far end of the room walked a large man dressed in black. His head was shaved and he was deeply tanned.

For several seconds she did not recognize him. The light from the one table lamp was dim and the figure remained at the end of the room. As she became adjusted to the light and the object of her gaze, she realized why the man appeared to be a stranger. The face had changed. The shining black hair was shaved off; the nose was altered, smaller and the nostrils wider apart; the ears were different, flatter against the head; even the eyes —where before there had been a Neapolitan droop to the lids—these eyes were wide, as if no lids existed. There were reddish splotches around the mouth and forehead. It was not a face. It was the mask of a face. It was striking. It was monstrous. And it was her son.

"Ulster! My God!"

"If you die right now of heart failure, you'll make fools out of several highly paid assassins."

The old woman tried to think, tried with all her strength to resist panic. She gripped the back of a chair until the veins in her aged hands seemed to burst from the skin.

"If you've come to kill me, there's little I can do now."

"You'll be interested to know that the man who ordered you killed will soon be dead himself. He was stupid."

Her son wandered toward the french window and checked the latch. He cautiously peered through the glass and was satisfied. His mother noticed that the grace with which he had always carried himself remained but there was no softness now, no gentle relaxation, which had taken the form of a slight aristocratic slouch. Now there was a taut, hard quality in his movement, accentuated by his hands—which were encased in skintight black gloves, fingers extended and rigidly curved.

Elizabeth slowly found the words. "Why have you come here?"

"Because of your obstinate curiosity." He walked rapidly to the hotel phone on the table with the lighted lamp, touching the cradle as if making sure it was secure. He returned to within a few feet of his mother and the sight of his face, now seen clearly, caused her to shut her eyes. When she reopened them, he was rubbing his right eyebrow, which was partially inflamed. He watched her pained look.

"The scars aren't quite healed. Occasionally they itch. Are you maternally solicitous?"

"What have you done to yourself?"

"A new life. A new world for me. A world which has nothing to do with yours. Not yet!"

"I asked you what you've done."

"You know what I've done, otherwise you wouldn't be here in London. What you must understand, now, is that Ulster Scarlett no longer exists."

"If that's what you want the world to believe, why come to me of all people?"

"Because you rightly assumed it wasn't true and your meddling could prove irksome to me."

The old woman steeled herself before speaking. "It's quite possible then that the instructions for my death were not stupid."

"That's very brave. I wonder, though, if you've thought about the others?"

"What others?"

Scarlett sat on the couch and spoke in a biting Italian dialect. "La Famiglia Scarlatti! That's the proper phrase, isn't it? . . . Eleven members to be exact. Two parents, a grandmother, a drunken bitch wife, and seven children. The end of the tribe! The Scarlatti line abruptly stops in one bloody massacre!"

"You're mad! I'd stop you! Don't pit your piddling theft against what I have, my boy!"

"You're a foolish old woman! We're beyond sums. It's only how they're applied now. You taught me that!"

"I'd put them out of your reach! I'd have you hunted down and destroyed!"

The man effortlessly sprang up from the couch.

"We're wasting time. You're concerning yourself with mechanics. That's pedestrian. Let's be clear. I make one phone call and the order is sent to New York. Within forty-eight hours the Scarlattis are snuffed out! Extinguished! It will be an expensive funeral. The foundation will provide nothing but the best."

"Your own child as well?"

"He'd be the first. All dead. No apparent reason. The mystery of the lunatic Scarlattis."

"You are mad." She was hardly audible.

"Speak up, Mother! Or are you thinking about those curly headed moppets romping on the beach at Newport, laughing in their little boats on the sound. Tragic, isn't it? Just one of them! Just one out of the whole lot might make it for you, and the Scarlatti tribe continues in glory! Shall I make my call? It's a matter of indifference to me."

The old woman, who had not moved, walked slowly toward one of the armchairs. "Is what you want from me so valuable that the lives of my family depend upon it?"

"Not to you. Only to me. It could be worse, you know. I could demand an additional one hundred million."

"Why don't you? Under the circumstances you know I'd pay it."

The man laughed. "Certainly you'd pay it. You'd pay it from a source that'd cause a panic in the ticker rooms. No, thank you. I don't need it. Remember, we're beyond sums."

"What is it you want?" She sat in the chair, crossing her thin arms on her lap.

"The bank letters for one. They're no good to you anyway, so there should be no struggle with your conscience."

She had been right! The concept had been right! Always trace the practical. The money.

"Bank letters?"

"The bank letters Cartwright gave you."

"You killed him! You knew about our agreement?"

"Come, Mother. A Southern ass is made vice-president of Waterman Trust! Actually given responsibility. We fol-

214

lowed him for three days. We have your agreement. At least his copies. Let's not fool each other. The letters, please."

The old lady rose from the chair and went into her bedroom. She returned and handed him the letters. He rapidly opened the envelopes and took them out. He spread them on the couch and counted them.

"Cartwright earned his money."

He gathered them up and casually sat down on the sofa.

"I had no idea those letters were so important."

"They're not, really. Nothing could be accomplished with them. All the accounts have been closed and the money . . . dispersed to others, shall we say."

"Then why were you so anxious to get them?" She remained standing.

"If they were submitted to the banks, they could start a lot of speculation. We don't want a great deal of talk right now."

The old woman searched her son's confident eyes. He was detached, pleased with himself, almost relaxed.

"Who is 'we'? What are you involved in?"

Again that grotesque smile from the crooked mouth underneath the unnatural nostrils. "You'll know in good time. Not by name, of course, but you'll know. You might even be proud but you'll never admit it." He looked at his wristwatch. "Down to business."

"What else?"

"What happened on the *Calpurnia*? Don't lie!" He riveted his eyes on the old woman's and they did not waver.

Elizabeth strained the muscles in her abdomen to help her conceal any reaction to the question. She knew that the truth might be all she had left. "I don't understand you."

"You're lying!"

"About what? I received a cablegram from a man named Boutier concerning Cartwright's death."

"Stop it!" He leaned forward. "You wouldn't have gone to the trouble of throwing everyone off with that York Abbey story unless something happened. I want to know where he is."

"Where who is? Cartwright?"

"I warn you!"

"I have no idea what you're talking about!"

"A man disappeared on that ship! They say he fell overboard."

"Oh, yes. I recall. . . . What has that to do with me?" Her look personified innocence.

Neither moved.

"You know nothing about the incident?"

"I didn't say that."

"What did you say, then?"

"There were rumors. Reliable sources."

"What rumors?"

The old woman weighed several replies. She knew that her answer had to have the ring of authenticity without any obvious errors in character or behavior. On the other hand, whatever she said had to reflect the sketchy extremes of gossip.

"That the man was drunk and belligerent. There'd been a struggle in the lounge. . . . He had to be subdued and carried to his stateroom. He tried to return and fell over the rail. Did you know him?"

A cloud of detachment covered Scarlett's answer. "No, he was no part of us." He was dissatisfied but he did not dwell on it. For the first time in several minutes he looked away from her. He was deep in thought. Finally he spoke. "One last item. You started out to find your missing son . . ."

"I started out to find a thief!" she interrupted sharply.

"Have it your way. From another point of view I simply moved up the calendar."

"That's not true! You stole from Scarlatti. What was assigned to you was to be used in conjunction with the Scarlatti Industries!"

"We're wasting time again."

"I wanted the point cleared up."

"The point is that you set out to find me and you succeeded. We agree on that fact?"

"Agreed."

"Now I'm telling you to say nothing, do nothing, and return to New York. Furthermore, destroy any letters or instructions you may have left concerning me."

"Those are impossible demands!"

"In that event my orders go out. The Scarlattis are dead! Go to your church and let them tell you how they've been washed in the blood of the lamb!"

Ulster Scarlett sprang up from the Victorian couch and before the old woman could adjust her eyes to his movement, he had reached the telephone. There wasn't the slightest hesitation on his part. He picked up the telephone without looking at her and waited for the switchboard to answer.

The old woman rose unsteadily. "Don't!"

He turned to face her. "Why not?"

"I'll do as you ask!"

He replaced the phone. "Are you sure?"

"I'm sure." He had won.

Ulster Scarlett smiled with his misshapen lips. "Then our business is concluded."

"Not quite." Elizabeth now would try, realizing that the attempt might cost her her life.

"Oh?"

"I'd like to speculate, for just a minute."

"On what?"

"For the sake of argument, supposing I decided to abandon our understanding?"

"You know the consequences. You couldn't hide from us, not for any length of time."

"Time, however, could be the factor on my side."

"The securities have been disposed of. No sense in thinking about that."

"I assumed they had been, or else you wouldn't have come here."

"This is a good game. Go on."

"I'm sure that if you hadn't thought of it yourself, someone would have told you that the only intelligent way of selling those securities would be on a currency basis in exchange for diminished value."

"No one had to tell me."

"Now it's my turn to ask a question."

"Go ahead."

"How difficult do you think it is to trace deposits, gold or otherwise, of that magnitude? I'll make it two questions. Where are the only banks in the world willing or even capable of such deposits?"

"We both know the answer. Coded, numbered, impossible."

"And in which of the great banking concerns of Switzerland is there the incorruptible man?"

Her son paused and squinted his lidless eyes. "Now you're the one who's insane," he answered quietly.

"Not at all. You think in small blocks, Ulster. You use large sums but you think in small blocks. . . . Word goes out in the marble halls of Bern and Zurich that the sum of one million American dollars can be had for the confidential exchange of information. . . ."

"What would you gain by it?"

"Knowledge! . . . Names! People!"

"You make me laugh!"

"Your laughter will be short-lived! . . . It's obvious that you have associates; you need them. Your threats make that doubly clear, and I'm sure you pay them well. . . . The question is—once they're known to me and I to them—will they be able to resist my price? Certainly you can never match it! In this we are not beyond sums!"

The grotesque face distorted itself further as a thick, drawlish laugh came forth from the misshapen mouth. "I've waited years to tell you that your slide-rule theories smell! Your stinking buy-me, sell-me manipulations are finished! You've had your way! It's finished! Dead! Gone! . . . Who are you to manipulate? With your conniving bankers! Your stinking little Jews! You're finished! I've watched you! Your kind is dead! . . . Don't talk to me about my associates. They wouldn't touch you or your money!" The man in black was in a rage.

"You believe that?" Elizabeth did not move. She asked a simple question.

"Completely!" Ulster Scarlett's unhealed flesh was red with the blood rushing to his head. "We have something else! And you can't touch us! Any of us! *There is no price for us!*"

"However, you'll grant—as with the bank letters—I could prove irksome. Only to a far greater degree. Do you wish to take that gamble?"

"You sign eleven death warrants! A mass burial! Is that what you want, Mother?"

"The answer to both our questions would seem to be no. This is now a more reasonable understanding."

The man-mask in black paused and spoke softly, precisely. "You're not my equal. Don't for one minute think you are!"

"What happened, Ulster? What happened? . . , Why?"

"Nothing and everything! I'm doing what none of you

218

are capable of doing! What has to be done! But you can't do it!"

"Would I . . . or we . . . want to?"

"More than anything in the world? But you haven't the stomachs! You're weak!"

The telephone rang, piercing the air.

"Don't bother to answer it," Ulster said. "It'll ring only once. It's merely a signal that my wife—the devoted whore—and her newest bedmate have left Claridge's."

"Then I assume our meeting is adjourned." She saw to her great relief that he accepted the statement. She noted also that in such a position he was dangerous. A tick was developing on the surface of his skin above his right eye. He again stretched his fingers in a slow deliberate motion.

"Remember what I say. You make one mistake . . ."

She interrupted before he could finish. "Remember who I am, young man! You're speaking to the wife of Giovanni Merighi Scarlatti! There is no need to repeat yourself. You have your agreement. Go about your filthy business. I have no further interest in you!"

The man in black strode rapidly to the door. "I hate you, Mother."

"I hope you benefit as much from those you hold less dear."

"In ways you'd never understand!"

He opened the door and slipped out, slamming it harshly behind him.

Elizabeth Scarlatti stood by the window and pulled apart the drapes. She leaned against the cold glass for support. The city of London was asleep, and only a scattering of lights dotted its concrete facade.

What in God's name had he done?

More important, who was paying attention to him?

What might have been mere horror turned into terror for he had the weapon. The weapon of power—which she and Giovanni innocently, productively provided.

They were, indeed, beyond sums.

Tears fell from her old eyes and that inner consciousness, which afflicts all human beings, was taken by surprise. She had not cried in over thirty years.

Elizabeth pushed herself away from the window and slowly wandered about the room. She had a great deal of thinking to do.

CHAPTER 28

In a room in the Home Office, James Derek took out a file. "Jacques Louis Bertholde, The Fourth Marquis of Chatellerault."

The dossier custodian entered the room. "Hello, James. Late hours tonight, I see."

"I'm afraid so, Charles. I'm taking out a copy. Did you get my request?"

"Right here. Fill me in and I'll sign for it. But please make it short. I've a card game in my office."

"Short and simple. The Americans suspect their embassy personnel of selling Yank securities undercover over here. This Bertholde travels in the diplomatic circles. There could be a connection with the Scarlatti fellow."

The dossier custodian made his appropriate notes. "When did this all take place?"

"About a year ago, as I understand it."

The custodian stopped writing and looked at James Derek. "A year ago?"

"Yes."

"And this American chap wants to confront embassy personnel *now?* Over *here?*"

"That's right."

"He's on the wrong side of the Atlantic. All American embassy personnel were transferred four months ago. There's no one there now—not even a secretary—who was in London a year ago."

"That's very strange," said Derek quietly.

"I'd say your American friend has a rather poor connection with his State Department."

"Which means he's lying."

"Which means he is."

Janet and Matthew, laughing, got off on the seventh floor and started down the corridor toward Elizabeth's suite. The length of their walk was approximately one hundred feet and they stopped four times to embrace and exchange kisses.

The girl took a key out of her purse and handed it to the field accountant.

He inserted it and simultaneously turned the knob before making any lateral motion with the key. The door opened and in a split second the field accountant was more sober than drunk.

He practically fell into the room.

Elizabeth Scarlatti was sitting on the Victorian couch in the dim light emanating from the single lamp. She did not move other than to look up at Canfield and her daughter-in-law.

"I heard you in the hallway."

"I told you to lock these doors!"

"I'm sorry, I forgot."

"The hell you did! I waited until I heard the latch and the bolt!"

"I ordered some coffee from room service."

"Where's the tray?"

"In my bedroom, which I presume to be private."

"Don't you believe it!" The field accountant ran toward the bedroom door.

"I apologize again! I called to have it taken away. I'm quite confused. Forgive me."

"Why? What's the matter?"

Elizabeth Scarlatti thought quickly and looked at her daughter-in-law as she spoke. "I had a most distressing telephone call. A business matter completely unrelated to you. It entails a great deal of money and I must make a decision before the British exchange opens." She looked at the field accountant.

"May I ask what's so important that you don't follow my instructions?"

"Several million dollars. Perhaps you'd care to help me. Should the Scarlatti Industries conclude the purchase of the remaining convertible debentures in Sheffield Cutlery and by exercising the conversions gain control of the company or not?"

Still uncertain, the field accountant asked, "Why is that so . . . distressing?"

"Because the company constantly loses money."

"Then you don't buy. That shouldn't keep you up all night."

The old woman eyed him coldly. "Sheffield Cutlery is one of the oldest, finest firms in England. Their product is superb. The problem is neither management nor labor conditions but a heavy influx of Japanese imitations. The question is, Will the purchasing public learn in time to reverse the trend?"

Elizabeth Scarlatti rose from the couch and went into her bedroom, closing the door behind her. The field accountant turned to Janet Scarlett. "Does she do this sort of thing all the time? Doesn't she have advisers?"

But Janet was still staring at the bedroom door. She took off her wrap and approached the field accountant. She spoke quietly. "She's not telling the truth."

"How do you know?"

"The way she looked at me when she was talking to you. She was trying to tell me something."

"Like what?"

The girl shrugged impatiently and continued in a hushed whisper. "Oh, I don't know, but you know what I mean. You're with a group of people, and you start to tell a whopper or exaggerate something, and while you do, you look at your husband or a friend who knows better . . . and they know they shouldn't correct you. . . ."

"Was she lying about that company she spoke of?"

"Oh, no. That's the truth. Chancellor Drew's been trying to persuade her to buy that firm for months."

"How do you know?"

"She's already turned it down."

"Then why did she lie?"

As Canfield started to sit down, his attention was drawn to the linen antimacassar on the back of the chair. At first he dismissed it and then he looked again. The material was crumpled as if it had been mangled or bunched together. It was out of place in an immaculate suite. He looked closer. There were breaks in the threads and the imprint of fingertips was unmistakable. Whoever had gripped the chair had done so with considerable force.

"What is it, Matthew?"

"Nothing. Get me a drink, will you?"

"Of course, darling." She went to the dry bar as Canfield walked around the chair in front of the french window. For no particular reason, he pulled apart the curtains and inspected the window itself. He turned the latch and pulled the left side open. He saw what he had begun to look for. The wood around the clasp was scratched. On the sill he could see where the paint had been discolored by the impression of a heavy coarse object, probably a rubber-soled boot or a crepe-soled shoe. Not leather; there were no scratches on the enamel. He opened the right side and looked out. Below were six stories straight down; above two floors to what he recalled was an acutely slanting roof. He pushed the window shut and locked it.

"What on earth are you doing?"

"We've had a visitor. An uninvited guest, you might say."

The girl stood absolutely still. "Oh, my God!"

"Don't be frightened. Your mother-in-law wouldn't do anything foolish. Believe that."

"I'm trying to. What are we going to do?"

"Find out who it was. Now get hold of yourself. I'll need you."

"Why didn't she say something?"

"I don't know, but you may be able to find out."

"How?"

"Tomorrow morning she'll probably bring up the Sheffield business. If she does, tell her you remember she refused to buy it for Chancellor. She'll have to give you an explanation of some kind."

"If Mother Scarlatti doesn't want to talk, she just won't. I know."

"Then don't press it. But she'll have to say something."

Although it was nearly three o'clock, the lobby had a flow of stragglers from late parties. They were mostly in evening dress, a great many were unbalanced and giggling, all were happily tired.

Canfield went to the desk clerk and spoke in a gentle, folksy tone. "Say, fella, I've got a little problem."

"Yes, sir. May we be of service?"

"Well, it's a bit touchy. . . . I'm traveling with Madame Elizabeth Scarlatti and her daughter. . . ."

"Oh, yes indeed. Mr. . . . Canfield, isn't it?"

"Sure. Well, the old girl's getting on, you know, and the people above her keep pretty late hours."

The clerk, who knew the legend of the Scarlatti wealth, was abject in apology. "I'm dreadfully sorry, Mr. Canfield. I'll go up myself at once. This is most embarrassing."

"Oh, no, please, everything's quiet now."

"Well, I can assure you it won't happen again. They must be loud, indeed. As I'm sure you're aware, the Savoy is the soundest of structures."

"Well, I guess they keep the windows open, but, please, don't say anything. She'd be pretty sore at me if she thought I talked to you about it. . . ."

"I don't understand, sir."

"Just tell me who they are and I'll talk to them myself. You know, friendly-like, over a drink."

The clerk couldn't have been happier with the American's solution. "Well, if you insist, sir. . . . In eight west one is the Viscount and Viscountess Roxbury, charming couple and quite elderly, I believe. Most unusual. However, they could be entertaining."

"Who's above them?"

"Above them, Mr. Canfield? I don't think . . ."

"Just tell me, please."

"Well in nine west one is . . ." The clerk turned the page. "It's not occupied, sir."

"Not occupied? That's unusual for this time of year, isn't it?"

"I should say unavailable, sir. Nine west one has been leased for the month for business conferences."

"You mean no one stays there at night?"

"Oh, they're certainly entitled to but that hasn't been the case."

"Who leased it?"

"The firm is Bertholde et Fils."

CHAPTER 29

The telephone beside James Derek's bed rang harshly, waking him.

"It's Canfield. I need help and it can't wait."

"That may possible be only your judgment. What is it?"

"Scarlatti's suite was broken into."

"What! What does the hotel say?"

"They don't know about it."

"I do think you should tell them."

"It's not that simple. She won't admit it."

"She's your problem. Why call me?"

"I think she's frightened. . . . It was a second-story."

"My dear fellow, her rooms are on the seventh floor! You're too fantastic! Or do the nasty men fly by themselves?"

The American paused just long enough to let the Englishman know he wasn't amused. "They figured she wouldn't open the door, which, in itself, is interesting. Whoever it was, was lowered from one of the rooms above and used a blade. Did you learn anything about Bertholde?"

"One thing at a time." Derek began to take Canfield seriously.

"That's the point. I think they are the same thing. Bertholde's company leased the rooms two floors above."

"I beg your pardon?"

"That's right. For a month. Daily business conferences, no less."

"I think we'd better have a talk."

"The girl knows about it and she's frightened. Can you put a couple of men on?"

"You think it's necessary?"

"Not really. But I'd hate to be wrong."

"Very well. The story will be anticipated jewel theft. Not uniformed, of course. One in the corridor, one in the street."

"I appreciate it. You beginning to wake up?"

"I am, confound you. I'll be with you in a half hour. With everything I've been able to dig up on Bertholde. And I think we'd better get at look at their suite."

Canfield left the phone booth and started back to the hotel. His lack of sleep was beginning to take effect and he wished he was in an American city where such institutions as all-night diners provided coffee. The English, he thought, were wrong in thinking themselves so civilized. No one was civilized without all-night diners.

He entered the opulent lobby and noted that the clock above the desk read quarter to four. He walked toward the ancient elevators.

"Oh, Mr. Canfield, sir!" The clerk rushed up.

"What is it?" Canfield could only think of Janet and his heart stopped.

"Just after you left, sir! Not two minutes after you left! . . . Most unusual this time of night. . . ."

"What the hell are you talking about?"

"This cablegram arrived for you." The clerk handed Canfield an envelope.

"Thank you," said a relieved Canfield as he took the cablegram and entered the open-grill elevator. As he rose from the ground floor he pressed the cable between his thumb and forefinger. It was thick. Benjamin Reynolds had either sent a long abstract lecture or there would be a considerable amount of decoding to be done. He only hoped he could finish it before Derek arrived.

Canfield entered his room, sat down in a chair near a floor lamp, and opened the cable.

No decoding was necessary. It was all written in simple business language and easily understood when applied to the current situation. Canfield separated the pages. There were three.

SORRY TO INFORM YOU RAWLINS THOMAS AND LIL-
LIAN IN AUTOMOBILE ACCIDENT REPEAT ACCIDENT PO-
CONO MOUNTAINS STOP BOTH ARE DEAD STOP KNOW
THIS WILL UPSET YOUR DEAR FRIEND E S STOP SUGGEST
YOU CARE FOR HER IN HER DISTRESS STOP TO WIMBLE-
DON BUSINESS STOP WE HAVE SPARED NO EXPENSE
AGAIN SPARED NO EXPENSE WITH OUR ENGLISH SUP-
PLIERS TO OBTAIN MAXIMUM QUOTAS OF MERCHANDISE
STOP THEY ARE SYMPATHETIC WITH OUR PROBLEMS OF
SCANDINAVIAN EXPORTS STOP THEY ARE PREPARED TO
AID YOU IN YOUR NEGOTIATIONS FOR FAIR REDUCTIONS
ON MAXIMUM PURCHASES STOP THEY HAVE BEEN TOLD
OF OUR COMPETITORS IN SWITZERLAND AGAIN SWIT-
ZERLAND AND THE COMPANIES REPEAT COMPANIES IN-
VOLVED STOP THEY KNOW OF THE THREE BRITISH
FIRMS IN COMPETITION STOP THEY WILL GIVE YOU ALL
ASSISTANCE AND WE EXPECT YOU TO CONCENTRATE
AGAIN CONCENTRATE ON OUR INTERESTS IN ENGLAND
STOP DO NOT AGAIN DO NOT ATTEMPT TO UNDERBID
OUR COMPETITORS IN SWITZERLAND STOP STAY OUT
OF IT STOP NOTHING CAN BE ACCOMPLISHED STOP

J. HAMMER WIMBLEDON NEW YORK

Canfield lit a thin cigar and placed the three pages on
the floor between his outstretched legs. He peered down
at them.

Hammer was Reynolds's code name for messages sent
to field accountants when he considered the contents to
be of the utmost importance. The word *again* was for
positive emphasis. The word *repeat* a simple inversion.
It denoted the negative of whatever it referred to..

So the Rawlinses—Canfield had to think for a minute
before he remembered that the Rawlinses were Boothroyd's in-laws—had been murdered. Not an accident.
And Reynolds feared for Elizabeth Scarlatti's life. Washington had reached an agreement with the British government to gain him unusual cooperation—no expense spared
—and in return had told the English of the Swedish
securities and the land purchases in Switzerland, which
were presumed to be related. However, Reynolds did not
specify who the men in Zurich were. Only that they
existed and three upstanding Englishmen were on the list.
Canfield recalled their names—Masterson of India fame;

Leacock of the British Stock Exchange; and Innes-Bowen, the textile magnate.

The main points Hammer made were to protect Elizabeth and stay out of Switzerland.

There was a light tapping on his door. Canfield gathered the pages together and put them in his pocket. "Who is it?"

"Goldilocks, confound you! I'm looking for a bed to sleep in." The crisp British accent belonged, of course, to James Derek. Canfield opened the door and the Englishman walked in without further greeting. He threw a manila envelope on the bed, placed his bowler on the bureau, and sat down in the nearest stuffed chair.

"I like the hat, James."

"I'm just praying that it may keep me from being arrested. A Londoner prowling around the Savoy at this hour has to have the look of immense respectability."

"You have it, take my word."

"I wouldn't take your word for a damn thing, you insomniac."

"Can I get you a whiskey?"

"God, no! . . . Madame Scarlatti didn't mention a thing to you?"

"Nothing. Less than nothing. She tried to divert my attention. Then she just shut up and locked herself in her bedroom."

"I can't believe it. I thought you two were working together." Derek withdrew a hotel key attached to the usual wooden identification tag. "I had a chat with the hotel bobby."

"Can you trust him?"

"It doesn't matter. It's a master key and he thinks I'm covering a party on the second floor."

"Then I'll get going. Wait for me, please. Grab some sleep."

"Hold on. You're obviously connected with Madame Scarlatti. I should do the reconnoitering."

The field accountant paused. There was merit in what Derek said. He presumed the British operative was far more adept at this kind of sleuthing than he was. On the other hand, he could not be sure of the man's confidence. Neither was he prepared to tell him very much and have the British government making decisions.

"That's brave of you, Derek, but I wouldn't ask it."

"Not brave at all. Numerous explanations under the Alien Order."

"Nevertheless, I'd prefer going myself. Frankly, there's no reason for you to be involved. I called you for help, not to do my work."

"Let's compromise. In my favor."

"Why?"

"It's safer."

"You've won a point."

"I'll go in first while you wait in the corridor by the lift. I'll check the rooms and then signal you to join me."

"How?"

"With as little energy as possible. Perhaps a short whistle."

Canfield heard the short, shrill whistle and walked quickly down the hallway to nine west one.

He closed the door and went to the source of the flashlight. "Everything all right?"

"It's a well-kept hotel suite. Perhaps not so ostentatious as the American variety, but infinitely more home-like."

"That's reassuring."

"More than you know. I really don't like this sort of work."

"I thought you people were famous for it."

This small talk covered the start of their rapid but thorough search of the premises. The floor plan of the rooms was identical to the Scarlatti suite two stories below. However, instead of similar furniture there was a long table in the center of the main room with perhaps a dozen chairs around it.

"Conference table, I presume," said Derek.

"Let's take a look at the window."

"Which one?"

Canfield thought. "Over here." He went toward the french windows directly in line with those of Elizabeth Scarlatti.

"Good point. Here." The Englishman edged Canfield out of the way as he directed the light.

On the wooden sill was a freshly made valley, which had gone through the paint to the wood grain. Where the wood met the outer stone there was a similar semi-circle, which had cut through the layers of dirt and turned that small portion of blackish stone to light gray. The ridge was approximately an inch and a half thick and obviously caused by the friction of a wide rope.

"Whoever it was is a cat," said Canfield.

"Let's look around." The two men walked first through the left bedroom door and found a double bed fully made up. The bureaus were empty and nothing but the usual stationery and corked pens were on the desk. The closets held nothing but hangers and cloth shoe repositories. The bathroom was spotless, the fixtures gleaming. The second bedroom to the right was the same except that the bedspread was mussed. Someone had slept or rested on it.

"Large frame. Probably six feet or over," said the Englishman.

"How can you tell?"

"Imprint of the buttocks. See here, below the half point of the bed."

"I wouldn't have thought of that."

"I have no comment."

"He could have been sitting."

"I said probably."

The field accountant opened the closet door. "Hey, shine the light here."

"There you are."

"Here it is!"

On the closet floor was a sloppily coiled pile of rope. Through the coils at the bottom were three wide straps of leather attached to the rope by metal clasps.

"It's an Alpine rig," said the English agent.

"For mountain climbing?"

"Precisely. Very secure. The professionals won't use it. Unsporting. Used for rescues, mainly."

"God bless 'em. Would it scale a wall at the Savoy?"

"Beautifully. Very quick, very safe. You were correct."

"Let's get out of here," said Canfield.

"I'll take that drink now."

"My pleasure." Canfield rose from the bed with difficulty. "Scotch whiskey and soda, friend?"

230

The American walked to a table by the window that served as his bar and poured two large quantities of whiskey into glasses. He handed one to James Derek and half raised his own in a toast.

"You do good work, James."

"You're quite competent yourself. And I've been thinking, you may be right about taking that rig."

"All it can do is cause confusion."

"That's what I mean. It could be helpful. . . . It's such an American device."

"I don't understand."

"Nothing personal. Just that you Americans are so equipment conscious, if you know what I mean. When you shoot birds in Scotland, you carry heavy millimeter cannon with you into the field. . . . When you fish in the Lowlands, you have six-hundred artifices in your tackle box. The American's sense of sportsmanship is equated with his ability to master the sport with his purchases, not his skill."

"If this is hate-the-American hour, you should get a radio program."

"Please, Matthew. I'm trying to tell you that I think you're right. Whoever broke into the Scarlatti suite was an American. We can trace the rig to someone at your embassy. Hasn't that occurred to you?"

"We can do what?"

"Your embassy. If it is someone at your embassy. Someone who knows Bertholde. The men you suspect of having been involved with the securities. . . . Even an Alpine rig has to be manipulated by a trained mountain climber. How many climbers can there be in your embassy? Scotland Yard could check it in a day."

"No. . . . We'll handle it ourselves."

"Waste of time, you know. After all, embassy personnel have dossiers just as Bertholde has. How many are mountain climbers?"

The field accountant turned away from James Derek and refilled his glass. "That puts it in a police category. We don't want that. We'll make the interrogations."

"Just as you say. It shouldn't be difficult. Twenty to thirty people at most. You should track it down quickly."

"We will." Canfield walked to his bed and sat down.

"Tell me," said the Englishman, finishing the last of

his whiskey, "do you have a current list of your embassy personnel? Up-to-date, that is?"

"Of course."

"And you're absolutely sure that members of the staff working there now were part of this securities swindle last year?"

"Yes. I've told you that. At least, the State Department thinks so. I wish you'd stop harping on it."

"I shan't any longer. It's late and I have a great deal of work on my desk which I've neglected." The British operative rose from the chair and went to the bureau where he had put his hat. "Good night, Canfield."

"Oh, you're leaving? . . . Was there anything in the Bertholde file? I'll read it but right now I'm bushed."

James Derek stood by the door looking down at the exhausted field accountant. "One item I'm sure you'll be interested in. . . . Several probably, but one comes to mind."

"What's that?"

"Among the marquis's athletic pursuits is mountain climbing. The imminent sportsman is, in fact, a member of the Matterhorn Club. He's also one of the few hundred who've scaled the north side of the Jungfrau. No mean feat, I gather."

Canfield stood up angrily and shouted at the Englishman. "Why didn't you say so, for Christ's sake?"

"I frankly thought you were more interested in his associations with your embassy. That's really what I was looking for."

The field accountant stared at Derek. "So it was Bertholde. But why? . . . Unless he knew she wouldn't open the door for anyone."

"Perhaps. I really wouldn't know. Enjoy the dossier, Canfield. It's fascinating. . . . However, I don't think you'll find much in it related to the American embassy. . . . But that's not why you wanted it, is it?"

The Britisher let himself out the door, closing it sharply behind him. Canfield stared after him, confused but too tired to care.

CHAPTER 30

The telephone awoke him.

"Matthew?"

"Yes, Jan?" He held the phone and the blood drained from his arm and it hurt.

"I'm in the lobby. I told Mother Scarlatti I had some shopping to do."

The field accountant looked at his watch. It was eleven thirty. He had needed the sleep. "What happened?"

"I've never seen her like this, Matthew. She's frightened."

"That's new. Did she bring up the Sheffield business?"

"No. I had to. She brushed it aside and said the situation had changed."

"Nothing else? Just that?"

"Yes. . . . There was something else. She said she was going to talk with you this afternoon. She says there are problems back in New York that have to be attended to. I think she's going to tell you that she's decided to leave England and go home."

"That's impossible! What did she say exactly?"

"She was vague. Just that Chancellor was a fool and that it was senseless throwing away time on a wild-goose chase."

"She doesn't believe that!"

"I know she doesn't. She wasn't convincing either. But she means it. What are you going to do?"

"Take her by surprise, I hope. Stay out shopping for at least two hours, will you?"

They made plans for a late lunch and said good-bye.

Thirty minutes later the field accountant walked across the Savoy lobby into the grill and ordered breakfast. It was no time to go without food. Without energy.

He carried the Bertholde file with him. He promised himself that he'd read through it, or most of it, at the table. He opened it and placed it to the left of his plate and started at the top of the first page.

Jacques Louis Aumont Bertholde, fourth marquis of Chatellerault.

It was a dossier like so many other dossiers on the very wealthy. Exhaustive details about the family lineage. The positions and titles held by each member for several generations in business, government, and society—all impressive sounding, all meaningless to anyone else. The Bertholde holdings—enormous—mainly, as Elizabeth Scarlatti had said, within British territories. The specific education of the subject in question and his subsequent rise in the world of commerce. His clubs—all very correct. His hobbies—automobiles, horse breeding, dogs—also correct. The sports he excelled in—polo, sailing, the Matterhorn and the Jungfrau—not only correct, but colorful, fitting. And finally the character estimates elicited from his contemporaries. The most interesting part and yet the part many professionals disregarded. The flattering contributions were generally supplied by friends or associates hoping to gain. The unflattering, by enemies or competitors with a wish to undermine.

Canfield withdrew a pencil and made two notations in the dossier.

The first was on page 18, paragraph 5.

No particular reason other than the fact that it seemed out 'of place—unattractive—and it contained the name of a city Canfield recalled was on Ulster Scarlett's European itinerary.

The Bertholde family had extensive interests in the Ruhr Valley, which were sold to the German Ministry of Finance several weeks before the assassination at Sarajevo. The Bertholde offices in Stuttgart and Tassing were closed. The sale caused considerable comment in French business circles and the Bertholde family was criticized by the States General and in numerous newspaper editorials. No collusion accused, however, due to explanation that the

German Finance Ministry was paying exorbitant prices. Explanation proved out. Following the war, the Ruhr Valley interests repurchased from the Weimar government. Offices in Stuttgart and Tassing reopened.

The second, on page 23, paragraph 2, referred to one of Bertholde's more recently formed corporations and included the following information.

The Marquis de Bertholde's partners in the importing firm are Mr. Sydney Masterson and Mr. Harold Leacock. . . .

Masterson and Leacock.

Both were on the Zurich list. Each owned one of the fourteen properties in Switzerland.

No surprise. They tied Bertholde to the Zurich contingent.

No surprise at all. Just comforting—in a professional way—to know that another piece of the puzzle fitted.

As he finished his coffee, an unfamiliar man in a Savoy waistcoat approached the field accountant.

"Front desk, sir. I have two messages."

Canfield was alarmed. He reached for the notes extended to him. "You could have had me paged."

"Both parties requested that we not do that, sir."

"I see. Thank you."

The first message was from Derek. "Imperative you contact me."

The second was from Elizabeth Scarlatti. "Please come to my suite at two thirty. It is most urgent. I cannot see you before then."

Canfield lit one of his thin cigars and settled back into the curved Savoy dining chair. Derek could wait. The Englishman probably had gotten word of Benjamin Reynolds's new arrangement with the British government and was either furious or apologetic. He'd postpone Derek.

Scarlatti, on the other hand, had made a decision. If Janet was right, she was folding up. Forgetting for the moment his own potential loss, he could never explain her reversal to Reynolds, or Glover, or anyone else at Group Twenty, for that matter. He had spent thousands of dollars on the premise that he had Elizabeth's cooperation.

The field accountant thought about the old woman's visitor, the fourth marquis of Chatellerault, veteran of the Matterhorn and the Jungfrau, Jacques Louis Bertholde. Why had he broken into the Scarlatti suite the way he had? Was it simply the locked door and the knowledge that it would remain locked? Was it to terrify Elizabeth? Or was he searching for something?

Just as he and Derek had searched in the darkness two floors above.

Once confronting her what could Bertholde have said to bend her will? What could he possibly say that would frighten Elizabeth Scarlatti?

He could promise the death of her son if he were still alive. That might do it. . . . But would it? Her son had betrayed her. Betrayed the Scarlatti Industries. Canfield had the unnatural feeling that Elizabeth would rather see her son dead than let him continue that betrayal.

Yet now she was retreating.

Again Canfield felt the inadequacy he had begun to feel aboard the *Calpurnia*. An assignment conceived of as theft had been complicated by extraordinary occurrences, extraordinary people.

He forced his mind back to Elizabeth Scarlatti. He was convinced she could "not see" him before two thirty because she was completing arrangements to return home.

Well, he had a shock in store for her. He knew she had had an early-morning visitor. And he had the Bertholde dossier.

The dossier she could refuse. The Alpine rig would be irresistible.

"I wrote in my note that I couldn't see you before two thirty! Would you please respect my wishes?"

"It can't wait. Let me in quickly!"

She opened the door in disgust, leaving it ajar as she walked back into the center of the room. Canfield closed it, loudly inserting the bolt. He spoke before she turned around to face him. "I've read the dossier. I know now why your visitor didn't have to open the door."

It was as if a pistol had been fired in front of her ancient face. The old woman turned and sprang her back forward and arched her neck. Had she been thirty years younger, she would have leapt upon him in fury. She spoke with an intensity he had never heard from her before.

"You unconscionable bastard! You're a liar! A thief! Liar! Liar! I'll have you spend the rest of your life in prison!"

"That's very good. Attack for attack! You've pulled it before but not this time. Derek was with me. We found the rig. An Alpine rig, he called it—which your visitor let down the side of the building."

The old woman lurched toward him, unsteady on her feet.

"For Christ's sake, relax! I'm on your side." He held her thin shoulders.

"You've got to buy him! Oh, my God! You've got to buy him! Get him here!"

"Why? Buy him how? Who?"

"Derek. How long have you known? Mr. Canfield, I ask you in the name of all that's holy, how long have you known?"

"Since about five o'clock this morning."

"Then he's talked to others! Oh, my God, he's talked to others!" She was beside herself, and Canfield was now frightened for her.

"I'm sure he has. But only to his immediate superiors and I gather he's pretty superior himself. What did you expect?"

The old woman tried with what strength she had left to regain control of herself. "You may have caused the murder of my entire family. If you've done that, I'll see you dead!"

"That's pretty strong language! You'd better tell me why!"

"I'll tell you nothing until you get Derek on that telephone."

The field accountant crossed the room to the telephone and gave the operator Derek's number. He talked urgently, quietly, for a few moments and turned to the old woman. "He's going in to a meeting in twenty minutes. He has a full report and they'll expect him to read it."

The old woman walked rapidly toward Canfield. "Give me that phone!"

He handed her both the stand and the receiver. "Mr. Derek! Elizabeth Scarlatti. Whatever this meeting is, do not go to it! I am not in the habit of begging, sir, but I implore you, do not go! Please, please do not speak to a soul about last night! If you do, you will be responsible for the deaths of a number of innocent people. I can say no more now. . . . Yes, yes, whatever you like. . . . I'll see you, of course. In an hour. Thank you. Thank you!"

She replaced the receiver on the hook and slowly, with great relief, put the telephone back on the table. She looked at the field accountant. "Thank God!"

The field accountant watched her as she spoke. He began to walk toward her. "Sweet mother of Jesus! I'm beginning to see. That crazy Alpine thing. The acrobatics at two in the morning. It wasn't just to scare you half to death—it was necessary!"

"What are you talking about?"

"Since early this morning I've thought it was Bertholde! And he'd come to you like that to scare hell out of you! But it didn't make sense. It wouldn't accomplish anything. He could have stopped you in the lobby, in a store, in the dining room. It had to be someone who couldn't do that! Someone who couldn't take a chance anywhere!"

"You're babbling! You're incoherent!"

"Sure, you're willing to call the whole thing off! Why not? You did what you'd set out to do! You found him! You've found your missing son, haven't you?"

"That's a lie!"

"Oh, no, it's not. It's so clear I should have thought of it last night. The whole damn thing was so weird I looked for insane explanations. I thought it was persuasion by terror. It's been used a lot these past few years. But it wasn't that at all! It was our celebrated war hero come back to the land of the living! Ulster Stewart Scarlett! The only one who couldn't risk stopping you outside. The only one who couldn't take a chance that you might not unlatch that bolt!"

"Conjecture! I deny it!"

"Deny all you like! Now I'm giving you a choice! Derek will be here in less than an hour. Either we straighten this out between us before then, or I walk out that door and cable my office that in my highly regarded professional opinion we've found Ulster Scarlett! And, incidentally, I'm taking your daughter-in-law with me."

The old woman suddenly lowered her voice to nearly a whisper. She walked haltingly toward the field accountant. "If you have any feeling whatsoever for that girl, you'll do as I ask. If you don't, she'll be killed."

It was now the field accountant's turn to raise his voice. It was no longer the shout of the angry debater, it was the roar of an angry man. "Don't you make any pronouncements to me! Don't you or your rotten bastard son make any threats to me! You may buy part of me, but you don't buy all of me! You tell him I'll kill him if he touches that girl!"

Pleading without shame, Elizabeth Scarlatti touched his arm. He withdrew it swiftly from her. "It's not my threat. Please, in the name of God, listen to me. Try to understand. . . . I'm helpless. And I can not be helped!"

The field accountant saw the tears roll down her wrinkled cheeks. Her skin was white and the hollows of her eyes were black with exhaustion. He thought, quite out of context with the moment, that he was looking at a tear-stained corpse. His anger ebbed.

"Nobody has to be helpless. Don't let anybody tell you that."

"You love her, don't you?"

"Yes. And because I do, you don't have to be quite so afraid. I'm a committed public servant. But far more committed to us than the public."

"Your confidence doesn't change the situation."

"You won't know that until you tell me what it is."

"You leave me no choice? No alternative?"

"None."

"Then God have mercy on you. You have an awesome responsibility. You are responsible for our lives."

She told him.

And Matthew Canfield knew exactly what he would do. It was time to confront the Marquis de Bertholde.

CHAPTER 31

Fifty-seven miles southeast of London is the seaside resort of Ramsgate. Near the town, on a field set back from the main road, stood a wooden shack no more than twenty feet by twenty. It had two small windows and in the early-morning mist a dim light could be seen shining through them. About a hundred yards to the north was a larger building—once a barn—five times the size of the shack. It was now a hangar for two small monoplanes. One of them was being wheeled out by three men in gray overalls.

Inside the shack, the man with the shaved head sat at a table drinking black coffee and munching bread. The reddish splotch above his right eye was sore and inflamed and he touched it continually.

He read the message in front of him and looked up at the bearer, a man in a chauffeur's uniform. The contents of the message infuriated him.

"The marquis has gone too far. The instructions from Munich were clear. The Rawlinses were *not* to be killed in the States. They were to be brought to Zurich! They were to be killed in *Zurich!*"

"There's no need for concern. Their deaths, the man and his wife, were engineered above suspicion. The marquis wanted you to know that. It has appeared as an accident."

"To whom? God damn it, to *whom?* Go shag, all of you! Munich doesn't want risks! In *Zurich* there would have been no risk!" Ulster Scarlett rose from the chair and walked to the small window overlooking the field.

His plane was nearly ready. He hoped his fury would subside before takeoff. He disliked flying when he was angry. He made mistakes in the air when he was angry. It had been happening more frequently as the pressures mounted.

God damn Bertholde! Certainly Rawlins had to be killed. In his panic over Cartwright's discovery Rawlins had ordered his son-in-law to kill Elizabeth Scarlatti. A massive error! It's funny, he reflected. He no longer thought of the old woman as his mother. Simply Elizabeth Scarlatti. . . . But to have Rawlins murdered three thousand miles away was insanity! How could they know who was asking questions? And how easily might the order be traced back to Bertholde?

"Regardless of what happened . . ." Labishe started to speak.

"What?" Scarlett turned from the window. He had made up his mind.

"The marquis also wanted you to know that regardless of what happened to Boothroyd, all associations with him are buried with the Rawlinses."

"Not quite, Labishe. Not quite." Scarlett spoke softly but his voice was hard. "The Marquis de Bertholde was ordered . . . commanded by Munich to have the Rawlinses brought to Switzerland. He disobeyed. That was most unfortunate."

"Pardon, monsieur?"

Scarlett reached for his flying jacket, which hung over the back of his chair. Again he spoke quietly, simply. Two words.

"Kill him."

"Monsieur!"

"Kill him! Kill the Marquis de Bertholde and do it today!"

"Monsieur! I do not believe what I hear!"

"Listen to me! I don't give explanations! By the time I reach Munich I want a cable waiting for me telling me that stupid son of a bitch is dead! . . . And, Labishe! Do it so there's no mistake who killed him. You! We can't have any investigations now! . . . Get back here to the field. We'll fly you out of the country."

"Monsieur! I have been with *le marquis* for fifteen years! He has been good to me! . . . I can not . . ."

"You what?"

"Monsieur . . ." The Frenchman sunk to one knee. "Do not ask me. . . ."

"I don't ask. I command! Munich commands!"

The foyer on the third floor of Bertholde et Fils was enormous. In the rear was an impressive set of white Louis XIV doors that obviously led to the sanctum sanctorum of the Marquis de Bertholde. On the right side were six brown leather armchairs in a semicircle—the sort that might be found in the study of a wealthy country squire—with a thick rectangular coffee table placed in front. On the table were neatly stacked piles of chic magazines—chic socially and chic industrially. On the left side of the room was a large white desk trimmed in gold. Behind the desk sat a most attractive brunet with spit curls silhouetted against her forehead. All this Canfield took in with his second impression. It took him several moments to get over his first.

Opening the elevator door, he had been visually overpowered by the color scheme of the walls.

They were magenta red and sweeping from the ceiling moldings were arcs of black velvet.

Good Christ! he said to himself. I'm in a hallway thirty-five hundred miles away!

Seated in the chairs beside one another were two middle-aged gentlemen in Savile Row clothes reading magazines. Standing off to the right was a man in a chauffeur's uniform, his hat off, his hands clasped behind his back.

Canfield approached the desk. The spit-curled secretary greeted him before he could speak. "Mr. Canfield?"

"Yes."

"The marquis would like you to go right in, sir." The girl spoke as she rose from the chair and started toward the large white doors. Canfield saw that the man seated on the left was upset. He uttered a few "Damns!" and went back to his magazine.

"Good afternoon, Mr. Canfield." The fourth marquis of Chatellerault stood behind his large white desk and extended his hand. "We have not met, of course, but an emissary from Elizabeth Scarlatti is a welcome guest. Do sit down."

Bertholde was almost what Canfield expected him to

242

be, except, perhaps, shorter. He was well-groomed, relatively handsome, very masculine, with a voice resonant enough to fill an opera house. However, in spite of his exuding virility—bringing to mind the Matterhorn and the Jungfrau—there was something artificial, slightly effete about the man. Perhaps the clothing. It was almost too fashionable.

"How do you do?" Canfield smiled, shaking the Frenchman's hand. "Is it Monsieur Bertholde? Or *Monsieur le Marquis?* I'm not sure which I should use."

"I could tell you several unflattering names given me by your countrymen." The marquis laughed. "But please, use the French custom—so scorned by our proper Anglicans. Plain Bertholde will do. Marquises are such an out-of-date custom." The Frenchman smiled ingenuously and waited until Canfield sat in the chair in front of his desk before returning to his seat. Jacques Louis Aumont Bertholde, fourth marquis of Chatellerault, was immensely likable and Canfield recognized the fact.

"I appreciate your interrupting your schedule."

"Schedules are made to be broken. Such a dull existence otherwise, yes?"

"I won't waste time, sir. Elizabeth Scarlatti wants to negotiate."

Jacques Bertholde leaned back in his chair and looked startled. "Negotiate? . . . I'm afraid I don't comprehend, monsieur. . . . Negotiate what?"

"She knows, Bertholde. . . . She knows as much as she needs to know. She wants to meet you."

"I'd be delighted—at any time—to meet Madame Scarlatti but I can't imagine what we have to discuss. Not in a business sense, monsieur, which I presume to be your . . . errand."

"Maybe the key is her son. Ulster Scarlett."

Bertholde leveled his gaze intently on the field accountant. "It is a key for which I have no lock, monsieur. I have not had the pleasure. . . . I know, as most who read newspapers know, that he vanished a number of months ago. But that is all I know."

"And you don't know a thing about Zurich?"

Jacques Bertholde abruptly sat up in his chair. "*Quoi?* Zurich?"

"We know about Zurich."

"Is this a joke?"

243

"No. Fourteen men in Zurich. Maybe you've got the fifteenth. . . . Elizabeth Scarlatti."

Canfield could hear Bertholde's breathing. "Where did you get this information? What do you refer to?"

"Ulster Scarlett! Why do you think I'm here?"

"I don't believe you! I don't know what you are talking about!" Bertholde got out of his chair.

"For God's sake! She's interested. . . . Not because of him! Because of you! And the others! She's got something to offer, and if I were you, I'd listen to her."

"But you are not me, monsieur! I'm afraid I must ask you to leave. There is no business between Madame Scarlatti and the Bertholde companies."

Canfield did not move. He remained in the chair and spoke quietly. "Then I'd better put it another way. I think you'll have to see her. Talk with her. . . . For your own good. For Zurich's good."

"You threaten me?"

"If you don't, it's my opinion that she'll do something drastic. I don't have to tell you she's a powerful woman. . . . You're linked with her son. . . . And she met with her son last night!"

Bertholde stood motionless. Canfield couldn't decide whether the Frenchman's look of disbelief was over the revelation of Scarlett's visit or his—the field accountant's—knowledge of it.

After a few moments Bertholde replied, "I know nothing of what you speak. It has nothing to do with me."

"Oh, come on! I found the rig! The Alpine rig! I found it at the bottom of a closet in your conference suite at the Savoy!"

"You what?"

"You heard me! Now, let's stop kidding each other!"

"You broke into my firm's private quarters?"

"I did! And that's just the beginning. We've got a list. You might know some of the names on it. . . . Daudet and D'Almeida, fellow countrymen, I think. . . . Olaffsen, Landor, Thyssen, von Schnitzler, Kindorf. . . . And, oh yes! Mr. Masterson and Mr. Leacock! Current partners of yours, I believe! There are several others, but I'm sure you know their names better than I do!"

"Enough! Enough, monsieur!" The Marquis de Bertholde sat down again, slowly, deliberately. He stared at Canfield. "I will clear my office and we will talk further.

People have been waiting. It does not look good. Wait outside. I will dispense with them quickly."

The field accountant got out of the chair as Bertholde picked up the telephone and pressed the button for his secretary.

"Monsieur Canfield will remain. I wish to finish the afternoon's business as rapidly as possible. With each person interrupt me in five minutes if I have not concluded by then. What? Labishe? Very well, send him in. I'll give them to him." The Frenchman reached into his pocket and withdrew a set of keys.

Canfield crossed to the large white double doors. Before his hand touched the brass knob, the door on his left opened swiftly, with great force.

"So sorry, monsieur," the man in uniform said.

"Voici les clefs, Labishe."

"Merci, Monsieur le Marquis! Je regrette. . . . J'ai un billet . . ."

The chauffeur closed the door and Canfield smiled at the secretary.

He wandered over to the semicircle of chairs, and as the two gentlemen looked up, he nodded pleasantly. He sat down on the end chair nearest the entrance to Bertholde's office and picked up the *London Illustrated News*. He noted that the man nearest him was fidgeting, irritable, quite impatient. He was turning the pages of *Punch*, but he was not reading. The other man was engrossed in an article in the *Quarterly Review*.

Suddenly, Canfield was diverted by an insignificant action on the part of the impatient man. The man extended his left hand through his coat sleeve, turned his wrist, and looked at the watch. A perfectly normal occurrence under the circumstances. What startled the field accountant was the sight of the man's cuff link. It was made of cloth and it was square with two stripes running diagonally from corner to corner. The small stripes were deep red and black. It was a replica of the cuff link that had identified the hulking, masked Charles Boothroyd in Elizabeth Scarlatti's stateroom on board the *Calpurnia*. The colors were the same as the paper on the marquis' walls and the black velvet drapes arcing from the ceiling.

The impatient man noticed Canfield's stare. He abruptly withdrew his hand into his jacket and placed his arm at his side.

"I was trying to read the time on your watch. Mine's been running fast."

"Four twenty."

"Thanks."

The impatient gentleman folded his arms and leaned back, looking exasperated. The other man spoke.

"Basil, you'll have a stroke if you don't relax."

"Well and good for you, Arthur! But I'm late for a meeting! I told Jacques it was a hectic day, but he insisted I come over."

"He can be insistent." '

"He can be bloody rude, too!"

There followed five minutes of silence except for the rustling of papers at the secretary's desk.

The large left panel of the white double doors opened and the chauffeur emerged. He closed the door, and Canfield noticed that once it was shut, the chauffeur twisted the knob to make sure it was secure. It was a curious motion.

The uniformed man went to the secretary and leaned over her desk, whispering. She reacted to his information with resigned annoyance. He shrugged his shoulders and walked quickly to a door to the right of the elevator. Canfield saw through the slowly closing door the flight of stairs he had presumed to be there.

The secretary placed some papers into a manila folder and looked over at the three men. "I'm sorry, gentlemen, the Marquis de Bertholde can not see anyone further this afternoon. We apologize for any inconvenience."

"Now see here, young lady!" The impatient gentleman was on his feet. "This is preposterous! I've been here for three-quarters of an hour at the explicit request of the Marquis! . . . Request be damned! At his instructions!"

"I'm sorry, sir, I'll convey your displeasure."

"You'll do more than that! You'll convey to Monsieur Bertholde that I am waiting right here until he sees me!" He sat down pompously.

The man named Arthur rose and walked toward the elevator.

"For heaven's sake, man, you'll not improve French manners. People have been trying for centuries. Come along, Basil. We'll stop at the Dorchester and start the evening."

"Can't do it, Arthur. I'm staying right where I am."

"Have it your way. Be in touch."

Canfield remained in his seat next to the impatient Basil. He knew only that he would not leave until Bertholde came out. Basil was his best weapon.

"Ring the marquis again, please, miss," said Basil.

She did so.

A number of times. And there was no response.

The field accountant was alarmed. He rose from his chair and walked to the large double doors and knocked. There was no answer. He tried opening both doors; they were locked.

Basil unfolded his arms and got out of his chair. The spit-curled secretary stood up behind her white desk. She automatically picked up the phone and started pressing the buzzer, finally holding her finger down upon it.

"Unlock the door," commanded the field accountant.

"Oh, I don't know . . ."

"I do! Get me a key!"

The girl started to open the top drawer of her desk and then looked up at the American. "Perhaps we should wait. . . ."

"Damn it! Give me the key!"

"Yes, sir!" She picked up a ring of keys and selecting one, separated it from the others, and gave the key to Canfield. He rapidly unlocked the doors and flung them open.

There in front of them was the Frenchman sprawled across the top of his white desk, blood trickling from his mouth; his tongue was extended and swollen; his eyes bulged from their sockets; his neck was inflated and lacerated just below the chin line. He had been expertly garroted.

The girl kept screaming but did not collapse—a fact that Canfield wasn't sure was fortunate. Basil began to shake and repeated "Oh, my God!" over and over again. The field accountant approached the desk and lifted the dead man's wrist by the coat sleeve. He let it go and the hand fell back.

The girl's screams grew louder and two middle-aged executives burst through the staircase doorway into the outer room. Through the double doors the scene was clear to both men. One ran back to the stairway, shouting at the top of his voice, while the other slowly, fearfully walked into Bertholde's room.

"Le bon Dieu!"

Within a minute, a stream of employees had run down and up the staircase, log-jamming themselves in the doorway. As each group squeezed through, subsequent screams and oaths followed. Within two minutes twenty-five people were shouting instructions to nonexistent subordinates.

Canfield shook the spit-curled secretary in an attempt to stop her screaming. He kept telling her to phone the police, but she could not accept the order. Canfield did not want to make the call himself because it would have required separate concentration. He wished to keep his full attention on everyone in sight, especially Basil, if that was possible.

A tall, distinguished-looking, gray-haired man in a double-breasted pin-stripe suit came rushing through the crowd up to the secretary and Canfield. "Miss Richards! Miss Richards! What in God's name happened?"

"We opened his door and found him like this! That's what happened," shouted the field accountant over the growing din of excited voices.

And then Canfield looked closely at the questioner. Where had he seen him before? Or had he? The man was like so many in the Scarlatti world. Even to the perfectly waxed moustache.

"Have you phoned the police?" asked the gentleman.

Canfield saw Basil pushing his way through the hysterical mob gathered by the office doors. "No, the police haven't been called," yelled the American as he watched Basil making headway through the crowd. "Call them! . . . It might be a good idea to close these doors." He started after Basil as if to push the doors shut. The distinguished-looking man with the waxed moustache held him firmly by the lapel.

"You say you found him?"

"Yes. Let go of me!"

"What's your name, young man?"

"What?"

"I asked you your name!"

"Derek, James Derek! Now, phone the police!"

Canfield took the man's wrist and pressed hard against the vein. The arm withdrew in pain and Canfield ran into the crowd after Basil.

The man in the pin-striped suit winced and turned to

the secretary. "Did you get his name, Miss Richards? I couldn't hear."

The girl was sobbing. "Yes, sir. It was Darren, or Derrick. First name, James."

The man with the waxed moustache looked carefully at the secretary. She had heard. "The police, Miss Richards. Phone the police!"

"Yes, sir, Mr. Poole."

The man named Poole pushed his way through the crowd. He had to get to his office, he had to be by himself. *They* had done it! The men of Zurich had ordered Jacques' death! His dearest friend, his mentor, closer to him than anyone in the world. The man who'd given him everything, made everything possible for him.

The man he'd killed for—willingly.

They'd pay! They'd pay and pay and pay!

He, Poole, had never failed Bertholde in life. He'd not fail him in death either!

But there were questions. So many questions.

This Canfield who'd just lied about his name. The old woman, Elizabeth Scarlatti.

Most of all the misshapen Heinrich Kroeger. The man Poole knew beyond a doubt was Elizabeth Scarlatti's son. He knew because Bertholde had told him.

He wondered if anyone else knew.

On the third-floor landing, which was now completely filled with Bertholde employees in varying stages of hysteria, Canfield could see Basil one floor below pulling himself downward by the railing. Canfield began yelling.

"Get clear! Get clear! The doctor's waiting! I've got to bring him up! Get clear!"

To some degree the ruse worked and he made swifter headway. By the time he reached the first-floor lobby, Basil was no longer in sight. Canfield ran out the front entrance onto the sidewalk. There was Basil about half a block south, limping in the middle of Vauxhall Road, waving, trying to hail a taxi. The knees of his trousers were coated with mud where he had fallen in his haste.

Shouts were still coming from various windows of Bertholde et Fils, drawing dozens of pedestrians to the foot of the company's steps.

Canfield walked against the crowd toward the limping figure.

A taxi stopped and Basil grabbed for the door handle.

As he pulled the door open and climbed in, Canfield reached the side of the cab and prevented the Englishman from pulling the door shut. He moved in alongside Basil, pushing him sideway to make room.

"I say! What are you doing?" Basil was frightened but he did not raise his voice. The driver kept turning his head back and forth from the street in front of him to the gathering crowds receding behind him. Basil did not wish to draw additional attention.

Before Basil could think further, the American grasped the Englishman's right hand and pulled the coat above his wrist. He twisted Basil's arm revealing the red and black cuff link.

"Zurich, Basil!" the field accountant whispered.

"What are you talking about?"

"You damn fool, I'm with you! Or I will be, if they let you live!"

"Oh, my God! Oh, my God!" Basil babbled.

The American released Basil's hand by throwing it downward. He looked straight ahead as if ignoring the Englishman. "You're an idiot. You realize that, don't you?"

"I don't know you, sir! I don't know you!" The Englishman was near collapse.

"Then we'd better change that. I may be all you have left."

"Now see here. I had nothing to do with it! I was in the waiting room with you. I had nothing to do with it!"

"Of course, you didn't. It's pretty damned obvious that it was the chauffeur. But a number of people are going to want to know why you ran. Maybe you were just making sure the job was done."

"That's preposterous!"

"Then why did you run away?"

"I . . . I . . ."

"Let's not talk now. Where can we go where we'll be seen for about ten or fifteen minutes? I don't want it to look as though we dropped out of sight."

"My club . . . I suppose."

"Give him the address!"

CHAPTER 32

"What the devil do you mean I was there?" James Derek shouted into the phone. "I've been here at the Savoy since midafternoon! . . . Yes, of course I am. Since three or thereabouts. . . . No, she's here with me." The Englishman suddenly caught his breath. When he spoke again his words were barely audible, drawn out in disbelief. "Good Lord! . . . How horrible. . . . Yes. Yes, I heard you."

Elizabeth Scarlatti sat across the room on the Victorian couch, absorbed in the Bertholde dossier. At the sound of Derek's voice she looked up at the Englishman. He was staring at her. He spoke again into the phone.

"Yes. He left here roughly at three thirty. With Ferguson, from our office. They were to meet Mrs. Scarlett at Tippin's and he was to proceed from there to Bertholde's. . . . I don't know. His instructions were that she remain in Ferguson's custody until he returned. Ferguson's to call in. . . . I see. For heaven's sake, keep me posted. I'll phone you if there're any developments here."

He replaced the telephone receiver on the hook and remained at the table. "Bertholde's been killed."

"Good God! Where's my daughter?"

"With our man. She's all right. He reported in an hour ago."

"Canfield! Where's Canfield?"

"I wish I knew."

"Is he all right?"

"How can I answer that if I don't know where he is?

We can presume he's functioning. He identified himself as me and left the scene!"

"How did it happen?"

"He was garroted. A wire around his throat."

"Oh!" Elizabeth suddenly, vividly recalled the picture of Matthew Canfield thrusting the cord in her face after Boothroyd's attempt on her life aboard the *Calpurnia.* "If he killed him, he must have had a reason!"

"What?"

"For killing him. He must have had to!"

"That's most interesting."

"What is?"

"That you would think Canfield had to kill him."

"It couldn't have happened otherwise! He's no killer."

"He didn't kill Bertholde either, if it's any comfort to you."

Her relief was visible. "Do they know who did?"

"They believe so. Apparently it was Bertholde's chauffeur."

"That's odd."

"Very. The man's been with him for years."

"Perhaps Canfield's gone after him."

"Not likely. The man left some ten to twelve minutes before they found Bertholde."

James Derek walked from the telephone table toward Elizabeth. It was obvious that he was upset. "In the light of what's just happened, I'd like to ask you a question. But, of course, you needn't answer. . . ."

"What is it?"

"I'd like to know how—or perhaps why—Mr. Canfield received a full clearance from the British Foreign Office."

"I don't know what that is."

"Come, madame. If you don't care to answer, I respect that. But since my name's been used in the killing of an influential man, I believe I'm entitled to something more than another . . . falsehood."

"Another . . . falsehood? That's insulting, Mr. Derek."

"Is it? And are you and Mr. Canfield still setting elaborate traps for embassy personnel who returned to the United States over four months ago?"

"Oh." Elizabeth sat down again on the couch. She was not concerned with the Englishman's complaint; she only wished Canfield was there to answer him. What she was concerned with was the agent's reference to the Foreign Office. "An unfortunate necessity."

"Most unfortunate. . . . I gather, then, that you don't care to answer."

"On the contrary, I have answered you." Elizabeth looked up at the Britisher. "I wish you'd explain. What is full clearance?"

"Extraordinary cooperation from the highest echelons of our government. And such decisions from the British Foreign Office are generally reserved for major political crises! Not a stocks-and-bonds struggle between squabbling millionaires. . . . Or, if you'll pardon me, a private citizen's personal tragedy."

Elizabeth Scarlatti froze.

What James Derek had just said was abhorrent to the head of Scarlatti. More than anything else she had to operate outside the boundaries of "highest echelon" scrutiny. For the sake of Scarlatti itself. Canfield's minor agency had seemed heaven-sent. Her arrangement with him gave her the facilities of official cooperation without answering to anyone of consequence. If she had wanted it otherwise, she would have commanded any number of men in either or both the legislative and executive branches of the United States government. It would not have been difficult. . . . Now, it seemed, Canfield's relatively unimportant department had grown in significance. Or perhaps her son had involved himself in an undertaking far more ominous than she had conceived.

Was the answer in the Bertholde dossier? Elizabeth wondered. "I gather from your tone that this full clearance is a new development."

"I was informed this morning."

Then it must be in the Bertholde dossier, thought Elizabeth. . . . Of course it was! Even Matthew Canfield had begun to perceive it! Only his perception had been based solely on the recognition of certain words, names. He had marked the pages. Elizabeth picked up the file.

"Following the war, the Ruhr Valley interests repurchased. . . . Offices in Stuttgart and Tassing . . ."

Tassing.

Germany.

An economic crisis.

The Weimar Republic.

A series of economic crises! A major and constant political crisis!

". . . partners in the importing firm are Mr. Sydney Masterson and Mr. Harold Leacock. . . ."

Masterson and Leacock. Zurich!

Tassing!

"Does the city of Tassing mean anything to you?"

"It's not a city. It is an outlying district of Munich. In Bavaria. Why do you ask?"

"My son spent a good deal of time and money there . . . among other places. Does it have any special meaning for you?"

"Munich?"

"I suppose so."

"Hotbed of radicalism. Breeding ground of malcontents."

"Malcontents? . . . Communists?"

"Hardly. They'd shoot a Red on sight. Or a Jew. Call themselves *Schutzstaffel*. Go around clubbing people. Consider themselves a race apart from the rest of the world."

A race apart.

Oh, God!

Elizabeth looked at the dossier in her hands. Slowly she replaced it in the manila envelope and stood up. Without saving a word to the Englishman, she crossed to her bedroom door and let herself in. She closed the door behind her.

James Derek remained in the center of the room. He didn't understand.

Inside her bedroom Elizabeth went to her writing desk where papers were scattered across the top. She sorted them out until she found the Zurich list.

She read each name carefully.

AVERY LANDOR, U.S.A.—*Oil*.

LOUIS GIBSON, U.S.A.—*Oil*.

THOMAS RAWLINS, U.S.A.—*Securities*.

HOWARD THORNTON, U.S.A.—*Industrial Construction*.

SYDNEY MASTERSON, GREAT BRITAIN—*Imports*.

DAVID INNES-BOWEN, GREAT BRITAIN—*Textiles*.

HAROLD LEACOCK, GREAT BRITAIN—*Securities*.

LOUIS FRANÇOIS D'ALMEIDA, FRANCE—*Railroads*.

PIERRE DAUDET, FRANCE—*Ship lines*.

INGMAR MYRDAL, SWEDEN—*Securities*.

CHRISTIAN OLAFFSEN, SWEDEN—*Steel*.
OTTO VON SCHNITZLER, GERMANY—*I. G. Farben*.
FRITZ THYSSEN, GERMANY—*Steel*.
ERICH KINDORF, GERMANY—*Coal*.

One might say that the Zurich list was a cross-section of the most powerful men in the Western hemisphere.

Elizabeth put the list down and reached for a leather-bound notebook in which she kept telephone numbers and addresses. She thumbed to the letter *O*.

Ogilvie and Storm, Ltd., Publishers, Bayswater Road, London.

She would phone Thomas Ogilvie and have him send her whatever information he could unearth on the *Schutz-staffel*.

She knew something about it already. She remembered reading its political name was the National Socialists and they were led by a man named Adolph Hitler.

CHAPTER 33

The man's name was Basil Hawkwood, and Canfield quickly pictured the trademark *hawkwood*—small letter *h*—as it appeared on a variety of leather goods. Hawkwood Leather was one of the largest firms in England, only a short distance behind Mark Cross.

The nervous Basil led Canfield into the huge reading room of his club, Knights. They chose two chairs by the Knightsbridge window, where there were no other members within earshot.

Basil's fear caused him to stutter, and when his words came, the phrases tumbled over one another. He assumed, because he wanted to assume, that the young man facing him would help him.

Canfield sat back in the comfortable chair and listened with incredulity to Hawkwood's story.

The chairman of Hawkwood Leather had been sending shipment after shipment of "damaged" leather goods to a little-known firm in Munich. For over a year the directors of Hawkwood accepted the losses on the basis of the "damaged" classification. Now, however, they had ordered a complete report on the excess malfunctions of the plants. The Hawkwood heir was trapped. There could be no more shipments for an indeterminate time.

He pleaded with Matthew Canfield to understand. He begged the young man to report and confirm his loyalty, but the boots, the belts, the holsters would have to come from someone else.

"Why do you wear the cuff links?" asked Canfield.

"I wore them today to remind Bertholde of my contribution. He presented them to me himself. . . . You're not wearing yours."

"My contribution doesn't call for them."

"Well, damn it, mine does! I haven't stinted in the past and I won't in the future!" Hawkwood leaned forward in his chair. "The present circumstances don't change my feelings! You can report that. God damn Jews! Radicals! Bolsheviks! All over Europe! A conspiracy to destroy every decent principle good Christian men have lived by for centuries! They'll murder us in our beds! Rape our daughters! Pollute the races! I've never doubted it! I'll help again. You have my word! Soon there'll be millions at our disposal!"

Matthew Canfield suddenly felt sick. What in God's name had he done? He got out of the chair and his legs felt weak.

"I'll report what you said, Mr. Hawkwood."

"Good fellow. Knew you'd understand."

"I'm beginning to." He walked rapidly away from the Englishman toward the arch to the outer hallway.

As he stood on the curb under the Knights' canopy waiting for a taxi, Canfield was numb with fear. He was no longer dealing with a world he understood. He was dealing with giants, with concepts, with commitments beyond his comprehension.

CHAPTER 34

Elizabeth had the newspaper and magazine articles spread over the couch. Ogilvie and Storm, publishers, had done an excellent job. There was more material here than Elizabeth or Canfield could digest in a week.

The National Socialist German Workers party emerged as ragtail fanatics. The *Schutzstaffel* were brutes but no one took them seriously. The articles, the photographs, even the short headlines were slanted in such a way as to give a comic-opera effect.

Why Work in the Fatherland
if You Can Dress Up
and Pretend It's Wagner?

Canfield picked up a portion of a Sunday supplement and read the names of the leaders. Adolf Hitler, Erich Ludendorff, Rudolf Hess, Gregor Strasser. They read like a team of vaudeville jugglers. Adolf, Erich, Rudolf, and Gregor. However, toward the end of the article his amusement waned. There were the phrases.

". . . conspiracy of Jews and Communists . . ."

". . . daughters raped by Bolshevik terrorists! . . ."

". . . Aryan blood soiled by scheming Semites! . . ."

". . . a plan for a thousand years! . . ."

Canfield could see the face of Basil Hawkwood, owner of one of the largest industries in England, whispering with great intensity many of these same words. He thought of the shipments of leather to Munich. The leather without the trademark *hawkwood*, but the leather

258

that became part of the uniforms in these photographs. He recalled the manipulations of the dead Bertholde, the road in Wales, the mass murders at York.

Elizabeth was sitting at the desk jotting down notes from an article. A picture was beginning to emerge for her. But it was incomplete, as if part of a background was missing. It bothered her, but she'd learned enough.

"It staggers your imagination, doesn't it?" said Elizabeth, rising from her chair.

"What do you make of it?"

"Enough to frighten me. An obscure but volatile political organization is being quietly, slowly financed by a number of the wealthiest men on earth. The men of Zurich. And my son is part of them."

"But why?"

"I'm not sure yet." Elizabeth walked to the window. "There's more to learn. However, one thing is clear. If this band of fanatics make solid progress in Germany—in the Reichstag—the men of Zurich could control unheard-of economic power. It's a long-range concept, I think. It could be brilliant strategy."

"Then I've got to get back to Washington!"

"They may already know or suspect."

"Then we've got to move in!"

"You can't move in!" Elizabeth turned back to Canfield, raising her voice. "No government has the right to interfere with the internal politics of another. No government has that right. There's another way. A far more effective way. But there's an enormous risk and I must consider it." The old woman brought her cupped hands up to her lips and walked away from Canfield.

"What is it? What's the risk?"

Elizabeth, however, did not hear him. She was concentrating deeply. After several minutes she spoke to him from across the room.

"There is an island in a remote lake in Canada. My husband, in a rash moment, bought it years and years ago. There are several dwellings on it, primitive but habitable. . . . If I put at your disposal whatever funds were necessary, could you have this island so guarded that it would be impregnable?"

"I think so."

"That's not good enough. There can be no element of doubt. The lives of my entire family would depend on

259

total isolation. The funds I mention are, frankly, limit-less."

"All right, then. Yes, I could."

"Could you have them taken there in complete secrecy?"

"Yes."

"Could you set all this up within a week?"

"Yes, again."

"Very well. I'll outline what I propose. Believe me when I tell you it is the only way."

"What's your proposal?"

"Put simply, the Scarlatti Industries will economically destroy every investor in Zurich. Force them into financial ruin."

Canfield looked at the prepossessing, confident old woman. For several seconds he said nothing, merely sucked breath through his teeth as if trying to formulate a reply.

"You're a lunatic," he said quietly. "You're one person. They're fourteen . . . no, now thirteen stinking rich fatcats. You're no match for them."

"It's not what one's worth that counts, Mr. Canfield. Not after a point. It's how rapidly one can manipulate his holdings. The time factor is the ultimate weapon in economics, and don't let anyone tell you otherwise. In my case, one judgment prevails."

"What does that mean?"

Elizabeth stood motionless in front of Canfield. Her speech was measured. "If I were to liquidate the entire Scarlatti Industries, there is no one on earth who could stop me."

The field accountant wasn't sure he understood her implication. He looked at her for a few seconds before speaking. "Oh? So?"

"You fool! . . . Outside of the Rothschilds and, perhaps a few Indian maharajas, I doubt there's another person in my position, or in our civilization, who can say that!"

"Why not? Why can't any of the men in Zurich do the same thing?"

The old woman was exasperated. She clasped her hands and brought the clenched fingers to her chin. "For a man whose imagination far exceeds his intelligence,

260

you astonish me. Or is it only fear that provokes your perception of larger things?"

"No question for a question! I want an answer!"

"It's all related, I assure you. The primary reason why the operation in Zurich can not and will not do as I can do is their own fear. Fear of the laws binding their commitments; fear of the investments, investors; fear of extraordinary decisions; fear of the panic which always results from such decisions. Most important of all, fear of financial ruin."

"And none of that bothers you? Is that what you're saying?"

"No commitments bind Scarlatti. Until I die, there is only one voice. I *am* Scarlatti."

"What about the rest of it? The decisions, the panics, the ruin?"

"As always my decisions will be executed with precision and foresight. Panic will be avoided."

"And so will financial ruin, huh? . . . You are the God damnedest, self-confident old lady!"

"Again you fail to understand. At this juncture I anticipate the collapse of Scarlatti as inevitable should I be called. There will be no quarter given."

Matthew Canfield now understood. "I'll be damned."

"I must have vast sums. Amounts inconceivable to you, which can be allocated by a single command. Money which can purchase massive holdings, inflate or depress entire markets. Once that kind of manipulation has been exercised, I doubt that all the capital on earth could put Scarlatti back together. It would never be trusted again."

"Then you'd be finished."

"Irrevocably."

The old woman moved in front of Canfield. She looked at him but not in the manner to which he was accustomed. She might have been a worried grandmother from the dry plains of Kansas asking the preacher if the Lord would allow the rains to come.

"I have no arguments left. Please allow me my last battle. My final gesture, as it were."

"You're asking an awful lot."

"Not when you think of it. If you return, it'll take you a week to reach Washington. Another week to compile everything we've been through. Days before you reach

261

those in government who should listen to you, if you can get them to listen to you at all. By my calculations that would be at least three or four weeks. Do you agree?"

Canfield felt foolish standing in front of Elizabeth. For no reason other than to increase the distance between them, he walked to the center of the room. "God damn it, I don't know what I agree with!"

"Give me four weeks. Just four weeks from today. . . . If I fail we'll do as you wish. . . . More than that I'll come to Washington with you. I'll testify, if need be, in front of one of those committees. I'll do whatever you and your associates think necessary. Further, I'll settle our personal account three times above that agreed upon."

"Suppose you fail?"

"What possible difference can it make to anyone but myself? There's little sympathy in this world for fallen millionaires."

"What about your family then? They can't spend the rest of their lives in some remote lake in Canada?"

"That won't be necessary. Regardless of the larger outcome, I'll destroy my son. I shall expose Ulster Scarlett for what he is. I'll sentence him to death at Zurich."

The field accountant fell silent for a moment and looked at Elizabeth. "Have you considered the fact that you might be killed?"

"I have."

"You'd risk that. . . . Sell out Scarlatti Industries. Destroy everything you've built. Is it worth that to you? Do you hate him that much?"

"Yes. As one hates a disease. Magnified because I'm responsible for its flourishing."

Canfield put his glass down, tempted to pour himself another drink. "That's going a little far."

"I didn't say I invented the disease. I said that I'm responsible for spreading it. Not simply because I provided the money but infinitely more important, because I implanted an idea. An idea which has become warped in the process of maturing."

"I don't believe that. You're no saint, but you don't think like that." He pointed toward the papers on the couch.

The old woman's weary eyes closed.

"There's a little of . . . that in each of us. It's all part of the idea. . . . The twisted idea. My husband and I devoted years to the building of an industrial empire. Since his death, I've fought in the marketplace—doubling, redoubling, adding, building—always acquiring. . . . It's been a stimulating, all-consuming game. . . . I've played it well. And sometime during all those years, my son learned what many observers failed to learn—that it was never the acquisition of profits or material gain that mattered—they were merely the by-products. It was the acquisition of power. . . . I wanted that power because I sincerely believed that I was equipped for the responsibility. The more convinced I became, it had to follow that others were not equipped. . . . The quest for power becomes a personal crusade, I think. The more success one has, the more personal it becomes. Whether he understood it or not, that's what my son saw happening. . . . There may be similarities of purpose, even of motive. But a great gulf divides us—my son and me."

"I'll give you the four weeks. Jesus Christ only knows why. But you still haven't made it clear to me why you want to risk all this. Throw away everything."

"I've tried to. . . . You're slow at times. If I offend, it's because I think you do understand. You're deliberately asking me to spell out an unpleasant reality." She carried her notes to the table by her bedroom door. As the light had grown dim, she turned on the lamp, causing the fringe on the shade to shimmy. She seemed fascinated by the movement. "I imagine that all of *us*—the Bible calls us the rich and mighty—wish to leave this world somewhat different from the way it was before us. As the years go by, this vague, ill-defined instinct becomes really quite important. How many of us have toyed with the phrases of our own obituaries?" She turned from the lamp and looked at the field accountant. "Considering everything we now know, would you care to speculate on my not-too-distant obituary?"

"No deal. That's another question."

"It's a snap, you know. . . . The wealth is taken for granted. Every agonizing decision, every nerve-racking gamble—they become simple, expected accomplishments. Accomplishments more to be scorned than admired because I'm both a woman and a highly competitive speculator. An unattractive combination. . . . One son lost in the Great War. Another rapidly emerging as a pompous incompetent, sought after for every wrong reason, dis-

263

carded and laughed at whenever feasible. And now this. A madman leading or at least a part of a growing band of psychopathic malcontents. . . . This is what I bequeath. What Scarlatti bequeaths, Mr. Canfield. . . . Not a very enviable sum, is it?"

"No, it isn't."

"Consequently, I'll stop at nothing to prevent this final madness . . ." She picked up her notes and went into the bedroom. She closed the door behind her, leaving Canfield in the large sitting room by himself. He thought for a moment that the old woman was on the verge of tears.

CHAPTER 35

The monoplane's flight over the channel had been uneventful—the wind calm, the visibility excellent. It was fortunate for Scarlett that such was the case, for the stinging irritation of his unhealed surgery coupled with the pitch of his fury would have made a difficult trip a disastrous one. He was hardly capable of keeping his mind on the compass bearings and when he first saw the Normandy coast, it looked unfamiliar to him. Yet he had made these very same sightings a dozen times.

He was met at the small airfield outside of Lisieux by the Paris contingent, consisting of two Germans and a French Gascon, whose guttural dialect nearly matched that of his associates.

The three Europeans anticipated that the man—they did not know his name—would instruct them to return to Paris. To await further orders.

The man had other intentions, insisting that they all sit uncomfortably together in the front seat while he occupied the entire space in the back. He ordered the car to Vernon, where two got out and were told to make their own way back to Paris. The driver was to remain.

The driver vaguely protested when Scarlett ordered him to proceed west to Montbéliard, a small town near the Swiss border.

"*Mein Herr!* That's a four-hundred-kilometer trip! It will take ten hours or more on these abysmal roads!"

"Then we should be there by dinner time. And be quiet!"

"It might have been simpler for *mein Herr* to refuel and fly . . ."

"I do not fly when I am tired. Relax. I'll find you some 'seafood' in Montbéliard. Vary your diet, Kircher. It excites the palate."

"Jawohl, mein Herr!" Kircher grinned, knowing the man was really a fine *Oberführer.*

Scarlett reflected. The misfits! One day they'd be rid of the misfits.

Montbéliard was not much more complex than an oversized village. The principal livelihood of its citizens was farm produce, much of which was shipped into Switzerland and Germany. Its currency, as in many towns on the border, was a mixture of francs, marks, and Swiss francs.

Scarlett and his driver reached it a little after nine in the evening. However, except for several stops for petrol and a midafternoon lunch, they had pushed forward with no conversation between them. This quiet acted as a sedative to Scarlett's anxiety. He was able to think without anger, although his anger was ever present. The driver had been right when he had pointed out that a flight from Lisieux to Montbéliard would have been simpler and less arduous, but Scarlett could not risk any explosions of temper brought on by exhaustion.

Sometime that day or evening—the time was left open —he was meeting with the Prussian, the all-important man who could deliver what few others could. He had to be up to that meeting, every brain cell working. He couldn't allow recent problems to distort his concentration. The conference with the Prussian was the culmination of months, years of work. From the first macabre meeting with Gregor Strasser to the conversion of his millions to Swiss capital. He, Heinrich Kroeger, possessed the finances so desperately needed by the National Socialists. His importance to the party was now acknowledged.

The problems. Irritating problems! But he'd made his decisions. He'd have Howard Thornton isolated, perhaps killed. The San Franciscan had betrayed them. If the Stockholm manipulation had been uncovered, it had to

266

be laid at Thornton's feet. They'd used his Swedish contacts and obviously he maneuvered large blocks of securities back into his own hands at the depressed price.

Thornton would be taken care of.

As was the French dandy, Jacques Bertholde.

Thornton and Bertholde! Both misfits! Greedy, stupid misfits!

What had happened to Boothroyd? Obviously killed on the *Calpurnia*. But how? Why? Regardless, he deserved to die! So did his father-in-law. Rawlins' order to kill Elizabeth Scarlatti was stupid! The timing had been insane! Couldn't Rawlins understand that she would have left letters behind, documents? She was far more dangerous dead than alive. At least until she'd been reached— as he had reached her, threatened her precious Scarlattis. Now, she could die! Now it wouldn't matter. And with Bertholde gone, Rawlins gone, and Thornton about to be killed, there'd be no one left who knew who he was. No one! He was Heinrich Kroeger, a leader of the new order!

They pulled up at L'Auberge des Moineaux, a small restaurant with a *buvette* and lodgings for the traveler or for those desiring privacy for other reasons. For Scarlett it was the appointed meeting place.

"Take the car down the road and park it," he told Kircher. "I'll be in one of the rooms. Have dinner. I'll call for you later. . . . I haven't forgotten my promise." Kircher grinned.

Ulster Scarlett got out of the car and stretched. He felt better, his skin bothered him less, and the impending conference filled him with a sense of anticipation. This was the kind of work he should always do! Matters of vast consequences. Matters of power.

He waited until the car was far enough down the street to obscure Kircher's rear-mirror view of him. He then walked back, away from the door, to the cobblestone path and turned into it. Misfits were never to be told anything that wasn't essential to their specific usefulness.

He reached an unlighted door and knocked several times.

The door opened and a moderately tall man with thick, wavy black hair and prominent, dark eyebrows stood in the center of the frame as if guarding an entrance, not welcoming a guest. He was dressed in a Bavarian-cut gray coat and brown knickers. The face was darkly cherubic, the eyes wide and staring. His name was Rudolf Hess.

"Where have you been?" Hess motioned Scarlett to enter and close the door. The room was small; there was a table with chairs around it, a sideboard, and two floor lamps, which gave the room its light. Another man who had been looking out the window, obviously to identify the one outside, nodded to Scarlett. He was a tiny, ugly man with birdlike features, even to the hawknose. He walked with a limp.

"Joseph?" said Scarlett to him. "I didn't expect you here."

Joseph Goebbels looked over at Hess. His knowledge of English was poor. Hess translated Scarlett's words rapidly and Goebbels shrugged his shoulders.

"I asked you where you have been!"

"I had trouble in Lisieux. I couldn't get another plane so I had to drive. It's been a long day so don't aggravate me, please."

"*Ach!* From Lisieux? A long trip. I'll order you some food, but you'll have to be quick. Rheinhart's been waiting since noon."

Scarlett took off his flying jacket and threw it on the sideboard shelf. "How is he?"

Goebbels understood just enough to interrupt. "Rheinhart? . . . Im-pa-tient!" He mispronounced the word, and Scarlett grinned. Goebbels thought to himself that this giant was a horrible-looking creature. The opinion was mutual.

"Never mind the food. Rheinhart's been waiting too long. . . . Where is he?"

"In his room. Number two, down the corridor. He went for a walk this afternoon but he keeps thinking someone will recognize him so he came back in ten minutes. I think he's upset."

"Go get him. . . . And bring back some whiskey." He looked at Goebbels wishing that this unattractive little man would leave. It wasn't good that Goebbels be there while Hess and he talked with the Prussian aristocrat. Goebbels looked like an insignificant Jewish accountant.

But Scarlett knew he could do nothing. Hitler was taken with Goebbels.

Joseph Goebbels seemed to be reading the tall man's thoughts.

"Ich werde dabei sitzen während Sie sprechen." He pulled a chair back to the wall and sat down.

Hess had gone out the corridor door and the two men were in the room alone. Neither spoke.

Four minutes later Hess returned. Following him was an aging, overweight German several inches shorter than Hess, dressed in a black double-breasted suit and a high collar. His face was puffed with excess fat, his white hair cropped short. He stood perfectly erect and in spite of his imposing appearance, Scarlett thought there was something soft about him, not associated with his bulk. He strutted into the room. Hess closed the door and locked it.

"Gentlemen. General Rheinhart." Hess stood at attention.

Goebbels rose from the chair and bowed, clicking his heels.

Rheinhart looked at him unimpressed.

Scarlett noticed Rheinhart's expression. He approached the elderly general and held out his hand.

"Herr General."

Rheinhart faced Scarlett, and although he concealed it well, his reaction to Scarlett's appearance was obvious. The two men shook hands perfunctorily.

"Please sit down, *Herr General.*" Hess was enormously impressed with their company and did not hide the fact. Rheinhart sat in a chair at the end of the table. Scarlett was momentarily upset. He had wanted to sit in that particular chair for it was the commanding position.

Hess asked Rheinhart if he preferred whiskey, gin, or wine. The general waved his hand, refusing.

"Nothing for me, either," added Ulster Scarlett as he sat in the chair to the left of Rheinhart. Hess ignored the tray and also took his seat. Goebbels retreated with his limp to the chair by the wall.

Scarlett spoke. "I apologize for the delay. Unforgivable but, I'm afraid, unavoidable. There was pressing business with our associates in London."

"Your name, please?" Rheinhart interrupted, speaking English with a thick Teutonic accent.

Scarlett looked briefly at Hess before replying. "Kroeger, *Herr General.* Heinrich Kroeger."

Rheinhart did not take his eyes off Scarlett. "I do not

think that is your name, sir. You are not German." His voice was flat.

"My sympathies are German. So much so that Heinrich Kroeger is the name I have chosen to be known by."

Hess interrupted. "Herr Kroeger has been invaluable to us all. Without him we would never have made the progress we have, sir."

"*Amerikaner.* . . . He is the reason we do not speak German?"

"That will be corrected in time," Scarlett said. In fact, he spoke nearly flawless German, but still felt at a disadvantage in the language.

"I am not an American, General. . . ." Scarlett returned Rheinhart's stare and gave no quarter. "I am a citizen of the new order! . . . I have given as much, if not more than anyone else alive or dead to see it come to pass. . . . Please remember that in our conversation."

Rheinhart shrugged. "I'm sure you have your reasons, as I have, for being at this table."

"You may be assured of that." Scarlett relaxed and pulled his chair up.

"Very well, gentlemen, to business. If it is possible, I should like to leave Montbéliard tonight." Rheinhart reached into his jacket pocket and took out a page of folded stationery. "Your party has made certain not inconsequential strides in the Reichstag. After your Munich fiasco, one might even say remarkable progress . . ."

Hess broke in enthusiastically. "We have only begun! From the ignominy of treacherous defeat, Germany will rise! We will be masters of all Europe!"

Rheinhart held the folded paper in his hand and watched Hess. He replied quietly, authoritatively. "To be masters of but Germany itself would be sufficient for us. To be able to defend our country is all we ask."

"That will be the least of your guarantees from us, General." Scarlett's voice rose no higher than Rheinhart's.

"It is the only guarantee we wish. We are not interested in the excesses your Adolf Hitler preaches."

At the mention of Hitler's name, Goebbels sat forward in his chair. He was angered by the fact that he could not comprehend.

"Was gibt's mit Hitler? Was sagen sie über ihn?"

Rheinhart answered Goebbels in his own tongue. "Er ist ein sehr storener geriosse."

"Hitler ist der Weg! Hitler ist die Hoffnung für Deutschland!"

"Vielleicht für Sie."

Ulster Scarlett looked over at Goebbels. The little man's eyes shone with hatred and Scarlett guessed that one day Rheinhart would pay for his words. The general continued as he unfolded the paper.

"The times our nation lives through call for unusual alliances. . . . I have spoken with von Schnitzler and Kindorf. Krupp will not discuss the subject as I'm sure you are aware. . . . German industry is no better off than the army. We are both pawns for the Allied Controls Commission. The Versailles restrictions inflate us one minute, puncture us the next. There is no stability. There is nothing we can count on. We have a common objective, gentlemen. The Versailles treaty."

"It is only one of the objectives. There are others." Scarlett was pleased, but his pleasure was short-lived.

"It is the only objective which has brought me to Montbéliard! As German industry must be allowed to breathe, to export unencumbered, so must the German army be allowed to maintain adequate strength! The limitation of one hundred thousand troops with over sixteen hundred miles of borders to protect is ludicrous! . . . There are promises, always promises—then threats. Nothing to count on. No comprehension. No allowance for necessary growth."

"We were betrayed! We were viciously betrayed in nineteen eighteen and that betrayal continues! Traitors still exist throughout Germany!" Hess wanted more than his life to be counted among the friends of Rheinhart and his officers. Rheinhart understood and was not impressed.

"*Ja.* Ludendorff still holds to that theory. The Meuse-Argonne is not easy for him to live with."

Ulster Scarlett smiled his grotesque smile. "It is for some of us, General Rheinhart."

Rheinhart looked at him. "I will not pursue that with you."

"One day you should. It's why I'm here—in part."

"To repeat, Herr Kroeger. You have your reasons; I have mine. I am not interested in yours but you are forced to be interested in mine." He looked at Hess and then over at the shadowed figure of Joseph Goebbels by the wall.

"I will be blunt, gentlemen. It is, at best, an ill-kept secret. . . . Across the Polish borders in the lands of the Bolshevik are thousands of frustrated German officers. Men without professions in their own country. They train the Russian field commanders! They discipline the Red peasant army. . . . Why? Some for simple employment. Others justify themselves because a few Russian factories smuggle us cannon, armaments prohibited by the Allied Commission. . . . I do not like this state of affairs, gentlemen. I do not trust the Russians. . . . Weimar is ineffectual. Ebert couldn't face the truth. Hindenburg is worse! He lives in a monarchial past. The politicians must be made to face the Versailles issue! We must be liberated from within!"

Rudolf Hess placed both his hands, palms down, on the table.

"You have the word of Adolf Hitler and those of us in this room that the first item on the political agenda of the National Socialist German Workers party is the unconditional repudiation of the Versailles treaty and its restrictions!"

"I assume that. My concern is whether you are capable of effectively uniting the diverse political camps of the Reichstag. I will not deny that you have appeal. Far more than the others. . . . The question we would like answered, as I'm sure would our equals in commerce, Do you have the staying power? Can you last? Will you last? . . . You were outlawed a few years ago. We can not afford to be allied with a political comet which burns itself out."

Ulster Scarlett rose from his chair and looked down at the aging German general. "What would you say if I told you that we have financial resources surpassing those of any political organization in Europe? Possibly the Western hemisphere."

"I would say that you exaggerate."

"Or if I told you that we possess territory—land—sufficiently large enough to train thousands upon thousands of elite troops beyond the scrutiny of the Versailles inspection teams."

"You would have to prove all this to me."

"I can do just that."

Rheinhart rose and faced Heinrich Kroeger.

"If you speak the truth . . . you will have the support of the imperial German generals."

CHAPTER 36

Janet Saxon Scarlett, eyes still shut, reached under the sheets for the body of her lover. He was not there, so she opened her eyes and raised her head, and the room spun around. Her lids were heavy and her stomach hurt. She was still exhausted, still a bit drunk.

Matthew Canfield sat at the writing desk in his undershorts. His elbows were on the desk, his chin cupped in his hands. He was staring down at a paper in front of him.

Janet watched him, aware that he was oblivious to her. She rolled onto her side so that she could observe him.

He was not an ordinary man, she thought, but on the other hand neither was he particularly outstanding, except that she loved him. What, she wondered, did she find so attractive about him? He was not like the men from her world—even her recently expanded world. Most of the men she knew were quick, polished, overly groomed and only concerned with appearances. But Matthew Canfield could not fit into this world. His quickness was an intuitive alertness not related to the graces. And in other respects there was a degree of awkwardness; what confidence he had was born of considered judgment, not simply born.

Others, too, were far more handsome, although he could be placed in the category of "good-looking" in a rough-hewn way. . . . That was it, she mused; he gave the appearance both in actions and in looks of secure independence, but his private behavior was different. In private he was extraordinarily gentle, almost weak. . . .

She wondered if he was weak. She knew he was deeply upset and she suspected that Elizabeth had given him money to do her bidding. . . . He didn't really know how to be at ease with money. She'd learned that during their two weeks together in New York. He'd obviously been told to spend without worrying about sums in order to establish their relationship—he'd suggested as much— and they'd both laughed because what they were doing on government funds was, in essence, spelling out the truth. . . . She would have been happy to pay the freight herself. She'd paid for others, and none were as dear to her as Matthew Canfield. No one would ever be so dear to her. He didn't belong to her world. He preferred a simpler, less cosmopolitan one, she thought. But Janet Saxon Scarlett knew she would adjust if it meant keeping him.

Perhaps, when it was all over, if it was ever to be all over, they would find a way. There had to be a way for this good, rough, gentle young man who was a better man than any she had ever known before. She loved him very much and she found herself concerned for him. That was remarkable for Janet Saxon Scarlett.

When she had returned the night before at seven o'clock, escorted by Derek's man Ferguson, she found Canfield alone in Elizabeth's sitting room. He'd seemed tense, edgy, even angry, and she didn't know why. He'd made feeble excuses for his temper and finally, without warning, he had ushered her out of the suite and out of the hotel.

They had eaten at a small restaurant in Soho. They both drank heavily, his fear infecting her. Yet he would not tell her what bothered him.

They'd returned to his room with a bottle of whiskey. Alone, in the quiet, they had made love. Janet knew he was a man holding on to some mythical rope, afraid to let go for fear of plunging downward.

As she watched him at the writing desk, she also in-stinctively knew the truth—the unwanted truth—which she had suspected since that terrible moment more than a day ago when he had said to her, "Janet. I'm afraid we've had a visitor."

That visitor had been her husband.

She raised herself on her elbow. "Matthew?"

"Oh. . . . Morning, friend."

"Matthew . . . are you afraid of him?"

Canfield's stomach muscles grew taut.

She knew.

But, of course, she knew.

"I don't think I will be . . . when I find him."

"That's always the way, isn't it? We're afraid of someone or something we don't know or can't find." Janet's eyes began to ache.

"That's what Elizabeth said."

She sat up, pulling the blanket over her shoulders, and leaned back against the headrest. She felt cold, and the ache in her eyes intensified. "Did she tell you?"

"Finally. . . . She didn't want to. I didn't give her an alternative. . . . She had to."

Janet stared straight ahead, at nothing. "I knew it," she said quietly. "I'm frightened."

"Of course you are. . . . But you don't have to be. He can't touch you."

"Why are you so sure? I don't think you were so sure last night." She was not aware of it, but her hands began to shake.

"No, I wasn't. . . . But only because he existed at all. . . . The unholy specter alive and breathing. . . . No matter how much we expected it, it was a shock. But the sun's up now." He reached for his pencil and made a note on the paper.

Suddenly Janet Scarlett flung herself down across the bed. "Oh, God, God, God!" Her head was buried in the pillow.

At first Canfield did not recognize the appeal in her voice, for she did not scream or shout out and his concentration was on his notes. Her muffled cry was one of agony, not desperation.

"Jan," he began casually. "Janet!" The field accountant threw down his pencil and rushed to the bed. "Janet! . . . Honey, please don't. Don't, please. Janet!" He cradled her in his arms, doing his best to comfort her. And then slowly his attention was drawn to her eyes.

The tears were streaming down her face uncontrollably, yet she did not cry out but only gasped for breath. What disturbed him were her eyes.

Instead of blinking from the flow of tears, they remained wide open, as if she were in a trance. A trance of horror.

276

He spoke her name over and over again.

"Janet. Janet. Janet. Janet. . . ."

She did not respond. She seemed to sink deeper and deeper into the fear which controlled her. She began to moan, at first quietly, then louder and louder.

"Janet! Stop it! Stop it! Darling, stop it!"

She did not hear him.

Instead she tried to push him away, to disengage herself from him. Her naked body writhed on the bed; her arms lashed out, striking him.

He tightened his grip, afraid for a moment that he might hurt her.

Suddenly she stopped. She threw her head back and spoke in a choked voice he had not heard before.

"God damn you to hell! . . . God damn you to hell!!"

She drew out the word "hell" until it became a scream.

Her legs spread slowly, reluctantly, apart on top of the sheet.

In that same choked, guttural voice she whispered, "You pig! Pig! Pig! Pig!"

Canfield watched her in dread. She was assuming a position of sexual intercourse, steeling herself against the terror which had enveloped her and which would progressively worsen.

"Janet, for God's sake, Jan. . . . Don't! Don't! No one's going to touch you! Please, darling!"

The girl laughed horridly, hysterically.

"You're the *card*, Ulster! You're the God damn jack of . . . jack of . . ." She quickly crossed her legs, one emphatically on top of the other, and brought her hands up to cover her breasts. "Leave me alone, Ulster! Please, dear God, Ulster! Leave me alone! . . . You're going to leave me alone?" She curled herself up like an infant and began to sob.

Canfield reached down to the foot of the bed and pulled the blanket over Janet.

He was afraid.

That she could suddenly, without warning, reduce herself to Scarlett's unwilling whore was frightening.

But it was there, and he had to accept it.

She needed help. Perhaps far more help than he could provide. He gently stroked her hair and lay down beside her.

Her sobs evened off into deep breathing as she closed

her eyes. He hoped she was sleeping but he could not be sure. At any rate, he would let her rest. It would give him the time to figure out a way to tell her everything she had to know.

The next four weeks would be terrible for her.

For the three of them.

But now there was an element which had been absent before, and Canfield was grateful for it. He knew he shouldn't have been, for it was against every professional instinct he had.

It was hate. His own personal hate.

Ulster Stewart Scarlett was no longer the quarry in an international hunt. He was now the man Matthew Canfield intended to kill.

CHAPTER 37

Ulster Scarlett watched the flushed, angry face of Adolf Hitler. He realized that in spite of his fury, Hitler had a capacity for control that was nothing short of miraculous. But then the man himself was a miracle. A historic man-miracle who would take them into the finest world imaginable on earth.

The three of them—Hess, Goebbels, and Kroeger—had driven through the night from Montbéliard to Munich, where Hitler and Ludendorff awaited a report of their meeting with Rheinhart. If the conference had gone well, Ludendorff's plan was to be set in motion. Each faction of the Reichstag possessing any serious following would be alerted that a coalition was imminent. Promises would be made, threats implied. As the Reichstag's sole member of the National Socialist party and its candidate for president the previous year, Ludendorff would be listened to. He was the soldier-thinker. He was slowly regaining the stature he had thrown away in defeat at the Meuse-Argonne.

Simultaneously and in twelve different cities anti-Versailles demonstrations would be staged, where the police had been paid handsomely not to interfere. Hitler was to travel to Oldenburg, in the center of the northwest Prussian territory, where the great military estates were slowly going to seed—massive remembrances of past glories. A huge rally would be mounted and it was planned that Rheinhart himself would make an appearance.

Rheinhart was enough to give credence to the party's military support. It was more than enough; it would be a momentary climax fitting their current progress. Rheinhart's recognition of Hitler would leave no room for doubt as to where the generals were leaning.

Ludendorff looked upon the act as a political necessity. Hitler looked upon it as a political coup. The Austrian lance corporal was never unmoved by the anticipation of Junker approval. He knew that it was his destiny to have it—demand it!—but nonetheless it filled him with pride, which was why he was furious now.

The ugly little Goebbels had just finished telling Ludendorff and Hitler of Rheinhart's remarks about the Austrian.

In the large rented office overlooking the Sedlingerstrasse, Hitler gripped the arms of his chair and pushed himself up. He stood for a moment glaring at Goebbels, but the thin cripple knew that Hitler's anger was not directed at him, only at his news.

"Fettes Schwein! Wir werden ihn zu seinen Landsort zurück senden! Lass ihm zu seinen Kühen zurück gehen!"

Scarlett was leaning against the wall next to Hess. As usual when the conversations taking place were in German, the willing Hess turned to Ulster and spoke quietly.

"He's very upset. Rheinhart may be an obstacle."

"Why?"

"Goebbels doesn't believe Rheinhart will openly support the movement. He wants all the advantages without getting his tunic dirty!"

"Rheinhart said he would. In Montbéliard he said he would! What's Goebbels talking about?" Scarlett found it necessary to watch himself. He really didn't like Goebbels.

"He's just told them what Rheinhart said about Hitler. Remember?" Hess whispered with his hand cupped in front of his mouth.

Scarlett raised his voice. "They should tell Rheinhart —no Hitler, no marbles! Let him go shag!"

"Was ist los?" Hitler glowered at Hess and Scarlett. "Was sagt er, Hess?"

"Lass Rheinhart zum Teufel gehen!"

Ludendorff laughed out of the corner of his mouth. "Das ist naiv!"

"Tell Rheinhart to do as we say or he's out! No troops! No weapons! No uniforms! No one to pay for it all! I don't pay! No place to train them without the inspection teams on his back! He'll listen!" Scarlett ignored Hess, who was rapidly translating everything the former said.

Ludendorff broke in on Hess as he finished interpreting.

"Man kann einen Mann wie Rheinhart nicht drohen. Er ist ein einflussreich Preusse!"

Hess turned to Ulster Scarlett. "Herr Ludendorff says that Rheinhart will not be threatened. He is a Junker."

"He's a frightened, overstuffed tin soldier, that's what he is! He's running scared. He's got the Russian shakes! He needs us and he knows it!"

Hess repeated Scarlett's remarks. Ludendorff snapped his fingers in the Heidelberg fashion, as if mocking a ridiculous statement.

"Don't laugh at me! I talked with him, not you! It's my money! Not yours!"

Hess did not need to translate. Ludendorff rose from his chair, as angry as Scarlett.

"Sag dem Amerikaner dass sein Gelt gibt ihm noch lange nicht das Recht uns Befehle zu geben."

Hess hesitated. "Herr Ludendorff does not believe that your financial contributions . . . as welcome as they are . . ."

"You don't have to finish! Tell him to go shag, too! He's acting just the way Rheinhart expects!" Scarlett, who had not moved from his position against the wall, pushed himself away and sprang forward effortlessly to his full height.

For a moment the aging, intellectual Ludendorff was physically afraid. He did not trust the motives of this neurotic American. Ludendorff had often suggested to Hitler and the others that this man who called himself Heinrich Kroeger was a dangerous addition to their working circle. But he had been consistently overruled because Kroeger not only possessed what appeared to be unlimited financial resources, but seemed to be able to enlist the support, or at least the interest, of incredibly influential men.

Still, he did not trust him.

Essentially because Ludendorff was convinced that this Kroeger was stupid.

"May I remind you, Herr Kroeger, that I possess a . . . working knowledge of the English language!"

"Then why don't you use it?"

"I do not feel it is—how is it said?—entirely necessary."

"It is now, damn it!"

Adolf Hitler suddenly clapped his hands twice, signifying an order of silence. It was an irksome gesture to Ludendorff, but his respect for Hitler's talents—which bordered on awe—made him accept such aggravations.

"Halt! Beide!"

Hitler stepped away from the table, turning his back on all of them. He stretched his arms, then clasped his hands behind him. He said nothing for several moments, yet no one interrupted his silence. For it was his silence, and Goebbels, whose love of theatrics was paramount, watched with satisfaction the effect Hitler was having on the others.

Ludendorff, on the other hand, played the game but remained annoyed. The Hitler he knew well was capable of poor judgment. Great vision, perhaps, but often slipshod in decisions of everyday practical realities. It was unfortunate that he also resented debate on such matters. It made it difficult for Rosenberg and himself, who knew they were the true architects of the new order. Ludendorff hoped that this particular instance was not going to be another case when Hitler overrode his sound analysis. Like himself, Rheinhart was a Junker, proud and unbending. He had to be handled artfully. Who could know this better than the former field marshal of the imperial army who was forced to maintain his dignity in the midst of tragic defeat. Ludendorff understood.

Adolf Hitler spoke quietly. "Wir werden wie Herr Kroeger sagt tun."

"Herr Hitler agrees with you, Kroeger!" Hess touched Scarlett's sleeve, delighted. He was forever being condescended to by the arrogant Ludendorff, and this was not a small victory over him. Rheinhart was a prize. If Kroeger was correct, Ludendorff would look foolish.

"Warum? Es ist sehr gefährlich."

Ludendorff had to argue although he knew at once it was no use.

"Sie sind zu Vorsichtig die unruhigen Zieten, Ludendorff. Kroeger hat recht. Aber wir werden einen Schritt weiter gehen."

Rudolf Hess expanded his chest. He looked pointedly at Ludendorff and Goebbels as he nudged Scarlett with his elbow.

"Herr Hitler says that our friend Ludendorff is mistakenly cautious. He is right. Ludendorff is always cautious. . . . But Herr Hitler wishes to elaborate on your suggestion. . . ."

Adolf Hitler began speaking slowly but firmly, lending a finality to each German phrase. As he continued he watched with satisfaction the faces of those listening. When he reached the end of his diatribe he spat out the words.

"Da ist Montbéliard!"

For each it was a different evaluation with an underlying common denominator—the man was a genius.

For Hess, Hitler's conclusion was equated with a startling flash of political insight.

For Goebbels, Hitler had once again demonstrated' his ability to capitalize on an opponent's fundamental weakness.

For Ludendorff, the Austrian had taken a mediocre idea, added his own boldness, and emerged with a piece of brilliant strategy.

Heinrich Kroeger—Scarlett—spoke. "What did he say, Hess?"

But it was not Rudolf Hess who answered. It was Erich Ludendorff, who did not take his eyes off Adolf Hitler. "Herr Hitler has just . . . solidified the military for us, Kroeger. In a brief statement he has won us the reluctant Prussians."

"What?"

Rudolf Hess turned to Scarlett. "General Rheinhart will be told that unless he does as we demand, the Versailles officials will be informed that he is secretly negotiating illegal procurements. It is the truth. Montbéliard can not be denied!"

"He is a Junker!" Ludendorff added. "Montbéliard is the key because it is the truth! Rheinhart can not disavow what he has done! Even if he should be tempted, there are too many who know—von Schnitzler, Kindorf. Even Krupp! Rheinhart has broken his word." And then Ludendorff laughed harshly. "The holy word of a Junker!"

Hitler smiled briefly and spoke rapidly to Hess, gesturing his head toward Ulster Scarlett.

"*Der Führer* admires and appreciates you, Heinrich," said Hess. "He asks what of our friends in Zurich?"

"Everything is proceeding on schedule. Several errors

have been corrected. We may lose one of the remaining thirteen. . . . It's no loss; he's a thief."

"Who is that?" Ludendorff exercised his very acceptable working knowledge of English.

"Thornton."

"What of his land?" Ludendorff again.

Scarlett, now Kroeger, looked at the academic Ludendorff, the military intellectual, with the contempt born of money. "I intend to buy it."

"Is that not dangerous?" Hess was watching Ludendorff, who had quietly translated what Scarlett said to Hitler. Both men showed signs of alarm.

"Not at all."

"Perhaps not to you personally, my dashing young friend." Ludendorff's tone was blandly incriminating. "Who knows where your sympathies will lie six months from now?"

"I resent that!"

"You're not a German. This isn't your battle."

"I don't have to be a German! And I don't have to justify myself to you! . . . You want me out? Fine! I'm out! . . . And with me go a dozen of the richest men on earth. . . . Oil! Steel! Industry! Steamship lines!"

Hess no longer tried to be tactful. He looked toward Hitler, throwing his arms up in exasperation.

Hitler did not need to be prompted for he knew exactly what to do. He crossed rapidly to the former general of the imperial German army and struck the old man lightly across the mouth with the back of his hand. It was an insulting action—the very lightness of the blow was akin to disciplining a small child. The two men exchanged words and Scarlett knew the old Ludendorff had been severely, cruelly rebuked.

"My motives seem to be questioned, Herr Kroeger. I was merely—how is it said?—testing you." He lifted his hand to his mouth. The memory of Hitler's insult was difficult for him. He struggled to suppress it.

"I was quite sincere, however, about the Swiss property. Your . . . work with us has been most impressive and undoubtedly noticed by many. Should the purchase be traced through you to the party, it might—how is it said—make useless the whole arrangement."

Ulster Scarlett answered with confident nonchalance.

He enjoyed putting the thinkers in their place. "No problems. . . . The transaction will be made in Madrid."

"Madrid?" Joseph Goebbels did not fully understand what Scarlett said, but the city of Madrid had a special connotation for him.

The four Germans looked at each other. None was pleased.

"Why is . . . Madrid so safe?" Hess was concerned that his friend had done something rash.

"Papal attaché. Very Catholic. Very much beyond reproach. Satisfied?"

Hess automatically spoke Scarlett's words in German.

Hitler smiled while Ludendorff snapped his fingers, now in sincere applause.

"How is this accomplished?"

"Very simple. Alfonso's court will be told that the land is being bought with White Russian money. Unless it's done quickly, the capital could be manipulated back into Moscow. The Vatican is sympathetic. So is Rivera. This won't be the first time such an arrangement's been made."

Hess explained to Adolf Hitler as Joseph Goebbels listened intently.

"My congratulations, Herr Kroeger. Be . . . cautious." Ludendorff was impressed.

Suddenly Goebbels began chattering, waving his hands in exaggerated gestures. The Germans all laughed and Scarlett wasn't sure whether the unattractive little fascist was making fun of him or not.

Hess translated. "Herr Goebbels says that if you tell the Vatican you can keep four hungry Communists from having a loaf of bread, the pope will let you repaint the Sistine Chapel!"

Hitler broke in on the laughter. "Was hörst du aus Zürich?"

Ludendorff turned to Scarlett. "You were saying about our friends in Switzerland?"

"On schedule. By the end of next month . . . five weeks say, the buildings will be completed. . . . Here, I'll show you."

Kroeger approached the table, taking a folded map from his jacket pocket. He spread it on the table. "This heavy blue line is the perimeter of the adjacent properties. This section . . . in the south is Thornton's. We extend west to here, north here to Baden, east to the outskirts of Pfäffikon. Approximately every mile and a quarter is a structure which can house fifty troops—eighteen in all. Nine hundred men. The water lines are down, the foundations are in. Each structure looks like a barn or a granary. You couldn't tell the difference unless you were inside."

"Excellent!" Ludendorff inserted a monocle in his left eye and looked closely at the map. Hess translated for a curious Hitler and a skeptical Goebbels. "This . . . perimeter between the . . . *Keserne* . . . barracks . . . is it fenced?"

"Twelve feet high. Wired by generators in each building for alarms. Patrols will be maintained twenty-four hours a day. Men and dogs. . . . I've paid for everything."

"Excellent. Excellent!"

Scarlett looked over at Hitler. He knew that Ludendorff's approval was never granted easily and in spite of their unpleasant encounter a few moments ago, Scarlett also realized that Hitler valued Ludendorff's opinion, perhaps above all others. It seemed to Scarlett that Hitler's penetrating stare, which was now directed at him, was a look of admiration. Kroeger controlled his own elation and quickly continued.

"The indoctrinations will be concentrated—each lasting four weeks with several days between sessions for transportation and housing. Each contingent has nine hundred men. . . . At the end of one year . . ."

Hess interrupted. "Prachtvoll! At the end of a year ten thousand trained men!"

"Ready to spread throughout the country as military units. Trained for insurgency!" Scarlett was fairly bursting with energy.

"No longer rabble, but the basis of an elite corps! Perhaps the elite corps itself!" Ludendorff himself was catching the younger man's enthusiasm. "Our own private army!"

"That's it! A skilled machine capable of moving fast, hitting hard, and regrouping swiftly and secretly."

As Kroeger spoke, it was Ludendorff who now turned his phrases into the German language for the benefit of Hitler and Goebbels.

But Goebbels was bothered. He spoke quietly, as if

this Kroeger might somehow catch the shaded meaning of his observations. Goebbels was still suspicious. This huge, strange American was too glib, too casual in spite of his fervor. In spite of the power of his money. Adolf Hitler nodded his head in agreement.

Hess spoke. "Quite rightly, Heinrich, Herr Goebbels is concerned. These men in Zurich, their demands are so . . . nebulous."

"Not to them they're not. They're very specific. These men are businessmen. . . . And besides, they're sympathetic."

"Kroeger is correct." Ludendorff looked at Ulster Scarlett, knowing that Hess would use the German tongue for the others. He was thinking as he spoke, not wishing Kroeger to have any time to formulate answers or comments. This Kroeger, although he did not speak their language fluently, understood far more than he let on, Ludendorff believed. "We have gone so far as to sign agreements, have we not? . . . Pacts, if you like, that with the emergence of our power on the political scene in Germany, our friends in Zurich will be given . . . certain priorities. . . . Economic priorities. . . . We are committed, are we not." There was no hint of a question in Ludendorff's last remark.

"That's right."

"What happens, Herr Kroeger, if we do not honor those commitments?"

Ulster Scarlett paused, returning Ludendorff's now questioning gaze. "They'd yell like sons of bitches and try to ruin us."

"How?"

"Any means they could, Ludendorff. And their means are considerable."

"Does that bother you?"

"Only if they succeeded. . . . Thornton's not the only one. They're all thieves. The difference is that the rest of them are smart. They know we're right. We'll win! Everyone likes to do business with the winner! They know what they're doing. They want to work with us!"

"I believe you're convinced."

"You're damn right I am. Between us we'll run things our way. The right way! The way we want to. We'll get rid of the garbage! The Jews, the Reds, the stinking little bourgeois bootlickers!"

Ludendorff watched the confident American closely. He was right, Kroeger was stupid. His description of the lesser breeds was emotional, not based upon the sound principles of racial integrity. Hitler and Goebbels had similar blind.spots but theirs was a pyramid logic in spite of themselves—they knew because they saw; they had studied as had Rosenberg and himself. This Kroeger had a child's mentality. He was actually a bigot.

"There is much in what you say. Everyone who thinks will support his own kind. . . . Do business with his own kind." Ludendorff would watch Heinrich Kroeger's actions carefully. Such a high-strung man could do great damage. He was a fever-ridden clown.

But then, their court had need of such a jester. And his money.

As usual, Hitler was right. They dare not lose him now.

"I'm going to Madrid in the morning. I've already sent out the orders concerning Thornton. The whole business shouldn't take any longer than two or three weeks, and then I'll be in Zurich."

Hess told Hitler and Goebbels what Kroeger had said. *Der Führer* barked out a sharp question.

"Where can you be reached in Zurich?" interpreted Ludendorff. "Your schedule, if it proceeds as it has, will require communication with you."

Heinrich Kroeger paused before giving his answer. He knew the question would be asked again. It was always asked whenever he went to Zurich. Yet he was always evasive. He realized that part of his mystique, his charisma within the party, was due to his obscuring the specific individuals or firms with which he did business. In the past he had left a single phone number or a post office box, or perhaps even the name of one of the fourteen men in Zurich with instructions to ask him for a code name.

Never direct and open.

They did not understand that identities, addresses, phone numbers were unimportant. Only the ability to deliver was essential.

Zurich understood.

These Goliaths of the world's great fortunes understood. The international financiers with their tangled labyrinths of manipulations understood perfectly.

288

He had delivered.

Their agreements with Germany's emerging new order insured markets and controls beyond belief.

And none cared who he was or where he came from.

But now, at this moment, Ulster Stewart Scarlett realized that these titans of the new order needed to be reminded of Heinrich Kroeger's importance.

He would tell them the truth.

He would say the name of the one man in Germany sought by all who drove for power. The one man who refused to talk, refused to be involved, refused to meet with any faction.

The only man in Germany who lived behind a wall of total secrecy. Complete political isolation.

The most feared and revered man in all Europe.

"I'll be with Krupp. Essen will know where to reach us."

CHAPTER 38

Elizabeth Scarlatti sat up in her bed. A card table had been placed at her side, and papers were strewn all over the immediate vicinity—the bed, the table, the entire walking area of the room. Some were in neat piles, others scattered. Some were clipped together and labeled by index cards; others discarded, ready for the trash basket.

It was four o'clock in the afternoon and she had left her room only once. That was to let in Janet and Matthew. She noted that they looked terrible; exhausted, ill, perhaps. She knew what had happened. The pressure had become too much for the government man. He had to break out, get relief. Now that he had, he would be better prepared for her proposal.

Elizabeth gave a final look at the pages she held in her hand.

So this was it! The picture was now clear, the background filled in.

She had said that the men of Zurich might have created an extraordinary strategy. She knew now that they had.

Had it not been so grotesquely evil she might have agreed with her son. She might have been proud of his part in it. Under the circumstances, she could only be terrified.

She wondered if Matthew Canfield would understand. No matter. It was now time for Zurich.

She got up from the bed, taking the pages with her, and went to the door.

Janet was at the desk writing letters. Canfield sat in a chair nervously reading a newspaper. Both were startled when Elizabeth walked into the room.

"Do you have any knowledge of the Versailles treaty?" she asked him. "The restrictions, the reparations payments?"

"As much as the average guy, I guess."

"Are you aware of the Dawes Plan? That wholly imperfect document?"

"I thought it made the reparations livable with."

"Only temporarily. It was grasped at by the politicians who needed temporary solutions. Economically it's a disaster. Nowhere does it give a final figure. If, at any time, a final figure is given, German industry—who pays the bill—might collapse."

"What's your point?"

"Bear with me a minute. I want you to understand. . . . Do you realize who executes the Versailles treaty? Do you know whose voice is strongest in the decisions under the Dawes Plan? Who ultimately controls the internal economics of Germany?"

Canfield put the newspaper down on the floor. "Yes. Some committee."

"The Allied Controls Commission."

"What are you driving at?" Canfield got out of his chair.

"Just what you're beginning to suspect. Three of the Zurich contingent are members of the Allied Controls Commission. The Versailles treaty is being executed by these men.- Working together, the men of Zurich can literally manipulate the German economy. Leading industrialists from the major powers to the north, the west, and the southwest. Completed by the most powerful financiers within Germany itself. A wolf pack. They'll make sure that the forces at work in Germany remain on a collision course. When the explosion takes place— as surely it must—they'll be there to pick up the pieces. To complete this . . . master plan, they need only a political base of operation. Believe me when I tell you they've found it. With Adolf Hitler and his Nazis. . . . With my son, Ulster Stewart Scarlett."

"My God!" Canfield spoke quietly, staring at Elizabeth. He had not fully understood the details of her recital, but he recognized the implications.

"It's time for Switzerland, Mr. Canfield."

He would ask his questions on the way.

CHAPTER 39

The cablegrams were all in English and except for the names and addresses of the designees, the words were identical. Each was sent to the company or corporation in which the person specified held the highest position. Time zones were respected, each cable was to arrive at its destination at twelve noon, on Monday, and each was to be hand-delivered to the individual addressee upon a signed receipt of acceptance.

Elizabeth Scarlatt wanted those illustrious corporations identified in writing. She wanted those receiving her cables to know that this was, above all, business.

Each cable read as follows:

> THROUGH THE LATE MARQUIS DE BERTHOLDE THE
> SCARLATTI INDUSTRIES THROUGH THE UNDERSIGNED
> ALONE HAVE BEEN INFORMED OF YOUR CONSOLIDA-
> TION STOP AS THE SINGLE SPOKESMAN FOR SCARLATTI
> THE UNDERSIGNED BELIEVES THERE EXIST AREAS OF
> MUTUAL INTEREST STOP THE ASSETS OF SCARLATTI
> COULD BE AT YOUR DISPOSAL UNDER PROPER CIR-
> CUMSTANCES STOP THE UNDERSIGNED WILL ARRIVE IN
> ZURICH TWO WEEKS HENCE ON THE EVENING OF NO-
> VEMBER 3 AT THE HOUR OF NINE O'CLOCK STOP THE
> CONFERENCE WILL TAKE PLACE AT FALKE HAUS
> > ELIZABETH WYCKHAM SCARLATTI

There were thirteen reactions, all separate, in many different languages, but each with a single ingredient common to all.

There was a fourteenth reaction, and it took place in the suite of rooms reserved for Heinrich Kroeger at Madrid's Hotel Emperador. The reaction was fury.

"I won't have it! It can't take place! They're all dead! Dead! Dead! Dead! She was warned! They're dead! Every God damned one of them! Dead. My orders go out tonight! Now!"

Charles Pennington, sent by Ludendorff to act as Kroeger's bodyguard, stood across the room looking out the balcony at the reddish, fan-shaped rays of the Spanish sun.

"Glorious! Simply glorious! . . . Don't be an ass." He didn't like to look at Heinrich Kroeger. In repose that tissued, patched face was bad enough. Angered, it was repulsive. It was now crimson with rage.

"Don't you tell me . . ."

"Oh, stop it!" Pennington saw that Kroeger continued to crush in his fist the telegram from Howard Thornton, which spelled out the Scarlatti conference in Zurich. "What bloody difference does it make to you? To any of us?" Pennington had opened the envelope and read the message because, as he told Kroeger, he had no idea when Kroeger would return from his meeting with the papal attaché. It might have been urgent. What he did not tell Kroeger was that Ludendorff had instructed him to screen all letters, phone calls—whatever—received by this animal. It was a pleasure.

"We don't want anyone else involved. We can't have anyone else! We can't! Zurich will panic! They'll run out on us!"

"They've all got the cables. If Zurich's going to run, you won't stop them now. Besides, this Scarlatti's the cat's whiskers if it's the same one I'm thinking of. She has millions. . . . Damned fortunate for us she wants to come in. I didn't think much of Bertholde—probably less than you did, smelly French Jew—but if he pulled this off, I doff my hat. Anyway, I repeat, what's it to you?"

Heinrich Kroeger glared at the stylish, effeminate Englishman who pulled at his cuffs, making sure they fell just below his jacket sleeve. The red and black cuff links were surrounded by the soft linen of his light blue shirt. Kroeger knew this appearance was deceptive. Like the social Boothroyd, Pennington was a killer who took emotional sustenance from his work. He also was held in high esteem by Hitler, even more so by Joseph Goebbels. Nevertheless, Kroeger had made up his mind. He could not risk it!

"This meeting won't take place! She'll be killed. I'll have her killed."

"Then I'll have to remind you that such a decision must be multilateral. You can not make it yourself. . . . And I don't think you'll find anyone else consenting."

"You're not here to tell me what to do!"

"Oh, but I am. . . . My instructions come from Ludendorff. And, of course, he knows about your message from Thornton. I wired him several hours ago." Pennington casually looked at his wristwatch. "I'm going out for dinner. . . . Frankly, I'd prefer eating alone but if you insist upon joining me, I'll tolerate your company."

"You little prick! I could break your God damn neck!"

Pennington bristled. He knew that Kroeger was unarmed, his revolver lay on the bureau in his bedroom, and the temptation was there. He could kill him, use the telegram as proof, and say that Kroeger had disobeyed. But then there were the Spanish authorities and a hasty retreat. And Kroeger did have a job to do. Strange that it involved Howard Thornton so completely.

"That's possible, of course. But then we could, no doubt, do each other in any number of ways, couldn't we?" Pennington withdrew a thin pistol from his chest holster. "For instance, I might fire a single bullet directly into your mouth right now. . . . But I wouldn't do it in spite of your provocation because the order is larger than either of us. I'd have to answer for my action—no doubt be executed for it. You'll be shot if you take matters into your own hands."

"You don't know this Scarlatti, Pennington. I do!"

How could she have known about Bertholde? What could she have learned from him?

"Of course, you're old friends!" The Englishman put away his pistol and laughed.

How! How? She wouldn't dare challenge him! The only thing she valued was the Scarlatti name, its heritage, its future. She knew beyond a doubt that he would stamp it out! How! Why?

"That woman can't be trusted! She can't be trusted!"

Charles Pennington pulled down his blazer so the

shoulders fell correctly, the jacket cloth concealing the slight bulge of his holster. He walked to the door in calm anticipation of *chorizo*. "Really, Heinrich? . . . Can *any* of us?"

The Englishman closed the door leaving only a faint aroma of Yardley's.

Heinrich Kroeger uncrumpled the telegram in his palm.

Thornton was panic-stricken. Each of the remaining thirteen in Zurich had received identical cablegrams from Elizabeth Scarlatti. But none save Thornton knew who he was.

Kroeger had to move quickly. Pennington hadn't lied. He would be shot if he ordered Elizabeth Scarlatti's death. That did not, however, preclude such an order after Zurich. Indeed, after Zurich it would be mandatory.

But first the Thornton land. He had instructed Thornton for his own safety to let it go. The frightened Thornton had not argued, and the idiot attaché was playing right into his hands. For the glory of Jesus and another blow against atheistic communism.

The money and title would be transferred within a week. Thornton was sending his attorney from San Francisco to conclude the negotiations by signature.

As soon as the land was his, Heinrich Kroeger would issue a warrant for death that no one could deny.

And when that misfit life was snuffed out, Heinrich Kroeger was free. He would be a true light of the new order. None would know that Ulster Scarlett existed.

Except one.

He would confront her at Zurich.

He would kill her at Zurich.

CHAPTER 40

The embassy limousine climbed the small hill to the front of the Georgian house in Fairfax, Virginia. It was the elegant residence of Erich Rheinhart, attaché of the Weimar Republic, nephew of the sole imperial general who had thrown his support to the German radical movement given the name of Nazi, by philosophy, a full-fledged Nazi himself.

The well-tailored man with the waxed moustache got out of the back seat and stepped onto the driveway. He looked up at the ornate facade.

"A lovely home."

"I'm pleased, Poole," said Rheinhart, smiling at the man from Bertholde et Fils.

The two men walked into the house and Erich Rheinhart led his guest to a book-lined study off the living room. He indicated a chair for Poole and went to a cabinet, taking out two glasses and a bottle of whiskey.

"To business. You come three thousand miles at a loathsome time of year for ocean travel. You tell me I am the object of your visit. I'm flattered, of course, but what can . . ."

"Who ordered Bertholde's death?" Poole said harshly.

Erich Rheinhart was astonished. He hunched his padded shoulders, placed his glass on the small table, and extended his hands, palms up. He spoke slowly, in consternation.

"My dear man, why do you think it concerns me? I mean—in all candor—you are either deluded as to my influence or you need a long rest."

"Labishe wouldn't have killed him without having been ordered to do it. Some one of enormous authority had to issue that order."

"Well, to begin with I have no such authority, and secondly I would have no reason. I was fond of that Frenchman."

"You hardly knew him."

Rheinhart laughed. "Very well. . . . All the less reason . . ."

"I didn't say you personally. I'm asking who did and *why*." Poole was betraying his normal calm. He had good reason. This arrogant Prussian held the key if Poole was right, and he wasn't going to let him go until he found out. He would have to press nearer the truth, yet not disclose it.

"Did Bertholde know something the rest of you didn't want him to know?"

"Now, you're preposterous."

"Did he?"

"Jacques Bertholde was our London contact! He enjoyed a unique position in England that approached diplomatic immunity. His influence was felt in a dozen countries among scores of the industrial elite. His death is a great loss to us! How dare you imply that any of us was responsible!"

"I find it interesting that you haven't answered my question." Poole was exasperated. "Did he know something the men in Munich might consider dangerous?"

"If he did, I have no idea what it might be!"

But Poole knew. Perhaps he was the only one who did know. *If he could only be sure.*

"I'd like another drink, please. Forgive my temper." He smiled.

Rheinhart laughed. "You're impossible. Give me your glass. . . . You're satisfied?" The German crossed to the liquor cabinet and poured. "You travel three thousand miles for nothing. It's been a bad trip for you."

Poole shrugged. He was used to the trips—some good, some bad. Bertholde and his odd friend, the misshapen Heinrich Kroeger, had ordered him over barely six months ago. His orders had been simple then. Pick up the girl, find out what she had learned from old Scarlatti. He'd failed. The Canfield man had stopped him. The solicitous lackey, the salesman-cum-escort had prevented it. But he hadn't failed his other orders. He'd followed the banker named Cartwright. He'd killed him and broken into the railroad station locker and gotten the banker's agreement with Elizabeth Scarlatti.

It was then that he had learned the truth of Heinrich Kroeger's identity. Elizabeth Scarlatti's son had needed an ally and Jacques Bertholde was that ally. And in return for that precious friendship, Ulster Scarlett had ordered Bertholde's death. The fanatic had commanded the death of the man who had made everything possible for him.

He, Poole, would avenge that terrible murder. But before he did, he had to confirm what he suspected was the truth. That neither the Nazi leaders nor the men in Zurich knew who Kroeger was. If that was the case, then Kroeger had murdered Bertholde to keep that identity secret.

The revelation might cost the movement millions. The Munich Nazis would know this, if they knew anything.

Erich Rheinhart stood over Poole. "A penny for your thoughts, my dear fellow? Here, a bourbon. You do not speak to me."

"Oh? . . . Yes, it's been a bad trip, Erich. You were right." Poole bent his neck back, closed his eyes, and rubbed his forehead. Rheinhart returned to his chair.

"You need a rest. . . . Do you know what I think? I think you're right. I think some damned fool *did* issue that order." Poole opened his eyes, startled by Erich Rheinhart's words. "Ja! In my opinion you are correct. And it must stop! . . . Strasser fights Hitler and Ludendorff. Ekhart rambles on like a madman. Attacking! Attacking! Kindorf screams in the Ruhr. Jodl betrays the Black Wehrmacht in Bavaria. Graefe makes a mess in the north. Even my own uncle, the illustrious Wilhelm Rheinhart, makes an idiot of himself. He speaks, and I hear the laughter behind my back in America. I tell you we are split in ten factions. Wolves at each other's throats. We will accomplish nothing! Nothing, if this does not stop!" Erich Rheinhart's anger was undisguised. He didn't care. He rose again from his chair. "What is most asinine is the most obvious! We can lose the men in Zurich. If we can not agree among ourselves, how long do you think they will stay with us? I tell you, these men are not interested in who has next week's power base in the Reichstag—not for its own sake. They don't care a Deutschemark for the glories of the new Germany. Or the ambitions of any nation. Their wealth puts them above political boundaries. They are with us for one reason alone—their own power. If we give them a single doubt that we are not what we claim to be, that we are not the emerging order of Germany, they will abandon us. They will leave us with nothing! Even the Germans among them!"

Rheinhart's fury abated. He tried to smile but instead drained his glass quickly and crossed to the cabinet.

If Poole could only be sure. "I understand," he said quietly.

"Ja. I think you do. You've worked long and hard with Bertholde. You've accomplished a great deal . . ." He turned around facing Poole. "That's what I mean. Everything that all of us have worked for can be lost by these internal frictions. The achievements of Funke, Bertholde, von Schnitzler, Thyssen, even Kroeger, will be wiped out if we can not come together. We must unite behind one, possibly two, acceptable leaders . . ."

That was it! That was the sign. Poole was now sure. Rheinhart had said the name! Kroeger!

"Maybe, Erich, but who?" Would Rheinhart say the name again? It was not possible, for Kroeger was no German. But could he get Rheinhart to use the name, just the name, once more without the slightest betrayal of concern.

"Strasser, perhaps. He's strong, attractive. Ludendorff naturally has the aura of national fame, but he's too old now. But mark me, Poole, watch this Hitler! Have you read the transcripts of the Munich trial?"

"No. Should I?"

"Yes! He's electric! Positively eloquent! And sound."

"He has a lot of enemies. He's banned from speaking in almost every *grafshaft* in Germany."

"The necessary excesses in a march to power. The bans on him are being removed. We're seeing to that."

Poole now watched Rheinhart carefully as he spoke.

"Hitler's a friend of Kroeger, isn't he?"

"Ach! Wouldn't you be? Kroeger has millions! It is through Kroeger that Hitler gets his automobiles, his chauffeur, the castle at Berchtesgaden, God knows what else. You don't think he buys them with his royalties, do

300

you? Most amusing. Last year Herr Hitler declared an income which could not possibly purchase two tires for his Mercedes." Rheinhart laughed. "We managed to have the inquiry suspended in Munich, fortunately. Ja, Kroeger is good to Hitler.

Poole was now absolutely sure. The men in Zurich did not know who Heinrich Kroeger was!

"Erich, I must go. Can you have your man drive me back to Washington?"

"But of course, my dear fellow."

Poole opened the door of his room at the Ambassador Hotel. Upon hearing the sound of the key, the man inside stood up, practically at attention.

"Oh, it's you, Bush."

"Cable from London, Mr. Poole. I thought it best that I take the train down rather than using the telephone." He handed Poole the cable.

Poole opened the envelope and extracted the message. He read it.

DUCHESS HAS LEFT LONDON STOP DESTINATION ASCERTAINED GENEVA STOP RUMORS OF ZURICH CONFERENCE STOP CABLE INSTRUCTIONS PARIS OFFICE

Poole pinched his aristocratic lips together, nearly biting into his own flesh in an attempt to suppress his anger.

"Duchess" was the code name of Elizabeth Scarlatti. So she headed for Geneva. A hundred and ten miles from Zurich. This was no pleasure trip. It was not another leg on her journey of mourning.

Whatever Jacques Bertholde had feared—plot or counterplot—it was happening now. Elizabeth Scarlatti and her son "Heinrich Kroeger" were making their moves. Separately or together, who could know.

Poole made his decision.

"Send the following to the Paris office. 'Eliminate Duchess from the market. Her bid is to be taken off our lists at once. Repeat, eliminate Duchess'."

Poole dismissed the courier and went to the telephone. He had to make reservations immediately. He had to get to Zurich.

There'd be no conference. He'd stop it. He'd kill the mother, expose the killer son! Kroeger's death would follow quickly!

It was the least he could do for Bertholde.

PART THREE

CHAPTER 41

The train clanged over the antiquated bridge spanning the Rhone River, into the Geneva station. Elizabeth Scarlatti sat in her compartment looking first down at the river barges, then at the rising banks and into the large railroad yard. Geneva was clean. There was a scrubbed look about it, which helped to hide the fact that scores of nations and a thousand score of business giants used this neutral city to further intensify conflicting interests. As the train neared the city, she thought that someone like herself belonged in Geneva. Or, perhaps, Geneva belonged to someone like herself.

She eyed the luggage piled on the seat facing her. One suitcase contained the clothes she needed, and three smaller bags were jammed with papers. Papers that contained a thousand conclusions, totaling up to a battery of weapons. The data included figures on the complete worth of every man in the Zurich group. Every resource each possessed. Additional information awaited her in Geneva. But that was a different sort of musketry. It was not unlike the *Domesday Book*. For what awaited her in Geneva was the complete breakdown of the Scarlatti interests. The legally assessed value of every asset controlled by the Scarlatti Industries. What made it deadly was her maneuverability. And opposite each block of wealth was a commitment to purchase. These commitments were spelled out, and they could be executed instantaneously by a cable to her attorneys.

And well they should be.

Each block was followed—not by the usual two columns designating assessed value and sales value—but three columns. This third column was an across-the-board cut, which guaranteed the buyer a minor fortune with each transaction. Each signified a mandate to purchase that could not be refused. It was the highest level of finance, returned through the complexities of banking to the fundamental basis of economic incentive. Profit.

And Elizabeth counted on one last factor. It was the reverse of her instructions but that, too, was calculated.

In her sealed orders sent across the Atlantic was the emphatic stipulation that every contact made—to complete the task teams of administrators had to work twelve-hour shifts night and day—was to be carried out in the utmost secrecy and only with those whose authority extended to great financial commitments. The guaranteed gains absolved all from charges of irresponsibility. Each would emerge a hero to himself or to his economic constituency. But the price was consummate security until the act was done. The rewards matched the price. Millionaires, merchant princes, and bankers in New York, Chicago, Los Angeles, and Palm Beach found themselves quartered in conference rooms with their dignified counterparts from one of New York's most prestigious law firms. The tones were hushed and the looks knowing. Financial killings were being made. Signatures were affixed.

And, of course, it had to happen.

Unbelievable good fortune leads to ebullience, and ebullience is no mate for secrecy.

Two or three began to talk. Then four or five. Then a dozen. But no more than that. . . . The *price*.

Phone calls were made, almost none from offices, nearly all from the quiet seclusion of libraries or dens. Most were made at night under the soft light of desk lamps with good pre-Volstead whiskey an arm's length away.

In the highest economic circles, there was a rumor that something most unusual was happening at Scarlatti.

It was just enough. Elizabeth knew it would be just enough. After all, the *price*. . . . And the rumors reached the men in Zurich.

Matthew Canfield stretched out across the seats in his own compartment, his legs propped over his single suitcase, his feet resting on the cushions facing him. He, too, looked out the window at the approaching city of Geneva. He had just finished one of his thin cigars and the smoke rested in suspended layers above him in the still air of the small room. He contemplated opening a window, but he was too depressed to move.

It had been two weeks to the day since he had granted Elizabeth Scarlatti her reprieve of one month. Fourteen days of chaos made painful by the knowledge of his own uselessness. More than uselessness, more akin to personal futility. He could do nothing, and nothing was expected of him. Elizabeth hadn't wanted him to "work closely" with her. She didn't want anyone to work with her—closely or otherwise. She soloed. She soared alone, a crusty, patrician eagle sweeping the infinite meadows of her own particular heaven.

His most demanding chore was the purchase of office supplies such as reams of paper, pencils, notebooks, and endless boxes of paper clips.

Even the publisher Thomas Ogilvie had refused to see him, obviously so instructed by Elizabeth.

Canfield had been dismissed as he was being dismissed by Elizabeth. Even Janet treated him with a degree of aloofness, always apologizing for her manner but by apologizing, acknowledging it. He began to realize what had happened. He was the whore now. He had sold himself, his favors taken and paid for. They had very little use for him now. They knew he could be had again as one knows a whore can be had.

He understood so much more completely what Janet had felt.

Would it be finished with Janet? Could it ever be finished with her? He told himself no. She told him the same. She asked him to be strong enough for both of them, but was she fooling herself and letting him pay for it?

He began to wonder if he was capable of judgment. He had been idle and the rot inside of him frightened him. What had he done? Could he undo it? He was operating in a world he couldn't come to grips with.

Except Janet. She didn't belong to that world either. She belonged to him. She had to!

The whistle on the train's roof screeched twice and the huge metal-against-metal slabs on the wheels began to grind. The train was entering the Geneva station, and Canfield heard Elizabeth's rapid knocking on the wall between their compartments. The knocking annoyed him. It sounded like an impatient master of the house rapping for a servant.

Which is exactly what it was.

"I can manage this one, you take the other two. Let the redcaps handle the rest."

Dutifully Canfield instructed the porter, gathered up the two bags, and followed Elizabeth off the train.

Because he had to juggle the two suitcases in the small exit area, he was several feet behind Elizabeth as they stepped off the metal stairway and started down the concrete platform to the center of the station. Because of those two suitcases they were alive one minute later.

At first it was only a speck of dark movement in the corner of his eye. Then it was the gasps of several travelers behind him. Then the screams. And then he saw it.

Bearing down from the right was a massive freight dolly with a huge steel slab across the front used to scoop up heavy crates. The metal plate was about four feet off the ground and had the appearance of a giant, ugly blade.

Canfield jumped forward as the rushing monster came directly at them. He threw his right arm around her waist and pushed-pulled her out of the way of the mammoth steel plate. It crashed into the side of the train less than a foot from both their bodies.

Many in the crowd were hysterical. No one could be sure whether anyone had been injured or killed. Porters came running. The shouts and screams echoed throughout the platform.

Elizabeth, breathless, spoke into Canfield's ear. "The suitcases! Do you have the suitcases?"

Canfield found to his amazement that he still held one in his left hand. It was pressed between Elizabeth's back and the train. He had dropped the suitcase in his right hand.

"I've got one. I let the other go."

"Find it!"

"For Christ's sake!"

"Find it, you fool!"

Canfield pushed at the crowd gathering in front of them. He scanned his eyes downward and saw the leather case. It had been run over by the heavy front wheels of the dolly, crushed but still intact. He shouldered his way against a dozen midriffs and reached down. Simultaneously another arm, with a fat, uncommonly large hand thrust itself toward the crumpled piece of leather. The arm was clothed in a tweed jacket. A woman's jacket. Canfield pushed harder and touched the case with his fingers and began pulling it forward. Instinctively, amid the panorama of trousers and overcoats, he grabbed the wrist of the fat hand and looked up.

Bending down, eyes in blind fury, was a jowled face Canfield could never forget. It belonged in that hideous foyer of red and black four thousand miles away. It was Hannah, Janet's housekeeper!

Their eyes met in recognition. The woman's iron-gray head was covered tightly by a dark green Tyrolean fedora, which set off the bulges of facial flesh. Her immense body was crouched, ugly, ominous. With enormous strength she whipped her hand out of Canfield's grasp, pushing him as she did so, so that he fell back into the dolly and the bodies surrounding him. She disappeared rapidly into the crowd toward the station.

Canfield rose, clutching the crushed suitcase under his arm. He looked after her, but she could not be seen. He stood there for a moment, people pressing around him, bewildered.

He worked his way back to Elizabeth.

"Take me out of here. Quickly!"

They started down the platform, Elizabeth holding his left arm with more strength than Canfield thought she possessed. She was actually hurting him. They left the excited crowd behind them.

"It has begun." She looked straight ahead as she spoke.

They reached the interior of the crowded dome. Canfield kept moving his head in every direction, trying to find an irregular break in the human pattern, trying to find a pair of eyes, a still shape, a waiting figure. A fat woman in a Tyrolean hat.

309

They reached the south entrance on Eisenbahn Platz and found a line of taxis.

Canfield held Elizabeth back from the first cab. She was alarmed. She wanted to keep moving.

"They'll send our luggage."

He didn't reply. Instead he propelled her to the left toward the second car and then, to her mounting concern, signaled the driver of a third vehicle. He pulled the cab door shut and looked at the crushed, expensive Mark Cross suitcase. He pictured Hannah's wrathful, puffed face. If there was ever a female archangel of darkness, she was it. He gave the driver the name of their hotel.

"Il n'y a plus de bagage, monsieur?"

"No. It will follow," answered Elizabeth in English.

The old woman had just gone through a horrifying experience, so he decided not to mention Hannah until they reached the hotel. Let her calm down. And yet he wondered whether it was him or Elizabeth who needed the calm. His hands were still shaking. He looked over at Elizabeth. She continued to stare straight ahead, but she was not seeing anything anyone else would see.

"Are you all right?"

She did not answer him for nearly a minute.

"Mr. Canfield, you have a terrible responsibility facing you."

"I'm not sure what you mean."

She turned and looked at him. Gone was the grandeur, gone the haughty superiority.

"Don't let them kill me, Mr. Canfield. Don't let them kill me now. Make them wait till Zurich. . . . After Zurich they can do anything they wish."

CHAPTER 42

Elizabeth and Canfield spent three days and nights in their rooms at the Hotel D' Accord. Only once had Canfield gone out—and he had spotted two men following him. They did not try to take him, and it occurred to him that they considered him so secondary to the prime target, Elizabeth, that they dared not risk a call out of the Geneva police, reported to be an alarmingly belligerent force, hostile to those who upset the delicate equilibrium of their neutral city. The experience taught him that the moment they appeared together he could expect an attack no less vicious than the one made on them at the Geneva station. He wished he could send word to Ben Reynolds. But he couldn't, and he knew it. He had been ordered to stay out of Switzerland. He had withheld every piece of vital information from his reports. Elizabeth had seen to that. Group Twenty knew next to nothing about the immediate situation and the motives of those involved. If he did send an urgent request for assistance, he would have to explain, at least partially, and that explanation would lead to prompt interference by the embassy. Reynolds wouldn't wait upon legalities. He would have Canfield seized by force and held incommunicado.

The results were predictable. With him finished, Elizabeth wouldn't have a chance of reaching Zurich. She'd be killed by Scarlett in Geneva. And the secondary target would then be Janet back in London. She couldn't stay at the Savoy indefinitely. Derek couldn't continue his security precautions ad infinitum. She would eventually leave, or Derek would become exasperated and careless. She, too, would be killed. Finally, there was Chancellor Drew, his wife, and seven children. There would be a hundred valid reasons for all to leave the remote Canadian refuge. They'd be massacred. Ulster Stewart Scarlett would win.

At the thought of Scarlett, Canfield was able to summon up what anger was left in him. It was almost enough to match his fear and depression. Almost.

He walked into the sitting room Elizabeth had converted into an office. She was writing on the center table.

"Do you remember the housekeeper at your son's house?" he said.

Elizabeth put down her pencil. It was momentary courtesy, not concern. "I've seen her on the few occasions I've visited, yes."

"Where did she come from?"

"As I recall, Ulster brought her back from Europe. She ran a hunting lodge in . . . southern Germany." Elizabeth looked up at the field accountant. "Why do you ask?"

Years later Canfield would reflect that it was because he had been trying to find the words to tell Elizabeth Scarlatti that Hannah was in Geneva that caused him to do what he did. To physically move from one place to another at that particular instant. To cross between Elizabeth and the window. He would carry the remembrance of it as long as he lived.

There was a shattering of glass and a sharp, terrible stinging pain in his left shoulder. Actually the pain seemed to come first. The jolt was so powerful that it spun Canfield around, throwing him across the table, scattering papers, and crashing the lamp to the floor. A second and third shot followed, splintering the thick wood around his body and Canfield, in panic, lurched to one side, toppling Elizabeth off her chair onto the floor. The pain in his shoulder was overpowering, and a huge splotch of blood spread across his shirt.

It was all over in five seconds.

Elizabeth was crouched against the paneling of the wall. She was at once frightened and grateful. She looked at the field accountant lying in front of her trying to hold his shoulder. She was convinced he had thrown himself over her to protect her from the bullets. He never explained otherwise.

312

"How badly are you hurt?"

"I'm not sure. It hurts like hell. . . . I've never been hit before. Never shot before. . . ." He was finding it difficult to speak. Elizabeth started to move toward him. "God damn it! Stay where you are!" He looked up and saw that he was out of the sight line of the window. They both were. "Look, can you reach the phone? Go on the floor. Stay down! . . . I think I need a doctor. . . . A doctor." He passed out.

Thirty minutes later Canfield awoke. He was on his own bed with the whole upper left part of his chest encased in an uncomfortable bandage. He could barely move. He could see, blurredly to be sure, a number of figures around him. As his eyes came into focus, he saw Elizabeth at the foot of the bed looking down at him. To her right was a man in an overcoat, behind him a uniformed policeman. Bending over him on his left was a balding, stern-faced man in his shirt sleeves, obviously a doctor. He spoke to Canfield. His accent was French.

"Move your left hand, please."

Canfield obeyed.

"Your feet, please."

Again he complied.

"Can you roll your head?"

"What? Where?"

"Move your head back and forth. Don't try to be amusing." Elizabeth was possibly the most relieved person within twenty miles of the Hotel D' Accord. She even smiled.

Canfield swung his head back and forth.

"You are not seriously hurt." The doctor stood erect.

"You sound disappointed," answered the field accountant.

"May I ask him questions, *Herr Doktor?*" said the Swiss next to Elizabeth.

The doctor replied in his broken English. "Yes. The bullet passed him through."

What one had to do with the other perplexed Canfield, but he had no time to think about it. Elizabeth spoke.

"I've explained to this gentleman that you're merely accompanying me while I conduct business affairs. We're totally bewildered by what's happened."

313

"I would appreciate this man answering for himself, madame."

"Damned if I can tell you anything, mister. . . ." And then Canfield stopped. There was no point in being a fool. He was going to need help. "On second thought, maybe I can." He looked toward the doctor, who was putting on his suit coat. The Swiss understood.

"Very well. We shall wait."

"Mr. Canfield, what can you possibly add?"

"Passage to Zurich."

Elizabeth understood.

The doctor left and Canfield found that he could lie on his right side. The Swiss *Geheimpolizist* walked around to be nearer.

"Sit down, sir," said Canfield as the man drew up a chair. "What I'm going to tell you will seem foolish to someone like you and me who have to work for our livings." The field accountant winked. "It's a private matter —no harm to anyone outside the family, family business, but you can help. . . . Does your man speak English?"

The Swiss looked briefly at the uniformed policeman.

"No, monsieur."

"Good. As I say, you can help. Both the clean record of your fair city . . . and yourself."

The Swiss *Geheimpolizist* drew up his chair closer.

He was delighted.

The afternoon arrived. They had timed the train schedules to the quarter hour and had telephoned ahead for a limousine and chauffeur. Their train tickets had been purchased by the hotel, clearly spelling out the name of Scarlatti for preferred treatment and the finest accommodations available for the short trip to Zurich. Their luggage was sent downstairs an hour beforehand and deposited by the front entrance. The tags were legibly marked, the train compartments specified, and even the limousine service noted for the Zurich porters. Canfield figured that the lowest IQ in Europe could know the immediate itinerary of Elizabeth Scarlatti if he wished to.

The ride from the hotel to the station took about twelve minutes. One-half hour before the train for Zurich departed an old woman, with a heavy black veil, accompanied by a youngish man in a brand-new fedora, his left arm in a white sling, got into a limousine. They were escorted by two members of the Geneva police, who kept their hands on their holstered pistols.

No incident occurred, and the two travelers rushed into the station and immediately onto the train.

As the train left the Geneva platform, another elderly woman accompanied by a youngish man, this one in a Brooks Brothers hat, and also with his left arm in a sling but hidden by a topcoat, left the service entrance of the Hotel D'Accord. The elderly woman was dressed in the uniform of a Red Cross colonel, female division, complete with a garrison cap. The man driving was also a member of the International Red Cross. The two people rushed into the back seat, and the young man closed the door. He immediately took the cellophane off a thin cigar and said to the driver, "Let's go."

As the car sped out the narrow driveway, the old woman spoke disparagingly. "Really, Mr. Canfield! Must you smoke one of those awful things?"

"Gevena rules, lady. Prisoners are allowed packages from home."

CHAPTER 43

Twenty-seven miles from Zurich is the town of Menziken. The Geneva train stopped for precisely four minutes, the time allotted for the loading of the railway post, and then proceeded on its inevitable, exact, fated ride up the tracks to its destination.

Five minutes out of Menziken, compartments D4 and D5 on Pullman car six were broken into simultaneously by two men in masks. Because neither compartment contained any passengers, and both toilet doors were locked, the masked men fired their pistols into the thin panels of the commodes, expecting to find the bodies when they opened the doors.

They found no one. Nothing.

As if predetermined, both masked men ran out into the narrow corridor and nearly collided with one another.

"Halt! Stop!" The shouts came from both ends of the Pullman corridor. The men calling were dressed in the uniforms of the Geneva police.

The two masked men did not stop. Instead they fired wildly in both directions.

Their shots were returned and the two men fell.

They were searched; no identifications were found. The Geneva police were pleased about that. They did not wish to get involved.

One of the fallen men, however, had a tattoo on his forearm: an insignia, recently given the term of swastika. And a third man, unseen, unmasked, not fallen, was first off the train at Zurich, and hurried to a telephone.

316

"Here we are at Aarau. You can rest up here for a while. Your clothes are in a flat on the second floor. I believe your car is parked in the rear and the keys are under the left seat." Their driver was English and Canfield liked that. The driver hadn't spoken a word since Geneva. The field accountant withdrew a large bill from his pocket and offered it to the man.

"Hardly necessary, sir," said the driver as he waved the bill aside without turning.

They waited until eight fifteen. It was a dark night with only half a moon shrouded by low clouds. Canfield had tried the car, driving it up and down a country road to get the feel of it, to get used to driving with only his right hand. The gas gauge registered *rempli* and they were ready.

More precisely, Elizabeth Scarlatti was ready.

She was like a gladiator, prepared to bleed or let blood. She was cold but intense. She was a killer.

And her weapons were paper—infinitely more dangerous than maces or triforks to her adversaries. She was also, as a fine gladiator must be, supremely confident.

It was more than her last *grande geste*, it was the culmination of a lifetime. Hers and Giovanni's. She would not fail him.

Canfield had studied and restudied the map; he knew the roads he had to take to reach Falke Haus. They would skirt the center of Zurich and head toward Kloten, turning right at the Schlieren fork and follow the central road toward Bulach. One mile to the left on the Winterthurstrasse would be the gates of Falke Haus.

He had pushed the car up to eighty-five miles an hour, and he had stopped at sixty within the space of fifty feet without causing a dislocation of the seats. The Geneva *Geheimpolizist* had done his job well. But then he was well paid. Damn near two years' wages at the going Swiss rate of Civil Service. And the car was licensed with the numbers no one would stop—for any reason—the Zurich police. How he had done it, Canfield didn't ask. Elizabeth suggested that it might have been the money.

"Is that all?" asked Canfield as he led Elizabeth Scarlatti toward the car. He referred to her single briefcase.

"It's enough," said the old woman as she followed him down the path.

"You had a couple of thousand pages, a hundred thousand figures!"

"They're meaningless now." Elizabeth held the briefcase on her lap as Canfield shut the car door.

"Suppose they ask you questions?" The field accountant inserted the key in the ignition.

"No doubt they will. And if they do, I'll answer." She didn't wish to talk.

They drove for twenty minutes and the roads were coming out right. Canfield was pleased with himself. He was a satisfied navigator. Suddenly Elizabeth spoke.

"There is one thing I haven't told you, nor have you seen fit to bring it up. It's only fair that I mention it now."

"What?"

"It's conceivable that neither of us will emerge from this conference alive. Have you considered that?"

Canfield had, of course, considered it. He had assumed the risk, if that was the justifiable word, since the Boothroyd incident. It had escalated to pronounced danger when he realized that Janet was possibly his for life. He became committed when he knew what her husband had done to her.

With the bullet through his shoulder, two inches from death, Matthew Canfield in his own way had become a gladiator in much the same manner as Elizabeth. His anger was paramount now.

"You worry about your problems, I'll worry about mine, okay?"

"Okay. . . . May I say that you've become quite dear to me. . . . Oh, stop that little-boy look! Save it for the ladies! I'm hardly one of them! Drive on!"

On Winterthurstrasse, three-tenths of a mile from Falke Haus there is a stretch of straight road paralleled on both sides by towering pine trees. Matthew Canfield pushed the accelerator down and drove the automobile as fast as it would go. It was five minutes to nine and he was determined that his passenger meet her appointment on time.

Suddenly in the far-off illumination of the head lamps, a man was signaling. He waved his hands, crisscrossing above his head, standing in the middle of the road. He was violently making the universal sign, stop—emergency. He did not move from the middle of the road in spite of Canfield's speed.

"Hold on!" Canfield rushed on, oblivious to the human being in his path.

As he did so, there were bursts of gunfire from both sides of the road. "Get down!" shouted Canfield. He continued to push the gas pedal, ducking as he did so, bobbing his head, watching the straight road as best he could. There was a piercing scream—pitched in a death note—from the far side of the road. One of the ambushers had been caught in the crossfire.

They passed the area, pieces of glass and metal scattered all over the seats.

"You okay?" Canfield had no time for sympathy.

"Yes. I'm all right. How much longer?"

"Not much. If we can make it. They may have gotten a tire."

"Even if they did, we can still drive?"

"Don't you worry! I'm not about to stop and ask for a jack!"

The gates of Falke Haus appeared and Canfield turned sharply into the road. It was a descending grade leading gently into a huge circle in front of an enormous flagstone porch with statuary placed every several feet. The front entrance, a large wooden door, was situated twenty feet beyond the center steps. Canfield could not get near it.

For there were at least a dozen long, black limousines lined up around the circle. Chauffeurs stood near them, idly chatting.

Canfield checked his revolver, placed it in his right-hand pocket, and ordered Elizabeth out of the car. He insisted that she slide across the seat and emerge from his side of the automobile.

He walked slightly behind her, nodding to the chauffeurs.

It was one minute after nine when a servant, formally dressed, opened the large wooden door.

They entered the great hall, a massive tabernacle of architectural indulgence. A second servant, also formally attired, gestured them toward another door. He opened it.

Inside was the longest table Matthew Canfield thought possible to build. It must have been fifty feet from end to end. And a good six to seven feet wide.

Seated around the massive table were fifteen or twenty men. All ages, from forty to seventy. All dressed in expensive suits. All looking toward Elizabeth Scarlatti. At the head of the table, half a room away, was an empty chair. It cried out to be filled, and Canfield wondered for a moment whether Elizabeth was to fill it. Then he realized that was not so. Her chair was at the foot of the table closest to them.

Who was to fill the empty chair?

No matter. There was no chair for him. He would stay by the wall and watch.

Elizabeth approached the table.

"Good evening, gentlemen. A number of us have met before. The rest of you I know by reputation, I can assure you."

The entire complement around the table rose as one body.

The man to the left of Elizabeth's chair circled and held it for her.

She sat down, and the men returned to their seats.

"I thank you. . . . But there seems to be one of us missing." Elizabeth stared at the chair fifty feet away directly in front of her eyes.

At that moment a door at the far end of the room opened and a tall man strutted in. He was dressed in the crisp, cold uniform of the German revolutionary. The dark brown shirt, the shining black belt across his chest and around his waist, the starched tan jodhpurs above the thick, heavy boots that came just below his knees.

320

The man's head was shaven, his face a distorted replica of itself.

"The chair is now taken. Does that satisfy you?"

"Not entirely. . . . Since I know, through one means or another, every person of consequence at this table, I should like to know who you are, sir."

"Kroeger. Heinrich Kroeger! Anything else, Madame Scarlatti?"

"Not a thing. Not a single thing . . . Herr Kroeger."

CHAPTER 44

"Against my wishes and my better judgment, Madame Scarlatti, my associates are determined to hear what you have to say." The grotesque shaven-headed Heinrich Kroeger spoke. "My position has been made clear to you. I trust your memory serves you well about it."

There were whispers around the table. Looks were exchanged. None of the men were prepared for the news that Heinrich Kroeger had had prior contact with Elizabeth Scarlatti.

"My memory serves me very well. Your associates represent an aggregate of much wisdom and several centuries of experience. I suspect far in excess of your own on both counts—collectively and individually."

Most of the men simply lowered their eyes, some pressing their lips in slight smiles. Elizabeth slowly looked at each face around the table.

"We have an interesting board here, I see. Well represented. Well diversified. Some of us were enemies in war a few short years ago, but such memories, by necessity, are short. . . . Let's see." Without singling out any one individual, Elizabeth Scarlatti spoke rapidly, almost in a cadence. "My own country has lost two members, I'm sad to note. But I don't believe prayers are in order for Messrs. Boothroyd and Thornton. If they are, I'm not the one to deliver them. But still, the United States is splendidly represented by Mr. Gibson and Mr. Landor. Between them, they account for nearly twenty percent of the vast oil interests in the American Southwest. To say nothing of a joint expansion in the Canadian Northwest Territories. Combined personal assets—two hundred and twenty-five million. . . . Our recent adversary, Germany, brings us Herr von Schnitzler, Herr Kindorf, and Herr Thyssen. I. G. Farben; the baron of Ruhr coal; the great steel companies. Personal assets? Who can really tell these days in the Weimar? Perhaps one hundred and seventy-five million, at the outside. . . . But someone's missing from this group. I trust he's successfully being recruited. I speak of Gustave Krupp. He would raise the ante considerably. . . . England sends us Messrs. Masterson, Leacock, and Innes-Bowen. As powerful a triumvirate as can be found in the British Empire. Mr. Masterson with half of the India imports, also Ceylon now, I understand; Mr. Leacock's major portion of the British Stock Exchange; and Mr. Innes-Bowen. He owns the largest single textile industry throughout Scotland and the Hebrides. Personal assets I place at three hundred million. . . . France has been generous, too. Monsieur D'Almeida; I now realize that he is the true owner of the Franco-Italian rail system, partially due to his Italian lineage, I'm sure. And Monsieur Daudet. Is there any among us who have not used some part of his merchant fleet? Personal assets, one hundred and fifty million. . . . And lastly, our neighbors to the north, Sweden. Herr Myrdal and Herr Olaffsen. Understandably"—here Elizabeth looked pointedly at the strange-faced man, her son, at the head of the table—"one of these gentlemen, Herr Myrdal, has controlling interest in Donnenfeld, the most impressive firm on the Stockholm exchange. While Herr Olaffsen's many companies merely control the export of Swedish iron and steel. Personal assets are calculated at one hundred and twenty-five million. . . . Incidentally, gentlemen, the term *personal assets* denotes those holdings which can be converted easily, quickly, and without endangering your markets. . . . Otherwise, I would not insult you by placing such meager limits on your fortunes."

Elizabeth paused to place her briefcase directly in front of her. The men around the table were aroused, apprehensive. Several were shocked at the casual mention of what they believed was highly confidential information. The Americans, Gibson and Landor, had quietly gone into the Canadian venture unannounced, without legal sanction, violating the U.S.-Canadian treaties. The Germans, von Schnitzler and Kindorf, had held secret conferences with Gustave Krupp—who was fighting desperately to remain neutral for fear of a Weimar takeover. If these conferences were made known, Krupp had sworn to expose them. The Frenchman, Louis François D'Almeida, guarded with his very life the extent of his ownership of the Franco-Italian rails. If it were known, it might well be confiscated by the republic. He had purchased the majority shares from the Italian government through plain bribery.

And Myrdal, the heavyset Swede, bulged his eyes in disbelief when Elizabeth Scarlatti spoke so knowingly about the Stockholm exchange. His own company had covertly absorbed Donnenfeld in one of the most complicated mergers imaginable, made possible by the illegal transaction of the American securities. If it became public knowledge, the Swedish law would step in, and he'd be ruined. Only the Englishmen seemed totally poised, totally proud of their achievements. But even this measure of equanimity was misleading. For Sydney Masterson, undisputed heir to the merchant domain of Sir Robert Clive, had only recently concluded the Ceylon arrangements. They were unknown in the import-export world and there were certain agreements subject to question. Some might even say they constituted fraud.

Huddled, quiet-toned conferences took place around the table in the four languages. Elizabeth raised her voice sufficiently to be heard.

"I gather some of you are conferring with your aides—I assume they are your aides. If I'd realized this meeting made provisions for second-level negotiators, I'd have brought along my attorneys. They could have gossiped among themselves while we continue. The decisions we reach tonight, gentlemen, must be our own!"

Heinrich Kroeger sat on the edge of his chair. He spoke harshly, unpleasantly. "I wouldn't be so sure of any decisions. There are none to be made! You've told us nothing which couldn't be learned by any major accounting firm!"

A number of the men around the table—specifically the two Germans, D'Almeida, Gibson, Landor, Myrdal, and Masterson—avoided looking at him. For Kroeger was wrong.

"You think so? Perhaps. But then I've overlooked you,

haven't I? . . . I shouldn't do that, you're obviously terribly important." Again, a number of the men around the table—excluding those mentioned—had traces of smiles on their lips.

"Your wit is as dull as you are." Elizabeth was pleased with herself. She was succeeding in this most important aspect of her appearance. She was reaching, provoking Ulster Stewart Scarlett. She continued without acknowledging his remark.

"Strangely obtained assets of two hundred and seventy million sold under the most questionable circumstances would necessitate a loss of at least fifty percent, possibly sixty percent of market value. I'll grant you the least, so I shall hazard an estimate of one hundred and thirty-five million dollars at the current rates of exchange. One hundred and eight, if you've been weak."

Matthew Canfield lurched from the wall, then held his place.

The men around the table were astonished. The hum of voices increased perceptibly. Aides were shaking their heads, nodding in agreement, raising their eyebrows unable to answer. Each participant thought he knew something of the others. Obviously, none were this knowledgeable of Heinrich Kroeger. They had not even been sure of his status at this table. Elizabeth interrupted the commotion.

"However, Mister Kroeger, surely you know that theft, when eminently provable, is merely subject to proper identification before steps can be taken. There are international courts of extradition. Therefore, it is conceivable that your assets might be calculated at . . . zero!"

A silence fell over the table as the gentlemen, along with their assistants, gave Heinrich Kroeger their full attention. The words *theft*, *courts*, and *extradition* were words they could not accept at this table. They were dangerous words. Kroeger, the man many of them vaguely feared for reasons solely associated with his enormous influence within both camps, was now warned.

"Don't threaten me, old woman." Kroeger's voice was low, confident. He sat back in his chair and glared at his mother at the opposite end of the long table. "Don't make charges unless you can substantiate them. If you're prepared to attempt that, I'm ready to counter. . . . If you or your colleagues were outnegotiated, this is no place to cry. You won't get sympathy here! I might even go so far as to say you're on treacherous ground. Remember that!" He kept staring until Elizabeth could no longer stand the sight of his eyes. She looked away.

She was not prepared to do anything—not with him, not with Heinrich Kroeger. She would not gamble the lives of her family more than she had already. She would not wager at this table the name of Scarlatti. Not that way. Not now. There was another way.

Kroeger had won the point. It was obvious to all, and Elizabeth had to rush headlong on so that none would dwell upon her loss.

"Keep your assets. They are quite immaterial."

Around the table the phrase "quite immaterial" when applied to such millions was impressive. Elizabeth knew it would be.

"Gentlemen. Before we were interrupted, I gave you all, by national groupings, the personal assets calculated to the nearest five million for each contingent. I felt it was more courteous than breaking down each individual's specific worth—some things are sacred, after all. However, I was quite unfair, as several of you know. I alluded to a number of—shall we say, delicate negotiations, I'm sure you believed were inviolate. Treacherous to you —to use Mr. Kroeger's words—if they were known within your own countries."

Seven of the Zurich twelve were silent. Five were curious.

"I refer to my cocitizens, Mr. Gibson and Mr. Landor. To Monsieur D'Almeida, Sydney Masterson, and of course, to the brilliant Herr Myrdal. I should also include two-thirds of Germany's investors—Herr von Schnitzler and Herr Kindorf, but for different reasons, as I'm sure they realize."

No one spoke. No one turned to his aides. All eyes were upon Elizabeth.

"I don't intend to remain unfair in this fashion, gentlemen. I have something for each of you."

A voice other than Kroeger's spoke up. It was the Englishman, Sydney Masterson.

"May I ask the point of all this? All this . . . incidental intelligence? I'm sure you've been most industrious—highly accurate, too, speaking for myself. But none of us

326

here have entered the race for a Jesus medal. Surely, you know that."

"I do, indeed. If it were otherwise, I wouldn't be here tonight."

"Then why? Why this?" The accent was German. The voice belonged to the blustering baron of the Ruhr Valley, Kindorf.

Masterson continued. "Your cablegram, madame—we all received the same—specifically alluded to areas of mutual interest. I believe you went so far as to say the Scarlatti assets might be at our joint disposal. Most generous, indeed. . . . But now I must agree with Mr. Kroeger. You sound as though you're threatening us, and I'm not at all sure I like it."

"Oh, come, Mr. Masterson! You've never held out promises of English gold to half the minor potentates in the backwaters of India? Herr Kindorf has not openly bribed his unions to strike with pledges of increased wages once the French are out of the Ruhr? Please! You insult all of us! Of course, I'm here to threaten you! And I can assure you, you'll like it less as I go on!"

Masterson rose from the table. Several others moved their chairs. The air was hostile. "I shall not listen further," said Masterson.

"Then tomorrow at noon the Foreign Office, the British Stock Exchange, and the board of directors of the English Importers Collective will receive detailed specifics of your highly illegal agreements in Ceylon! Your commitments are enormous! The news might just initiate a considerable run on your holdings!"

Masterson stood by his chair. "Be damned!" were the only words he uttered as he returned to his chair. The table once again fell silent. Elizabeth opened her briefcase.

"I have here an envelope for each of you. Your names are typed on the front. Inside each envelope is an accounting of your individual worths. Your strengths. Your weaknesses. . . . There is one envelope missing. The . . . influential, very important Mr. Kroeger does not have one. Frankly, it's insignificant."

"I warn you!"

"So very sorry, Mr. Kroeger." Again the words were rapidly spoken, but this time no one was listening. Each one's concentration was on Elizabeth Scarlatti and her briefcase. "Some envelopes are thicker than others, but none should place too great an emphasis on this factor. We all know the negligibility of wide diversification after a certain point." Elizabeth reached into her leather case.

"You are a witch!" Kindorf's heavy accent was now guttural, the veins stood out in his temples.

"Here. I shall pass them out. And as each of you peruse your miniature portfolios I shall continue talking, which, I know, will please you."

The envelopes were passed down both sides of the table. Some were torn open immediately, hungrily. Others, like the cards of experienced poker players, were handled carefully, cautiously.

Matthew Canfield stood by the wall, his left arm smarting badly in the sling, his right hand in his pocket, sweatily clutching his revolver. Since Elizabeth had identified Ulster Scarlett with the 270 million, he could not take his eyes off him. This man called Heinrich Kroeger. This hideous, arrogant son of a bitch was the man he wanted! This was the filthy bastard who had done it all! This was Janet's personal hell.

"I see you all have your envelopes. Except, of course, the ubiquitous Mr. Kroeger. Gentlemen, I promised you I would not be unfair and I shan't be. There are five of you who can not begin to appreciate the influence of Scarlatti unless you have, as they say in cheap merchandising, samples applicable to you alone. Therefore, as you read the contents of your envelopes, I shall briefly touch on these sensitive areas."

Several of the men who had been reading shifted their eyes toward Elizabeth without moving their heads. Others put the papers down defiantly. Some handed the pages to aides and stared at the old woman. Elizabeth glanced over her shoulder at Matthew Canfield. She was worried about him. She knew he, at last, faced Ulster Scarlett, and the pressure on him was immense. She tried to catch his eye. She tried to reassure him with a look, a confident smile.

He would not look at her. She saw only the hatred in his eyes as he stared at the man called Heinrich Kroeger.

"I shall delineate alphabetically, gentlemen. . . . Monsieur Daudet, the Republic of France would be reluctant to continue awarding franchises to your fleet if they were aware of those ships under Paraguayan flag which carried supplies to France's enemies in time of war." Daudet remained motionless, but Elizabeth was amused to see the three Englishmen bristle at the Frenchman. The predictable, contradictory British!

"Oh, come, Mr. Innes-Bowen. You may not have run ammunition, but how many neutral ships were loaded off how many piers in India with textile cargoes bound for Bremerhaven and Cuxhaven during the same period? . . . And Mr. Leacock. You can't really forget your fine Irish heritage, can you? The Sinn Féin has prospered well under your tutelage. Monies funneled through you to the Irish rebellion cost the lives of thousands of British soldiers at a time when England could least afford them! And quiet, calm Herr Olaffsen. The crown prince of Swedish steel. Or is he the king now? He might well be, for the Swedish government paid him several fortunes for untold hundreds of tons of low-carbon ingot. However, they didn't come from his own superior factories. They were shipped from inferior mills half a world away— from Japan!"

Elizabeth reached into her briefcase once again. The men around the table were like corpses, immobile, only their minds were working. For Heinrich Kroeger, Elizabeth Scarlatti had placed the seal of approval on her own death warrant. He sat back and relaxed. Elizabeth withdrew a thin booklet from her briefcase.

"Lastly we come to Herr Thyssen. He emerges with the least pain. No grand fraud, no treason, only minor illegality and major embarrassment. Hardly a fitting tribute to the house of August Thyssen." She threw the booklet into the center of the table. "Filth, gentlemen, just plain filth. Fritz Thyssen, pornographer! Purveyor of obscenity. Books, pamphlets, even motion pictures. Printed and filmed in Thyssen warehouses in Cairo. Every government on the Continent has condemned the unknown source. There he is, gentlemen. Your associate."

For a long moment no one spoke. Each man was concerned with himself. Each calculated the damage that could result from old Scarlatti's disclosures. In every instance the loss was accompanied by degrees of disgrace. Reputations could hang in balance. The old woman had issued twelve indictments and personally returned twelve verdicts of guilty. Somehow, no one considered the thirteenth, Heinrich Kroeger.

Sydney Masterson pierced the belligerent air with a loud, manufactured cough. "Very well, Madame Scarlatti, you've made the point I referred to earlier. However, I think I should remind you that we are not impotent men. Charges and countercharges are parts of our lives. Solicitors can refute every accusation you've made, and I can assure you that lawsuits for unmitigated slander would be in the forefront. . . . After all, when gutter tactics are employed, there are expedient replies. . . . If you think we fear disdain, believe me when I tell you that public opinion has been molded by far less money than is represented at this table!"

The gentlemen of Zurich took confidence in Masterson's words. There were nods of agreement.

"I don't for one second doubt you, Mr. Masterson. Any of you. . . . Missing personnel files, opportunistic executives—sacrificial goats. Please, gentlemen! I only contend that you wouldn't welcome the trouble. Or the anxiety which goes with such distasteful matters."

"*Non*, madame." Claude Daudet was outwardly cool but inwardly petrified. Perhaps his Zurich associates did not know the French people. A firing squad was not out of the question. "You are correct. Such troubles are to be avoided. So, then what is next? What is it you prepare for us, eh?"

Elizabeth paused. She wasn't quite sure why. It was an instinct, an intuitive need to turn around and look at the field accountant.

Matthew Canfield had not budged from his position by the wall. He was a pathetic sight. His jacket had fallen away from his left shoulder revealing the dark black sling, his right hand still plunged in his pocket. He seemed to be swallowing continuously, trying to keep himself aware of his surroundings. Elizabeth noticed that he now avoided looking at Ulster Scarlett. He seemed, in essence, to be trying to hang on to his sanity.

"Excuse me, gentlemen." Elizabeth rose from her chair and crossed to Canfield. She whispered quietly to him. "Take hold of yourself. I demand it! There's nothing to fear. Not in this room!"

Canfield spoke slowly, without moving his lips. She

could barely hear him, but what she heard startled her. Not for its content, but for the way in which he said it. Matthew Canfield was now among the ranks in this room in Zurich. He had joined them; he had become a killer, too.

"Say what you have to say and get it over with. . . . I want him. I'm sorry, but I want him. Look at him now, lady, because he's a dead man."

"Control yourself! Such talk will serve neither of us." She turned and walked back to her chair. She stood behind it while she spoke. "As you may have noticed, gentlemen, my young friend has been seriously wounded. Thanks to all of you . . . or one of you, in an attempt to prevent my reaching Zurich. The act was cowardly and provocative in the extreme."

The men looked at each other.

Daudet, whose imagination would not stop conjuring pictures of national disgrace or the firing squad, answered quickly. "Why would any here take such action, Madame Scarlatti? We are not maniacs. We are businessmen. No one sought to prevent your coming to Zurich. Witness, madame, we are all here."

Elizabeth looked at the man called Kroeger.

"One of you violently opposed this conference. We were fired upon less than a half hour ago."

The men looked at Heinrich Kroeger. Some were becoming angry. This Kroeger was, perhaps, too reckless.

"No." He answered simply and emphatically, returning their stares. "I agreed to your coming. If I'd wanted to stop you, I'd have stopped you."

For the first time since the meeting began, Heinrich Kroeger looked at the sporting goods salesman at the far end of the room, half concealed in the poor light. He had reacted with only moderate surprise when he realized Elizabeth Scarlatti had brought him to Zurich. Moderate because he knew Elizabeth's penchant for employing the unusual, both in methods and personnel, and because she probably had no one else around she could browbeat into silence as easily as this money-hungry social gadfly. He'd be a convenient chauffeur, a manservant. Kroeger hated the type.

Or was he anything else?

Why had the salesman stared at him? Had Elizabeth

told him anything? She wouldn't be that big a fool. The man was the sort who'd blackmail in a minute.

One thing was sure. He'd have to be killed.

But who had tried to kill him previously? Who had tried to stop Elizabeth? And why?

The same question was being considered by Elizabeth Scarlatti. For she believed Kroeger when he disavowed the attempts on their lives.

"Please continue, Madame Scarlatti." It was Fritz Thyssen, his cherubic face still flushed with anger over Elizabeth's disclosure of his Cairo trade. He had removed the booklet from the center of the table.

"I shall." She approached the side of her chair but did not sit down. Instead, she reached once more into her briefcase. "I have one thing further, gentlemen. With it we can conclude our business, and decisions can be made. There is a copy for each of the twelve remaining investors. Those with aides will have to share them. My apologies, Mr. Kroeger, I find I haven't one for you." From her position at the end of the table she distributed twelve slender manila envelopes. They were sealed, and as the men passed them down, the investors taking one apiece, it was apparent that each found it difficult not to rip open the top and withdraw the contents at once. But none wished to betray such obvious anxiety.

Finally, as each of the twelve held his envelope in front of him, one by one the men began to open them.

For nearly two minutes the only sound was the rustling of pages. Otherwise, silence. Even breathing was seemingly suspended. The men from Zurich were mesmerized by what they saw. Elizabeth spoke.

"Yes, gentlemen. What you hold in your hands is the scheduled liquidation of the Scarlatti Industries. . . . So that you have no illusions of doubt concerning the validity of this document, you will note that after each subdivision of holdings is typed the names of the individuals, corporations, or syndicates who are the purchasers. . . . Every one of those mentioned, the individuals as well as the organizations, are known to each of you. If not personally, then certainly by reputation. You know their capabilities, and I'm sure you're not unaware of their ambitions. Within the next twenty-four hours they will own Scarlatti."

For most of the Zurich men Elizabeth's sealed information was the confirmation of the whispered rumors. Word had reached them that something unusual was taking place at Scarlatti. Some sort of unloading under strange circumstances.

So this was it. The head of Scarlatti was getting out.

"A massive operation, Madame Scarlatti." Olaffsen's low Swedish voice vibrated throughout the room. "But to repeat Daudet's question, what is it you prepare us for?"

"Please take note of the bottom figure on the last page, gentlemen. Although I'm quite sure you all have." The rustle of pages. Each man had turned swiftly to the final page. "It reads seven hundred and fifteen million dollars. . . . The combined, immediately convertible assets of this table, placed at the highest figure is one billion, one hundred and ten million. . . . Therefore, a disparity of three hundred and ninety-five million exists between us. . . . Another way to approach this difference is to calculate it from the opposite direction. The Scarlatti liquidation will realize sixty-four point four percent of this table's holdings—if, indeed, you gentlemen could convert your personal assets in such a manner as to preclude financial panics."

Silence.

A number of the Zurich men reached for their first envelopes. The breakdowns of their own worth.

One of these was Sydney Masterson, who turned to Elizabeth with an unamused smile. "And what you're saying, I presume, Madame Scarlatti, is that this sixty-four point plus percent is the club you hold over our heads?"

"Precisely, Mr. Masterson."

"My dear lady, I really must question your sanity . . ."

"I wouldn't, if I were you."

"Then I shall, Frau Scarlatti." I. G. Farben's von Schnitzler spoke in a disagreeable manner, lounging back in his chair as if toying verbally with an imbecile. "To accomplish what you have must have been a costly sacrifice. . . . I wonder to what purpose? You can not buy what there is not to sell. . . . We are not a public corporation. You can not force into defeat something which does not exist!" His German lisp was pronounced, his arrogance every bit as unattractive as reputed. Elizabeth disliked him intensely.

"Quite correct, von Schnitzler."

"Then, perhaps"—the German laughed—"you have been a foolish woman. I would not wish to absorb your losses. I mean, really, you can not go to some mythical *Baumeister* and tell him you have more funds than we—therefore, he must drive us out into the streets!"

Several of the Zurich men laughed.

"That, of course, would be the simplest, would it not? The appeal to one entity, negotiating with one power. It's a shame that I can't do that. It would be so much easier, so much less costly. . . . But I'm forced to take another road, an expensive one. . . . I should put that another way. I have taken it, gentlemen. It has been accomplished. The time is running out for its execution."

Elizabeth looked at the men at Zurich. Some had their eyes riveted on her—watching for the slightest waver of confidence, the smallest sign of bluff. Others fixed their stares on inanimate objects—caring only to filter the words, the tone of her voice, for a false statement or a lapse of judgment. These were men who moved nations with a single gesture, a solitary word.

"At the start of tomorrow's business, subject to time zones, enormous transfers of Scarlatti capital will have been made to the financial centers of the five nations represented at this table. In Berlin, Paris, Stockholm, London, and New York, negotiations have already been completed for massive purchases on the open market of the outstanding shares of your central companies. . . . Before noon of the next business day, gentlemen, Scarlatti will have considerable, though, of course, minority ownership in many of your vast enterprises. . . . Six hundred and seventy million dollars' worth! . . . Do you realize what this means, gentlemen?"

Kindorf roared. *"Ja!* You will drive up the prices and makes us fortunes! You will own nothing!"

"My dear lady, you are extraordinary." Innes-Bowen's textile prices had remained conservative. He was overjoyed at the prospects.

D'Almeida, who realized she could not enter his Franco-Italian rails, took another view. "You can not purchase one share of my property, madame!"

"Some of you are more fortunate than others, Monsieur D'Almeida."

Leacock, the financier, the gentlest trace of a brogue in his cultivated voice, spoke up. "Granting what you say, and it is entirely possible, Madame Scarlatti, what have we suffered? . . . We have not lost a daughter, but gained a minor associate." He turned to the others who, he hoped, would find humor in his analogy.

Elizabeth held her breath before speaking. She waited until the men of Zurich were once again focused on her.

"I said before noon Scarlatti would be in the position I outlined. . . . One hour later a tidal wave will form in the Kurfuerstendamm in Berlin and end in New York's Wall Street! One hour later Scarlatti will divest itself of these holdings at a fraction of their cost! I have estimated three cents on the dollar. . . . Simultaneously, every bit of information Scarlatti has learned of your questionable activities will be released to the major wire services in each of your countries. . . . You might sustain slander by itself, gentlemen. You will not be the same men when it is accompanied by financial panic! Some of you will remain barely intact. Some will be wiped out. The majority of you will be affected disastrously!"

After the briefest moment of shocked silence, the room exploded. Aides were questioned peremptorily. Answers were bellowed to be heard.

Heinrich Kroeger rose from his chair and screamed at the men. "Stop! Stop! You damn fools, stop it! She'd never do it! She's bluffing!"

"Do you really think so?" Elizabeth shouted above the voices.

"I'll kill you, you bitch!"

"You are demented, Frau Scarlatti!"

"Try it . . . Kroeger! Try it!" Matthew Canfield stood by Elizabeth, his eyes bloodshot with fury as he stared at Ulster Stewart Scarlett.

"Who the hell are you, you lousy peddler?" The man called Kroeger, hands gripping the table, returned Canfield's stare and screeched to be heard by the salesman.

"Look at me good! I'm your executioner!"

"What!"

The man called Heinrich Kroeger squinted his misshapen eyes. He was bewildered. Who was this parasite? But he could not take the time to think. The voices of the men of Zurich had reached a crescendo. They were now shouting at each other.

Heinrich Kroeger pounded the table. He had to get control. He had to get them quiet. "Stop it! . . . Listen to

335

me! If you'll listen to me, I'll tell you why she can't do it! She can't do it, I tell you!"

One by one the voices became quieter and finally trailed off into silence. The men of Zurich watched Kroeger. He pointed at Elizabeth Scarlatti.

"I know this bitch-woman! I've seen her do this before! She gets men together, powerful men, and frightens them. They go into panic and sell out! She gambles on *fear*, you cowards! On fear!"

Daudet spoke quietly. "You have answered nothing. Why can't she do as she says?"

Kroeger did not take his eyes off Elizabeth Scarlatti as he replied. "Because to do it would destroy everything she's ever fought for. It would collapse Scarlatti!"

Sydney Masterson spoke just above a whisper. "That would appear to be obvious. The question remains unanswered."

"She couldn't live without that power! Take my word for it! She couldn't live without it!"

"That's an opinion," said Elizabeth Scarlatti facing her son at the opposite end of the table. "Do you ask the majority of those at this table to risk everything on your opinion?"

"God damn you!"

"This Kroeger's right, honey." The Texas drawl was unmistakable. "You'll ruin yourself. You won't have a pot to piss in."

"Your language matches the crudity of your operations, Mr. Landor."

"I don't give pig piss for words, old lady. I do about money, and that's what we're talkin' about. Why do you want to pull this here crap?"

"That I'm doing it is sufficient, Mr. Landor. . . . Gentlemen, I said time was running out. The next twenty-four hours will either be a normal Tuesday or a day which will never be forgotten in the financial capitals of our world. . . . Some here will survive. Most of you will not. Which will it be, gentlemen? . . . I submit that in light of everything I've said, it's a poor fiscal decision wherein the majority allows the minority to cause its destruction."

"What is it you want of us?" Myrdal was a cautious bargainer. "A few might rather weather your threats than accept your demands. . . . Sometimes I think it is all a game. What are your demands?"

"That this . . . association be disbanded at once. That all financial and political ties in Germany with whatever factions be severed without delay! That those of you who have been entrusted with appointments to the Allied Controls Commission resign immediately!"

"No! No! No! No!" Heinrich Kroeger was enraged. He banged his fist with all his might upon the table. "This organization has taken years to build! We will control the economy of Europe. We will control all Europe! We will do it!"

"Hear me, gentlemen! Mr. Myrdal said it's a game! Of course, it's a game! A game we expend our lives on. Our souls on! It consumes us, and we demand more and more and more until, at last, we crave our own destruction. . . . Herr Kroeger says I can't live without the power I've sought and gained. He may be right, gentlemen! Perhaps it's time for me to reach that logical end, the end which I now crave and for which I'm willing to pay the price. . . . Of course, I'll do as I say, gentlemen. I welcome death!"

"Let it be yours, then, not ours." Sydney Masterson understood.

"So be it, Mr. Masterson. I'm not overwhelmed, you know. I leave to all of you the necessity of coping with this strange new world we've entered. Don't think for a minute, gentlemen, that I can't understand you! Understand what you've done. Most horridly, why you've done it! . . . You look around your personal kingdoms and you're frightened. You see your power threatened—by theories, governments, strange-sounding concepts which eat away at your roots. You have an overpowering anxiety to protect the feudal system which spawned you. And well you should, perhaps. It won't last long. . . . But you will *not* do it this way!"

"Since you understand so, why do you stop us? This undertaking protects all of us. Ultimately yourself as well. Why do you stop us?" D'Almeida could lose the Franco-Italian rails and survive, if only the remainder could be saved.

"It always starts that way. The greater good. . . . Let's say I stop you because what you're doing is a far greater blemish than it is a cure. And that's all I'll say about it!"

"From you, that's ludicrous! I tell you again, she won't do it!" Kroeger pounded the flat of his hand on the table, but no one paid much attention to him.

"When you say time is running out, Madame Scarlatti, how do you mean it? From what you said, I gathered time had run out. The expensive road had been taken. . . ."

"There's a man in Geneva, Mr. Masterson, who's awaiting a phone call from me. If he receives that phone call, a cable will be sent to my offices in New York. If that cable arrives, the operation is canceled. If it doesn't, it's executed on schedule."

"That's impossible! Such complexity untangled with a cablegram? I don't believe you." Monsieur Daudet was certain of ruin.

"I assume considerable financial penalties by the action."

"You assume more than that, I would suspect, madame. You'll never be trusted again. Scarlatti will be isolated!"

"It's a prospect, Mr. Masterson. Not a conclusion. The marketplace is flexible. . . . Well, gentlemen? Your answer?"

Syndey Masterson rose from his chair. "Make your phone call. There's no other choice, is there, gentlemen?"

The men of Zurich looked at each other. Slowly they began to get out of their chairs, gathering the papers in front of them.

"It's finished. I am out of it." Kindorf folded the manila envelope and put it in his pocket.

"You're a beastly tiger. I shouldn't care to meet you in the arena with an army at my back." Leacock stood erect.

"You may be bullshitter, but I'm not gonna slip on it!" Landor nudged Gibson, who found it difficult to adjust.

"We can't be sure. . . . That's our problem. We can't be sure," said Gibson.

"Wait! Wait! Wait a minute!" Heinrich Kroeger began to shout. "You do this! You walk out! You're dead! . . . Every God damn one of you leeches is dead! Leeches! Yellow-bellied leeches! . . . You suck our blood; you make agreements with us. Then you walk out? . . . Afraid for your little businesses? You God damn Jew bastards! We don't need you! Any of you! But you're going to need us! We'll cut you up and feed you to dogs! God damn swine!" Kroeger's face was flushed. His words spewed out, tumbling over one another.

"Stop it, Kroeger!" Masterson took a step toward the raving man with the splotched face. "It's finished! Can't you understand? It's finished!"

"Stay where you are, you scum, you English fairy!" Kroeger drew the pistol from his holster. Canfield, standing by Elizabeth, saw that it was a long-barreled forty-five and would blast half a man's body off with one shot.

"Stay where you are! . . . Finished! Nothing's finished until I say it's finished. God damn filthy pigs! Frightened little slug worms! We're too far along! . . . No one will stop us now! . . ." He waved the pistol toward Elizabeth and Canfield. "Finished! I'll tell you who's finished! She is! . . . Get out of my way." He started down the left side of the table as the Frenchman, Daudet, squealed.

"Don't do it, monsieur! Don't kill her! You do, and we are ruined!"

"I warn you, Kroeger! You murder her and you'll answer to us! We'll not be intimidated by you! We'll not destroy ourselves because of you!" Masterson stood at Kroeger's side, their shoulders nearly touching. The Englishman would not move.

Without a word, without warning, Heinrich Kroeger pointed his pistol at Masterson's stomach and fired. The shot was deafening and Sydney Masterson was jackknifed into the air. He fell to the floor, blood drenching his entire front, instantaneously dead.

The eleven men of Zurich gasped, some screamed in horror at the sight of the bloody corpse. Heinrich Kroeger kept walking. Those in his path got out of his way.

Elizabeth Scarlatti held her place. She locked her eyes with those of her killer son. "I curse the day you were born. You revile the house of your father. But know this, Heinrich Kroeger, and know it well!" The old woman's voice filled the cavernous room. Her power was such that her son was momentarily stunned, staring at her in hatred as she pronounced his sentence of execution. "Your identity will be spread across every front page of every newspaper in the civilized world after I'm dead! You will be hunted down for what you are! A madman, a murderer, a thief! And every man in this room, every investor in Zurich, will be branded your associate if they let you live this night!"

An uncontrollable rage exploded in the misshapen eyes of Heinrich Kroeger. His body shook with fury as he lashed at a chair in front of him sending it crashing across the floor. To kill was not enough. He had to kill at close range, he had to see the life and mind of Elizabeth Scarlatti detonated into oblivion in front of his eyes.

Matthew Canfield held the trigger of his revolver in his right-hand pocket. He had never fired from his pocket and he knew that if he missed he and Elizabeth would die. He was not sure how long he could wait. He would aim in the vicinity of the approaching man's chest, the largest target facing him. He waited until he could wait no longer.

The report of the small revolver and the impact of the bullet into Scarlett's shoulder was so much of a shock that Kroeger, for a split second, widened his eyes in disbelief.

It was enough, just enough for Canfield.

With all his strength he crashed into Elizabeth with his right shoulder sending her frail body toward the floor out of Kroeger's line of sight as he, Canfield, flung himself to the left. He withdrew his revolver and fired again, rapidly, into the man called Heinrich Kroeger.

Kroeger's huge pistol went off into the floor as he crumpled over.

Canfield staggered up, forgetting the unbearable pain in his left arm, which had been crushed under the weight of his own body. He leaped on Ulster Stewart Scarlett, wrenching the pistol from the iron grip. He began hitting the face of Heinrich Kroeger with the barrel. He could not stop.

Destroy the face! Destroy the horrible face!

Finally he was pulled off.

"*Gott!* He's dead! Halt! Stop! You can do no more!" The large, strong Fritz Thyssen held him.

Matthew Canfield felt weak and sank to the floor.

The men of Zurich had gathered around. Several helped Elizabeth, while the others bent over Heinrich Kroeger.

Rapid knocking came from the door leading to the hall.

Von Schnitzler took command. "Let them in!" he ordered in his thick German accent.

D'Almeida walked swiftly to the door and opened it. A number of chauffeurs stood at the entrance. It occurred to Canfield as he watched them that these men were not simply drivers of automobiles. He had good reason. They were armed.

As he lay there on the floor in terrible pain and shock, Canfield saw a brutish-looking blond man with close-cropped hair bent over the body of Heinrich Kroeger. He pushed the others away for the briefest instant while he pulled back the misshapen lid of one eye.

And then Canfield wondered if the agony of the last hours had played tricks with his sight, corrupted the infallible process of vision.

Or had the blond man bent his head down and whispered something into Heinrich Kroeger's ear?

Was Heinrich Kroeger still alive?

Von Schnitzler stood over Canfield. "He will be taken away. I have ordered a coup de grace. No matter, he is dead. It is finished." The obese von Schnitzler then shouted further commands in German to the uniformed chauffeurs around Kroeger. Several started to lift up the lifeless form but they were blocked by the blond man with the close-cropped hair. He shouldered them out of the way, not letting them touch the body.

He alone lifted Heinrich Kroeger off the floor and carried him out the door. The others followed.

"How's she?" Canfield gestured toward Elizabeth, who was seated in a chair. She was staring at the door through which the body had been taken, staring at the man no one knew was her son.

"Fine! She can make her call now!" Leacock was trying his best to be decisive.

Canfield rose from the floor and crossed to Elizabeth. He put his hand on her wrinkled cheek. He could not help himself.

Tears were falling down the ridges of her face.

And then Matthew Canfield looked up. He could hear the sound of a powerful automobile racing away. He was bothered.

Von Schnitzler had told him he'd ordered a coup de grace.

341

A mile away, on the Winterthurstrasse, two men dragged the body of a dead man to a truck. They weren't sure what to do. The dead man had hired them, hired them all to stop the automobile heading to Falke Haus. He had paid them in advance, they had insisted upon it. Now he was dead, killed by a bullet meant for the driver of the automobile an hour ago. As they dragged the body over the rocky incline toward the truck, the blood from the mouth sprewed onto the perfectly matted waxed moustache.

The man named Poole was dead.

PART FOUR

CHAPTER 45

Major Matthew Canfield, aged forty-five—about to be forty-six—stretched his legs diagonally across the back of the army car. They had entered the township of Oyster Bay, and the sallow-complexioned sergeant broke the silence.

"Getting close, Major. You better wake up."

Wake up. It should be as easy as that. The perspiration streamed down his face. His heart was rhythmically pounding an unknown theme.

"Thank you, Sergeant."

The car swung east down Harbor Road toward the ocean drive. As they came closer to his home, Major Matthew Canfield began to tremble. He grabbed his wrists, held his breath, bit the front of his tongue. He could not fall apart. He could not allow himself the indulgence of self-pity. He could not do that to Janet. He owed her so much.

The sergeant blithely turned into the blue stone driveway and stopped at the path, which led to the front entrance of the large beach estate. The sergeant enjoyed driving out to Oyster Bay with his rich major. There was always lots of good food, in spite of rationing, and the liquor was always the best. No cheap stuff for the Camshaft, as he was known in the enlisted man's barracks.

The major slowly got out of the car. The sergeant was concerned. Something was wrong with the major. He hoped it didn't mean they'd have to drive back to New York. The old man seemed to have trouble standing up.

"Okay, Major?"

345

"Okay, Sergeant. . . . How'd you like to bunk in the boathouse tonight?" He did not look at the sergeant as he spoke.

"Sure! Great, Major!" It was where he always bunked. The boathouse apartment had a full kitchen and plenty of booze. Even a telephone. But the sergeant didn't have any signal that he could use it yet. He decided to try his luck. "Will you need me, Major? Could I call a couple of friends here?"

The major walked up the path. He called back quietly. "Do whatever you like, Sergeant. Just stay away from that radiophone. Is that understood?"

"You betcha, Major!" The sergeant gunned the engine and drove down toward the beach.

Matthew Canfield stood in front of the white, scalloped door with the sturdy hurricane lamps on both sides.

His home.

Janet.

The door opened and she stood there. The slightly graying hair, which she would not retouch. The upturned nose above the delicate, sensitive mouth. The bright, wide, brown searching eyes. The gentle loveliness of her face. The comforting concern she radiated.

"I heard the car. No one drives to the boathouse like Evans! . . . Matthew. Matthew! My darling! You're crying!"

CHAPTER 46

The plane, an Army B-29 transport, descended from the late-afternoon clouds to the airport in Lisbon. An Air Force corporal walked down the aisle.

"Please buckle all seat belts! No smoking! We'll be down in four minutes." He spoke in a monotone, aware that his passengers had to be important, so he would be more important, but courteous, when he had to tell them something.

The young man next to Matthew Canfield had said very little since their takeoff from Shannon. A number of times the major tried to explain that they were taking air routes out of range of the *Luftwaffe*, and that there was nothing to worry about. Andrew Scarlett had merely mumbled understood approval and had gone back to his magazines.

The car at the Lisbon airport was an armored Lincoln with two OSS personnel in the front. The windows could withstand short-range gunfire, and the automobile was capable of 120 miles an hour. They had to drive thirty-two miles up the Tejo River road to an airfield in Alenguer.

At Alenguer the man and boy boarded a low-flying, specially constructed Navy TBF with no markings for the trip to Bern. There would be no stops. Throughout the route, English, American, and Free French fighters were scheduled to intercept and protect to the destination.

At Bern they were met by a Swiss government vehicle, flanked by a motorcycle escort of eight men—one at the front, one at the rear, and three on each side. All were armed in spite of the Geneva pact, which prohibited such practices.

They drove to a village twenty-odd miles to the north, toward the German border. Kreuzlingen.

They arrived at a small inn, isolated from the rest of civilization, and the man and boy got out of the car. The driver sped the automobile away, and the motorcycle complement disappeared.

Matthew Canfield led the boy up the steps to the entrance of the inn.

Inside the lobby could be heard the wailing sound of an accordion, echoing from what was apparently a sparsely populated dining room. The high-ceilinged entry room was inhospitable, conveying the feeling that guests were not welcome.

Matthew Canfield and Andrew Scarlett approached the counter, which served as a front desk.

"Please, ring through to room six that April Red is here."

As the clerk plugged in his line, the boy suddenly shook. Canfield grabbed his arm and held him.

They walked up the stairs, and the two men stood in front of the door marked with the numeral six.

"There's nothing I can tell you now, Andy, except that we're here for one person. At least that's why I'm here. Janet. Your mother. Try to remember that."

The boy took a deep breath. "I'll try, Dad. Open the door! Jesus! Open the door!"

The room was dimly lit by small lamps on small tables. It was ornate in the fashion the Swiss felt proper for tourists—heavy rugs and solid furniture, overstuffed chairs and much antimacassar.

At the far end sat a man in half shadow. The spill of light angled sharply down across his chest but did not illuminate his face. The figure was dressed in brown tweeds, the jacket a combination of heavy cloth and leather.

He spoke in a throaty, harsh voice. "You are?"

"Canfield and April Red. Kroeger?"

"Shut the door."

Matthew Canfield closed the door and took several steps forward in front of Andrew Scarlett. He would cover the boy. He put his hand in his right coat pocket.

"I have a gun pointed at you, Kroeger. Not the same gun but the same pocket as last time we met. This time I won't take anything for granted. Do I make myself clear?"

"If you like, take it out of your pocket and hold it against my head. . . . There's not much I can do about it."

Canfield approached the figure in the chair.

It was horrible.

The man was a semi-invalid. He seemed to be paralyzed through the entire left portion of his body, extending to his jaw. His hands were folded across his front, his fingers extended as though spastic. But his eyes were alert.

His eyes.

His face. . . . Covered over by white splotches of skin graft below gray short-cropped hair. The man spoke.

"What you see was carried out of Sevastopol. Operation Barbarossa."

"What do you have to tell us, Kroeger?"

"First, April Red. . . . Tell him to come closer."

"Come here, Andy. By me."

"Andy!" The man in the chair laughed through his half-closed mouth. "Isn't that nice! Andy! Come here, Andy!"

Andrew Scarlett approached his stepfather and stood by his side, looking down at the deformed man in the chair.

"So you're the son of Ulster Scarlett?"

"I'm Matthew Canfield's son."

Canfield held his place, watching the father and son. He suddenly felt as though he didn't belong. He had the feeling that giants—old and infirm, young and scrawny—were about to do battle. And he was not of their house.

"No, young man, you're the son of Ulster Stewart Scarlett, heir to Scarlatti!"

"I'm exactly what I want to be! I have nothing to do with you." The young man breathed deeply. The fear was leaving him now, and in its place Canfield saw that a quiet fury was taking hold of the boy.

"Easy, Andy. Easy."

"Why? . . . For him? . . . Look at him. He's practically dead. . . . He doesn't even have a face."

"Stop it!" Ulster Scarlett's shrill voice reminded Canfield of that long-ago room in Zurich. "Stop it, you fool!"

"For what? For you? . . . Why should I? . . . I don't know you! I don't want to know you! . . . You left a long time ago!" The young man pointed to Canfield. "He took over for you. I listen to him. You're nothing to me!"

"Don't you talk to me like that! Don't you dare!"

Canfield spoke sharply. "I've brought April Red, Kroeger! What have you got to deliver! That's what we're here for. Let's get it over with!"

"He must understand first!" The misshapen head nodded back and forth. "He must be made to understand!"

"If it meant that much, why did you hide it? Why did you become Kroeger?"

The nodding head stopped, the ashen slit eyes stared. Canfield remembered Janet speaking about that look.

"Because Ulster Scarlett was not fit to represent the new order. The new world! Ulster Scarlett served his purpose and once that purpose was accomplished, he was no longer necessary. . . . He was a hindrance. . . . He would have been a joke. He had to be eliminated. . . ."

"Perhaps there was something else, too."

"What?"

"Elizabeth. She would have stopped you again. . . . She would have stopped you later, just the way she stopped you at Zurich."

At Elizabeth's name, Heinrich Kroeger worked up the phlegm in his scarred throat and spat. It was an ugly sight. "The bitch of the world! . . . But we made a mistake in twenty-six. . . . Let's be honest, I made the mistake. . . . I should have asked her to join us. . . . She would have, you know. She wanted the same things we did. . . ."

"You're wrong about that."

"Hah! You didn't know her!"

The former field accountant replied softly without inflection. "I knew her. . . . Take my word for it, she despised everything you stood for."

The Nazi laughed quietly to himself. "That's very funny. . . . I told her she stood for everything I despised. . . ."

"Then you were both right."

"No matter. She's in hell now."

"She died thinking you were dead. She died in peace because of that."

"Hah! You'll never know how tempted I was over the years, especially when we took Paris! . . . But I was waiting for London. . . . I was going to stand outside Whitehall and announce it to the world—and watch Scarlatti destroy itself!"

"She was gone by the time you took Paris."

"That didn't matter."

"I suppose not. You were just as afraid of her in death as you were when she was alive."

"I was afraid of no one! I was afraid of nothing!" Heinrich Kroeger strained his decrepit body.

"Then why didn't you carry out your threat? The house of Scarlatti lives."

"She never told you?"

"Told me what?"

"The bitch-woman always covered herself on four flanks. She found her corruptible man. My one enemy in the Third Reich. Goebbels. She never believed I'd been killed at Zurich. Goebbels knew who I was. After nineteen thirty-three she threatened our respectability with lies. Lies about me. The party was more important than revenge."

Canfield watched the destroyed man below him. As always, Elizabeth Scarlatti had been ahead of all of them. Far ahead.

"One last question."

"What?"

"Why Janet?"

The man in the chair raised his right hand with difficulty. "Him. . . . Him!" He pointed to Andrew Scarlett.

"Why?"

"I believed! I still believe! Heinrich Kroeger was part of a new world! A new order! The true aristocracy! . . . In time it would have been his!"

"But why Janet?"

Heinrich Kroeger, in exhaustion, waved the question aside. "A whore. Who needs a whore? The vessel is all we look for. . . ."

Canfield felt the anger rise inside him, but at his age and in his job, he suppressed it. He was not quick enough for the boy-man beside him.

Andrew Scarlett rushed forward to the overstuffed chair and swung his open hand at the invalid Kroeger. The

351

slap was hard and accurate. "You bastard! You filthy bastard!"

"Andy! Get back!" He pulled the boy away.

"Unehelich!" Heinrich Kroeger's eyes were swimming in their sockets. "It's for you! That's why you're here! You've got to know! . . . You'll understand and start us up again! Think! Think the aristocracy! For you . . . for you. . . ." He reached with his slightly mobile hand to his inside jacket pocket and withdrew a slip of paper. "They're yours. Take them!"

Canfield picked up the paper and without looking at it handed it to Andrew Scarlett.

"They're numbers. Just a lot of numbers."

Matthew Canfield knew what the numbers meant, but before he could explain, Kroeger spoke. "They're Swiss accounts, my son. My only son. . . . They contain millions! Millions! But there are certain conditions. Conditions which you will learn to understand! When you grow older, you'll know those conditions have to be met! And you'll meet them! . . . Because this power is the power to change the world! The way we wanted to change it!"

The man-boy looked at the deformed figure in the chair. "Am I supposed to thank you?"

"One day you will."

Matthew Canfield had had enough. "This is it! April Red has his message. Now I want it! What are you delivering?"

"It's outside. Help me up and we'll go to it."

"Never! What's outside? Your staff members in leather coats?"

"There's no one. No one but me."

Canfield looked at the wreck of a man in front of him and believed him. He started to help Heinrich Kroeger out of the chair.

"Wait here, Andy, I'll be back."

Major Matthew Canfield, in full uniform, helped the crippled man in brown tweeds down the stairs and onto the lobby floor. In the lobby, a servant brought over the crutches discarded by the Nazi when he first ascended the staircase to his room. The American major and the Nazi went out the front door.

"Where are we going, Kroeger?"

"Don't you think it's time you called me by my right

352

name? The name is Scarlett. Or, if you will, Scarlatti."

The Nazi led them to the right, off the driveway, into the grass.

"You're Heinrich Kroeger. That's all you are to me."

"You realize, of course, that it was you, and you alone who caused our setback in Zurich. You pushed our time-table back a good two years. . . . No one ever suspected. . . . You were an ass!" Heinrich Kroeger laughed. "Perhaps it takes an ass to portray an ass!" He laughed again.

"Where are we going?"

"Just a few hundred yards. Hold your pistol up, if you like. There's no one."

"What are you going to deliver? You might as well tell me."

"Why not? You'll have them in your hands soon enough." Kroeger hobbled along toward an open field. "And when you have them, I'm free. Remember that."

"We have a deal. What is it?"

"The Allies will be pleased. Eisenhower will probably give you a medal! . . . You'll bring back the complete plans of the Berlin fortifications. They're known only to the elite of the German High Command. . . . Underground bunkers, rocket emplacements, supply depots, even the Führer's command post. You'll be a hero and I'll be nonexistent. We've done well, you and I."

Matthew Canfield stopped.

The plans of the Berlin fortifications had been obtained weeks ago by Allied Intelligence.

Berlin knew it.

Berlin admitted it.

Someone had been led into a trap, but it was not him, not Matthew Canfield. The Nazi High Command had led one of its own into the jaws of death.

"Tell me, Kroeger, what happens if I take your plans, your exchange for April Red, and don't let you go? What happens then?"

"Simple. Doenitz himself took my testimony. I gave it to him two weeks ago in Berlin. I told him everything. If I'm not back in Berlin in a few days, he'll be concerned. I'm very valuable. I expect to make my appearance and then . . . be gone. If I don't appear, then the whole world knows!"

Matthew Canfield thought it was the strangest of ironies. But it was no more than he had anticipated. He had

353

written it all down in the original file, sealed for years in the archives of the State Department.

And now a man in Berlin, unknown to him except by reputation, had reached the same conclusion.

Heinrich Kroeger, Ulster Stewart Scarlett—was expendable.

Doenitz had allowed Kroeger—bearing his false gifts— to come to Bern. Doenitz, in the unwritten rule of war, expected him to be killed. Doenitz knew that neither nation could afford this madman as its own. In either victory or defeat. And the enemy had to execute him so that no doubts existed. Doenitz was that rare enemy in these days of hatreds. He was a man his adversaries trusted. Like Rommel, Doenitz was a thorough fighter. A vicious fighter. But he was a moral man.

Matthew Canfield drew his pistol and fired twice.

Heinrich Kroeger lay dead on the ground.

Ulster Stewart Scarlett was—at last—gone.

Matthew Canfield walked through the field back to the small inn. The night was clear and the moon, three-quarters of it, shone brightly on the still foliage around him.

It struck him that it was remarkable that it had all been so simple.

But the crest of the wave is simple. Deceptively simple. It does not show the myriad pressures beneath that make the foam roll the way it does.

It was over.

And there was Andrew.

There was Janet.

Above all, there was Janet.

ABOUT THE AUTHOR

ROBERT LUDLUM is the author of sixteen novels published in nineteen languages and twenty-three countries with worldwide sales in excess of one hundred sixty million copies. His works include *The Scarlatti Inheritance, The Osterman Weekend, The Matlock Paper, The Rhinemann Exchange, The Gemini Contenders, The Chancellor Manuscript, The Road to Gandolfo, The Holcroft Covenant, The Matarese Circle, The Bourne Identity, The Parsifal Mosaic, The Aquitaine Progression, The Bourne Supremacy, The Icarus Agenda, Trevayne* and *The Bourne Ultimatum.* He lives with his wife, Mary, in Florida.